DATE

MAR 0 5 2021

NOO_____NY'S

ALSO BY ECHO HERON

NONFICTION:
Intensive Care; The Story of a Nurse
Condition Critical; The Story of a Nurse Continues
Tending Lives; Nurses on the Medical Front

NOVELS:
Mercy: a novel

MYSTERIES:
The Adele Monsarrat series:
       Pulse
       Panic
       Paradox
       Fatal Diagnosis

NOON AT TIFFANY'S

an historical, biographical novel

ECHO HERON

HERON
QUILL
PRESS

2012

Noon at Tiffany's is a work of historical fiction. Apart from the known actual people, events and locales that figure in the narrative, some of the names, characters, places and incidents are the products of the author's imagination or are used fictitiously. Any resemblance to current events or to living persons is entirely coincidental.

Published in the United States by Heron Quill Press, LLC.

Noon at Tiffany's:
an historical, biographical novel /Echo Heron

ISBN: 978-1-938439-47-6

Printed in the United States of America 2012

www.EchoHeron.com

Cover design by Daniel Magil/ danmagil.com
Top cover photo by Steven Vermillion
Photo of Clara Wolcott courtesy of Linda Alexander
Bottom cover image: Tiffany Daffodil leaded lamp/designer:
Clara Driscoll/Telome4/CC-BY-SA 1.0
Book design: PenWorthyLLC
Interior images used by permission from Jupiter Images.

In memory of Clara Pierce Wolcott Driscoll Booth
December 15, 1861 – November 6, 1944

When I see her mosaics, lamps and windows now, I see my sister's soul. I have always thought of Clara as one of the special heroines of God's world. We have been singled out to enjoy the blessing of her companionship; we have walked in her light. Her memory is a star that will move on before us to the end.

Emily Wolcott, 1944

AUTHOR'S NOTE

I began writing this book in January 2007, after hearing a National Public Radio broadcast about the discovery of a cache of 1,330 letters written between 1853 and the 1930s. The majority of this collection is made up of the weekly round robin letters circulated among Clara Wolcott, two of her three sisters, Emily and Kate, and their mother, Fannie. What makes these letters so noteworthy is the secret revealed within their yellowed pages—that Clara was, in fact, the designer of the iconic Tiffany lamps and of many of the glass and mosaic pieces that Louis C. Tiffany claimed were his own designs.

For most of my writing life I have endeavored to champion remarkable women who unjustly go unrecognized simply because they are women. By the time I had finished reading Clara's letters, in which she gives vivid accounts of her daily life in turn-of-the-century New York City, I felt I had to bring this incredible woman out from behind Louis Tiffany's shadow and into her own light. There was no doubt in my mind that not only was Clara Wolcott an extraordinary woman, years ahead of her time, she was also unquestionably one of America's most prolific and original artists.

Since Clara's letters form the foundation of this book, I have used sections of the Wolcott letters and diary entries to fashion portions of the dialogue, story lines and scenes. I also relied on my own intuition based on my research into the events and mood of the place and time.

I derived my characterization of Louis Comfort Tiffany's personality and psychology from the abundant source materials available, including but not limited to his biographers and memoirists. Although I relied on my research to form Louis Tiffany's diary entries, they are conjectural, since few of his personal accounts are in existence.

In the instance of Clara's visit to the church in Troy, NY, the particular windows I describe in that scene are invented, although in fact, Troy's St. Paul's, St. John's and St. Joseph's do have a magnificent collection of Tiffany Studios windows.

While I have tried to capture the essence of truth, if not always the precision of factual detail, in depicting the events and characters in this book, I have not hesitated to bend personalities, time, and events to suit the fictional needs of a novel. I trust what liberties I have taken will be forgiven.

If you will, take a closer look at the book cover. The pensive woman in the photograph is Clara. I think, after all these years of silence, she would be honored for you to read her story.

Round robin (round rob·in)

Noun

a letter, notice, or the like, circulated from person to person in a group, often with individual comments being added by each individual in turn.

1888 ~ 1892

~ 1 ~

May 7, 1888
Tiffany Glass Company
333-35 Fourth Avenue at East Twenty-fifth Street,
Manhattan

A TEAM OF WILD-EYED HORSES rounded the corner at a reckless speed at the same moment that Clara Wolcott and her younger sister reached the middle of the intersection. Frozen in mid-step, Clara focused instinctively on the panicked driver, who stood on the dray's platform, straining against the reins for control. She heard screams as the horses veered sharply at the last second, sending the overloaded cart up onto two wheels, where it teetered and then righted itself with a loud crash. The animals thundered past with only an inch to spare.

Clara let out a breath and tightened her grip on the handle of her portfolio, somewhat pleased at her increasing ability to take these daily death-defying events in stride. When she'd first arrived in New York, merely the sound of an approaching wagon had turned her weak-kneed. She gave her skirts a perfunctory shake and resumed her brisk pace through the cloud of dust.

Josie ran after her, clutching her hat. "For God's sake, won't you please slow down?"

"Prestigious businessmen such as Mr. Tiffany don't like to be kept waiting by anyone, especially two poverty-stricken newcomers who come begging favors," Clara shouted over the noise of the carriages.

"We aren't poverty-stricken, and you aren't a newcomer, Clara. You've been in New York for well over a year."

"Which is why you should listen to me when I tell you that being late for an interview practically guarantees you'll soon be poverty-stricken."

Clara continued toward the Tiffany building, giving no indication that beneath her composed exterior, she was a mass of roiling nerves. It still didn't seem possible that she was about to present her work to Louis Tiffany. If meeting the magnate wasn't pressure enough, her mother and sisters were sure to have told every living soul within a fifty-mile radius of their farm in Ohio that she and Josie were, at this very moment, heading into an interview that would determine their fate. They would assuredly be the main topic of conversation at every supper table throughout Tallmadge and Kent for weeks.

They were halfway across the building lobby when a stout gentleman, intent on his pocket watch, collided with Clara, knocking the portfolio from her hand and the derby from his head.

"Watch where you're going!" he growled, retrieving his hat.

Clara turned a withering eye on him. Even after a year of being subjected to the coarse manners that prevailed among the men of New York, she still had difficulty coming to grips with their disregard for women. No man in Tallmadge—or even Cleveland—would ever think of behaving so poorly.

"I beg your pardon, sir, but I think you would be better advised to go where you're watching!"

"What impudence! Women shouldn't be allowed to barge about the streets like wild animals!"

"And you, sir, need to be reeducated in the basics of how a civilized man should behave in polite society."

His face suffused with color, he stalked off, his hat lopsided.

She retrieved her case, stealing a glance at her sister. Hand pressed against the middle of her chest, as if to smother the pain that often resided there, Josie was pale, her face beaded with perspiration. Clara averted her gaze. Any other day she would have insisted they sit and rest, but today she couldn't allow Josie's poor health to delay them. A position at Tiffany's was her entrance into a world she'd dreamed of since the moment she realized her life's purpose was to create art. If her sister wanted to fit into the life of a New York artist, she would have to grow tougher skin.

Clara caught sight of herself in one of the mirrors that lined the lobby walls and stopped to make sure she was presentable. She'd gone without lunch for a week so she could afford to rent the blue taffeta gown that flowed over the length of her figure. Cut tight across her slender waist and hips, but draped full over the bustle, the garment was so recently out of fashion that only the most observant dressmaker would know it was last year's style.

Josie came to stand next to her. Both women were considered attractive by current standards, though they were of a completely different cast of features. Clara's hazel eyes, prominent cheekbones and sensuous mouth gave her a marked exotic appearance, contrasting sharply with Josie's girlish, wholesome mien.

She glanced at the lobby clock and grabbed Josie's hand. "We have to hurry!"

Three steps into the climb, she spied an unattended elevator cage and did an about face. "Let's use the lift."

Josie stopped short. "I won't ride in that contraption. We'll plummet to our deaths."

"Don't be silly. Elevators are a modern marvel. We'll shoot up three stories in a matter of seconds and emerge looking as fresh as if we had stepped out of a bandbox."

Josie blotted her face and neck with a hanky she pulled from her sleeve. "I'd rather rush and look like a beggar than risk my life in that mechanical deathtrap."

Privately thankful she didn't have to demonstrate her ignorance of how to actually operate the machine, Clara nonetheless gave an exasperated sigh before following her sister up the stairs.

Clara had just raised a hand to knock on the door displaying the name *Louis C. Tiffany* in gold script when a rush of raw panic overtook her. Closing her eyes, she did a quick review of her work. Surely, it was as good as any she'd seen in the galleries, and, despite his great wealth and notoriety, Louis Tiffany couldn't help but recognize that. After all, he was a fellow artist—though, in her private estimation, his paintings and stained glass lacked passion and confidence. It was her belief that his true talent lay in his innovative and flamboyant architectural designs.

As she lifted her hand again, a strikingly handsome gentleman in a beige pongee suit opened the door. He made no attempt to greet them, but rather stared at Clara as if he were seeing a ghost. The moment might have been awkward had she not also been rendered speechless by the physical reality of Louis Tiffany. The slim, elegantly groomed gentleman before her did not conform to the fat and jowly exterior she'd imagined. Unsure of what to say or do, she smiled.

He reanimated at once. "Forgive me. Please come in. I am Louis Tiffany."

Clara breached the rules of genteel feminine conduct and extended her hand before he did. "I am Miss Clara Wolcott, and this is my sister, Miss Josephine Wolcott."

"You're directly on time," he said shaking her hand. "A few seconds early in fact. I assume you had no trouble finding your way?"

"I'm quite familiar with this part of the city," she replied, remedying the quiver in her voice by clearing her throat. "And I do try to be punctual, despite carriage drivers' consistent attempts to run me over."

He didn't appear to be listening, nor had he given up her hand. Rather, he was again absorbed in studying her. Unable to restrain herself, Clara openly examined him in return. He was inarguably good-looking, a man who could easily turn women's heads. His careless dark curls looked tossed about, as if he'd been caught in a windstorm—a contrast to the neatly trimmed beard and mustache. His broad forehead, wide mouth and straight nose were perfectly formed, but it was his eyes that commanded attention. Large and brilliant blue, they had a sharp, penetrating quality, like that of a bird of prey. They gave her the eerie feeling he could look inside her and know her thoughts.

A man standing half-hidden in the darkest corner coughed and stepped forward.

Tiffany dropped her hand at once. "May I introduce Mr. Henry Wyckoff Belknap, the artistic director here at Tiffany Glass," he paused and then added, ". . . second to myself, of course."

The diminutive, impeccably dressed gentleman stepped out of the shadows, greeting them with a bow and a kind smile. He was so slender and youthful looking, he could easily have passed as a young boy.

"Please sit down, ladies." Mr. Tiffany gestured toward the two chairs that faced his desk. He placed himself directly in front of them, adjusted his pince-nez and commenced reading a document she recognized as her résumé.

Blinded by the glare from the window behind him, she dug her heels into the rug and tried unsuccessfully to push back the heavy chair. Not to be deterred, she positioned herself in Tiffany's shadow in order to judge his reactions.

"I see here that after high school you taught for a short time?"

Relieved that he hadn't started with a more challenging line of inquiry, Clara nodded. "Yes, I took a position teaching in a private girls' school, but didn't care for the work. My aim in life has always been to be a designer."

She pulled her portfolio onto her lap and began unfastening the straps. "As I mentioned in my letter, I've taken the liberty of bringing some of my— "

"After you gave up your teaching position, you enrolled in the Western Reserve School of Design for Women where you graduated first in your class with honors. Is this correct?"

"Yes. While I was in— "

He fixed her with a look. "When did you discover your path as an artist, and, how did you end up here in my office?"

She took his direct manner as an invitation to answer in kind. "It was my mother who recognized my talent early on and sent me to Cleveland. While there, I soon learned of the exalted role the arts play in New York City. After that, there was no question that New York was where I wanted to be.

"A few years later, my closest friend, Alice Gouvy, proposed we move here and attend the Art Students' League together. To help cover expenses, I took a position modeling for Mr. Waldo's illustration classes; he's the gentleman who told me Tiffany's was looking for women artists with experience in—"

"You also write that you are in excellent health, take daily exercise, and enjoy opera and the theater?"

Momentarily perplexed by the sudden turn of the interview's focus, she recalled George Waldo's warning that Tiffany had a reputation for being eccentric and that she shouldn't worry if he had a sudden turn to the fanciful.

"I walk a great deal, and when I'm able to afford the theater, I like—"

"Ah, the theater, one of my favorite entertainments." Tiffany regarded her with unconcealed amusement. "Whom do you consider to be the greatest actors on the stage today, Miss Wolcott?"

She thought for a moment. "Without doubt I would say Sarah Bernhardt and, of course, Mr. Booth. He is by far the greatest tragedian of our age, and Miss Bernhardt has a most eloquent manner of speech. I believe she—"

"But Mr. Booth is the brother of John Wilkes Booth, the man who assassinated President Lincoln, is he not?"

"Yes," she replied hesitantly, "though the relation does not appear to have affected his acting abilities. Indeed, from what I've read, all three Booth brothers have proved themselves to be highly talented thespians, irrespective of any wayward political beliefs they may have held."

"I see." Tiffany pinched the corners of his mouth and resumed reading. A moment later, his eyes lit up with a modicum of excitement. "You held a managerial position with Ransom and Company in Cleveland designing Moorish-style fretwork and furniture?"

Happy to be returned to the safe ground of her résumé, she brightened. "Yes, I was head designer there for two years and managed fifteen workers who—"

"I have a great fondness for that style," Tiffany cut in. "I employ the Moorish influence in many of my own architectural endeavors, in both interiors and exteriors."

"While I agree Moorish design is intriguing," she said, not at all convinced that giving her unsolicited opinion was in her best interest, especially since it didn't entirely agree with his ideas, "and the Moorish influence is fine for broad use in architecture, as you have brilliantly demonstrated in your building on Lenox Hill, my own tastes and interests lean toward Oriental simplicity for interiors. It seems much more suited to decorative elegance and personal comfort. The Japanese style of minimal decoration and clean lines is, in my estimation, the most—"

In the corner, Mr. Belknap lapsed into a fit of coughing that scarcely disguised his laughter. She left off at once, afraid that Tiffany might have taken umbrage at her having voiced her thoughts so freely. Except, instead of a scowl, Tiffany was beaming. At a loss to understand why, she entertained the idea that he might be toying with her.

Tiffany returned his attention to her résumé. "After Ransom's you came to New York and studied at the Metropolitan Museum Art School? Your emphasis was on—"

"Yes," she replied, only dimly aware of having cut him off mid-sentence. "What I wanted to do was—"

He shot her a look. Eyebrows raised, Tiffany smiled so broadly, she could see his back teeth. Briefly, both Wolcott sisters unconsciously mimicked his expression.

"This is most satisfactory, Miss Wolcott!" He tapped the paper. "You say here that you studied architectural decoration?"

"Clara was the only woman in the entire architectural decoration division," Josie broke in. "She graduated first in her class."

"What my sister has neglected to say is that I had a great deal of help from the other students. I assure you, they were as qualified as I—"

Mr. Tiffany thrust his hand toward her. Momentarily confused, she thought perhaps a handshake was his way of terminating the interview. She was about to extend her hand when she realized he merely wished to see her portfolio.

He placed the leather case on his desk and opened it with a reverence she would not have expected of him. Mr. Belknap stepped closer, and for what seemed an extensive amount of time, the two men stood side by side, silently considering her work. It pleased her to see they didn't rush through the watercolors and sketches, but rather spent whole minutes examining each image. Mr. Belknap picked out several watercolors, pouring over each one with the excitement a child might have experienced upon seeing a long-awaited gift.

Tiffany lowered the best of her hummingbird illustrations and regarded her with a respect that had not been there before, as if he'd seen her soul though her art. Remaining perfectly still, she held her breath.

"First rate work, Miss Wolcott," he said quietly. "You have an excellent eye for color and detail. We are of a similar artistic leaning. Like you, I find my muse in nature. You've hit upon exactly the sort of thing I'm looking for in an artisan."

She let out a sigh of relief. "Thank you. I have other examples of my work, including my designs from Ransom's. If you'd like, I'll bring the rest around tomorrow."

"That won't be necessary," he said, handing back her case. "What you have here is more than acceptable. I need no further proof of your capabilities."

He seemed to retreat into deeper thought, fixing on something she couldn't even guess at. Within the space of a single breath, he'd put a distance between himself and everyone in the room. It crossed her mind that he might be trying to find the words to tell her that her capabilities, though 'first rate,' weren't quite good enough for Tiffany's, when he motioned to Mr. Belknap.

"After I've finished writing out instructions, I'd like you to escort the ladies downstairs and introduce them to Mr. Bracey." He turned abruptly to Josie. "Where are you and your sister residing at present, Miss Wolcott?"

Stricken, Josie looked to Clara, who answered for her. "My sister and I are living at Miss Todd's boardinghouse near Fort Greene Park in Brooklyn. Perhaps you know of the place?"

As soon as the words were out of her mouth, Clara wanted to call them back. It was not likely Louis Tiffany would be on familiar terms with boardinghouses, let alone the people who inhabited them.

Tiffany pointedly ignored her, never taking his eyes off Josie. "You write in your application letter that you've registered for the fall session at the Art Students' League, yet you also wish to have an apprenticeship at Tiffany's?"

Josie answered so softly he was required to lean close. "I, well, we, meaning my mother and sisters, thought it best if I were to have some practical experience along with my studies."

He regarded her for a long while before resuming in a gentler tone. "You're seventeen, Miss Wolcott, a most tender age. I'm afraid having a position here, plus studying at the League will be a strain on your health."

"I assure you it won't," she said. "As you say, I'm young, which provides me with the strength I'll need for a demanding schedule."

He gave her a last searching look and took his seat behind the massive desk. Absently he stroked his beard, then set to writing. For several minutes, the only sounds were the creak of his chair and the scratch of his pen.

A quarter of an hour later, the sisters stole a questioning glance at one another. Clara was about to clear her throat, when he put down his pen and folded the sheaf of papers.

"Daniel Bracey, our head man in the glass department, will show you around the workroom and answer any questions you might have."

Clara rose from her chair, but Tiffany motioned for her to remain seated. "Your duties as artisan-designer in my stained-glass window and mosaic department are fairly straightforward. When the orders come in, I'll meet with you to explain what the client wants. Mostly, you'll be designing ecclesiastical windows, though of late we are acquiring quite a few private clients who want specially designed windows for their homes.

"When you've sketched out your designs and made note of the colors you wish to use for each piece, you'll bring them to me. If I approve them, you'll then make a cartoon—a large drawing—the same dimensions as the actual windows. "

For a brief moment he searched her face, as if half expecting her to protest. "Once that's completed, you will select and cut your glass. Make sure to keep an account of each pound and piece of glass used, and how much time you spend on each task.

"Mr. Bracey and the men will then set the cames . . ." He saw their confusion and sighed. "Cames are the strips of lead that hold the glass pieces together." He waited for their nods of understanding before continuing. "At that point, I'll view the piece, make my criticisms, and then you'll make the changes I ask for. Is this clear?"

"Yes," Clara replied, with a confidence she did not feel.

"Considering your previous experience, I'll review your position after a six-month probation period. If you've shown yourself to be competent and your work meets my expectations, I'll advance you to a managerial position. The other girls need someone assertive to guide them. You are to report next Monday, 8 a.m. sharp. Tardiness is not tolerated here at Tiffany's for any reason."

Clara moved forward in her chair, "Thank you, Mr. Tiffany. I'm looking forward to—"

"Your hours," he continued, "are Monday through Friday from eight to five, and Saturdays from eight to three-thirty. Based on what I've seen of your skills, and considering the responsibilities of your position, I'm setting your wage at ten dollars and fifty cents a week."

He shifted his attention to Josie. "As for you, Miss Wolcott, I think—"

"It is said I have great promise as an artist," Josie said quickly.

He looked about to laugh, but then changed his mind. "In that case, you shall start as your sister's assistant. Your pay will be five dollars per week. However, once the League is back in session, you should concentrate on your studies. At that time, your hours and wages will be decreased by half. You may arrange your schedule to what best suits your purpose. Is that agreeable to you?"

"Yes, sir. I'm very grateful. I hope—"

Abruptly, Tiffany stood and went to the door, an indication the interview was at an end.

As if waking from a dream, Clara rose slowly. It didn't seem real that one of the most famous and successful men in New York had just hired her. The interview could not have lasted longer than a half hour, and yet she felt her life was changed forever.

They followed him into the hallway, where he handed his instructions to Mr. Belknap. "Give these to Mr. Bracey, Henry, and make sure the Misses Wolcott are given a tour of the department before they leave. Good day, ladies."

Elated, Clara all but curtsied. "Thank you, Mr. Tiffany. I can't express how pleased I—"

Without further ceremony, Louis Tiffany took a step back and closed the door.

Afraid they would burst into laughter should they look at one another, the sisters directed their attention to Mr. Belknap, who seemed as bewildered as they.

He cleared his throat. "Well then, ladies, follow me if you would to our new elevator." To Clara's chagrin, Josie insisted they use the stairs.

The Window and Mosaic Department was an open workroom, one wall of which was made up of enormous windows that filled the room with light. Awed by the sheer size of the place, Clara let her eyes wander to the partially completed leaded windows spread out on huge easels, and then to the finished ones hanging from the ceiling, sending rays of color in all directions. Racks of colored glass in every shade one could imagine were placed in the center of the room. It was, she thought, like wandering into a thieves' cave and finding a mountain of treasure.

Mr. Belknap pressed a handkerchief to his neck. "You should take care not to wear your best clothes, and don't forget to bring aprons and comfortable shoes."

A dour-looking man approached. Not waiting for introductions, he took the instructions out of Belknap's hand and began to read, his expression one of vexation.

Well-acquainted with the prejudice men held against women who sought jobs rather than husbands, Clara saw her work would be cut out for her trying to sway this man into thinking of her as a colleague rather than an enemy out to steal jobs away from men.

For the better part of an hour, Mr. Bracey lectured in his Irish brogue as to where each tool was stored, and to whom they were to speak and to whom they were not. He was particularly adamant that they take their instruction from him and only him, adding at the end that any 'female nonsense,' such as unnecessary talking, giggling, smiling or flirting, would be grounds for immediate dismissal. He punctuated the end of his discourse with an emphatic 'bah!' and strode away.

Clara was about to wish the back of his head a sour good day when Josie marched after him, chatting cheerfully as she went: "I detect from your accent that you must be from Ireland, Mr. Bracey. I've heard that your country is beautiful with all those green hills surrounded by nothing but ocean and sky. I hope to see it for myself someday. Surely you miss your homeland?"

The Irishman eyed Josie as he would if he were seeing her for the first time. His gruffness eased, and he swiftly removed his cap as if he had just remembered his manners. "Aye Miss, 'tis a grand place, but there's no good in missin' it now. I'm here an' this is where I'll be when I meet me Maker."

"But still," Josie smiled, "I'd love to hear about your Ireland and the people there. Perhaps someday you might tell me about it?"

Mr. Bracey hunched up his shoulders, fighting the smile that threatened to make a mockery of his well-practiced scowl. "Aye, perhaps."

"Lovely. I look forward to seeing you on Monday. I'm sure my sister and I will learn a great deal under your capable direction."

Clara tried to duplicate her sister's smile, though she knew it held none of the same magic. For her efforts, Mr. Bracey managed to reward her with the barest of nods.

It was a start.

———§———

Mr. Belknap was waiting for them in the hall. "May I escort you ladies to the station?"

Clara opened her mouth to accept his offer when she changed her mind. Mr. Belknap was obviously a man of culture—it might do well to impress him by demonstrating her interest in the performing arts. After all, hadn't she just professed a love of theater?

"I'm sorry, but we've made plans to meet friends at Madison Square. We have tickets to attend the rehearsals at the Metropolitan Opera House this afternoon."

Puzzled, Josie turned to look at her. "But we aren't going to—"

"Of course we're going to make it on time—if we hurry," Clara quickly cut in. "Besides, the . . ." she threw out the fanciest name she could think of, " . . . the Vanderlings said they'd wait for us."

Belknap looked baffled. "Rehearsals? I wasn't aware there were rehearsals this early in the year. Is it Wagner or have the stockholders finally managed to overthrow German opera once and for all? I've heard they're bringing back Italian opera now that Verdi is so popular in Europe."

Snagged by her own piece of fiction, Clara stammered. "I . . . it's um. . . it's . . ."

"It's a Wagnerian opera," Josie said with conviction. "*Das Rheingold.*"

Clara stared at her.

"It's one of my favorites." Josie finished.

Belknap opened the outside door. "In that case I won't delay you. I'll stop in on Monday to see how you're doing. Until then, ladies, I wish you a pleasant day."

With a firm grip on her sister's arm, Clara whirled about, her skirt swirling as they wended their way toward Madison Avenue. Once they were out of earshot, she turned, eyebrows raised. "*Das Rheingold?*"

**Miss Todd's Boardinghouse
32 Oxford Street, Brooklyn**

Clara and Josie unpinned their hats and sank gratefully into the mountain of pillows lining the couch. The small room they called home had been made cozy with the addition of lace curtains and several vases of daisies and cornflowers.

"Mr. Belknap seemed the perfect gentleman," Josie said.

"Definitely that, although he was quite . . ." Clara paused, unsure of the word she wanted.

"Short?"

Clara laughed. "Not so much short as delicate and exceedingly well-groomed."

"Did you notice his shoes?"

"His shoes?"

"They were half the size of yours."

Clara lifted her skirt to reveal dusty lace-up boots of a most unladylike size. Picking up a sketchpad and charcoal stick she began sketching. "Mr. Bracey was ready to throw us to the devil until you worked your magic on him."

"Oh, Mr. Bracey's all right," Josie said. "A little prickly on the outside, but I expect he'll come round. I thought Mr. Tiffany a bit strange, the way he was cross and restless and tender all at the same time."

Josie lay back, and Clara saw the pose she'd been looking for. "Hold that position right there. Turn your head a little to the left."

"George said Mr. Tiffany went a little mad after his first wife and son died."

"Wealth and prominence in society don't always mean one is guaranteed an untroubled life, Jo."

"When I think of how happy we are here with nothing except a bed and a few pieces of clothing, and how lucky we are to have our family, I feel sorry for him. I don't think I'd like being rich—you'd never know whether someone loved you for yourself or your wealth."

Without looking up from her drawing, Clara smiled. Of her three sisters, it was Josie who always went right to the heart of a person.

From out in the hall came the familiar whistle of Mr. Driscoll, the widower who rented the room across from theirs. Neither sister could remember at what point he'd fallen into the habit of reading to them each evening, but it soon became the highlight of their day. Mr. Driscoll was blessed with an actor's knack for lending each character a unique personality and vitality with a simple change of voice. He made scenes and characters come alive as vividly as if they were assembled on a stage before them. With his pug nose and deeply cleft chin, their neighbor had about him a craggy, weatherworn look that on more than one occasion made him a worthy subject for their sketches.

Mr. Driscoll stood in the doorway, tipping an invisible hat. "Miss Todd has rung the first bell for dinner, and I thought I'd see about escorting you ladies downstairs."

"Then you shall be the first to know that we're hired on at Tiffany's," Clara said.

"It was exciting," Josie added. "Mr. Tiffany was much taken with Clara's work, and Mr. Belknap, the art director, was—"

"Mr. Henry Wyckoff Belknap?"

Clara looked surprised. "Do you know him?"

"Several years ago I represented Mrs. Belknap in the purchase of a commercial building. They're a wealthy family, leading patrons of the arts and tight with the Tiffanys. Belknap is a splendid chap, although his mother . . . " he hesitated. "Well, suffice to say Catherine Belknap is a widow who leans heavily upon her son." He turned to Josie. "How did you fare with Mr. Tiffany?"

"He had few questions for me, but I was only applying as an apprentice."

"Consider yourself lucky, my girl," Mr. Driscoll said, holding back a smile. "I know for a fact that Tiffany is meticulous in his business dealings, especially when it comes to the people who work for him, no matter how minor the position may be. I've heard that he once raked a twelve-year-old messenger boy over the coals for two hours before giving him the job. The poor lad ended up in Chambers Street Hospital with nervous prostration."

"I've also heard that Mr. Tiffany wields his walking stick like a weapon." Alice Gouvy stood in the doorway smiling. Her voice was huskier than one might expect from such a petite woman, though it did not detract from her beauty. "However, having grown up with the Wolcott girls in Tallmadge, Mr. Driscoll, I can assure you they've all been taught never to back away from adversity without a good fight."

She took Clara's hands. "I couldn't help but overhear the news. Congratulations—I think."

Clara smiled warmly at the woman she'd loved like a sister most of her life. "Is there anything else we should know before the next time we come face to face with this destroyer of young children?"

"I know of some things." George Waldo said, and entered their room somewhat out of breath from running up the stairs. Looking cheerful, he tossed his hat onto the sofa and bent to kiss Josie on the forehead. "I've come to see if Mr. Tiffany left you in one piece," he said. "Over dinner I want to hear every detail of the interview."

"You're staying for dinner?" Alice asked, eyebrows raised. "How did you manage to talk Miss Todd into that *again*? It must be the third time this week."

George moved about the room compulsively touching or rearranging things while he spoke. "I have a commission to do an illustration for a story about the suffragist movement, and when I arrived, I couldn't help but notice how closely Miss Todd resembles Susan B. Anthony. Seizing the opportunity, I asked if she'd sit for me. She was so pleased about having her likeness in *Scribner's* she convinced me to stay for dinner."

Though accustomed to George's inability to remain still or quiet for any length of time, Clara regarded him with a certain amount of fascination. She picked up his hat and hung it on the coat rack. "So what other secrets do you know about Mr. Tiffany that you haven't already told us?"

George thought for a moment. "You should be aware that he was born with a lazy tongue and has a tendency to lisp at times."

Doubtful, Clara gave him a look. "How is it possible that a family as wealthy as the Tiffanys didn't hire a speech coach for him?"

"I believe Charles Tiffany had his own ideas about how to rid his son of the impediment. From what I've heard, he thought speech training was a form of mollycoddling. He employed much harsher forms of treatment for Louis—namely, his fists and a rod."

Her eyes flickered up to his. "Surely that's just malicious hearsay?"

"I'm afraid not. The old man is supposedly quite the tyrant. Evidently, Louis eventually gained enough control over his lisp, that you never hear it—unless he's nervous or in an ill-temper."

George wandered over to the desk and began going through Clara's portfolio, rocking on his heels. "Why didn't you ask me to go over your work before you took it to Tiffany?" He held one of her butterfly watercolors to the light.

Taking the painting from him, Clara returned it to her case. "I did. You said you were too busy."

"You should have asked Mr. McBride; he's the one with the keenest eye."

"Actually, he was the first person I asked, but he was too busy with his art classes. I then appealed to Dudley Carpenter, but he was rushing to finish a commissioned portrait for a woman in Queens, and Alice and Josie are much too biased."

Incredulous, George stopped preening before the mirror. "You asked Dudley to peruse your work before you asked me? Why, Dud is only a child! He wouldn't know something good if it hit him in the nose."

"Dudley is only two years younger than you are," Josie pointed out.

"True enough," Alice said, "although I agree Dudley does look younger, due to his slender build."

George glanced down at his paunch and frowned. "In a good wind, that boy would blow over to New Jersey and never be seen again. At least I have some substance."

"Quite a bit, I'd say," Clara gave a quick glance at the strained buttons of his waistcoat and turned her attention to Mr. Driscoll. "Since we won't be obliged to entertain Mr. Waldo this evening, we were hoping you might indulge us by reading a chapter or two from *The Bostonians?*"

Making as deep a bow as his arthritic hips would allow, Francis Driscoll winked. "At your service, Mademoiselles."

27 East Seventy-second Street
Lenox Hill, Manhattan

Henry Belknap and Louis Tiffany emptied their brandy snifters as they gazed out over East Seventy-second Street from the turret window of Tiffany's Lenox Hill mansion. Below, the last horsecars of the night rolled by, harnesses creaking as the horses strained against their breastcollars.

Over Henry's protests, Louis handed him a cigar and refilled his brandy snifter. "Have a seat."

Reluctantly giving up the night air, Henry sank into a chair opposite his host and surveyed the room. With Persian carpets, potted palms, hanging baskets, copper vats, stuffed peacocks, ceramic elephants and iridescent dragon tiles crammed in every available space, not one clear inch of floor, wall or ceiling was visible. He found the random assortment of clutter suffocating.

"I've had a letter from Sam Clemens," Louis said. "He'd like us to finish the transom window for the Hartford house before he and his wife leave to go abroad. I thought perhaps the new girl, Miss . . . Miss . . ." He waved his cigar, struggling to recall the name.

"Wolcott," Henry said. "Clara and Josephine."

"Oh, right. I thought I'd have the elder girl, Clara, work on the transom. It shouldn't be too difficult a project. She seems capable enough, don't you think?" He lit his cigar and held out the match.

Henry declined, glancing warily at the cigar that Tiffany had forced on him. The smell alone made him sick. "Capable? My God man, from what I saw of her work, she's miles beyond capable, she's positively gifted. You've struck gold in hiring the woman, but I expect you already know that."

Louis blew smoke rings into the air between them. "I admit her work was intriguing, but then again, women naturally have a superior sense of color and design. I hope Miss Wolcott will follow through and stick with it. I've hired other promising girls, but in the end they're all the same, running off to get married or to have their illegitimate babies."

Henry sensed that Clara Wolcott was different—intelligent and fully alive, completely unlike the crowds of pallid, tightly corseted women who regularly infested his mother's parlor. He thought of those women as flocks of puffy-winged birds, who flitted from one overheated parlor to another, engaging in insipid gossip, every last one of them topped with preposterously large hats that always reminded him of festooned ships on seas of hair. Forsaking any kind of higher education, the lot of them had had nothing but marriage fed to them starting with their mother's milk, as if the getting of husbands was their only purpose in life.

"But don't you get the feeling that this woman is somehow . . ." Henry paused to think of the right word, "remarkable?"

Louis shifted his gaze from the window back to Henry. "How do you mean?"

"Talent and maturity aside, she has a sense of purpose about her, as if she's determined to be successful. There's not a hint of artifice about her, and she says what she means."

"Yes, well, she certainly has her own ideas about things." Tiffany drained his glass and, before the residue could gather at the bottom, poured another measure. "As long as she doesn't allow her own purposes to interfere with mine, she'll get on all right."

Growing up next door to the Tiffanys, Henry had circulated within Louis's world long enough to have witnessed a man who could, when it suited his ego, be kind and generous. By the same token, he'd also seen the cold-blooded and destructive scoundrel, who seemed devoid of both principle and conscience. Time and again, he'd watched the man sign his own name to what others created without thinking twice. Henry looked down at his hands. "Perhaps you should allow her that."

Louis took the cigar from his mouth. "Allow her what?"

"To explore her own depth instead of being kept within the strict confines of what Tiffany's requires of her. She just might surprise you."

"I'll be the one to determine when and if she is to be given more responsibility. For now, she'll do as I tell her. I detected a trace of insolence about her."

A smile came to Henry's lips as he recalled the manner in which Miss Wolcott had maintained her purpose, despite Tiffany's offensive habit of interrupting and then wandering off the subject at hand. It was a rare few who were ever successful in getting their own views across when disagreeing with him. "I doubt Miss Wolcott has ever had an insolent thought in her life."

"If you truly believe that, you are a fool," Louis scoffed. "If the women of your generation aren't kept in check, they'll soon be wearing pants and voting. The very idea is perverse. The next thing we know, women will be running for political office."

"That might not be a bad thing. At least we'd be free of war."

"In that case, you are not only politically naïve, my friend, but it's obvious you have never been married. If you had, you would know that the old proverb about women being the gentler sex is a complete myth.

"She is a fine-looking woman, I'll admit to that. Too tall, but not without allure."

Henry nodded in agreement. "She has a graceful charm about her that makes her seem beautiful."

"A graceful charm," Louis repeated, his face reflecting a sudden sadness. "Do you know, Henry, that when I opened my office door today, I thought for a moment she was May. The resemblance is astonishing, don't you think?"

Mildly surprised, Henry shook his head. Louis rarely mentioned the first Mrs. Tiffany or the grim circumstances surrounding her and their son's untimely deaths. "I remember seeing her at Mother's afternoon teas, but I was only twelve."

Louis's gaze wandered to the window. "I was sure it was May come back from the grave to take me to task for . . . everything."

"Everything?"

"My son's death, her illness, her death. My behavior was . . ." Tiffany sighed. "I was young and selfish. I didn't have enough sense to realize how much she meant to me or how much I would miss her. She had a frail constitution; I should never have insisted on dragging her halfway around the world while she was with child."

He let his head fall back. "My father blamed me for their deaths, of course; to this day he never misses an opportunity to throw it in my face." He waved a hand. "I shouldn't dwell on it—it's much too maudlin."

In the ensuing silence, Henry searched for words of solace. Finding none, he rose to leave. "I'd better be getting home. Mother will be sending out the militia if I'm not there to bid her goodnight and bring her her valerian. It seems the tisane is never so effective as when made by my own hands."

Louis squinted, as if sizing him up. "How is it you aren't married yet, Henry? When I was your age, I was long married and awaiting the birth of my second child."

"I'm particular when it comes to women," Henry said, suddenly uneasy. "I've not met many who interest me."

"And," Louis added smugly, "I suspect there are even fewer of whom your mother approves. I wouldn't call that particular." Louis studied the end of his cigar. "Peculiar is more like it."

Ignoring the jibe, Henry picked up his coat and bid his host goodnight. He'd grown accustomed to Tiffany's galling nature long ago. It was just one of the many things he would have to warn Miss Wolcott about.

——§——

By the time she burrowed under the covers next to Josie, Clara was too excited to sleep. A light breeze, heavy with the scent of blooming peonies, set the lace curtains moving in a fairy dance that held her mesmerized.

"If Mr. Driscoll proposed, would you accept?" Josie asked.

Clara plumped her pillow. "Just because he reads to us and sometimes treats us to an ice cream doesn't mean he wants to marry me, Josie. Mr. Driscoll is an affable and agreeable companion, who has friendly affections toward both of us, and that's all there is to the matter."

"There's more to it than that. You seem to have forgotten that when you and Alice moved in, Mr. Driscoll was here only temporarily while his Manhattan flat was being renovated. Doesn't it strike you as odd that he has continued on here long after the renovations were completed?"

"Mr. Driscoll is financially prudent. I'm sure he rents out his flat for five times what he pays here."

"You aren't looking at the facts, Clara. He spends all his free time with us, and he's always happy when he sees you. Now that I think about it, you seem particularly cheerful when he's around."

"You could also say that I'm particularly cheerful when I'm in the company of George, Dudley, or Mr. McBride. That doesn't mean I want to marry any of them. I'm twenty-six years old, Jo. Mr. Driscoll is a lovely gentleman, but marriage to a widower thirty-one years older than I, and one whom I know very little about?" She gave Josie a disparaging look. "I don't waste my time thinking of things that will never happen."

"But you're so well suited to each other," Josie insisted, "Like Mama's glass mantel clock."

"What, pray tell, does *that* mean?"

"When you look at the back of the clock you can see the gears and intricate parts working; each piece balances another to produce perfect time without effort." Josie looked at her, as if the answer were obvious. "Don't you see? That's how you and Mr. Driscoll are together."

Clara got out of bed and perched on the edge of the windowsill. "It's a charming image, and for all I know, it might be true, but you've ignored the most important factor."

"You mean that he hasn't asked for your hand yet?"

She rolled her eyes. "No, I mean that married women aren't allowed to work at Tiffany's."

Outside, a light rain fell, bringing with it a cool breeze. Below, she could hear water trickling from the eaves into the rain barrel. "I've worked hard to get to where I am now, let alone how much Mama had to sacrifice to send me to art school."

"I suppose," Josie stared up at the ceiling, "but if something happens to me, I don't want you to be alone here without family."

"Nothing is going to happen to you. You mustn't think that way."

She was distracted by a small spotted skipper moth that landed on a fold of the curtain. "Come for your portrait, have you?" As if it understood, the moth fluttered its wings, giving her a close-up view of forewings banded with bright orange, and the patch of silver that marked each hindwing. She took up her sketchpad and drew the moth in detail, down to the clubbed ends of its antennae, leaving off only when the breeze turned chilly.

Crawling in next to Josie's warmth, she watched a spot of cream moonlight creep across the floor until her eyes grew heavy. First thing in the morning she would send word to her mother that her life as an artist was about to blossom.

——§——

Louis unclipped the small key from his watch chain and unlocked the compartment hidden at the back of the top drawer in his desk. He withdrew a leather-bound diary and sat down to write.

Lenox Hill
May 7, 1888

Louise with child. December confinement. I feel it is too soon after the twins' birth, but I leave that side of women's business to her physician. I told Louise this one had best be a son for my father's sake. Four girls and a son, who is likely sterile from mumps, is certain to send the Tiffany name into extinction.

There will be no sons from brother Burnie, to be sure. I doubt the drunken lout could stay sober long enough to get a woman with child. The only good thing about Burnie is that he is the one subject on which Father and I agree.

Belknap here tonight to discuss company matters, but left early to attend his mother. He is in dire need of distance from that suffocating grasp. I don't put stock in this brand of filthy gossip, but, as of late, I've heard his name bandied about at the club. He possesses a flawless sense of what will sell, but no matter — such loathsome behavior, if true, or if made common knowledge, would not be tolerated.

Father regularly reminds me that sales are slow, even though Stanford White brought in a contract for ten large windows to install in his latest architectural feat. I must remember to send him a gold and emerald cravat pin from Father's shop.

I've hired a new artisan, Miss Clara Wolcott. I suspect she is a diamond of the first water. An excellent eye for color, and her sense of balance and rhythm unusually good. Superb lines and shading. Her sample rendering of a butterfly with its wings pushed backward by the wind stays with me. It was so lifelike I dared not touch it, lest the creature fly off the paper. She will learn leaded glass, and then we'll see about designing. She lingers in my thoughts, though I dare say that is due to her strong likeness to May.

I hear the nurse attending to the wailing twins, who are suffering with summer colds. Little Charles has sneaked away from the nursery to beg me once again for a pony, Simpkins interrupts to ask if I want a bath drawn, and Louise is insisting I come to bed.

Dear God, how I wish I were in Morocco out on the dunes with nothing more than water, brandy, canvas and paint.

Louise is on the stair. (I'm hunted down like a beast!)   L.C.T.

~ 2 ~

HAD SHE FORESEEN what her life would become in the nine months since she'd taken the position at Tiffany's, Clara would have dismissed it as fantasy. In a matter of weeks after she had designed her first windows, Mr. Tiffany put her in charge of the women's glass cutting department. Almost immediately, there began a never-ending stream of orders for her work.

By the end of the day, it was all she could do to find her way home and fall into bed. The only time she had to write her letter for the round robin was while she ate her lunch. Clearing a place on her worktable, she put her sandwich and coffee to one side and carefully dipped her pen.

Noon at Tiffany's
March 8, 1889

Dearest Mama and sisters Kate and Emily,

The round robin arrived this morning. I couldn't wait until this evening, so read it as I walked to work, depending on luck to keep me from falling off curbs or bumping into lampposts. I will try to get this written and posted before I return to the madness awaiting me in the workroom. There's been a flurry of chaos here, with the getting up of four large windows for a rush order and finishing the windows Mr. Tiffany took away from the men's department. In some ways the work seems to be a mountainous undertaking, but I try to look at it in detail and only with reference to the next minute, perhaps the next hour. When it seems overwhelming and I'm about to jump into the Hudson, I think of the long years I've struggled to get to this place, and my confidence is restored.

I remain enthralled with this shining Mecca of New York, which provides limitless opportunities to the enterprising artists who flock here in great number. The thought that there's an abundance of collectors who pay handsomely for what these same artists produce leaves me wild with impatience to get my work into the public eye.

On Sunday, I walked by the Tiffany mansion on Lenox Hill at the head of Madison Avenue. You should see it, Mama—the structure is a magpie's nest of bizarre Moroccan design elements that somehow make the place rhythmic. The New York Times reported that it's viewed by many to be the most brilliant architectural feat in all of New York. I'd give my eyeteeth to explore the innards of that beast.

Mr. Belknap has invited Josie and me to a lecture at the Metropolitan Museum of Art. My opinion of him rises a little each day, and I've almost forgotten that when standing next to him, I look like a clumsy, ill-groomed giantess. We share a good many opinions of people, art, and politics. At 28, he is but a year older than I, and yet he's one of the worldliest men I've ever known.

Mr. Tiffany is a dichotomy. On one hand he's a boorish, avaricious man and on the other, a sensitive artist. Yes, he is handsome, but not to my taste, for I have the disadvantage of seeing the ugly side of him much too often.

Please assure Grandmother that electric lights aren't all they're cracked up to be. They have none of the warmth of gas lamps, though one does see much better.

Josie is well, all ailments at bay. More importantly, she is happy.

Love, Clara

P.S. The boarders have taken in a stray kitten we've named Ida B. Smith. She's the sorriest thing you ever saw. Miss Todd said that cats always begin washing themselves as soon as they feel loved. Evidently, Ida has never felt quite loved enough, so I've decided to give her a bath. I thought I'd—

"Excuse me, Miss?"

Her mouth full of bread and a slice of yesterday's roast beef, Clara broke off writing.

"I dunno what ya must be thinkin' on that Saint Anne window." Daniel Bracey took off his cap and slapped it against his leather apron.

It had taken time, but she'd managed to coax him from the pit of disapproval up the steep hill of acceptance. However, while she may have gained his respect, his devotion belonged entirely to Josie.

"How do ya expect the men to came them wee bits an' pieces in her hands?"

"Well, Mr. Bracey," Clara smiled, "I expect the men to do them very carefully. Please, won't you sit down and share this apple with me?"

"I'm not wantin' no apples, Miss. I come to find out how the men is 'sposed to use cames fer pieces of glass no bigger than a splinter."

She nodded in understanding of his dilemma. "You wouldn't happen to have a pocket knife, would you?"

Mr. Bracey produced a jackknife from his pocket and handed it over.

She commenced slicing the apple into sections. "Saint Anne was the mother of the Virgin Mary, was she not?"

"Aye, but I dunno what that's got to do with the—"

"What I mean to say is that Saint Anne is a special saint. She's the grandmother of Jesus Christ Himself, after all."

At the mention of Jesus, Mr. Bracey bowed his head. "True enough, Miss. In Ireland she's the patron saint of the childless."

Clara bit into a slice of apple and held one out to him. He hesitated, and then took it. Diplomacy was, she thought, rather like fishing: you had to offer the bait at the right moment.

"Did you know, Mr. Bracey, that this window is going all the way to Saint Augustine, Florida, to be used in the main church there?"

"Ah, no. Where the windows go 'taint none of me business."

"It's going into an alcove devoted specifically to Saint Anne. Think of all the poor childless couples who will come from miles around to kneel before this very window and pray to Saint Anne for the blessing of children. Later, when they've been blessed, they'll bring their wee ones to see this magnificent window of Saint Anne, perfect in her likeness."

She pressed another apple section on him. "We owe those people the most realistic and beautiful window we can possibly produce." She paused. "More than that, we owe Saint Anne a lovely set of hands with which to receive and bless those poor people."

He chewed thoughtfully. "Well, I suppose."

She handed him the remaining apple slice. "Only the other day, Josie told Mr. Tiffany that your workmanship is perfection itself and that she's honored to have you as her tutor."

A faint smile broke at the corners of his mouth. "A fine gal, that one."

"Yes, and you're a clever artisan, so I have no doubt you'll find a way to lead the details in Saint Anne's hands. I and the other girls have faith in your talents and trust your work completely." Slowly, but surely, she was reeling in the line.

He finished the last section of apple, all trace of irritation gone. "All right then, I might undo the cames an' use a wee strip of lead instead of the full width." Warming to the idea, he smiled at his own inventiveness.

"Or, you might use thin copper strips; it would look more delicate."

Mr. Bracey smiled. "A grand idea. I could make the cames thin as wire."

On his way out, he collided with Josie. The two blushed, smiled and bowed with the deepest respect, as if they were meeting for the first time and didn't, in fact, work together nine hours a day.

Josie set her sketchbook on the worktable. "I thought you might give me your opinion on these."

Clara wiped her hands on her apron before examining the twenty or so detailed drawings of elegant dresses. "These are the best designs you've done so far," she said when she finished. "You could easily design for *Godey's* or *Harper's Bazaar*."

Josie searched her face. "Do you mean that, or are you simply being kind because I'm your sister?"

"You know very well I don't give false flattery. You need to show these to George. He must know someone at one of the fashion magazines."

Josie ceased smiling and removed the book from Clara's hands. "They aren't ready to be viewed by anyone except you. I don't even want Alice to see them. "

"They *are* ready. Don't hold yourself back, Jo; believe in your talent. You were designing dresses for dolls before you were five. Mama is convinced you're going to end up in Paris designing for Charles Worth.

"Talk to George tonight. If you sold even a few of your designs it would bring in extra money, and Lord knows we need it."

——§——

Clara was using the maulstick to draw the finishing touches at the top of a landscape cartoon, when someone with a heavy step entered the workroom.

"Miss Wolcott! I demand an explanation for every one of these charges."

Lowering the stick, she took the time to lean it against the wall before turning to confront W. Pringle Mitchell, Louis Tiffany's vice president and manager. As usual, he was bristling with indignation, exactly as he had been when he'd knocked into her on the day of her interview. Since that moment, he'd continued to plague her, second-guessing her every decision and niggling over every expenditure, right down to the number of pencils she used.

He stood before her glowering, his side whiskers precisely barbered and his clothes faultlessly pressed from the cuffs of his pants to his stiff, white collar.

"What have I done now, Mr. Mitchell?" she asked wearily. "Have you discovered the three cents I embezzled from the company?"

"I'm glad you find this a joking matter, Miss Wolcott," he said, shaking an order sheet in her face "Though I assure you, I'm not amused. Who authorized you to order this absurd amount of glass?" He took a pencil from behind his ear and began slapping it against the paper as a sort of punctuation.

"Look at this here." (Snap!) "This is the most expensive glass we have." (Snap!) "You go too far. At this rate, you'll run Tiffany's into the ground. You must stop this constant flow of expense." (Snap! Snap!) "Explain yourself!"

Clara pulled the order sheet from Mr. Mitchell's grip and went down the list an item at a time. "This order for the patterned dark green glass was for the lilies on the Saint Anne window. Now, I suppose I could have made do with the lighter, cheaper color, but then there would have been no contrast with the other leaves—it would have looked out of place, and we know what Mr. Tiffany would have done about that, now, don't we?" She made a sound like breaking glass.

Stifled laughter came from the women who were pretending not to listen as they bent to their task of cutting glass.

Mr. Mitchell started to protest, but she cut him off. "Then there's this order for the cobalt glass. Terribly expensive, I know, but that was to replace a section of the Jesus at Galilee window that went under Mr. Tiffany's cane. Since he specifically asked for the cobalt, you might take the issue up with him.

"This order here for the number five pink glass? That was for the flowers in the Saint Joseph and Virgin Mary window. Mr. Tiffany wanted deep pink, but since I'm endeavoring to keep my charges down, I went with the number five instead of the number six, hoping it wouldn't be noticed and thus end up under Mr. Tiffany's cane. So, you might say I actually saved the company money with that order."

Except for the barely audible grinding of his teeth, Mr. Mitchell remained silent.

She went to the next item. "Then, of course, there's this gold glass for Jesus' halo in the crucifixion window. Again, frightfully expensive, but it *is* for Jesus' halo. I think the Son of God deserves a gold halo, don't you, Mr. Mitchell?"

"You're an insolent woman!" Mitchell ripped the paper from her hands. "I don't know what Mr. Tiffany was thinking when he hired you. We simply cannot have this kind of spending!" He lowered his voice. "It wasn't until you got here that we've had to put out so much for glass."

She took off her spectacles, her patience spent. "Which is exactly why the quality of the windows has soared. Don't think for one moment people haven't noticed. Orders have doubled in the last three months. Mr. Tiffany is pleased with this higher quality work, and I have serious doubts he'll ever be satisfied with mediocre products again."

"To the devil with higher quality! You're going to bankrupt us!"

"I'm doing no such thing! I'll even go so far as to say that once you cease your insufferable interfering with my department, the company will become even more productive."

Opening and closing his mouth like a beached fish, Mr. Mitchell stalked out, slamming the door behind him with a cry of outrage.

She sat down and rubbed her eyes, as the women converged on her.

"What's he got against you, Miss Wolcott?" asked Miss Hodgins, a pretty woman with hair the color of burning embers. "He's always harping at you about one thing or another. Honestly, if I didn't know to the contrary,

I'd say you was married to the disagreeable lout on account of the way you two bicker so professional-like."

Too worn out to laugh, Clara smiled. "I believe Mr. Mitchell belongs to that breed of men who don't approve of self-governing women."

Miss Ring, the department's best glasscutter, made a face. "We heard he's a relation of Mr. Tiffany, and that's the only reason Mr. Tiffany keeps him around."

Clara lifted the maulstick to its original position. "Mr. Tiffany's sister is married to Mr. Mitchell's uncle." She hesitated. "Which, I suppose, is where the expression 'a monkey's uncle' originated."

When the laughter died away, she resumed work on the cartoon until her eyes gave out. She was in the ladies' convenience splashing her face with water, when Josie appeared in a state of agitation. "You've got to come quickly. Mr. Tiffany is here for the Cane Criticism. He says he has to do it now, because his father has made other plans for him tomorrow morning."

Mr. Bracey was waiting for her in the hall. He ran alongside her as she made her way to her office. "Should I undrape all them windows fer His Majesty or no?"

"Uncover the four finished ones," she directed, searching frantically for her writing pad while smoothing down her hair. "Josie, have all the girls gather to one side of Mr. Tiffany the way he likes, and tell them this time there shall be no giggling, sobbing or fainting."

She removed her apron, glad she'd worn the less threadbare of her two white lawn waists. Pinching color into her otherwise pale cheeks, she hurried into the main workroom where Louis Tiffany was already perched on a tall stool. Head tilted and both hands clasped around one knee, he squinted at Saint Anne with great intensity.

Off to the side, her girls stood at attention like soldiers in formation. Though it would not have been evident to the casual observer, she could see they were flustered by the unscheduled visit, each one nervously holding her breath, awaiting his approval. Daniel Bracey and Josie stood behind them, waiting for the drama to unfold.

Clara hurried to his side. "I'm sorry, Mr. Tiffany. I wasn't aware you were coming for the criticism today."

He gave her a withering glance. "I specifically told Mr. Mitchell to inform you of the schedule change. It must have slipped your mind."

"Mr. Mitchell never gave me your message," she said without a trace of the irritation she felt.

"No matter." He pointed his cane at Saint Anne. "This is quite good. You've selected exactly the right color for her face. The lilies are perfect."

Tiffany slipped off the stool and stepped closer to the window, a furrow beginning between his brows. He began pacing, which she knew from experience was not a good sign.

"What about the hands?" He looked at her in disbelief. "Why aren't they finished?"

"Mr. Bracey and I were discussing that earlier. He's come up with the brilliant idea of using copper for caming the finely detailed portions, like Saint Anne's hands. He's ordered the copper and should have it by tomorrow. I'm sure you'll be pleased with the result."

Tiffany nodded to Mr. Bracey. "Very good, Daniel. I look forward to seeing it completed."

Clara winked at the women—one window approved with no broken glass was cause for celebration.

He shifted his attention to Jesus at Galilee, staring at the window for a long while before breaking into a wide smile. "You've outdone yourself on this one, Miss Wolcott. It is superb."

"Thank you," she said, her spirits lifting. "It was your choice of cobalt blue for the water that balanced it perfectly, although I'm not so sure Mr. Mitchell approved of the cost."

"Mr. Mitchell be hanged," Tiffany said offhandedly, already inspecting the next window, with its depiction of Saint Joseph and the Virgin Mary in a garden of flowers. He cocked his head. "The richness of your color selection is exceptional, but I don't think the Virgin's crown is quite the right color." He raised his cane and let the tip rest against the glass.

A tremendous impulse to wrest the cane out of his hand and throw it across the room caused her to take an involuntary step toward him. The window had been particularly difficult; she'd spent hours of her own free time, coming in early and leaving after closing in order to bring it to perfection.

Before she could check herself, she let out a little cry, as Tiffany jabbed his cane into each of the crown's sections. One by one the pieces fell to the floor and shattered.

"Perhaps it might do better to change these sections to a deep gold.

You agree, don't you, Miss Wolcott?"

No matter what she said, she couldn't win. If she agreed with him, she would betray her own sense that the gold would ruin the restful quality of the window. If she disagreed, he would accuse her of impertinence and perhaps destroy the entire window.

"But, Mr. Tiffany, might not the gold . . . " her voice slid to a whisper, ". . . defeat the tranquility of the window's other muted colors?"

His cane swung up. Flinching, she quickly covered her face. When she opened her eyes, Louis was still looking at the window, the cane resting on his shoulder. "To my eye, the right color is as essential to these windows as notes are to the composer. Since I'm the colorist here, I want to see gold glass in the Lady's crown, and so you shall place gold glass in the Lady's crown." He turned to her. "You *will* do that, won't you?"

The headache that had been threatening to blind her crouched behind her eyes like a panther waiting to strike. That he found it necessary to browbeat her was insulting; that he did it in front of the rest of the department was deplorable.

Tiffany frowned at the Crucifixion at Golgotha window, his fingers drumming on the head of his cane.

"Is something wrong, Mr. Tiffany?" She fought to keep the apprehension out of her voice. It was best to remain calm.

Taking a piece of paper from his breast pocket, he looked from it to the window, his mouth set in a hard line.

She stepped back, discreetly motioning to the four women closest to him to do the same.

"This is wrong." He checked the paper again and turned his icy gaze on her. "What are the dimensions of this window?"

A bolt of panic twisted her stomach into a knot. "Six feet by four. Mr. Mitchell said you wanted the size changed. He said— "

He moved closer to the window, using his pince-nez to examine the lower panel. "And what in the blazes are those brown things at the base of the cross?"

She forced herself to look where he was pointing. "Those are the rocks you requested."

His eyes fixed on hers, hard and accusing. "I asked for gray rockth!" he shouted, "Not lumpth of something that resembles what you'd find on the floor of a livery."

She checked her notes. "But Mr. Mitchell said you wanted brown rocks because the gray was too expen—"

The cane came down against the lower half of the window, shattering the figures of the Virgin and two Roman soldiers. Multicolored shards of glass flew in every direction. She shielded her eyes, hoping the women remembered to turn their heads and cover their faces with both hands as she'd instructed.

"Do not *dare* contradict me!" he screamed. "I would never have asked for brown rockth!" He struck the window again, sending Mary Magdalene's head spinning in Clara's direction.

A sharp, stabbing pain above her left eye caused her to jump back from the destruction. Unbidden, an image of a guillotine blade flashed through her mind and then vanished. She waited until she was sure the demolition was over before unshielding her eyes. Tiffany stood before her gaping at the destroyed window, as if he couldn't fathom who had done such a thing. Behind her, she heard Miss Barnes, the youngest and most sensitive of her flock, run sobbing from the room.

"About the rocks," Clara began, careful to keep her voice neutral, "Mr. Mitchell refused to purchase the gray glass I originally ordered, because it was too expensive. He assured me you wanted brown rocks instead. I argued against it, but he wouldn't budge. He said—"

"I don't give a damn what Mitchell told you," Tiffany shouted, as he made for the door, glass crunching under his shoes. "Remake the window eight feet by five. Change the figures to fit the new scale and make the rocks three shades of gray. While you're about it, make the sky a lighter blue, but not too light, and add another mourner—a woman—to the right of the frame. I want her in ochre robes. No halo."

At the door he shouted into the otherwise silent room. "Have all four windows complete and ready for my criticism and shipment by next Wednesday morning."

She ran after him. "But Mr. Tiffany, you can't expect us to—"

"I not only expect it of you," he barked, "I demand it. If you and the other girls hope to keep your positions here, you'll do as I say." He disappeared into the hall, his booming voice echoing behind him. "Wednesday morning. First thing!"

The instant his voice died away, they began picking up the larger pieces of glass, while Mr. Bracey swept up the rest. "'Tis a shameful waste of good glass," he muttered. "Half a fortune in glass right here on the floor."

"I'd like to tell that Mr. Mitchell a thing or two," Miss Hodgins added, picking slivers of blue glass out of her shawl. "It was plain spite, him giving us the wrong measures. His Majesty ain't much better, either. He ought to be locked away—he's like a crazy man."

Clara looked at the shattered window. The waste in time and labor galled her.

Miss Ring took a step toward her. "Miss Wolcott, you've been cut."

When she touched the stinging place on her forehead, her fingers came away slick with blood. She pressed her handkerchief against the wound. "It's only a scratch. Nothing to be concerned about. However, if I do bleed to death before the day is out, please notify Mr. Tiffany that I won't be in tomorrow."

A few girls giggled, though most remained grim.

Miss Griffin voiced what was on all their minds. "How are we going to get an entire new window done by Wednesday? The selection alone is going to take that long. Cutting all those pieces for the soldiers' tunics and Mary's robes in four days, plus the other repairs? It's an impossible task to put on us, and none of us can afford to be let go."

She looked into their solemn faces and forced down her own frustration. "First, we should congratulate ourselves that of the four windows, two and most of a third were well received. I'm immensely proud of you and your fine efforts. If we're all willing to work extra, I know we can remake this window and finish the others by Wednesday. I must ask that you all commit to working two or more extra hours each day, including Saturday."

At the smattering of protests, Clara held up a hand. "Finishing the window in four days will keep our positions safe, and at the same time prove to Mr. Tiffany that we're made of sturdy stuff. We need to show Mr. Mitchell and Mr. Tiffany that we can handle anything they throw at us."

One by one the women nodded their consent, and with that, the mood in the room was changed. The infusion of energy bound them together as co-conspirators.

Clara squared her shoulders. "All right then, ladies, onward into the Coliseum and let's see what we can do with those lions."

Tiffany's
March 12, 1889

Dearest Ones,

    We've just now accomplished the impossible and resurrected the Crucifixion window, which fell mortally wounded under Mr. Tiffany's cane. As it turns out, Mr. Tiffany's judgment was correct—the window was made better with his suggestions. A rare mixture of businessman and artist, he seems to have escaped that terrible disorder that routinely afflicts the wealthy class—extremely bad taste in art.

    After dinner I'm going to Dudley's apartment for a rehearsal of Mr. McBride's medieval play. I play the King's wicked cousin, who plots against the life of the beautiful princess—to be played by our lovely Alice. If wickedness is the only quality necessary, I feel sure of my success in my part. George is quite pleased with his role as the torturer and does not share my anxiety over acting roles. When told he'd have to gouge out the princess's eyes, he positively beamed.

Love, Clara

P.S. It's hard to believe the Great Blizzard was just one year ago. To honor those who perished, I recited Tennyson's poems on death while we worked.

~ 3 ~

Noon at Tiffany's
June 5, 1889

Dearest Ones,

I have time for only a short note and a buttered roll. Once I dig myself out from under Tiffany's latest avalanche of work, I'll respond to all the robins I've let fly by with nary a peep.

Mama, why all this fretting about Reverend Cutler? Of course I approve of his desire to court you—he's a fine man. If his company makes you happy and gives you solace, then please accept him at once without concern for us. We know better than anyone what a beautiful and extraordinary woman you are. I'm overjoyed at the prospect of a romance for you. You have been a widow for far too long.

It's astonishing how much one can care for cats. Ida B. Smith, the little beast, has steadily advanced into my affections. Miss Todd, however, does not share those same sentiments. At the sound of the dinner bell last night, we entered the dining room only to find the chicken platter empty and the cat, visibly swelled, fast asleep on the napkins. We contemplated the scene with some dismay, until Josie said quite earnestly, "Do you think she'll die?" This amused us all, except Miss Todd.

I am turning into a regular bon vivant. Friday night, George, Dudley, Alice and I are to attend New York City's Annual Artists' Soiree at the plush Dakota Hotel. It is said that the drawing rooms are forty-nine feet long, the ceilings, eighteen feet high, and the mahogany floors are inlaid with silver!

I can hardly wait to attend. It is the event of the year, and I hope to make myself better known to my peers. I will give you a full account in the next robin.

Love, Clara

June 7, 1889
The Dakota Hotel

CLARA LEANED AGAINST Alice, drinking in the splendor of the Dakota Hotel ballroom. Swirls of pastel gowns, accented by the men's black-and-white evening dress, lent an air of regality to the festivities going on around them. "I'll wager there's more artistic talent in this room than in the entire Metropolitan Museum."

Alice looked over her fan. "And I would bet there will soon be a plethora of paintings entitled 'The Soiree' flooding every gallery in New York."

George appeared, towing Dudley Carpenter by the sleeve. Without any attempt at subtlety, Dudley commandeered the chair closest to Alice. His infatuation with her was no secret, considering that she was the subject of most of his paintings. Unfazed by his adoration, Alice treated him in the same manner she would a tiresome younger brother.

"We have a rather lively group attending this evening," George said. "Although we did have to endure several rounds of boring exchanges of opinion."

"Personally," Dudley drawled in his Tennessee accent, "I enjoy listening to people discuss the purpose of art."

"It was a lot of hot air from a bunch of overweening nitwits," George growled.

"As usual, Mr. Waldo and I disagree," Dudley said, brushing invisible lint off his lapel with fingers faintly stained by oil paint. "I found the discussions, revivifying, especially for those of us who feel that art puts people in awe of human capability and leaves them inspired."

"Revivifying?" George frowned. "My dear boy, the only revivifying going on in any of that twaddle was Mr. McBride's discourse on the origin of artistic talent."

"Artistic talent is a question that's been debated since humans began scratching pictures on cave walls," Alice broke in. "Is it God-given, passed down through the blood, or obtained through study?"

"As an art instructor," George began, "I can tell you unequivocally that it's acquired through rigorous training."

"What's your verdict, Miss Wolcott?" Henry Belknap approached with a bored-looking Louis Tiffany trailing behind.

Clara tensed, at once aware of her décolletage. The gown of deep lavender silk was one of Alice's castoffs that Josie had made over by ripping out the high collar and sewing in a low neck with a frill of lace. She couldn't imagine what her sister had been thinking, cutting away so much fabric. She leaned close to Alice. "Give me your fan."

The desperation in her voice caused Alice to turn in alarm. "Are you feeling faint, dearest? You look flushed. Are you ill? Shall I send George for a glass of water?"

Giving Alice a look, she yanked the fan from her hand, flipped it open and held it against her exposed flesh. Tiffany came up behind her, placing his hand on the back of her chair. She could feel his breath flowing over her neck like warm waves. Uncomfortably aware of his hand so near her bare shoulder, she shifted, pressing the fan closer.

"So, Miss Wolcott," Henry resumed, "is the artist born or made?"

"Artists are born. To believe anything else is folly." She gave her answer with such equanimity it seemed to end the debate, until George shook his head.

"That's absurd. All you have to do to dispel that theory is to attend one of my illustration classes. At the beginning of the term, the new students are undisciplined scribblers; by the end, many of them are quite acceptable artists."

"You're speaking of technique," Dudley said. "There's no comparison to be made between the true artist and simply a talented amateur who learns the correct way to wield a pen and brush. Anyone, even a chimpanzee, can learn art technique."

"I believe Miss Wolcott is referring to something more transcendental," Alice said.

All eyes went to Clara. "The true artist's drive to create resides in his soul," she said quietly. "When I work, I'm driven by a passion that comes through my soul, and into these hands. I know every one of you has felt that same intensity—I've seen it in your faces."

"What you are referring to, Mr. Waldo," Tiffany said, "is the physical training and technical refinement of a person who believes himself to have talent because he has some glorified and romantic notion of an artist's life. Those poor souls find out soon enough that their brush is never quite equal to their imaginations. The artist's gift can't be learned—or taught."

George opened his mouth to protest, but Louis held up a finger. "That isn't to say the true artist doesn't need your services in refining his technique, but don't mistake that for instilling talent. That gift belongs to the true artist from his first breath to his last."

Dudley sighed impatiently. "Be reasonable, George. Non-artists don't view the world in the same way an artist does. Place an artist and a common man in a jail cell, the artist will perceive how the light cuts through the bars and makes shadows and glare; he'll see texture and design in the concrete walls. The ordinary man will see only the ugliness of his prison."

George crossed his arms over his chest. "I would wager that if those same men were in that cell together for a year, and the artist carefully instructed the other man in the way he saw things, the ordinary man would soon begin to see things in the same way."

"You would lose," Alice said matter-of-factly. "You might teach an ordinary man how to paint a flower, but there would be no part of his soul in the finished product."

Henry Belknap broke the awkward silence that followed. "Although I practice my art through the lens of a camera, I know what it is to feel such lofty passions. I also know the suffering an artist feels when the critics criticize and destroy his work."

"Artists and critics go hand in glove," Clara said. "For myself, I welcome critics— they're a propelling force behind the quality of the artist's work."

"Speaking of suffering," Tiffany said, "If you'll excuse me, I need to make my way home. The new baby is afflicted with colic, and Mrs. Tiffany prefers not to suffer alone." He looked to Henry. "Mr. Belknap, shall we share a cab?"

"I think I'll stay awhile. I want to bask in the abundance of natural talent that presently surrounds me."

"The man is a pompous ass," George growled the moment Tiffany was out of earshot. "He preaches to us? A man who rides on the backs of other artists' work?"

Clara touched his hand. "He meant nothing against you personally."

"How can you, of all people, defend him?"

"Whether or not you agree with how he conducts himself, George, it's beneath you to make such disparaging remarks about another artist."

No one said anything more until Henry struck up a conversation about the opulence of the flocked wallpaper, speculating as to whether the flock tufts were shedding poisonous dust into the air. An incurable hypochondriac, George covered his nose and mouth with his handkerchief, refusing to remove it despite Dudley's teasing.

"Although we're spellbound by all this talk of wallpaper," Clara said, rising from her chair, "I think Miss Gouvy and I will join Miss Griffin and mingle among the throngs. I want to learn more about the women who are fed up with being barred from participation in national artists' societies and have formed The Women's Art Club. I hear they're signing their work using initials or a special mark, so as not to give away their gender, and having great success as a result."

As they proceeded into the room, Mr. Belknap excused himself from the men and fell in behind her and Alice. "I was wondering if I might join you two ladies?"

Clara hesitated, and then nodded. She'd hoped to speak to the other women without the constraint a gentleman's presence would place on their conversations.

"I enjoyed your views on the passion of true artists, Miss Wolcott," Henry began. "I'm convinced you're a sentimentalist."

"You are sadly mistaken on that account," she said drily.

Henry smiled. "Unless my memory fails me, I do believe that was you sitting next to me at *La Traviata*, sobbing into your hanky."

"That isn't fair, Mr. Belknap. Every person in the audience was in tears. If I remember correctly, you were soaking your own handkerchief long before I even unfolded mine."

"I take exception to that assumption," Henry said. "Something was in my eye."

"Something from the flocked wallpaper no doubt. No, I'm definitely not one who wallows in sentimentality."

Alice made a face. "Excuse me, but aren't you the person who begged Miss Todd to let you take in that fleabag of a stray cat now known as Ida

B. Smith? A reasonable person would have left the pitiful thing on the doorstep, or deposited it on someone else's stoop."

They came to the circle of women where Miss Griffin was waxing euphoric about the use of the new Kodak camera in art. "Oh, all right." Clara sighed, "I admit to being a bit of a sentimental fool from time to time, but I do try not to let it interfere with my life."

With her words left hanging in the air, they looked at one another and broke into laughter.

Lenox Hill
June 7, 1889

Louise talks of having yet another child, but I am reluctant. Six seems enough for any family, although I do long for another son, which would please Father as well.

Miss Wolcott attended the Dakota soiree. There is something about her that draws me, though were I called on to explain, I could not.

I am clearing the land for the construction of a simple summer home in Laurel Hollow, overlooking Cold Spring Harbor in Long Island. It is only an hour and ten minutes from Manhattan by train and trotter. I plan on having a magnificent garden, a clock tower, and a fountain pool for lilies and bog plants. I have dubbed the place, 'The Briars,' as the land is covered with them.

I have not touched brush to canvas for far too long. I am too weighted down with all the cares of business and home. I fear the muse has deserted me.

Dear God how I long for a life where I might touch fire!   L.C.T.

~ 4 ~

Dear Mama, et al,

It has been a week of health mishaps here at Tiffany's and elsewhere. Three of my girls and Frank (my deaf errand boy) are down with the grippe, so it falls upon me to take up the slack.

Josie had a fainting spell on Monday last. Mr. Tiffany insisted on calling in a doctor (at his expense, thank God, as we'd exceeded the weekly budget), who informed us she is anemic and will need to rest for a month on a diet of rare beef, green vegetables, fruit and honey.

The following day, Miss Ring received a serious cut to two of her "best" fingers. Despite the deluge of blood, I managed to get her to the hospital for mending without fainting myself. I took her home on the streetcar and made sure she was supplied with enough food and tea to last a few days. The poor girl was so weak I dared not leave her alone until her mother could come from New Jersey.

On Thursday, George had a fit of sorts, while we were at Henry Belknap's new apartment on Union Square rehearsing for another of Mr. McBride's plays. He didn't come around for five minutes, by which time we were frightened out of our wits. When he revived, he was confused, like someone with brain fever. Mr. Belknap insisted George stay on with him, which is a good thing since he is a far better nurse than any of us.

Not to be outdone, Ida B. Smith escaped up the chimney and didn't return until the following day, with half an ear missing and covered with bites.

Besides our regular work, Mr. Tiffany has charged me with creating a fairy garden window for Mrs. Tiffany's sewing room. I was ordered to Lenox Hill to take measurements. To my great disappointment, instead of being given a grand tour, I was escorted directly to a cramped little room in the attic via the servants' stairs.

It was such a plain room, containing only a rickety table and chairs, a torn rag rug, and an upright Steinway. It's apparently used for school and piano lessons as well as sewing. My every spare moment goes into this window. There are so many flowers—each petal and leaf requires precise color selections and cutting until my eyes feel certain to fall out. Mrs. Tiffany isn't at all uppity. I wish she had more influence over her husband.

To top off the week, one of my best selectors—a poor little fool of a girl—announces she is to be married tomorrow and must leave. She is seventeen. Her husband is barely eighteen and makes $10 a week. She was earning $5.50 here and was to be raised in two months to $7. How are these girls gullible enough to believe marriage will provide them with a better life? I wanted to slap her. Instead, I handed over her last week's pay and wished her well.

If that wasn't enough to test my patience, Miss Agnes Northrop, one of Tiffany's longest-tenured floral designers, has found it necessary to nit-pick my designs. She's a bit in love with Mr. Tiffany, so I often feel we have a turncoat in our camp.

As a final painful blow, Alice moved out of Miss Todd's and in with her aunt, who lives north of Central Park and is currently suffering from rheumatism. It does save her money, but I miss having her comforting presence at Miss Todd's.

I must leave off here. Mr. Tiffany has arrived and is shouting at the top of his lungs.

Love, Clara

P.S. We can use whatever produce, dried herbs and cheese you care to ship. In exchange, Miss Todd will give us a reduced rate on our board. Whatever you send will be appreciated by all, since it will be of better *quality and cheaper than anything that can be purchased in the city. Don't bother about the shipping cost—Miss Todd will gladly pay the $1 fee.*

P.P.S. Yes, by all means attend the Harvest Fair with Reverend Cutler, Mama. If there is gossip, what of it? Pay no heed. You and the Reverend are pillars of the community.

September 4, 1889

ENGROSSED IN CHOOSING the right shade of glass for Jesus' halo in the Last Supper window, Clara had little else on her mind except color, hue and light. It was the part of making the windows she loved best, for it was when they came alive.

As the clock inched past the closing hour, Daniel Bracey was anxious to lock up and get over to McSorley's for the one libation Mrs. Bracey allowed him each week. He noisily moved chairs and easels about the room, and finally resorted to clearing his throat with theatrical volume.

"You needn't stay on my account, Mr. Bracey," she said, holding a piece of yellow glass to the light. "Mr. Tiffany wants this window done by Thursday, so I may as well make good use of the light while I still have it."

Mr. Bracey frowned. "An' who might be escortin' ya home, Miss? 'Tain't proper fer a lady to be alone out on the streets after dark."

The man removed his cap and pushed a shock of auburn hair out of his eyes. "An' with all that business with Jack Ripper over there in London? It gives me the shivers. If anythin' happened to ya, Miss . . . " Mr. Bracey made the sign of the cross, "Jesus, Mary, 'n Joseph an' all the martyred saints, Mr. Tiffany would skin me alive an' throw what were left to the dogs."

She knew he meant well, but just for once she wished he would leave without a fuss. "Thank you for your concern, Mr. Bracey, but you needn't worry. Mr. Driscoll will be here at six to escort me to my boardinghouse."

"Ah, well, that's all right then. Have ya got yer keys?"

"Yes, Mr. Bracey," she sighed. "Rest assured my keys are on my person at all times, even when I sleep."

"If ya please, Miss, give me regards to Miss Josephine. God willin' she'll be right as angels afore long." He removed his cap and a shaft of sun fell across the upper portion of his face. For an instant she was distracted by his eyes, which were exactly the shade of green she needed for her secret project.

"I'll make sure to tell her. Have a good night." She returned her attention to the halo, hoping his leave-taking was drawing to a close. She was itching to get to the bins of scrap glass. There were bound to be a few pieces of green left over from the "Sermon on the Mount" window.

She slipped off her spectacles and rubbed her eyes, listening to the bill and coo of pigeons on the ledge outside the open window and the rough-voiced cab drivers shouting to their horses. The moment she heard the rumble of the basement delivery door that heralded Mr. Bracey's departure from the building, she rushed to her private workroom and slid the wooden fruit crate out from under her desk. Pulling off the top, she feasted her eyes on her prize creation.

Not only unique, it served a practical purpose as well. It was just the sort of thing to generate the talk Mr. Tiffany was seeking for his showroom. She didn't like thinking about her work in terms of profits, but the piece did bring with it the possibility of extra income.

From the basket of discarded shards, she chose a sliver of green and commenced to work.

———§———

Francis Driscoll paused over his letter and stared out the drawing room window. After a moment he resumed writing.

I imagine you, dearest Mary, in a sunny orchard, harvesting
apples to give to the poor. I miss you with all my heart and hope
that someday we shall be reunited. Perhaps then—

Without so much as a nod, Josie entered the drawing room and settled near the fireplace. Despite the warm glow of afternoon light, the normally cheerful girl looked drawn, her eyes red-rimmed and swollen.

In an instant he crossed the room and took her hands in his. "Your hands are cold as ice. Are you ill, my dear?"

"No," she replied, barely above a whisper. "I've received a letter from my mother insisting that I return home."

Uneasiness gripped him. "Has someone in your family fallen ill?"

She picked at an invisible snag in the weave of her skirt. "No, it's only that my mother fears I place too much of a burden on Clara. Since the doctor forbade me to continue on at Tiffany's, she's had to carry my share of the expenses. She's barely able to afford our rent, let alone my tuition at the Art League."

"Why have you and Clara never mentioned your financial worries? Didn't you consider that I might be able to offer assistance or advice?"

"Our mother taught us not to bother people outside the family with our troubles. But to be honest, Mr. Driscoll, you seem more like my family than some of my actual relations."

Touched by the girl's unaffected openness, he slipped an arm around her thin shoulders. "Surely there must be something I can do to ease your troubles?"

"I was thinking . . ." She looked away, suddenly shy. ". . .that as a man of business, you must know a great many people. Perhaps you might inquire whether any of them have need of a governess or a lady's companion?

"It's gentle work, and I am amiable. My embroidery and sewing are above reproach, I read well, and I have a neat hand. I could pour tea for guests, and see to it that the lady of the house took her medicine at the correct times. I might even be able to manage the household, if it didn't require physical labor."

The buoyancy that was her nature returned. "When I've earned enough, I could take up my art lessons again without being a burden." She touched his arm, a sudden anxiety overtaking her. "Mr. Driscoll, I don't think it would be wise to mention this to Clara. She feels we trespass upon your time and goodwill far too often as it is."

Driscoll kissed both her hands. "I won't betray your trust. I shall put my mind to finding a solution to your predicament. You needn't worry another moment."

"Are you certain? I'd feel terrible if this were in any way an imposition."

"Not at all. In the meantime, go upstairs and pin on your loveliest hat. We'll go to Tiffany's together to fetch your sister. The exercise will do you good."

He watched her climb the stairs, hardly able to suppress the urge to shout for joy. It was the opportunity he'd been waiting for. Dictates of society being what they were, offering financial assistance to the Wolcotts would require that he first ask for Clara's hand in marriage. The prospect sent his heart racing.

He went to the cabinet where Miss Todd kept the sherry for medical emergencies and poured himself a good measure. Once married, he might help Clara establish a small shop-studio of her own, one in which she and Josephine could produce all manner of artistic froufrou. With their artistic talents and his business acumen, such an enterprise might even prove profitable.

His spirits soared at the thought of playing the role of benefactor. The effects of the sherry having worked on him, he was sure his life was about to take on new meaning.

——§——

She knew she should put the piece away, but could not—at least not while the sun was still shining. Holding the glass to the light, Clara admired the reflected patterns of red and yellow dancing across the walls.

"What do you have there, Miss Wolcott?"

Startled, she instinctively thrust the piece inside the crate and threw her apron over the top. In the doorway stood the last two people in the world she wanted to see. Had it been Mr. Tiffany alone, she would not have felt such foreboding, but the sight of Mr. Mitchell made her stomach cramp with fear.

"I asked you a question, Miss Wolcott." Mitchell pushed past Louis. "I expect an answer. What are you hiding there?"

Before she could respond, he tossed aside her apron and grabbed at the fragile glass. At the sight of his clumsy hands mauling her work, Clara pushed him aside and plucked the shade out of the crate. She held the glass lampshade to the last of the day's light. Immediately a kaleidoscope of color lit up every corner of the room. A shaft of red fell across Louis Tiffany's face.

"Mr. Tiffany!" Her voice was urgent. "If you would please direct your attention here."

Tiffany stepped closer, his eyes focused on the vision of vibrant red poppies nestled like rubies among intricately veined leaves of liquid green, all on a background of deep yellow.

"It's a design I've been working on for some time. I wanted to wait until it was completed before showing it to you. I was hoping to . . ."

Tiffany was no longer listening. He set aside his walking stick and took the shade gently from her hands. Examining it closely, he seemed mesmerized by the colors and the fluid curve of the piece.

Design sketches and odd bits of cartoons scattered under her fingers as she rifled through the confusion of papers in her desk. She found her drawing for the lamp base and held it out to him. "I thought the base should be of copper or brass."

Pulling a pencil from her hair, she pointed at the four finely detailed poppy leaves that made up the feet of the base, their delicate stems weaving together in an exquisite and harmonious pattern that twisted up the length of the metal arm. "Inlaid here in these narrow panels between the stems will be mosaic tiles in colors complementary to the glass."

"Hideous!" Mitchell blurted. "It is the ugliest thing I've ever seen. No one would be foolish enough to buy such unappealing frippery. The production costs alone would put us out of business."

She whirled on him. "It is *not* hideous! Truth be told, it's the most original and interesting thing in the place! If you don't believe me, Mr. Mitchell, display this lamp in the showroom, and we'll just see how well it sells."

Tiffany took the shade to Clara's desk and sat down.

"Out of the question!" retorted Mitchell. "However, since we've caught you red-handed, might I inquire what business you have wasting company time and materials on this useless enterprise?"

"I beg your pardon!" she snapped, her voice high and loud. She promptly lowered it—sounding like a fishwife would get her nowhere. "I created this piece on my own time. As for the materials, every inch of the shade has come from scraps I recovered from the dustbins or scrap glass that I purchased with my own money."

Unrelenting in his attack, Mitchell shook his head. "That makes no difference whatsoever. You did not have my permission to engage in this this waste of company resources. You simply took it upon yourself to—"

"This is ingenious, Miss Wolcott," Tiffany said quietly, turning the lampshade so that the glass sparkled. "I applaud you."

"Louis!" Mitchell pushed her aside. "The cost of producing this design would exceed any profit we might realize from its sale, if indeed it sold at all."

Tiffany held up a hand. "I've said nothing about putting it into production." He returned his attention to the shade. "How did you come by this design?"

Cautiously she crossed in front of Mitchell. "Last winter being what it was with so much snow, Josephine talked incessantly about how much she longed for the bright colors of the other seasons. That became the seed of an idea that took root and blossomed when I saw how our landscape windows come alive when the light shines through them.

"I thought, why not a stained glass lampshade sporting colorful designs from nature? What could be more cheerful than all those colors on a dreary winter day?"

Tiffany nodded. "And the shape?"

"It seemed to match the natural lines of the flowers." She leaned over him, running her fingers down the curve of the shade. "You can see here how I used copper wire to mimic the fine veins of the leaves. It worked . . ."

She was at once acutely aware of him, the side of his face so close to hers she could smell the faint scent of apples on his breath. Tiffany caught her fingers under his. With the lightest of pressure, he caressed her hand, and then released it.

The event was so subtle and unexpected that, for an instant, she doubted it had actually happened. She resumed her thought, her words slow and halting. "It worked quite well as you can see. I wasn't sure at first how I would make the detail stand out, but—"

"Louis, please!" Mitchell broke in. "I don't understand how you could possibly entertain this preposterous notion for one moment. This thing would never sell to our class of clientele. It's more fitting as a carnival novelty item.

"Surely you don't mean to indulge the fanciful artistic whims of a woman who hasn't the first idea about designing for the higher classes of society, who, if I might be so bold as to remind you, are the cornerstone of our business."

With great care Tiffany placed the shade on the desk and fixed Mitchell with a cold stare, his jaw clenching spasmodically.

Clara held her breath, incredulous that Mr. Mitchell seemed oblivious to the change in Mr. Tiffany's eyes. Anyone who knew him even a little would know enough to heed their chilly warning.

"Honestly, Louis," Mitchell resumed, "your artistic judgment seems to be flagging. Perhaps we should ask your father's opinion in this matter, before we go off on any frivolous tangents."

Tiffany jabbed a finger in his direction. "Be quiet! When I want an evaluation of a design, I'll ask an artist, not a business manager." He threw back his shoulders. "Simply because you're related to my sister by marriage doesn't entitle or qualify you to critique the work produced by my artists—that's my business; money and accounting are yours.

"This piece is neither hideous nor preposterous, and if you possessed one iota of artistic refinement, you'd know that. It is, as Miss Wolcott has so shrewdly pointed out, the most innovative thing in the factory."

He turned to her. "I'm taking you off the Last Supper window effective immediately. You shouldn't be working on the mundane when you could be designing pieces like this. I'll notify the men in the glass and metal department to provide you with whatever you need in the way of supplies." He paused then added, "Within reason."

"Thank you, Mr. Tiffany. I promise I'll—"

"I want more sketches for these sorts of things. Make them exotic, but continue using nature as a stimulus and a harmonizer. When you have everything completed, you will meet with me so I can review what you've done. Is this agreeable?"

"Yes, of course. I'll design as many as you like. I'll—"

Tiffany stopped her with a look. "Miss Wolcott, understand that I'm granting you permission to complete this one sample. I'm not issuing any guarantees that we'll put it into production. The lamp must earn the approval of all members of the management before we can consider such a thing. It will be scrutinized from every standpoint, artistic and . . ." he nodded to the still fuming Mr. Mitchell, "commercial."

He hooked the end of his cane over his arm and removed his pince-nez. "You may carry on with what you were about. Good afternoon."

Before she could reply, they were gone; Louis Tiffany in a blaze of unassailable importance, and Pringle Mitchell in an evil temper. She plunked herself down on the windowsill, scarcely believing her luck. Of course, Mr. Mitchell would increase his efforts to sabotage her work, but for now she couldn't have planned a more successful introduction of her lamp design.

She leaned over the sill, breathing in the chill air of the early evening. Her eye was caught by a streak of orange above the setting sun. Taking out her notebook she began sketching ideas for lampshades as quickly as they popped into her head. She was working on her third rendering of a large goldfish entwined in pond lilies when a soft knock signaled the arrival of Mr. Driscoll.

Lenox Hill
September 26, 1889

Dined with H.O. Havemeyer at the club. My visit to Emile Galle's glass factory this summer impressed him, for he has commissioned me to decorate his home. He is a slippery bastard. I'll need to take care lest he tries to cheat me out of the fortune I stand to make from the job. Father would never let me live it down.

I encountered Belknap and Clara Wolcott at the new Metropolitan exhibition. They seem to regard the rest of the world with shared smugness, as if there were a joke in the works and they alone knew what it was. I admit I resented not being invited into their circle. Even more troubling was the sight of her on his arm. Still and all, I'm relieved to see Belknap in the company of a woman other than his mother.

Tomorrow the board decides on my glass lampshade idea. I'll try to collar Mitchell, who will assuredly knock the proposal down, as I suspect Father has already poisoned the waters.

Little Annie Olivia is ill again. The sweet child cries for me, but I cannot tolerate seeing her suffer. L.C.T.

~ 5 ~

Dear Ones,

When I returned from Tiffany's, I found Ida B. Smith camped by the fire grate. She refused to eat or drink and yowled piteously if touched. One of the boarders, Miss Julia Alling (of the Tallmadge Allings), claims to know all about cats. She examined Ida B. and said the poor thing was in a bad way, with nothing to be done about it. Seventy-five cents of chloroform gave her a peaceful death (Ida B., not Miss Alling).

Miss Todd sent for the ASPCA, but they refused to come, so I wrapped Ida in one of my old undergarments and laid her out in a gift box. I asked Abe (Miss Todd's colored handyman) if we could deposit her in the waste can. He informed us it was against the law, so I decided to put her in the river, but the washerwoman said I'd better not if I didn't want to be arrested on suspicion. Miss Alling predicted someone was sure to see me and call the police, who would drag the river and undoubtedly find a dead baby—a fish having meanwhile made off with Ida B—and I would end up in the Tombs.

So, off I trudged to the board of health (ironically across from the Tombs), where I announced that I had a dead cat in the box. After some amusement at Ida B.'s expense, they said they didn't want her and directed me to the Department of Public Docks men, who, as could be expected, didn't want her either.

At two this morning, I gave Ida B. Smith a proper burial under Miss Todd's peony bushes, grateful to the dear little thing for dying while the ground was still pliable.

Henry Belknap has asked George and me to accompany him to the Metropolitan lecture series on Charles Rennie Macintosh's European Arts and Crafts Movement. It's a delight to see how perfectly George and Henry's personalities are in balance—a floating bubble and a rock.

Speaking of rocks—as in millstones around my neck—Miss Northrop has been particularly critical of my work as of late. I refuse to be offended, preferring to believe she is jealous of my inventiveness. Her own work is excellent, but predictable.

Much love, Clara

P.S. Emily, my dear sister, taking into account how you love to tell people what to do and correct them when they make innocent mistakes, it's clear that in choosing the teaching profession, you have chosen a fitting vocation. Because of your diligence in returning all of my letters with the spelling errors circled in red, I have been shamed into purchasing a proper dictionary. I've discovered all manner of fine words, for instance, "punctilious" and "nitpicking."

September 27, 1889

L OUIS PLACED THE velvet drape over the lamp and set it to one side of his desk.

Henry threw up his hands in exasperation. "You would think just one of the other board members would have voted in favor of the lamps, especially after hearing Mrs. Tiffany's declaration that she wanted several permanently installed in your entry hall, so they would be the first and last pieces of decoration seen by your guests. For God's sake, every woman in New York knows that Louis and Louise Tiffany set the trend in home decoration."

"None of that matters now," Louis said. "We need to move forward with the windows."

"But what folly not to recognize the design's potential!" Henry fumed, "The minute Mitchell started bleating about financial instability and production costs, they all followed like sheep. Why can't they understand that taking chances is the only way to get ahead in this business?"

"The board is about money, Henry. They're afraid that if we start producing new things, it will divert business away from the windows and mosaics. No amount of praise or testimonial is going to change their position. Until Tiffany Glass is more securely rooted, we have to abandon the lamp idea." He tapped his pencil and stared fixedly out the window. After a minute he threw the pencil across the room. "Damn it! I want these lamps in the showroom."

Henry planted both hands on Louis's desk. "That's the spirit! I say we put them on display now . . . today."

Louis averted his eyes.

"What the blazes, Louis? Don't tell me you're in agreement with these cretins!"

"Don't be an ass, Henry. I want the piece in the showroom as much as you do, but I gave the board the power to override my decisions with a majority vote, and I'm bound to honor their decision."

At the lie, Henry bit his tongue. It was common knowledge that Charles Tiffany had handpicked the board of directors before providing the seed money for his son's company. The unwritten rule, strictly adhered to, was that none of his son's business ventures were to go forward without his approval.

Louis lifted the drape once more. "I am tempted to send it to the showroom despite the veto."

"We'd be deluged with orders," Henry urged.

"That's the problem. As long as my fa—" He caught himself. "As long as Mitchell can convince the board that the production cost of a single unit can't be recouped in the retail price, my hands are tied."

"That's absurd! They know perfectly well that we could charge far more than the cost of making such an item."

"Knowing they can is one thing; actually giving their permission to do so is an entirely different matter." Louis slapped his knees and stood abruptly. "But—there it is, and there's no changing their minds for the time being. Miss Wolcott will have to return to her work on the windows. I'll break the news on Monday. The sooner she knows, the sooner she'll get over her disappointment."

"Make sure to tell her that you and I supported the idea," Henry said. "I prefer she not think that we all went against it."

"About Mitchell's accusation this morning, Henry, that business about your interest in the lamp being tied to a more personal interest in Miss Wolcott? I think in the future it might be wise for you to guard against fraternizing so closely with the hired women."

He halted Henry's protest with a look. "You have Miss Wolcott's reputation to think of. Your association might foster jealousies and malicious gossip among the other girls, which, in turn, could ultimately hurt production. While I'm the first to admit she is a charming woman, you need keep in mind that Miss Wolcott is only a hired worker and you are a director. You should find a young woman of your own station. If I were your age and single again, I'd be—"

"Your counsel regarding my social life is not appreciated," Henry blurted. "I get quite enough of that from my mother." Halfway out the door, he turned. "And really, Louis, you should make up your mind as to how I am to be condemned. Only a short time ago you were suggesting something quite different from romancing the women employees."

Louis stared at the door for several minutes before grabbing his hat and cane. Making a mad dash for the street, he hailed a cabriolet. "Tiffany and Company on West Union Square at Fifteenth Street," he called to the driver, "and don't spare the horse."

From the window of the cab, Louis watched his father cross Fifteenth Street. Walking as tall and straight as a soldier, Charles Lewis Tiffany made a dignified impression in his formal silk top hat and double-breasted Chesterfield. The stubborn set of his mouth between a bristly hard mustache and full white beard revealed a determined man, who knew what was rightfully his. As he turned into his establishment, he nearly collided with a fashionably dressed matron. Charles bowed, tipped his hat in apology and entered the store.

Louis got down from the cab, but did not immediately release his hold on the handrail. He stood for several moments, trying to get his nerves under control, aware that the cabbie awaited direction. "Wait for me," he said finally, and crossed the street.

Larkin, Tiffany and Company's head clerk, greeted him stiffly. For as long as Louis could remember, the old codger had been Charles' personal guard, protecting him from the rabble who dared to intrude on his precisely ordered world. Larkin included Louis as one of those to be kept away.

Louis brushed past him and entered his father's office without knocking. Charles looked up from his writing, pen arrested in midstroke. At once his eyes took on the cool, distrustful expression they always held whenever his son came into his presence.

"Louis," Charles gave a curt nod, "to what do I owe this visit?"

"Why did you reject the lamp, Father? You know full well how much I value the project. Haven't you drilled it into my head since I was old enough to walk that the Tiffany men are born with an uncanny knack for divining the taste and fashion of the times?"

"Yes," Charles hissed, "and in that statement you will find the answer to your first question. Colored bits of glass fabricated into a wild design of flowers and leaves are not what our class of clientele wants. It is neither tasteful nor fashionable—nor is it art."

The older man shook his head "I can't even imagine Mrs. Astor or Mrs. J. P. Morgan purchasing such a silly thing. They wouldn't have it, because it is simply not fine enough for our people."

"They *would* have it and be eager to get it!" Louis countered. "People of all classes—especially the elite—are bored with the old standards. With a new century approaching, they want modern styles—more color, more light, and natural lines. People look to me to give them fashionable decoration. The lamp is uniquely beautiful. It has all the things our clath— our kind of people want. They—"

Charles stopped him with a dismissive wave of the hand. "Like any fad, it would soon fall out of favor. The old standards you deem beneath you will endure for time immemorial. Our people want quality and value that will last for centuries, items they can hand down through generations with pride.

"It is easy to imagine a woman a hundred years from now saying to her daughter, 'Here is the Tiffany diamond-and-ruby necklace that once belonged to your great-great grandmother, as exquisite and stylish today as it was then.' I assure you no one will be passing on one of these silly lamps that had sat for years in someone's dusty attic."

"You're wrong, Father. It is exactly what the younger generations are looking for. They desperately want to break away from the antiquated standards and embrace the new. This lamp reflects those desires. It's far more avant-garde than anything you've designed in years."

"Make peace with my decision," Charles said sternly. "I'll not provide a penny for this foolish project, and therefore it will fail."

"Why can't you allow me *my* vision, Father? I've been experimenting with different typeth of glath that the world has never theen—" Louis took a careful breath "before."

Charles made no effort to hide his look of disgust.

Louis wanted to scream and rip the tongue out of his head. It was his lisp—that evil thing his father most hated about him. Summoning a last vestige of control, he went on more slowly, taking great pains to make his tongue obey and enunciate each word. "There is nothing like these lamps. People will clamor for them."

Charles shook his head. "Just remember that windows and mosaics are your stock-in-trade. You can indulge your artistic whims after I am dead. If you must stray from the windows, take commissions for your exotic interior design and decoration. There's no shortage of men with too much money whose tastes run to that sort of nonsense. Keep your attentions on your windows and conform to the standard. Stop playing the rebel artist."

"But Father, that is what I am; a rebel in glass. I want to make glass art that will draw the attention of the world. Why can't you have faith in my worth as an artist?"

"I did," Charles said crisply. "I gave you a fortune to build a Tiffany family home. In return, you built a crazy house that no one who likes to sleep soundly at night would live in." He whirled his hands in the air "Turrets, fountains, foreign gewgaws hanging from the ceilings like an overdone Christmas tree."

"The Tiffany Mansion is an innovative architectural masterpiece." Louis protested. "The greatitht architects in the world have said as much."

"I admit the house is imposing on some level, but it isn't a home; it's the creation of an eccentric dreamer who thinks he is a great artist. You have always been a foolish man, Louis. It is a condition caused by your mother and me. We spoiled you with our coddling."

"Coddling?" Louis cried. "Your memory is faulty, Father. I was barely fourteen when you sent me away to spend three miserable years imprisoned in that godforsaken military academy, thleeping on a hard board. You never once allowed me to come home, even though I begged you in letter after letter. I doubt that could be called coddling!"

Charles took up his pen and resumed writing. "Stop your sniveling. I won't give my approval to this folly of yours, and that is my final word. It's fool's gold and nothing more. If you want to produce such things, you will have to do it with your own money or wait until I'm dead. I refuse to discuss this further. Give my regards to Louise, and tell her that your mother and I will see her and the grandchildren at dinner this evening. Good-day."

The familiar hurt lodged in Louis's chest, making his throat ache. "I am forty-one years old and yet you dithmith me as if I were a meddling child. What is it, Father? Are you jealous of my triumphs? Are you afraid I'll thteal your thunder?" He brought his fist down on his father's desk, making the inkwell jump.

Charles fixed him with a cold stare.

"You are wrong this time, Father! The lamp and the things that follow it will make my fortune. I shall eclipth you. I'll rise to prominenth without your money or your damned approval!" One angry sweep of his cane across the surface of the desk sent papers, pens and ink tray to the floor.

Charles sprang to his feet, calling for Larkin.

With amazing speed for a man of his age, Larkin bounded up the stairs, his eyes going from Charles to Louis and coming to rest on the long splash of ink soaking into the expensive carpet. "My son was just leaving, Larkin," Charles said, his voice flat. "Please see to it that a cab is called."

As he brushed past his father, Louis brought his mouth close to Charles' ear. "You would do well to remember the Tiffany modus operandi, old man," he whispered. "It is the obligation of the son to honor the father, then follow the urge to surpass him."

—— § ——

The Metropolitan Opera House
1411 Broadway, Manhattan

As Desdemona lay dead upon the stage, Clara leaned close to whisper in Mr. Driscoll's ear, "You see? *This* is what comes of marriage."

To her dismay, her witticism did not produce the expected response. Mr. Driscoll took on a stricken expression, as if she'd told him a close relative had died. Not knowing what to make of him, she directed her attention back to the stage where Othello was deep into his lament.

Mr. Driscoll had been jittery and unlike himself all week. Clara glanced over at Josephine, who, unlike Mr. Driscoll, was in unusually high spirits, despite their mother's continued insistence that she return home to Ohio—a prospect that as a rule reduced Josie to a state of wretchedness.

When the last bows were taken and the house lights came up, a familiar mane of dark hair caught Clara's eye. In the box closest to the stage, Henry Belknap was helping to arrange an evening cape about the shoulders of an older, elegantly appointed woman. The close resemblance between the two left no doubt of their familial relationship. Both disturbed and fascinated by the overt proprietary attitude that the imposing dowager displayed toward her son, Clara could not take her eyes off the pair.

As if summoned, Henry turned and found her at once. The warmth of his smile drew the attention of his mother, who searched the sea of faces for the object of her son's interest. When the dowager's eyes met Clara's, she fixed her with such a powerful look of distaste, that Clara felt it almost as a physical blow. The old woman touched Henry's arm, questioning.

His smile vanished, replaced with an expression that Clara had seen on the faces of prisoners who were paraded out of the Tombs and made to shovel snow off the city streets. He leaned close to his mother with a conspiratorial air and, after an exchange of words, shook his head. Assured that there was no threat of infiltration into their sealed circle of two, Mrs. Belknap resumed arranging her evening cloak.

Clara, painfully aware that she hadn't even warranted a second glance, drew herself up to her full height and took Mr. Driscoll's arm. Wearing a smile bereft of pleasure, she allowed herself to be led out of the theater.

The moment the threesome arrived at home, Josie retired to her room, using exhaustion as her excuse.

This mystified Clara. Only a half hour before, it was Josie who had insisted that they walk from the station instead of hailing a cab, and it was Josie who had kept such an energetic pace that both Clara and Mr. Driscoll had difficulty keeping up with her. The girl's unending chatter about the ladies' evening dresses, the weather and the effect the different seasons had on artists left her wondering if Josie had mistakenly indulged in a glass of champagne instead of lemon squash during the intermission.

She was about to excuse herself, when Mr. Driscoll touched her shoulder.

"Clara? If you would please join me in the drawing room, there's a personal matter I'd like to discuss."

Surprised by his use of her Christian name, she looked at him more closely, mildly alarmed at how flushed he was. Mr. Driscoll waited until she was settled on the settee before delving into his subject. "Have I ever spoken to you of my wife?"

"I don't believe so," Clara said, arranging her skirts around her. "You do have a tendency to play your cards rather close to the vest, Mr. Driscoll."

He chuckled. "I suppose that is the way of most men in my business. Discretion is the better part of making a good deal. Why, I remember once when I was first—"

"You were speaking about your wife?" She was tired and wanted to go to bed.

"Ah, yes. Catherine was a devout woman, although fanaticism might better describe her religious zeal. Our daughter, Mary, was a docile child. By the time she was ten, she'd been so beaten down by her mother's strenuous daily catechism and stern rules, that there wasn't an ounce of self-will or joy left in her. I tried to intervene, but Mrs. Driscoll was not to be deterred in her mission." He made a helpless gesture. "She put Mary in a convent at the age of thirteen."

Horrified, Clara pulled back. "But surely you could have withheld your consent?"

"I never gave my consent; it was solely her mother's doing. When Mrs.

Driscoll died a few years later, I went to the Mother Superior to demand that my daughter be released. I was informed that her soul was committed to God, and any further attempt on my part to see her would be denied. I challenged this but learned soon enough there was no reasoning with the church."

Clara imagined being bullied into joining some primitive cloister and felt a burst of gratitude for her mother's wisdom in giving her daughters the freedom to choose how, and even if, they wanted to make religion part of their lives.

"Is there some way in which I can assist?" she asked, unable to fathom why he was revealing the intimate details of his life. "Perhaps you'd like me to accompany you to the convent?"

He shook his head. "I am telling you this so that you might understand how alone I've been. I miss having the gentle influence of a woman in my life. I want my life to be more than an endless succession of days filled with business and meaningless talk. Until I met you, I'd barely been able to discern one day from the next. May I speak plainly?"

She managed a ghost of a smile, apprehension settling in her stomach like a block of ice. "Of course."

He went to the cabinet and poured them each a glass of sherry.

She raised her eyebrows. "Is it that bad, Mr. Driscoll? Shall I brace myself?"

Maintaining a serious demeanor, he set her sherry on the table in front of her. "I am not a young man, Clara, however I am a successful one. I beg you, do not take offense at my trespassing into your private matters, but I've recently been made aware that you are in need of financial assistance. In short, I wish to relieve you of your difficulties."

A surge of anxiety brought her to her feet. "I'm sorry, but I have a long day ahead of me tomorrow, and I'd like to retire to my room. Perhaps we could have this discussion some other time?"

He touched her hand. "Please, let me finish."

Reluctantly, she sat back down.

"Besides offering security, I wish to provide you with a comfortable life—trips abroad and perhaps a studio where you could work. We might even open a gallery shop where Josephine could have her own dressmaker's studio.

"Of course, it goes without question that Josephine would share our home and continue her art studies. We'd have a jolly time of it, if you would . . . I mean, if you'd like to—"

Out of patience, Clara stood abruptly. "Mr. Driscoll! What are you proposing?"

"Why, that is exactly what I'm doing: proposing. I am asking you to be my wife."

She fixed her attention on the portrait of President Harrison on the wall behind him. More than anything, she wanted to bolt up the stairs and barricade the door against him and his offers.

He gripped her hands. "I may not seem like a man capable of harboring tender affections, but I love you, Clara. I've loved you from the first."

Alarmed, she forcibly pulled her hands out of his grasp and hid them under her cape. "I'm at a loss for words; you've caught me by surprise."

"Surprise? Why, every boarder here knows of my feelings for you. Even the servants have their suspicions. I am a man who wears his heart on his sleeve."

That his intimate feelings for her were common knowledge distressed her almost as much as his proposal. The misery she felt showed plainly on her face. "I must have time to think this through."

"Take all the time you need, my dear. I'm not so vain as to imagine you harbor the same feelings for me, but I pray that in time you might come to love me."

He hesitated, and when he spoke again, his words were rushed and lurching. "Rest assured that I won't . . . I would not require you to . . ." He drained his glass. "At my age, I have no need for more progeny, nor would I want to subject you to the dangers of confinement, unless, of course . . . What I mean to say is that I realize you are young and vital, and if you harbored any such desires, I would . . . I could accommodate your wishes, although I'm not the sort of man to demand that you perform the duties of . . . that you fulfill the wifely obligations of the ah . . . marriage bed."

Clara hurriedly made her way to the door. "While I appreciate your honesty, Mr. Driscoll, I'm not—"

"My dearest." He took a step toward her, his arms open.

Thinking he meant to kiss her, she shied away in disgust.

He lowered his arms, the hurt evident on his face. "Your happiness is of the utmost importance to me," he said softly. "I won't press you for an answer now. I only wish to free you from your difficulties, not add to them."

"I don't mean to appear dismissive, Mr. Driscoll, but it's late, and my mind is occupied with matters at work."

Mr. Driscoll kissed her hand. "I understand. Shall I see you at breakfast?"

"No. I have a meeting with Mr. Tiffany first thing in the morning, so I'll be leaving earlier than usual." She withdrew her hand and shoved it under her cape, surreptitiously wiping away his touch. "Good night."

She grasped the newel post, and in her haste to escape, tripped over the first step. Embarrassed, she regained her poise and started up the stairs. After all, it wasn't as if she'd been given a death sentence; she'd simply been asked for her hand in marriage.

In their room, it wasn't difficult to surmise from Josie's ragged breathing and a laughable attempt at feigned sleep, that she'd been eavesdropping.

"Whatever possessed you to tell Mr. Driscoll of our difficulties?" Clara asked, lowering herself onto the edge of the bed. "Do you have any idea of the trouble your foolish meddling has caused?"

Josie sat up, tangled in the confusion of bedding. "I only asked him to help me find a position. How was I to know he'd use that as a reason to propose?"

Clara turned on her. "You don't have the constitution for any situation other than commissions for fashion design, and how many of *those* do you think will find their way to Miss Todd's boardinghouse and be handed to you on a silver platter?"

"My constitution is fine," Josie shot back.

"Then you are either deluded or deaf! The doctor said your heart couldn't withstand strain of any sort." She pressed her palms hard against her eyes. "I don't know how you did it, Jo, but somehow you've managed to create a disaster."

"You're being dramatic. Mr. Driscoll would do anything to make you happy. We . . . you would want for nothing. You could have a home of your own with a hired woman to cook and keep house. Mama, Emily and Kate wouldn't have to worry about tuitions and the cost of keeping up the farm. I could stay in New York and continue my lessons, and you could . . . you could . . . " She bit her lip. "Oh. I forgot."

"You *forgot*?" Clara said, her temper flaring, "Forgot that as a married woman I'd be required to give up my work? Forgot the possibility that I might someday be granted a position as head designer for Tiffany's, the most prestigious design firm in New York? How could you, Josie?"

"But Mr. Driscoll is an honorable man. Aunt Josephine always says that a marriage based on romantic love fades like cut flowers, but marriage to an honorable man is as strong as an oak."

"Aunt Josephine is a spinster," Clara retorted. "She's not exactly the best person to be giving sermons on the finer points of marriage."

"All right," Josie groaned, "I'll write to Mama. Perhaps Kate and I can start our own dressmaking business. With her sewing skills and my designs, I'll bet I could earn enough over the winter to come back next fall and finish my lessons. Of course, by that time you'll be head manager of Tiffany's, earning as much money as Mr. Belknap and Mr. Driscoll put together." Filled with a dreamer's confidence, Josie lay back smiling, happy with her reinvented world.

Clara shook her head and sighed. "All right, Jo. Don't write to Mama yet. We won't make any decisions until we've looked at all our options."

With the discovery of the ragged tear in the hem of her gown, Clara was sure there were evil forces at work trying to knock her down. It would be at least two more seasons before she could afford a new evening dress, and maybe not even then. A tailor could make it right, but might charge as much as a dollar to replace the panel with the right match of silk. There was no room for such a luxury with the weekly budget already stretched by Josie's tonics and special diet. She would have to purchase a cheap piece of trim and ask Josie to fix it as best she could.

The gown slipped from her fingers and lay crumpled between her feet. Making no move to retrieve it, she glanced around the room, taking in the abundant signs of their poverty. Inside the armoire were two well-worn nightgowns, numerous sets of cotton underwear handed down from her grandmother, one pair of heavy stockings, two sad-looking waists and two skirts, all of which had been made over and patched a half dozen times. Her only serviceable pair of flat work shoes were falling apart, and the black broadcloth coat she'd purchased at a seconds sale hung at the back of the wardrobe next to the linen traveling suit her mother had worn before the Civil War. The thought of suffering through another New York winter with only the thin coat to protect her brought her to despair. Mr. Driscoll's proposal would free them from poverty, but marriage was the last thing she wanted.

She worked her hair into a braid and stepped out of her petticoats. His words about wifely duties and sharing a bed made her insides shrivel. Not that she was ignorant about that type of passion. After all, she was the favored confidante for girls who told her, in unrestrained detail, about their torrid romantic adventures. While these colorful narratives both fascinated and embarrassed her, they also left her in awe of the girls' effortless ability to flow to emotional depths she could not even begin to imagine.

She scrubbed her face and neck, doubt already tearing at the edges of her decision to refuse him. For a woman of twenty-seven, the likelihood of receiving further marriage proposals was slim to none.

Shedding the steel cage of her corset, she checked her image in the mirror. If she wanted to be presentable for her meeting with Mr. Tiffany she would have to rise earlier than the others in order to have enough warm water for a bath and shampoo. There was nothing to be done about the poor condition of her skirts, but she would take care to wear the nicer of her two waists—the one Mr. Tiffany once complimented.

Once her lamp designs were in production, she was sure to receive a substantial increase in pay. With that, they could manage on their own. Her spirits lifted by the thought, she crawled into bed next to Josie.

In good conscience she couldn't allow Mr. Driscoll to make such a generous offer, especially since she didn't return his feelings. Be it her last marriage proposal or not, she was resolute—she would wait whatever number of days was considered proper etiquette, and then kindly, but firmly, refuse Mr. Driscoll's offer.

Lenox Hill
September 29, 1889

Sleep impossible, as I am still tortured by the thoughtless lack of vision on the part of the 'King of Diamonds.' I pray for the day I'm freed from Father's iron chancellorism and in charge of my own fate.

Halfway through family dinner tonight, Burnie arrived with a woman of low character, both of them reeking of drink. Without regard for my children, my wife or our mother, he goaded father for money. He was shameless, using language so vile Louise was forced to take the children to the nursery. When Father refused his demands, he stormed from the house with his whore in tow, but not without first smashing my best Moroccan vase to bits. One might think we are of no better breeding than the human vermin who inhabit Five Points.

Last night's dream will not leave me. Clara, dressed in flowered robes, finds me wandering the desert and feeds me petals from the cloth. I pull her down to lie with me and then awaken with the feel of her lips still on mine. A maddening passion lingered, until I was driven to seek relief from a much-surprised Louise.

I have begun drafting plans for the architectural masterwork that will someday be my home. L.C.T.

~ 6 ~

Dear Ones,

I have a few minutes before I meet with Mr. Tiffany about my lamp designs. I'm nervous as a cat, but hopeful.

Someday, I'd like to live in the country and combine artwork and gardening. I could also teach artisans how to make the things that appeal to the wealthy. It seems to me there would be enough money in that to make for a comfortable and productive life.

Don't worry anymore about the broken harness, Mama. Bring it to the blacksmith without delay, and tell him to send me his bill.

I must leave off here to make myself presentable. I try to follow Mr. Belknap's example of good grooming, although I stop short of manicured nails. My hands are put to hard use in this workplace, so I doubt I shall ever have the luxury of having pretty hands.

How lovely that Rev. Cutler painted the parlor and all three bedrooms, and in just two days! Thank him for us and give him our best regards.

Love to all, Clara

P.S. Mama: I haven't forgotten to have my photos taken—I'm just waiting to be better looking.

CLARA SWAYED, GRIPPING the edge of Louis Tiffany's desk for support. She was having difficulty keeping her voice steady. "I don't understand. People are certain to notice my lamps. I thought that was what you wanted."

"Miss Wolcott," Louis began, regret lacing his voice, "There is no question that these designs would draw attention, if displayed. Unfortunately, the board has determined that Tiffany's cannot justify spending money on a new project at this time. That's not to say we won't reconsider these and similar designs in the future."

He put his arm gently about her shoulders. "Please, sit down. You look unwell." Lowering her into the chair, he did not let go right away. Even with the disappointment still settling inside her, she was acutely aware of his face being so near that she was able to make out the small white striations that lined the blue of his eyes. She gave him a questioning glance that sent him back to his desk.

"I'm sorry for your disappointment, but you mustn't take this personally, Miss Wolcott—it's business. As soon as the company is stable, we'll review the lamp designs again, but for now I must ask that you return to your work in the window department."

Without stopping to consider what she was doing, she got to her feet, glaring at him. "How could you allow this? Are you not the owner of this company? Surely you can order—"

"No, I cannot!" he shouted. "The board has made its decision, and I refuse to second-guess them on your account."

She drew back as if jerked by a rope, a deep blush replacing her pallid complexion. "In that case, I must ask . . . no, I *insist* on an increase in my salary."

From his astonished expression, she guessed no other female employee had ever spoken to him in such a manner. "I appreciate my employment here, but I'm barely able to afford room and board. Considering the quality of my work, I think I deserve a higher wage."

"If I give in to your request, how long will it be before you insist on another increase?" Louis said between clenched teeth. "I can just imagine the idea spreading like influenza among the other girls. Within no time there would be a line of women outside my office door, demanding their due, as if Tiffany Glass were a charity instead of a business."

He picked up a piece of paper from his desk and slammed it down. "The rest of the board would never grant such a request. It's out of the question."

The thought of the thousands of hours she'd worked to oblige his demands filled her with despair and anger. "Begging your pardon, Mr. Tiffany, but my responsibilities and contributions to this company far outweigh those of the men. Yet, for all my efforts, I receive less than half what they are paid. And, while I appreciate being appointed assistant manager, as near as I can tell, I am the *only* manager."

Louis jumped to his feet, the veins in his neck standing out. "How dare you! I will not tolerate your attempts to erode my authority, Miss Wolcott." He paused and swallowed. "You are a talented employee, and there may be some merit to your boldness, but you've far overstepped your boundaries. For as much as I'd like to help you, I don't have the authority to raise your salary or your status. You'll have to take up those matters with Mr. Mitchell."

He flung open the door. "You have tried my patience to the limit. If you'll excuse me, I have other business to which I must attend."

She picked up her drawings and the lamp and turned to leave.

"I'll retain the design sketches and the lamp, Miss Wolcott. Leave them."

At a loss to understand, she looked from him to the things in her hands. They were her creations; they belonged to her as surely as a child belongs to his mother. "But . . . they're mine. I made them. You can't— "

Louis brought the heavy ebony cane against the door with such force as to split the wood. The piercing noise was like the retort of a pistol shot. He poised the cane for a second strike. "That lamp and every one of those drawings belong to me! You were paid to create them. Return them to my desk immediately!"

Mindful of his cane, she obeyed.

Louis forced a smile. "You shall see them in due time, when the company is ready for them. Now if you would be so kind." He made a stiff sweeping gesture toward the hall.

Mustering as much dignity as she could, she strode out of his office. The door slammed behind her with enough force to rattle the hall windows.

She stood motionless, then crouched down to run her fingers over the spoiled wood. Disappointment and frustration gathered in her throat like stones. When the tears came, she rose and walked away without a backward glance.

With the exception of the violence Louis Tiffany had inflicted on his office door, Clara left out nothing when relating the details of their meeting to Josie.

By turns, Josie received the news with dismay, disgust, and finally, indignation. "What a wretched man! He's no better than a thief."

"It's done and forgotten," Clara sighed. "I'll consider myself lucky if I still have a position by tomorrow."

"Oh, yes," Josie cried, a tinge of hysteria to her voice, "a position in which you slave long after everyone else has gone home, a job that uses up every last drop of your energy and time and pays so little you can't even afford a new hat!" The pillow she threw across the room missed the wall and sailed out the open window.

Clara grabbed her by the shoulders. "Don't! The doctor said—"

"I don't care what the doctor said! If this means I have to go home to Tallmadge, I'll die. I'm not like Kate. It's all well and good for her to be cooped up on the farm with nothing to do but fret with Mama over what color the wallpaper print should be or how many jars of peaches to put up. If it's Emily they want me to emulate, they should give up now. The way she always has her nose in some boring math book, she barely knows what day it is.

"I hate Tallmadge! I hate the way Mama hovers over me day and night, telling me what to wear, what to eat, when to sleep. My only worth is in fashion design. It's essential I live in New York."

Better than anyone, Clara understood how her sister felt. "All right, Jo. I'll try to find a way to keep you here. Mr. Mitchell's father is an editor at *Hearth and Home*. Perhaps Mr. Belknap could speak to him about looking at your portfolio. But, for now, we'll continue on as we are for as long as we can. After that, we'll just take it one catastrophe at a time."

Lenox Hill
September 30, 1889

I keep thinking of one of the proverbs stenciled on the gable beams of this House—'Good folks are scarce, take care of me'—and I am like a marble rolling between wrath and regret. I've written two notes of apology to the lady and discarded both. I can't seem to think straight around her.

Today, in the graceful line of her neck where the pulse is visible, I saw a mark of the palest tan. I wanted to touch that warm flesh more than I have ever wanted to touch any woman in my life.

I read these words and think I must be losing my mind. She is only a hired artisan. I must keep my attention on business and the money. L.C.T.

~ 7 ~

October 2, 1889
Miss Todd's Boardinghouse

THE MORNING BROUGHT with it perfect autumn weather, which added to Josie's euphoria over putting her plan into motion. The moment Clara left for work, she was on her feet and tiptoeing the length of the halls, listening for anyone who might still be milling around. The usual sounds of the servants clearing away the breakfast things were a good indication most of the boarders had gone for the day.

She paused in front of Julia Alling's room and set her ear against the door. While she liked the young woman in general, Miss Alling's tendency toward long-winded gossip was off-putting. Should she suspect there was a covert scheme in the works, she would spoil everything by telling anyone who would listen all about it.

Settling in with a copy of the *Times*, Josie went through the advertisements. The majority of situations for women called for wet nurses, cooks, maids, washerwomen or factory workers. She considered an ad for governess, but the employer required that the applicant speak fluent French. She was about to give up, when her eye fell on an ad misplaced on the Public Notices page.

> *WANTED: Refined woman of good breeding. Must be well-spoken, possess tact, and have a good memory for detail. A neat and legible hand preferred.*
> *Call at side entrance of Chatham House, #11 E 66th St. no later than 5 p.m. on October 2nd.*

Josie's mood lifted at once. It would be easy finding her way to the Broadway trolley, and the conductor could direct her to Chatham House from there. If she started at once, she'd be back before anyone knew she was gone. She pinned her hat into place and folded the three remaining dollars of her Tiffany earnings into her purse. It was more than she'd need, but in Manhattan, you never knew when there would be an extra expense.

She paused. There were dangers to venturing out alone; the papers were full of accounts of women who were murdered in unspeakable ways. She shook off the thought—surely in the light of day she wouldn't have to worry about such things.

By the time she boarded the Broadway Trolley, the weather had turned uncomfortably warm. Seeking a cooling breeze, Josie stuck her head out the window and immediately her hat sailed over the tracks and out of sight.

She made unsuccessful efforts to extricate herself from the grasp of several gentlemen, who made it their business to restrain her from jumping out. The moment the trolley stopped, she left the car and ran in the direction of where she had last seen her hat.

At the corner of Leonard Street and Broadway, the reek of urine, mixed with the decaying flesh of a horse carcass left in the street to rot made her sick. She pressed her handkerchief over her nose and mouth and quickly moved on.

In front of her, a street hawker with pans and a pile of old clothes clattered over the uneven cobblestones, shouting out his wares in a shrill voice that stabbed her ears. She was about to ask him for directions, when she caught a glimpse of her hat in the soiled hands of a street urchin. Dodging people and costermonger carts, she caught the child by the shoulder. "Excuse me, but that's my hat. Give it to me at once."

The girl whirled about and regarded her with such fear that Josie took a step back. She raised a hand to reassure the girl that she meant no harm, but the child ran. Josie dashed after her, doing her best to catch up, despite the effort it took to breathe. They turned a corner and then another. The waif looked over her shoulder to gauge the distance between them, tripped over a discarded crate and went sprawling. Stunned by her fall, she sobbed where she lay.

Josie wrenched the hat out of her hand and hastily pinned it onto her head. "Why did you run away?" she asked, surveying the child more closely. Under the clothes that were scarcely more than rags tied together, the girl was pitifully thin. Josie knelt and gently wiped away the girl's tears. With a few months of proper food, baths and clean clothes, she could see that the child might prove to be quite pretty.

The youngster scrambled to her feet. "I ain't got no hat. Yer a rich lady; you got plenty. You gunta call the coppers to throw me in the Tombs?"

"Of course not. What's your name?"

"Pearl."

"Have you eaten today?"

Pearl shook her head.

Josie took a toffee from her pocket and held it out. "Are you hungry?"

Nodding shyly, Pearl snatched the sweet and popped it into her mouth, still wrapped. Before Josie could protest, she'd chewed through the paper and swallowed it.

"We always hungry," Pearl said matter-of-factly. "We don't get nothin' to eat 'cept what we steal off carts. Sometimes me and my brothers sneak uptown and find good eats in them fancy hotel garbages. Once we got us a hunk a ham and some old butter, but the rats got us so bad, Mam say we can't go there no more."

The image of children fighting rats for food made Josie shudder. "Don't you have any food at home?"

"Sometimes Mam take me with her to the butcher for scrap soup bones when we got money, which ain't hardly ever. That's when we gotta beg or go to the garbages."

Josie took a dollar from her pocket and placed it securely in the girl's hand.

Pearl stared at the bill in disbelief before closing her fist around it. "What I got to do fer this?"

"You have to promise to bring it straight to your mother and tell her that it must be spent on food and nothing else. Do you give me your solemn promise?"

Pearl nodded once, and took off running. At the end of the block, she turned, waved, and vanished from view.

Josie looked around at the drab streets crowded with ramshackle buildings. Nothing was familiar, and there were no cabs in sight, only rickety wagons laden with rags and half-rotten vegetables. She walked in the direction she thought might be Broadway, only to find herself twenty minutes later back where she'd started. Despite the oppressive heat, a chill swept through her when she realized there were no other women to be seen, and several of the men who passed by had leered and made lewd gestures.

"What yer lookin' fer, girlie?"

Josie spun around.

The gravel voice belonged to a rickety old man sitting on the steps of a building that looked to be in ruins. His clothes were in no better condition than the buildings surrounding him, and his shoes were little more than strips of leather held onto his feet with twine.

"Excuse me, sir. Could you direct me to the Broadway trolley line? I need to get to Chatham House on East Sixty-sixth Street."

The old man opened his mouth, revealing a dark cavern full of blackened stumps that were once teeth. The sound that came out of him was more like a squeaky door than laughter. Thinking he might be drunk or afflicted with softening of the brain, she turned to leave.

"Hold on there," he said, getting his breath. "Yer a ways from the line. We got a Chatham Street, but yer don't wanna be goin' down there. You git yerself kilt yer go any farther down that way."

"Killed?" Her mouth went dry. "Why would anyone want to murder me? I've done nothing wrong."

Upon hearing this, he let out another long, dry cackle that ended in a violent fit of coughing. "That's rich," he wheezed, dust rising off his trousers as he slapped his knees. "That's a good story fer the boys."

Her fear gave way to annoyance. "If you can't direct me to Broadway, can you at least tell me where I am?"

He pulled back in surprise. "Why, yer in Five Points, lady. The devils what live down this way just as soon cut yer throat if they think yer got somethin' worth killin' yer fer."

Five Points! Her chest tightened. Miss Alling once told her that each morning the police went into Five Points with carts to remove the bodies of people murdered the day before. George called it a "hornet's nest of evil unfortunates."

The old man was watching her. "Ya better git on wit ya quick, girlie, 'fore they takes notice of ya." He stretched out a bony finger and pointed. "Take yerself down this here street. Don't stop an' don't turn nowhere. Broadway's down to the end."

Thanking him, Josie picked up her skirts and hurried in the direction he pointed. His squeaky cackle followed her until she broke into a run to get clear of the sound. She slowed only when the pain in her chest became too much to bear.

The first drops of rain fell in heavy splatters. Not wanting to ruin her dress, she ducked into an alleyway where the eaves of the buildings were so close together as to form a protective covering. She leaned against one of the buildings to catch her breath, mindful of the rats that scurried around her, careful not to let them crawl onto her skirts. She had her eye on a particularly aggressive rodent, when a slight change in the light captured her attention. Silhouetted against the light of the alleyway entrance, two boys watched her with predatory interest.

The taller one wore a cheap cap that shaded his face, but not enough to hide his grin. Next to him, a bone-thin youth stood with his head cocked and his thumbs hooked into the edges of his pockets. His eyes were small and ringed with the dark shadows that often branded consumptives.

"Well, well, what have we got here?" The tall boy sauntered toward her, light on his feet. "Looks like we trapped us a fancy lady. What's yer name?"

Mute with fear, Josie stepped back.

The boy's lips slid into a cocky grin that transformed into a sneer. "I'll lay ya odds this here fine lady gots herself a fat purse under them fancy skirts."

She jumped back at the same instant he leapt at her. He landed so near, she could see the rings of dirt that collared his neck. Screaming for help, she ran further into the alley, hiding in the deepest shadow of the buildings. Somewhere a window banged open—or closed, she couldn't be sure. Again she screamed, praying her cries wouldn't be mistaken for a complaining horse or the screech of a cat.

"Gimme yer purse." He raised a menacing hand, advancing in long strides. "Give it quick, or I'll give ya somethin' to be scared about."

"I lost it," she lied. "Don't you think I would have taken a cab if I had money?"

While they mulled over the logic of her explanation, she darted around them, but the older boy was quicker than she anticipated. He pulled her into the crook of his arm and squeezed her neck.

"Yer lyin'! Now gimme yer purse or git hurt."

She twisted out of his grip and fled, shrieking as she ran. He grabbed for her, missed, and stumbled. She made it as far as the street when the other boy caught the ribbon trim of her sleeve.

With a strength that didn't seem possible for such a thin body, he yanked her off her feet. Her face smashed into the sidewalk sending a blinding flash of pain through her head. Before she could rise, the first boy was on her, slapping her hard across the mouth. She fell back onto the pavement retching. When she tried to rise, he kicked at her legs until she collapsed.

Closing her eyes so she would not have to witness her own murder, she hoped they'd be quick about it.

Rough hands ripped open the bodice of her dress. Other hands searched her pockets. While they spoke in what sounded like a foreign language, someone lifted her skirts and began unlacing her boots. Her hair was being yanked about, when there came the shrill sound of a whistle followed by a confusion of running footsteps and shouts. The invading hands disappeared.

She lay still until she was sure they were gone. With numb hands, she covered herself with what was left of her bodice and dragged herself to her feet. Rainwater soaked through her torn stockings, and for a brief instant she forgot about the heavy ache in her chest as she tried to make sense of why they had taken her shoes.

Her hand went to her neck, and then to her head. Her grandmother's locket, along with her hat and gold hatpin were gone. She moaned long and loud, until it became a cry of pure despair. When she lifted her head, to her amazement, the old man who had given her directions was on the other side of the street, shouting and waving at someone in the distance. She stumbled toward him smiling, glad for the sight of someone familiar.

She was only a few feet away when a bolt of pain ripped through her, chest to spine. Falling onto the cold mud of the street, she tried for one last breath before allowing the darkness to take her.

The women looked up from their work, delighted to see Mr. Belknap making his way toward Miss Wolcott's worktable. A furtive tug of sleeves traveled from one woman to the next. There was talk that Miss Wolcott and Mr. Belknap were stepping out, and although there was some skepticism, they built on anything that involved romance, especially when it was between one of their own and one of the higher-ups.

As if on cue, each girl held up the glass she was cutting, feigning a sudden deep interest in its translucency. Clara glanced up, momentarily baffled by the sight of twenty-one women peering at her through pieces of colored glass.

Mr. Belknap greeted her with his customary courteous manner, though the slight pinch around his eyes betrayed the fact that he was there on a grim errand.

She squared her shoulders. "I'm disappointed Mr. Tiffany has chosen not to come himself," Clara said in a low voice, "but as you've been sent to do his dirty work for him, please dismiss me and get it over with. I'll vacate my post as soon as I've packed my personal belongings."

"Dismiss you? I've not come to dismiss you." He turned his back to the girls, who were now openly gaping at them, and spoke in a whisper. "Clara, I need to speak with you privately. It's urgent."

Without waiting for a reply, he pulled her into her private workroom and firmly closed the door behind them. From his somber expression, she surmised he had come to tell her something that would change her life. A quiet sadness settled inside her, preparing her for the news he was about to give.

"Please get your coat and hat. I'm here to accompany you to Chambers Street Hospital. I have a private cab waiting outside. I'll explain what little I know on the way."

The floor seemed to spin out from under her. "It's Josie," she whispered. "Is she dead?"

"No, but she's been in some sort of an accident." Henry lowered her to a chair and began chaffing her hands.

"An accident? But why would they bring her from Brooklyn to a hospital in Manhattan?"

"Didn't Josie come with you into the city this morning?"

"Of course not. She would never . . ." She shook her head. "There must be some mistake. Perhaps it isn't Josie at all. Who told you this?"

"A messenger boy was sent from the hospital. I assumed Josie, or someone who knows her, told them where you worked." He helped her to her feet. "We need to go. There's no time to waste."

An irrational urge to scream welled up inside her, and for a moment, she thought she might come unhinged enough to give in to the impulse. Instead she removed her apron and carefully folded it. Fighting down the dread, she took her jacket and hat from the closet, and without pausing to put them on, walked through the workroom.

The girls stared after her, each one aware that something was terribly wrong. Miss Griffin waved her hand. "Miss Wolcott? Aren't you feeling well? Where are you going?"

Clara stopped. "Carry on with what you're doing, ladies," she said without turning to face them. If she saw the concern in their eyes, she would break down, and until she knew for certain what awaited her, it was better to remain numb. "When you've finished with that, I trust you to select your own pieces and cut them. If you need help, Mr. Bracey will assist. Do your best—just as you always do."

~ 8 ~

THE STREETS WERE a blur as the cab raced through the city. She stared out the window trying to make sense of what Henry was telling her. That her sister would have gone to Five Points was inconceivable in and of itself, let alone that she'd gone without a chaperone.

The moment Henry handed her down from the cab, she ran to the hospital entrance, imploring a God she was not entirely sure of to let her sister be alive. Inside the lobby she stopped a young nurse pushing a cart stacked with folded bed linens.

"May I help you, Miss?"

"Word has reached me that my sister, Josephine Wolcott, was brought here a short time ago. Can you please tell me where I might find her?"

The nurse screwed up her face in an effort at concentration. "You don't mean the one who came in from Five Points?"

"Yes, Josephine Wolcott. Please, will you take me to her?"

The nurse's neutral expression changed to one of undisguised disgust. "I'm sure I couldn't help you," she said, pushing past her. "You'll have to speak to the matron about that one. I don't cater to them that's in the common ward."

Clara stepped in the path of the cart, stopping it with her foot. "Excuse me." Her voice was firm. "Perhaps I didn't make myself clear. My sister has been injured in an accident. I wish to see her immediately, or, if that isn't possible, I want to speak to the doctor treating her or to the matron in charge."

"I'm sure I don't know where Miss Grennan is at the moment." The nurse pushed around her and was about to continue on her way when

Henry appeared at Clara's elbow.

Stony-faced, he placed a hand on the cart. "You will find the ward matron or the doctor and bring one of them to us without further delay. If someone with authority isn't here within five minutes, I will personally see to it that you're dismissed before the end of the day. Do you understand?"

The nurse curtsied. "Yes, sir. Sorry, sir. It's just that the girl who came in was . . ." she glanced at Clara, curtsied again, and hurried off, leaving her cart in the middle of the lobby.

Clara clutched Henry's arm. "I'm frightened. What if Josie's dead?"

"She isn't. You were summoned to the hospital; the dead are taken to the police station."

A heavy woman in an immaculate white apron appeared on the other side of the lobby. The enormous ring of keys that hung from her waist clanked rhythmically against a foot-long crucifix. Her graying hair was held back by a white linen scarf, after the fashion of Catholic nuns.

She made her way toward them with a light step that belied her large frame. The young nurse trailed sheepishly behind her. "I'm Miss Grennan, the ward matron here," she said with a trace of an Irish brogue. "Would you be the ones inquirin' after Miss Wolcott?"

"I'm her sister, Clara Wolcott. Please tell me she's all right."

The woman peered over the top of her spectacles. "You say you're her sister?" There was doubt in the question.

Clara answered with growing impatience. "Yes, I've already told the nurse that. I want to know my sister's condition and what has happened to her. If you can't tell me, I demand to see the physician who is treating her."

The Ward Matron looked from Clara to Henry, scanning him head to foot. "And who might you be?"

"I am Mr. Henry Belknap, and I find this reluctance to answer Miss Wolcott's question about her sister's condition tantamount to cruelty. I'm well acquainted with the members of the board of this hospital, and you may be sure they'll be made aware of the shoddy treatment to which we've been subjected. Now, either take Miss Wolcott to her sister straightaway, or stand aside and we'll find her ourselves, even if we have to search every square inch of this building with the aid of the police!"

Miss Grennan's eyes flickered in recognition of his name. She pushed her spectacles back to the bridge of her nose and, without further delay, moved toward the stairs. "If you please, Miss, follow me. Your sister is in the women's common ward."

She glanced back at Henry. "Sorry sir, but men aren't allowed in the women's wards, except during visiting hours on Wednesday and Sunday. Today is Tuesday."

Henry waved Clara on. "I'll wait here. Take as long as you need."

Giving him a grateful smile, she ran after Miss Grennan, who was already halfway up the stairs.

Miss Grennan walked at a fast clip, though not as fast as Clara would have wished. After a maze of corridors, the matron led her through a set of swinging doors that opened onto a long, narrow room crowded with twenty or more cots lining each side.

Women of every age and description lay huddled on the dingy sheets. Yet, in spite of her revulsion, she could not stop herself from looking. Everywhere her eyes went she saw feverish, sunken eyes, toothless mouths and diseased or damaged flesh. Many of the poor wretches were wasted away to nothing more than flesh-covered skeletons, while others seemed to float on sagging pillows of fat. Two elderly women, whose skin was gray and mottled, lay side by side so perfectly still she was sure they were no longer among the living. Groans and cries of pain echoed off the walls. Several of the women could be heard begging for water or morphine. Only one prayed—a sickly girl who looked to be in the last days of her confinement.

A heavy stench caught in Clara's throat, forcing her to press her lapel scarf over her nose and mouth. She followed the matron down the constricted path that lay between the ends of the cots and redirected her gaze to the sway of the matron's hem, which went still at the end of the row.

Clara lifted her eyes to the battered creature lying on sheets filthy with blood and dirt. The orbits around the girl's eyes were greatly swollen, and the rest of her face was so marred with cuts and bruises, she wasn't at all sure it was Josie. She desperately searched for some small feature that was exclusively Josie's, and reflexively jerked back.

"She isn't breathing!" she gasped, pulling on Miss Grennan's arm. "Dear God, is she dead?"

"No, no. Of course not," Miss Grennan chided, picking up Josie's wrist to count her pulse. "Her breathing's shallow is all; it's common after they get the morphine. She was hysterical when they brought her in, you know. Dr. Mackley gave her an injection so she wouldn't work herself into a state that might cause her heart to fail.

"Cafferty—he's the copper that collared the two hooligans that got hold of her down at Five Points—he told me that some old codger saw 'em followin' her and fetched the law. Cafferty said they roughed her up, but . . ." Miss Grennan lowered her voice to a whisper, "they didn't violate the poor girl, thank sweet Jesus for *that*, Miss. You can't say her guardian angel wasn't watching over her today."

Clara wondered where the guardian angel was while her sister was being assaulted. Taking Jo's hand, she flinched at the cold flesh and began rubbing warmth into her fingers.

"Dr. Mackley is Chambers Street house surgeon," Miss Grennan went on. "He's the best in the city. He thinks she's going to be all right, but he says your sister has a sort of heart dropsy and the shock probably caused some damage. He's sent to the chemist for special medicines—she won't be able to get along without them."

The matron paused. "I hope you don't mind me asking, Miss, but you seem like a decent sort. What do you think your sister might've been doing down in Five Points? Most of the women we see from there are a bad lot. Anyone with the sense of a hen knows you can't go in there and come out same as what you went in."

Bewildered, Clara shook her head. "I can't imagine how my sister came to be in that dreadful place, but I'm certain it was not her intention to be there. It's a mystery only Josephine will be able to solve for us."

Miss Grennan fingered her keys. "I'll be plain with you Miss—we put her here in the common ward 'cause we thought she was a prostitute. When she wakes, we'll bring her upstairs to the private ladies' ward. It might cost you some, but it's got windows and it's quieter. They get their feed first, so the food is hot. She'll rest better up there, too. Nights down here . . ." Miss Grennan waved a hand in the general direction of the ward, "sometimes the women get to acting crazy. Some of 'em can be downright foul, if you understand my meaning."

Clara had no idea what Miss Grennan was hinting at, but from the matron's expression, she was fairly certain she didn't want to know. "How long will she have to be in the hospital?"

"Dr. Mackley won't let her leave until he's certain she's out of danger;

but that being said, he wouldn't dare keep one of the private ward beds occupied for too long either." The matron cocked her head to the side and studied Josie's inert body. "I reckon she'll be able to go home in a week's time. Now if you'll excuse me, Miss, I'll make arrangements to have your sister taken to the ladies' ward."

After the matron was gone, Clara inspected every inch of her sister's bruised and swollen face. "Josie? You're safe now. Please wake up."

Josie opened her eyes as far as the swelling would allow and winced at the light. Seeing Clara, she struggled to sit up, speaking in fits and starts, forcing her damaged lips to form the words.

"You should have seen it, Clara. There was this little girl who took my hat and ate garbage and . . . and . . ." She closed her eyes. "I almost escaped, except my heart hurt and I couldn't breathe. Those boys they . . . they were going to kill me! It was the old man who saved me." She gripped Clara's hand. "We have to find him and give him something—maybe a new pair of shoes and some money. Maybe we could find him some work at Miss Todd's. He could sleep in the furnace room."

"I'll see what we can do," Clara said quietly, "but you're safe now, and Dr. Mackley says you must rest. You have to—"

"They took everything—all the money I saved, grandmother's locket, even my hat and shoes." She let loose with a hysterical giggle. "My hat and shoes. Can you imagine? What would street boys want with those?"

Clara pulled her close, trying to absorb as much of the hurt as she could. She stroked Josie's hair, humming the first tune to come into her head. A dozen notes into "La donna è mobile," she felt her sister relax. "You mustn't worry any more about it," she whispered. "The police have recovered most of your things, including your shoes, which . . ." she attempted a lighthearted laugh, "they've probably polished for you."

Josie turned her face to the wall and sighed—a gentle, sad sound. "Now there'll be more doctor bills and medicines," she said, her voice growing faint as sleep overcame her. "I'll have to go to the Christian charities and ask for a dress. Alice and I can trim it with Miss Todd's old wreath ribbon."

Clara tucked Josie's hand under the covers and hurried to the lobby, where she related the facts to Henry. When she was finished, he led her to a nearby bench.

"I had a brilliant idea while you were gone," he said. "I'm going to stay at my club, and I want you to use my apartment. It's comfortable, and you could look after Josie yourself. I'll arrange to have my physician come by as often as you think necessary. It would be no inconvenience to me, and it would provide your sister with a private place to recover."

"Thank you, Henry, but I'm afraid she's much too ill to be moved. However, I am going to call upon you to help in another way."

"I'll do whatever I can, just name it."

"Please telephone Miss Todd and tell her Josie has been taken ill with the grippe and that we're staying with friends in the city for the time being. She'll press you for details, so you'll have to plead ignorance. In the morning, inform Mr. Tiffany that I won't be in until after noon. Tell him I made an emergency visit to the dentist—just the thought of a dentist makes him weak in the knees, so he won't ask anything further."

Clara hesitated. "This next request might prove impossible even for you, but if you have it within your power to ensure that news of this incident doesn't find its way into the newspapers, I'll be eternally grateful. Should word of this get into the gossip mills, Josie's reputation will be forever tarnished, and that would be a worse cruelty than anything she has endured today."

"The *Times* editor and the police commissioner are acquaintances of mine," Henry said. "I'll make sure not one word of this appears in any paper or gossip mill in New York."

"There is one more thing, Henry, but I have to come up with a plan first. When I've figured it out, I'll call on you. Until then, I think we should carry on as if nothing has happened."

————§————

The upstairs ward windows were open, letting in fresh air and light, while the smell of clean linen lent the ward a sense of wellbeing. The patients were of an altogether different sort, just as the ward matron had promised. Respectable married women occupied most of the beds, with the rest being taken up by shop girls and elderly widows.

Once Josie was settled, Miss Grennan brought Clara a tray weighted down with a generous bowl of steaming barley soup, a thick slice of brown bread and butter, a sliver of sausage, and a pot of hot, sweet tea. With her first bite, she realized how hungry she was and finished off the meal in haste. But even as the food revived her, she was assailed by guilt over eating provisions that might have gone to one of the unfortunate women in the common ward.

Confident that Josie would not wake for some time, she made her way to the front steps of the hospital, where a fine rain turned her hair into a Medusa-like mass of curls. She had to smile at the thought that with her hair sticking out at all angles, anyone passing by would think she was a madwoman making her escape.

She began walking, sorting out the day's events and their probable ramifications as she went. A few blocks later she came to a chapel, its doors open and the lamps lit, as if she were expected. Silence engulfed her as she slipped into the last pew and kneeled on the hard wood of the kneeling bench. The stained glass window behind the altar portrayed Jesus' agony in the Garden at Gethsemane. It was to that suffering God that she directed her simple prayer.

"I don't understand," she whispered. "Why have I been blessed with this gift if I'm not to use it? Surely my dream is not to end so soon."

Her throat ached with the effort of holding back her sorrow. When she couldn't stand it any longer, she wept. No revelations came from on high, yet, by the time her knees had gone numb, she knew the path she would take. As for her art, she would manage what she could, although to what end she couldn't say—that she would leave to fate.

Getting to her feet, she leaned out over the pew and exhaled in a long, keening note, just as she'd seen the Irish washerwomen do before rolling up their sleeves and plunging their arms into the scalding water of the washtubs.

October 13, 1889
Ft. Greene Park, Brooklyn

The heavy mourning veil draped over the top of Josie's hat made it impossible to tell anything was amiss underneath. This was evidenced by the fact that none of the Sunday morning strollers took notice of the trio as they descended the hospital steps and climbed into the private cab.

They were a half-mile away from Miss Todd's before anyone spoke.

"Let's go over the plan once more," Henry said, "just in case we run into problems."

Clara glanced out the cab window to check their location. "It's very simple. The boardinghouse is always deserted on Sundays between nine and eleven. We'll arrive a little after ten. I'll go in first to make sure there's no one left hanging about."

She fished in her purse for a handkerchief. "If the coast is clear, I'll wave my hanky from the front door. Henry, you will then escort Josie inside and up to our room."

"But what if someone is there?" Josie asked, her fingers stealing under the veil to touch her swollen face. "Like Miss Alling?"

"Say nothing, and above all don't stop. I'll create some sort of diversion, while the two of you slip past me before anyone is the wiser. I'll just say Mr. Belknap is calling with his sister-in-law from Denver."

Henry sighed. "I still think it would be much safer to do this at midnight."

Josie shook her head. "That's exactly when everybody in the house is feeling peckish and searching around for something to eat. It's practically a mob scene in the parlor."

Just kitty-corner from Miss Todd's, Clara alighted from the cab. As she started for the boardinghouse, Henry stuck his head out the window. "If this doesn't work, I think we should use my idea of rolling her up inside a carpet and carrying her upstairs. It worked for Cleopatra."

Miss Todd's Boardinghouse
October 20, 1889

Dear Aunt Harriet and Uncle Joseph,

We have a little mystery here at Miss Todd's that you may find interesting. As I mentioned in my last letter, Miss Josephine Wolcott was unexpectedly struck down with a bad case of grippe (or so we were told), while visiting Clara at Tiffany's. Some doctor we've never heard of insisted she wasn't well enough to return to Miss Todd's, so Clara took her to the home of a Miss Smith (we'd never heard of her before either), where Josie allegedly stayed for some time.

Then, one morning last week, Clara announced that Josie was back in residence. We were all greatly surprised, since none of us, including the house servants, had seen her return. Of course, we all wanted to welcome her home, but according to Clara, the doctor insisted she was not to have any social calls whatsoever for fear of triggering a relapse.

Josephine remained locked in their room, even taking all her meals there. On one occasion, I did try to speak to her through the door in case she was in need of something, but received no answer. Thinking I might find her dead on the floor, I attempted to enter and found the door locked! Being the conscientious woman I am, I attempted to peer through the keyhole, but my view was blocked by something draped over the doorknob.

The following day everyone was instructed by an irate Clara that under no circumstances was Josephine to be disturbed, and if we wished to communicate with her, we should stick to writing letters.

I thought the situation rather peculiar, and there were speculations that Josephine might be suffering from some deadly disease, like typhoid or scarlet fever, that could very well infect us all. With my rooms being directly down the hall from theirs, you can imagine my concern. Just as I was about to insist on knowing what was afoot in the name of safety, the Misses Wolcott appeared at the dinner table one evening as if nothing had happened. Everyone was so astonished, nary a word was said about the strange affair.

Please, if you hear of anything there in Tallmadge that might shed some light on this mystery, do let me know.

Your loving niece, Miss Julia Alling

Tiffany's
October 31, 1889

Dearest Mama and sisters Kate and Emily,

Josie is fully recovered from her spell with the grippe and is occupied with designing a winter wardrobe for the hoity-toity ladies she reads about.

George's most recent series of fits left him ill for days. The doctor, one of the best in the city, believes it may be a brain virus or epilepsy. It's disconcerting to see him so wan and still, when he's normally as busy as a hummingbird.

Work is relentless, and the strain on my eyes is almost beyond endurance. When I'm able to get free of Tiffany's, I'll see about being fitted for new spectacles.

Mama, I'm happy that Reverend Cutler has finally declared his love for you. We've all been waiting for this momentous occasion. Considering you've known each other for twenty years, I wouldn't call his declaration frivolous. I just hope he doesn't take quite so long to ask for your hand.

I'm meeting with Mr. Tiffany now on an important matter and must not be late.

I love you all, Clara

Lenox Hill
October 31, 1989

This morning, Clara gave notice of her betrothal to Mr. Driscoll. I doubt I shall ever find someone with her talent. I'm shattered, as there is no doubt her departure will mean financial loss for the company. My offers of increased salary and a higher position failed to persuade her to stay. To make matters worse, three of the department's best girls have given notice as well, saying they do not wish to work under anyone else. To have that type of loyalty from my own board would make me a happy man.

Miss Northrop will have to fill her position, and while she is a fine artisan, she does not posses that which marks Clara's work as extraordinary.

Just the idea of her absence leaves a hole in my life. Until today I didn't know how much I depended on seeing her each morning. As Father says, I make my own follies. L.C.T.

~ 9 ~

November 4, 1889

Dearest Clara,

Your three letters came all together, and they are stunners. You may be sure I would go farther than New York to walk you down the aisle on Thanksgiving Day.

Certainly Mr. Driscoll is a marvel of generosity. I didn't think there were any such men left in the world. As your betrothed, it is natural that Mr. Driscoll should look out for you, and in this instance the game is worth the candle; but that he should take up our poor Josie, stranded and penniless in that Babel city, and set her on her feet, shows a divine soul.

You must not fret. This man knows that you are independent, proud-spirited and quite willing to work to support yourself and the rest. If you hadn't given to others till all was gone, you would have something for yourself. But now you should allow Mr. Driscoll to take over your cares. I think it's more embarrassing for Josie than for you, but I hope she will be as sensible about it as she is thankful. I shall write a letter to Mr. Driscoll, for he is now a partner in <u>my</u> matters.

With love, Mama

Franklin Square Station
Manhattan

T HE SIGHT OF the black ostrich feather joggling over the heads of the other passengers emerging from the train made Clara smile.

Weary of being overlooked in crowds due to her small stature, Alice had hit upon the idea of redecorating her hats with tall feathers and grand sprays of flowers to give her height. Her millinery creations were so fantastic as to have gained a certain amount of notoriety throughout Manhattan.

Alice flung herself into Clara's arms and then drew back, her eyes full of concern. "What is it, dearest? You look . . . worn out."

Fully aware that the normal landscape of her face had changed, Clara tucked Alice's hand securely under her own. "Worn out doesn't even begin to describe how I feel. If you don't mind, let's wait before we head to Miss Todd's. I could use some fresh air. I've been cooped up all day with Kate and Emily, writing the three hundred and sixty-seven wedding announcements Mr. Driscoll insisted we send out."

She caught Alice's shocked expression. "Not only that, but he insisted on purchasing them at Dempsey and Carroll's. It was a ridiculous waste of money. I could easily have done without and purchased something useful, like a new pen and ink set for Josie, or a camera to make photographic studies of plants and flowers for my designs."

They found an empty bench near the station and seated themselves. Under the streetlamp, a recent dusting of snow sparkled like tiny diamonds on the sidewalk. Alice pulled a wool scarf from her valise and wrapped it around her neck. "How did Mr. Tiffany take the news of your departure?"

"He was upset. I don't think he really believed I'd actually leave." Clara looked away. The truth of it was that Louis Tiffany had been beside himself, ranting and raving so that by the time she left his office, she'd felt guilty, as if she'd betrayed him in some way.

"He got himself all in a flap," she resumed. "Mr. Platt, the company treasurer, wasn't too happy about it either. Mr. Mitchell, on the other hand, was so elated at the news of my departure that I thought he was going to throw me over his shoulder and carry me out of the building right then and there."

As they laughed, Clara studied her closest friend. Alice's fair skin and delicate features created a kind of graceful beauty that struck her as something remarkable. She leaned over and kissed Alice's cheek. "I'd go mad if I didn't have you to talk to."

"Is it leaving Tiffany's that's troubling you?"

"That's part of the inventory, I suppose, but there are other matters to keep me awake at night."

"Josie?"

"No. She's recovered well enough, but her color remains poor and she's often unable to catch her breath. It's her spirit that's slow to heal, although her overall outlook has brightened considerably since she learned of my betrothal. She designed every piece of my travel wardrobe. That being said, she's not happy about having to return to Tallmadge while we're on our wedding trip." Clara laughed. "She even tried to convince Mr. Driscoll that going to Florida, Cuba, Mexico *and* California was excessive."

A sharp wind caused both women to pull their coats snugly about their necks.

"Forgive me if this is too personal a matter," Alice began, "but is there some trouble between you and Mr. Driscoll?"

"Not trouble. It's more that I have grave doubts about marrying him. I'm having nightmares, and this morning Kate told me that when I pace in the middle of the night, I sound like a woman trying to get away from herself."

"But, Clara, this is a common state of mind among new brides."

Clara made a fist, the soft kid glove pulling tight across her knuckles. "Bride!" she said in disgust, "I hate the very word. It seems to be the only one that defines me now, as if I were a sort of secondary accessory belonging to Mr. Driscoll.

"I hate that I must ask for money. I hate that I'm now dependent on someone else for every basic need. Above all, I despise the fact that I can be myself only in a limited fashion." She angrily wiped away tears. "I can assure you not many brides feel *this* way before marriage!

"Oh, I suppose we get on well enough, and he is refined to a certain degree, although his nature is more suited to matters of the business trade than the world of art, but I don't love him as a woman should love a husband."

"You could break the engagement. You wouldn't be the first bride to back out."

"Four days before the wedding?" Clara looked at Alice as if she'd gone mad. "The humiliation and gossip would ruin us. What's done is done. I've committed myself."

Alice put an arm around her. "If you really feel this way, how do you expect this union to bring you any joy?"

"Is anyone ever truly happy for longer than a fleeting moment or two? People look to love for happiness. I've always seen folly in that. I'm a practical woman, and this is the most sensible plan available."

Alice threw up her hands. "For Heaven's sake, Clara, morganatic marriages went out of style eons ago. I know you feel this is the only way out for you and Josie, but I fear for your peace of mind."

Clara pulled Alice to her feet. "You shouldn't listen to me when I get like this. Mr. Driscoll is a kind and generous man. He'll provide for me and Jo, plus I'll not have to worry about any confinements." Alice puzzled for a moment and then laughed abruptly when Clara's meaning became clear. "Oh, I see. How did you and Mr. Driscoll come to that resolution?"

"Actually, it was Mr. Driscoll who brought it up. We've agreed that ours will be a chaste marriage unless I change my mind." She arched an eyebrow. "And I assure you there'll be snow in Hell before that ever comes to pass."

"There aren't many men who would agree to something like that," Alice said, shaking her head. "Have you decided on a place to live?"

"Mr. Driscoll decided for us. He leased a large suite of rooms on the eighth floor of the San Remo, the new residence hotel on Central Park West at Seventy-fifth Street—the one with the two towers. He thinks the park view will be beneficial to Josie's health.

"I was dead set against it at first, because of the expense, but then Mr. Driscoll saw an advertisement in the *New York Times* that read: 'If you wish to avoid the drudgery of housekeeping and the cares of cooking, the residential suites at the Hotel San Remo are what you've been looking for.'" Clara snorted. "He knew at once it was perfect for me."

"Go ahead and shock me," Alice said eagerly. "What do they charge for rent?"

"Somewhere around seven thousand dollars a year, plus another six dollars a week per person for meals. I don't know how Mr. Driscoll affords it, and he doesn't tell me. The one thing he's adamant about is that we never discuss finances.

"He's given us free rein to furnish the rooms as we see fit. If truth be told, I'm more excited about arranging the suite than I am about getting married." Clara started to laugh and then checked herself. "Don't think me ungrateful. I'm well aware that not many unmarried women over the age of twenty-five are likely to find a respectable wealthy gentleman, who will wed them, whisk them off on exotic travels, put them up in expensive hotel suites *and* provide for their family."

"I don't think of you as ungrateful in the least," Alice said, all trace of amusement gone. "My view of the arrangement is that it isn't an equal exchange, but rather a socially condoned robbery. Some great wrong has been done to our sex, so that we are continually forced into accepting these unsuitable situations." She shook her head in disappointment. "And I was so sure Mr. Belknap would propose."

"Henry and I might have made a better match of temperaments, but his mother would never have allowed it. Besides," Clara gave Alice a meaningful glance, "you've been part of the art community long enough to know there are men who are happier in the company of other men." She paused before adding, "He's asked George to move in."

"You mean *with* him?"

"Of course I mean *with* him."

They linked arms and resumed walking toward the trolley.

"I want to hear all about your gown," Alice said.

"You're going to do more than hear about it. You've been chosen to make a hat for my wedding trip. And when you finish that, I'm locking you in with Kate and Emily until those absurd announcements are finished."

——§——

Thanksgiving, November 28, 1889

Bathed in the flickering light of a multitude of candles, Clara stood alone in the vestibule, while her mother was in the choir loft conferring with the violinists.

She caught sight of a regal-looking bride reflected in the beveled windows and raised her bouquet of white chrysanthemums to make sure it was really her reflection. Through the filmy veil, her face appeared serene and flawless, like that of a porcelain doll.

The gown had been made especially for her at Mr. Driscoll's insistence and expense. The cream silk brocade that made up the bodice and draped skirts flowed from a yoke of Brussels lace that extended shoulder to shoulder. From the circlet of orange blossoms that crowned her head, a fine tulle veil cascaded over her shoulders to the floor.

The heady fragrance of the orange blossoms mingled with the scent of burning candles to create an intoxicating perfume that made her dizzy. She peered through the crack between the nave doors. Kate, Emily and Josie, each in her best gown, stood on the steps of the altar. Opposite them, Mr. Hulse, the groom's best man and business partner, was checking his pocket watch, while Mr. Driscoll looked on. In contrast to her sisters, who fairly sparkled in their wedding party euphoria, the two older men looked positively mournful.

She located Alice by the tall branches of holly berry shooting up from her hat. Next to Alice, George chattered away to Henry, who was turned in his seat staring expectantly at the nave doors. In the last row sat several of her girls.

She would have liked to be with them, at someone else's wedding, gossiping about Mr. Tiffany's latest Cane Criticism and Destruction. The thought made her smile, Mr. Tiffany's cane and Mr. Mitchell's thumb-screwing notwithstanding.

A gust of cold wind sliced through the church doors, wrapping the veil around her face like a shroud. An overwhelming panic seized her, as she frantically plucked at the suffocating veil. The future awaiting her at the end of the aisle was not hers. How could she have allowed it to go this far? Whirling around, she tore blindly at the church door handles, sure she would die if she didn't get away.

"Clara?" Her mother's quiet voice cut through her terror.

Before she could turn, Fannie gently pulled her back from the door and searched her daughter's eyes through the veil. "What is it, my darling? You're trembling."

Clara let go of the bouquet and buried her face in the stiff silk of her mother's dress. "I don't know, Mama. I . . .I'm . . ."

Fannie cradled her until she stopped trembling. Clara pulled back and looked into her mother's eyes. In them she found the love and strength that had been the ultimate saving graces of her life. The strangling hysteria loosened its grip and receded. "I'm sorry," she shifted her attention to the floor. "I've lost one of my pearl buttons. I thought I'd look for it on the steps."

Fannie lifted Clara's arms and examined the line of tiny pearl buttons that ran the length of each tapering sleeve. "You are mistaken, dear. You see? Every pearl is in place. Your vision must have been clouded by your veil."

She stared intently into her daughter's eyes, speaking in a low voice. "Now listen to me. You are my firstborn, and I know the concerns of your heart as if they were mine. This is not the end of your life. You *will* rise to your dream, because it comes from a source that is greater than yourself. Your purpose has been clear since the day you were born. Right now, you might feel like a midnight traveler, not knowing which way to go, but have faith that some day you will be free to show the world who you are. Whatever fears haunt your dreams, remember that you are made of sturdier stuff—you have already proven it so."

She knelt to pick up the bouquet that lay at their feet and placed it back in Clara's hand. Straightening the bridal veil, Fannie kissed her just as the first exquisite notes of Vivaldi's "Largo" sounded high and clear throughout the church. On cue, the doors to the nave opened.

Fannie linked her arm through Clara's and, with great majesty, walked her to the altar.

Lenox Hill
November 28, 1889

Could there be a day more clouded? It is done—Clara married. Nothing to be thankful for this day.   L.C.T.

~ 10 ~

Dearest Mama,

The wedding photograph of you and of Reverend Cutler came this morning. How beautiful you look! It's a comfort knowing you are both happy in this union.

Considering the ease with which I've taken to married life, my previous fears now seem foolish. Mr. Driscoll and I arrived home last week, and as we sailed into New York Harbor, I was reminded of how alive and beautiful this city is in its ever-changing glory. Like the loyal darlings they are, Alice and Dudley were there to welcome the SS Normannia and escort us back to the San Remo.

It's a relief to pick up life where we left it, me to my little atelier and Mr. Driscoll to his business. Alice and I will meet Josie at the train tomorrow. You can be sure I'll make her recite every detail of your wedding party, so I can at least imagine I was there.

Next Sunday, I'll resume our weekly gatherings (my version of a salon). One of the San Remo's young Irish housemaids has agreed to pose for the group. This child has a glorious mane of thick red hair that I would kill puppies to have. Honestly, she about knocks your eyes out with her beauty. As far as I can tell, she's the only female who can pry Dudley's eyes away from Alice.

Mama, I'm sending two sturdy binders, which you can use to preserve all our round robins. Who knows, someday they may be of value to someone.

Love to all, C.

CLARA WIPED HER sculpting tools free of clay, while studying the people assembled in her studio. Alice and Dudley sketched the red-haired maid, as she peeled the dinner potatoes. George and his brother, Edwin, concentrated on Mr. Driscoll, who posed with a briar pipe as the ideal salty sea dog. Off to the side, Mr. McBride sketched the well-traveled and adventurous Mrs. Dennison, while she astounded them with her firsthand accounts of life and death on the Ogowe River in the French Congo.

Clara let her eyes wander back to Edwin Waldo. Tall and slender, with dark shadowed eyes that never quite met anyone's gaze, he was George's polar opposite in more ways than physical appearance. He rarely spoke, and, as near as any of them could tell, he never smiled. He did appear to be reasonably intelligent and his drawings were surprisingly good, but other than the fact he had moved from New Jersey to take a position at the University Settlement House on the Lower East Side, he'd offered little information about himself.

Still, he intrigued her, though she wasn't at all sure why.

He caught her staring and quickly moved out of her line of view. Blushing, she returned her attention to the clay bust. They were still under Mrs. Dennison's spell, when a maid appeared in the studio doorway holding a calling card.

"Mrs. and Miss Price are callin' downstairs, Ma'am. Shall I say ya aren't at home, or do ya want I should bring 'em up?"

Alice paused in her drawing. "Isn't Mrs. Price the woman who owns the farmstead next to your mother's?"

Clara nodded. "She wrote last week saying she and her daughter would be in New York visiting relatives." She turned back to the maid. "Please tell them we aren't at home. I'll call on them tomorrow."

"Oh, let them come up," Mr. Driscoll urged. "If we don't receive them now, Mrs. Price will waste no time telling everyone in Tallmadge about the deterioration in our manners. She'll no doubt blame me, saying I'm a discourteous lout."

"Go ahead, Clara," Mr. McBride said, setting down his pencil. "Mrs.

Dennison can finish her tale after your callers have left. We were ready for refreshments anyway."

Mrs. Dennison got to her feet and stretched. "Personally, I could use a good cup of tea. My throat is dry as a bone from talking your ears off."

George jumped up, waving his hands. "Wait! I won't be able to think of anything else until I know what happened to the natives of that last village after the Fang Tribe captured them."

"Oh, well," said Mrs. Dennison, "The Fang ate them, of course." She looked off dreamily. "I must say I did enjoy the Fang—they were so full of fire and go!"

Clara was arranging cups alongside the samovar, when the expansive girth of Mrs. Price entered the parlor. By the time the older woman's requirements for a footstool and extra pillows were fulfilled, introductions made and refreshments served, mother and daughter were comfortably settled in on the sofa.

There followed the usual exchange of pleasantries about the weather, and then the long-winded report on Tallmadge births, deaths, marriages and disgraces. Throughout the discourse, Mrs. Price moved a steady steam of sandwiches and teacakes from plate to mouth.

Mr. McBride and George listened in quiet amusement, lips pursed, as if digesting each piece of gossip for future use in blackmail.

"Your rooms are so spacious." Mrs. Price shifted the bulk of her upper body about in order to scrutinize the parlor. "A bit bare, but you've arranged everything so well, one would hardly notice the . . . lack of things."

"Thank you," Clara smiled, "I've abandoned the smothering clutter style and adopted the modern minimalist approach in order to promote relaxation to both mind and body." She hesitated, and then added, "There's so much less to dust that way."

Failing to grasp what the others found so amusing, Mrs. Price craned her neck in order to see what lay beyond the archway that led to the rear of the flat. "How many rooms do you have here?"

"Besides the parlor, there are three bedrooms, a modern bathroom and a kitchenette," Josie replied. "Then, there's Clara's and my studio, and the sun porch at the back. Mr. Driscoll calls that his 'phrontistery.'"

Miss Violet Price let out a startling, high-pitched whinny. "Did you hear that, Mother? A phrontistery!"

All eyes went to the thin, anemic woman outlandishly attired in a blue serge sailor suit, trimmed with a surfeit of red and white ribbons. A too-narrow face and prominent overbite marred any beauty she might have had, but in her eyes was a look of innocence that held a certain appeal.

"A phrontistery!" Miss Price screeched, her ringlets bouncing like carriage springs. "It sounds like a place where monks go to pray and grow ferns."

George, a look of mischief in his eye, opened his mouth to remark, when Clara shot him a warning glance. Looking disappointed, he sank back into his chair.

"Clara's mother declares you're a living saint, Mr. Driscoll," Mrs. Price said, ignoring her daughter's outburst.

Mr. Driscoll gave a wry smile. "Mrs. Cutler is as kind as she is misguided about my sainthood. As a matter of fact, I'm afraid I must tarnish my halo and abandon this pleasant company within the hour. I've been called to my office by an important client who insists on discussing business matters today."

A look of shock and disbelief crossed Mrs. Price's face as she reached for another sandwich. "But surely no business is carried out on *Sunday*."

"When dealing with wealthy clients in a city where real estate is the supreme business trade, Sunday is the same as any other day of the week," Mr. Driscoll said. "The sad truth be told, there are entire weeks when I am away so often, I don't see my wife and sister-in-law at all."

Alarmed, Mrs. Price swiveled around to Clara. "Gracious, however do you and Josie manage here alone?"

"In light of the number of visitors we receive each day, we can scarcely claim to be alone," Clara replied.

"I can vouch for that," Alice laughed. "We all visit so often, the housemaids think we live here."

Josie poured another round of tea. "We have much to keep us busy, what with theater events, galleries to visit and lectures to attend, and there's always our studio, which we share with our friends."

"A wonderful studio it is, too," Mr. McBride added. "It's been the site for many an interesting and informative conversation, particularly when our literary friends join us. Take, for example, Mrs. Dennison here. She's traveled extensively throughout Africa and has authored a fascinating book about the various tribes."

Mrs. Price made a dismissive gesture. "Yes, yes, I'm sure it's all very interesting, but while this sort of frivolity might be all well and good for unmarried women, Clara has a husband to consider." She looked imploringly to Mr. Driscoll. "For goodness sake, sir, whatever must you think of your wife's . . ." she searched for an acceptable word that wasn't open to misunderstanding, "outside activities?"

Mr. Driscoll lowered his head to hide his smile. "Well, I think of them in the same manner any sensible man would, Mrs. Price—with great interest. My wife and sister-in-law derive as much pleasure from their artwork and outside activities as I do from my business. It's important that they expand their thinking in any way they find enjoyable."

Edwin Waldo cleared his throat. "Consider, Madam, that the knowledge and experience these women gain through their explorations of the world beyond their doorstep, they share with the rest of us. Thus, we are all enriched. It seems a much more enlightened way to live than being confined in one place everyday with little or no exposure to anything more than a variety of embroidery stitches. Don't you agree?" His radiant smile was so astonishingly attractive and genial that for a moment they all stared, spellbound by his dramatic transformation.

Mrs. Price frowned. "But surely," she said, her voice growing tight with annoyance, "once you begin your family, you won't have time for—"

Alice rapidly picked up a plate of cakes and held it so that it blocked eye contact between Mrs. Price and Clara. "You must ask Clara about their next trip to Europe."

"Yes," Clara said, joining in the effort to stay clear of subjects that would prove incendiary, "Mr. Driscoll, Josie and I hope to visit the House of Worth in Paris, where Jo is to submit her designs for critique. After that, we'll proceed to London to attend the conference on women's rights."

"Women's rights?" Mrs. Price picked at her black fichu, as if the silk were strangling her. Glancing around at their grinning faces, she set her cup down, a sheep among wolves. "Violet and I really must be going," she said, brushing crumbs from her bodice. "I don't want to be late for dinner."

As discretely as possible for a woman of her size, she began rocking, in order to gain purchase so that she might rise from the couch. With an exasperated sigh, Miss Price finally gave her mother's rump a shove that catapulted her to her feet.

—§—

Mrs. Dennison, posing as Annie Oakley, held a toy rifle at the ready, her wide-brimmed hat pushed back on her head. As they sketched, Clara listened to the tides of conversation flow and ebb, and then began all over again with new thoughts. The openness of their talk made her feel she was part of a remarkable and loyal family.

Mr. McBride exchanged his inkpen for a watercolor brush. "I understand Mr. Tiffany has crossed over from the Moorish influence to the art nouveau style."

"Art nouveau is more than a mere style, dear man," George said. "It's the art of the future. Lalique, Beardsley, Galle, even Toulouse-Lautrec are using it now."

Mrs. Dennison lowered her rifle. "Art nouveau?"

"New art," Josie said without looking up from her drawing. "It's a modern style of incorporating nature into decoration and architectural design—curling vines, flowers and such. Clara has been using it for years in most of her designs, long before it became the trend."

"By the way, I ran into Mr. Tiffany yesterday," Clara said. "He's searching for new designs for his showroom."

They stopped what they were doing and stared, waiting for something more— something scandalous. "That was all he said?" Alice asked. "That he wants new designs? Nothing more personal?"

Clara returned their stares. "For goodness sakes, what did you expect; some tawdry tale of illicit romance? I was only an employee, not his lost love."

"You were Mr. Tiffany's best designer," Josie reminded her in a spiky tone. She had never forgiven him for turning down the lamp designs. "I suspect he would give his eyeteeth to have you back."

George wore the grin of a true gossipmonger. "I wouldn't be too sure about not being his lost love either. From what Henry tells me, Tiffany frequently asks after you. He's even working on trying to change the company policy that bans married women from working there."

Though the news pleased her more than she was willing to let on, she scoffed at the idea. "Mr. Tiffany can talk about changing policies all he wants, but his father will never allow it. Now, Mrs. Dennison, if you would be so kind as to tell us another of your adventures?"

While the woman spun another yarn, Clara began sketching out a new design for a snapdragon tea screen made of glass.

The Briars
September 28, 1891

Havermeyer continues to criticize my plans for the renovation of his home. The clod knows nothing about architectural design. Were it not for the generous commission, I would have walked away from this project months ago.

Louise and the children will soon return to Lenox Hill for her confinement. If this one is a girl, we must relinquish all hope of having a son, as the doctor feels it would be too perilous for her to conceive another child. I have advised Lou that it's her responsibility to make sure there are no further confinements. I weary of my wife's long retreats from social entertainments. On the other hand, it leaves me free to attend the theater and other amusements as often as I like. Stanford White has proven to be a much more amusing companion.

I met the Francis Driscolls at the Women's Infirmary Charity Ball. One might easily mistake the gentleman for Clara's grandfather rather than her husband. He's decent enough, but obviously suffering from poor health and a slowing of the mind.

I was glad to find she and I are still friendly. She spoke of her numerous ideas for high-scale decorative glass items, and I was like a man dying of thirst, unable to reach the river only inches from my mouth.

Annie, my effervescent sprite, sits at my feet, while the rest of my children occupy themselves nearby. It is a pretty sight. I leave off and go collect my paints and canvas to capture the moment. L.C.T.

Lenox Hill
October 11, 1891

A girl delivered this day. Father tried his best to appear happy for Lou's sake, but I recognized that spasm of disapproval on the right side of his mouth. Lou and I make no such pretenses—we are sorely disappointed.

We've left the obligation of naming the child to May-May, who has chosen for her stepsister the silly name of Dorothy Trimble: Trimble for our dear friend, Mrs. Trimble, and Dorothy after some heroine in one of those vulgar romance novels she is so fond of reading.

I suspect father sees my inability to produce large numbers of male heirs to the throne as another of my many failures. There is nothing to be done about it now.

The commotion drives me to The Garden Theater to see the lovely Miss Lillian Russell in rehearsal. Perhaps she will agree to share a late dinner with me. L.C.T.

~ 11 ~

February 18, 1892
Hotel San Remo

CLARA STUDIED THE bust of Mr. Driscoll with a critical eye. "I never appreciated what a handsome man Mr. Driscoll is until I started this sculpture."

"It's his patient nature that makes him attractive," Alice said, closing her book. "What other man would allow a constant invasion of his home by a crowd of possessed artists? The poor man is forever being called upon to pose in foolish costumes, and the patience he shows George is positively saintly."

Clara let her thumb and fingers find their natural place on the sculpting tool. Setting the wire against the soft clay, she removed a thin strip. She leaned back, amazed as always at how the smallest alteration transformed the whole. "I remember when Josie was still having her Five Points nightmares, Mr. Driscoll was the only one who could calm her. He'd lull her to sleep with stories he made up as he went."

Putting away her tools, she sank down onto the couch next to Alice and waited for the muscles in her neck and shoulders to relax. "He was so tender with her, I almost wished I could love him in the way other wives love their husbands."

"Do you think he ever regrets not having a conventional marriage?"

"I've wondered, although he seems perfectly content to remain as we are." She wound a lock of hair around her finger. "He's not well, Alice.

Between him and Josie competing to see who can be the most short of breath and still be alive, I sometimes feel as though I live in a hospital."

She rose and went to the window. The moon was over Central Park, coating every tree with silver. She opened her locket watch and felt a brief stab of concern—it was nearly an hour past the time Mr. Driscoll promised to be home.

"He insists he's healthy as an ox, but I think his mind is failing. Twice this week, he took the wrong train and left his case with all his important papers in a cab. Then yesterday, he overlooked his appointment with the dentist."

"Failing to remember an appointment with the dentist isn't a matter of forgetfulness," Alice said wryly, "it's a matter of survival. Why don't you simply tell him your concerns?"

"It does no good. He changes the subject or speaks in vague terms and then abandons the topic altogether. For the last year, he's been promising to purchase a building where Josie and I might start up a gallery shop, but then he forgets all about it until I bring it up again. I hate pressing him on the matter, but I need to work, and I want to earn my own money. Occupying my time by going to the theater and galleries is amusing for only so long. I need to do something useful. Every sketch and sculpture I've created sits in this room unseen.

"I'm restless. This summer I was so desperate I almost . . ." She glanced over at Alice, considering how much to disclose. Alice wasn't likely to judge her, but still, she needed to be prudent. "Do you remember last August when George and I were supposed to go on a sketching trip around the city, but he had one of his fits?"

"How could I forget? He cut his head on the corner of your hall table, and Dr. Hydecker had to sew him up. George was more upset that he'd kept you from going than he was about his wound."

"But I did go—with Edwin Waldo. After everyone left, the two of us went out alone." She searched Alice's face for signs of disapproval.

Alice looked blank. "I'm sorry, were you expecting me to be shocked? You were two artists in search of a subject in broad daylight. I see nothing improper in that."

"He . . . he took me into Chinatown, so we could draw scenes from what he called 'real life.'"

The slight twitch of concern between Alice's eyes warned her against saying more. Edwin had not only taken her to the Chinatown markets, where people sometimes went to purchase rugs or other oriental goods, he'd dared to lead her into the seamy heart of the place.

'Real life' was like walking into another world. There was a danger there that excited her. It was a feast for the senses, with its exotic sights and smells—not all of them pleasant. She'd seen men and women coupling in doorways and stepped over bodies lying in the street. She thrilled to the vivid array of colors—reds mixed with purples and gold, and pastels of every hue. In the first hour she'd used up an entire sketchpad and depleted every color in her paint box. It was the first time since her marriage that she'd felt truly alive.

"Surely, as soon as you knew where you were, you made him take you away from there?" It wasn't a question, but rather an assumption.

"Of course," Clara lied, "but I was tempted to stay." She looked aimlessly around the room. "I hate being cooped up for months on end! I wish I could just go off on my own."

"Perhaps we should have Mr. McBride write another play," Alice suggested, "one in which you can play the villain. That should liven you up a little."

"I don't want to act in some silly play, Alice. I want to be doing something that has real meaning." She checked her watch again. "I hope Mr. Driscoll hasn't forgotten that he's reading the final chapter of *Treasure Island* tonight. The residents have already moved chairs into the ballroom; it promises to be a full house."

The hard, insistent knock that came an hour later did not alarm her, for she intuited the importance of this particular summons. With a resigned sigh she opened the door to what fate had brought her.

February 21, 1892
Hotel San Remo

Numb with exhaustion Clara measured out several drops of peppermint oil into a glass of warm water and prepared to rinse her husband's mouth. For the two days since he'd been carried home half-conscious between two policemen, Francis Driscoll had labored for his every breath.

She'd insisted on tending to him herself, never leaving his bedside except when exhaustion forced her into a few moments of fitful sleep. Alice made sure to keep her fed and in constant supply of hot tea or coffee, while Josie tactfully turned away well-wishers and the morbidly curious.

Clara moistened a piece of cotton with the peppermint water and daubed it over his parched lips. Francis's eyes flew open, a crazed, frightened expression twisting his features into an ugly mask. He searched the room, frantically tugging at her sleeve.

"What is it, dear? Do you need more sedative? Shall I send Josie upstairs to fetch Dr. Hydecker?"

Mr. Driscoll shook his head, his lips moving without sound. He turned pleading eyes on the glass of water. His thirst had been relentless, though she dared not go against Dr. Hydecker's orders that his patient was to be restricted to only a few ounces of water, so as not to overburden his failing heart. It was an order she found hard to enforce.

She propped him up with extra pillows and pressed the glass to his lips. "Rinse your mouth and spit out the rest. Remember what Dr. Hydecker told you about the—"

Francis grasped her arm, knocking the glass to the floor. She moved to pick up the shattered pieces, but he held her fast with a strength that shocked and frightened her.

"I'm done for," he rasped. "Forgive me. I forgot . . ." He pulled her close. The fetid smell of his breath brought the bile to the back of her throat.

"I meant to, Clara, but I—"

Summoned by the sound of breaking glass, both Alice and Josie appeared in the doorway.

"Alice, run upstairs and bring Dr. Hydecker," Clara ordered, unable to keep the alarm out of her voice. "Tell him it's urgent. Josie, make hot compresses. His legs and hands are cold as ice."

Josie did not move, but gaped at the wild-eyed man struggling for air. "Do it now!" Clara shouted. "Go!"

Josie's skirts swished as she vanished into the dark of the hallway at a run.

"Out of time," Mr. Driscoll panted. "Forgive me."

She stroked the side of his face. "You've done nothing to forgive. You are—"

His fingers dug deeper into her flesh. "I failed you both. Forgive—"

Clara eased her arm from his grip and pushed what was left of his hair back from his forehead. His face distorted in a grimace of pain, as his eyes rolled back into his head.

She glanced nervously toward the door, desperately wanting the doctor to appear. "You mustn't tax yourself, Francis. Dr. Hydecker said—"

His eyes bored into hers. "Let me go!" He struck out with his fists, kicking at the bedclothes. "I've got to . . . got to . . ."

She fought to gain control of his hands, watching in horror as the sickly gray of his skin took on a mottled purple hue. She captured one hand as his body arched, went rigid, and began to jerk. Bloody foam oozed from between his clenched teeth and down his chin.

She threw herself on top of him to stop the bucking motions of his body. He was still thrashing when his bladder released, soaking the front of her dress.

Dr. Hydecker hurried into the room, a napkin still tucked into his collar, his suspenders hanging loose at his sides. Undoing the clasps of his medical bag, he removed a glass syringe and vial.

"Help him!" Clara gasped. "For God's sake, do something!"

Quickly filling the syringe, he pushed her away from the bed and injected his seizing patient. Within seconds, the seizure lost its grip, leaving Driscoll's body limp.

Clara approached the bed and peered into her husband's face. His eyes were glazed. "Francis? I forgive you for whatever it is you believe you've done. I . . ."

Francis sat up with a jerk and sucked in a breath with the force of a drowning man breaking through the water's surface. For several seconds he stared at her, then fell back onto the bed, air escaping his lungs in an eerie moan as his eyes shifted toward the ceiling, fixed in an unseeing stare.

She waited for his next breath. When it didn't come, Dr. Hydecker pressed his stethoscope to Francis's chest and listened, at the same time feeling for a pulse. A moment later he straightened. "I'm sorry, Mrs. Driscoll, but your husband has—"

"No!" She shook her head, not wanting to hear the word. She brought Mr. Driscoll's hand to her lips, the cool, clammy feel of his skin proof of what she did not want to believe.

Dr. Hydecker let out a breath that spoke of his frustration at failing to keep death at bay. He dismantled the glass syringe and wrapped the pieces in a cloth soaked in disinfectant. The smell turned her stomach.

"How could this happen?" she whispered.

"He wouldn't let me help him," he said more to himself than to her. "For the last two years he has refused every medication I prescribed and ignored all my advice. There was nothing I could do."

From one of the other rooms came the sound of Josie weeping. Clara knew she should go to her, but could not make herself leave Mr. Driscoll. Her mind refused to focus on the enormity of what had taken place. She stepped back and heard the crunch of glass under her shoe. Dropping to her knees she began picking up the shards, unaware of the glass stabbing into her flesh.

The doctor pulled her to her feet and examined the cuts to her hands and fingers. When he had finished cleaning her wounds with antiseptic, he called for Alice to take her to her room and put her to bed. Once she was bathed and in her nightgown, Clara refused to get into bed. "It isn't right that I should be in here, while Mr. Driscoll is in there alone," she argued, slipping into her wrapper. "I need to see to the arrangements."

"Dr. Hydecker and I will wait for the undertaker," Alice said. "Tomorrow will be soon enough to be making arrangements. You should rest now and tomorrow—"

"You don't understand!" Clara pulled away. "I'm his wife; I should be with him."

She reached the door just as Dr. Hydecker returned with a glass of water into which he had stirred a packet of sleeping powder. "Drink this. I've given your sister the same draught. Hopefully, you'll both sleep through the night."

"I don't want sleep! If I don't make myself useful, I'll lose my mind."

"You're in no condition to be of use to anyone, Mrs. Driscoll." He put the drink in her hand. "You've had a grave shock and need to conserve your strength. You'll need it in the days to come."

He turned to Alice. "I'll call on Mrs. Driscoll and her sister first thing in the morning. If you have further need of me tonight, don't hesitate to knock on my door. Should I be out attending another patient, my wife is a trained nurse and will be able to care for Mrs. Driscoll and her sister until my return. For now, we should leave Mrs. Driscoll to her rest and retire to the parlor."

As soon as they were gone, Clara set aside the potion. She refused to take the easy way through her grief. Instead, she would take firm hold of the sorrow and pull it into herself, letting it whip and roil until it was done with her. Opening the door a crack, she peered into the parlor, where Alice and the doctor sat talking with their backs to her. Noiselessly, she tiptoed into Francis's room.

In death, he did not look like the man he'd been in life. She didn't know this placid face. The face of the Francis Driscoll she knew had never been this still, not even when he slept.

Not knowing what else to do, she removed his nightshirt and bathed him, scrubbing away all trace of blood and soil. When she was finished, she took up her sketchpad and pens and began drawing; searching for the man she'd known. In each line, curve and crosshatch, she remembered him—his kindness, his quick smile and the voice that could mesmerize a roomful of people. She recalled his sincerity when he vowed to love her for the remainder of his life.

By the time she finished the portrait of her dead husband, she'd found her grief.

Hotel San Remo
February 23, 1892

Dear Family,
You need not come. The worst is over, and the most important things done. I can manage the rest alone. Henry Belknap, George and his brother, Edwin, have been my towers of strength, doing all manner of things to make life easier for us in our time of grieving. Alice, my guardian angel, has not left my side. Now, if only I could sleep. Kate, please send a box of dried chamomile and a jug of Mrs. Price's best honey. They may help.

Josie maintains a good attitude, although I think this is a show for my benefit. Emily, please send her some of your humorous drawings of our relatives. They are the only things that might bring a genuine smile to her lips.

Everything has happened so fast. It's the oddest thing, but I keep thinking I'm going to wake up and the last few days will all have been a bad dream.

Love, Clara

March 1, 1892
27 Park Place, Manhattan

Inside the dimly lit office of John C. Dugro, Esq., Clara debated whether or not there were windows behind the books, stacked floor to ceiling against the walls. She decided there were, and turned her attention to the aged Mr. Dugro.

Magnifying glass held in one tremulous hand, the attorney examined the parchment that was Francis Driscoll's last will and testament. The cramped and dusty room was so quiet she could hear his beard scrape over the starched collar of his shirt.

To her left, Mr. Hulse leaned on his walking stick and studied the stacks of books with interest, craning his head every so often in an attempt to read the titles. The three gentlemen to her right were, as near as she could make out, legal representatives of a church in New Jersey.

For what seemed an interminably long time, no one spoke or made any sound other than the sighs and clearing of throats one usually hears at such solemn occasions. She began to doubt the wisdom of having come alone to the reading, though there wasn't anyone suitable to accompany her. Alice was indisposed, due to a bad bout of the grippe; George wouldn't have been able to sit still for five minutes, let alone two hours; and Josie—well, Josie was still hiding inside her cocoon of grief.

Her own mourning had followed a less traditional course. She'd made endless sketches of Mr. Driscoll, until there were no more places to put them. Once she'd finished with that, she set to putting things in order, scrubbing the suite top to bottom, and then scrubbing it again until exhaustion forced her to her bed, where, for three days, she slept like someone in a coma. When she awoke, she was ready to break free of the imprisonment of mourning and get on with the business of making her way.

Josie implored her to mourn in the way of other widows, but she could not bring herself to be so false. Death was a fact of life. She'd made the conscious choice to deal with it practically, planning for their future survival and not moldering in some darkened room, squandering precious time.

Her thoughts returned to the subject of Mr. Driscoll's will. He'd never discussed his financial arrangements for her, though he often assured her that she would never have cause to worry. Regardless, she was determined to have a studio and gallery shop of her own.

Mr. Dugro cleared his throat. "I will now commence with the reading of the last will and testament of Mr. Francis S. Driscoll. Unless any of you have an objection to my doing so, I won't bore you with the legal preambles and minutiae, but will go directly to the bequests." He solemnly looked at each of them, in turn. Assured of their consent, he held his magnifying glass over the document and began to read.

"I, Francis S. Driscoll, residing at Miss Todd's Boardinghouse, 32 Oxford Street, Brooklyn, New York, being sick of body, but sound of mind and memory, and considering the certainty of death and the uncertainty of time thereof, and being desirous of setting my worldly affairs in order, do hereby make and publish this document as my last will and testament on this twenty-seventh day of November, eighteen eighty-nine."

The blood drained from her face as she pushed unsteadily to her feet.

Mr. Dugro looked at her over the tops of his spectacles. "Mrs. Driscoll? Is something wrong?"

"With all due respect, sir, this can't be the correct document. We were married November twenty-eighth of that year, one day after he made this will. There must be a more recent will, or surely Mr. Driscoll made a codicil to this one."

Mr. Dugro didn't change his expression or the imperturbable lawyerly drone of his voice. "Unless Mr. Driscoll hired another solicitor to draw up a new will, I am afraid this is the only one he left behind." He pursed his lips and added, "Mr. Driscoll did make several appointments with me in the last six months, saying that he wanted to draw up a new will, though I regret to say he never kept any of them, nor did he discuss with me what revisions he wanted to make."

She lowered herself to the chair, her heart beating hard enough to make her teeth rattle.

Forgive me. I forgot . . .

Her breath grew shallow, as the truth of the matter came to her. She loosened the buttons of her collar. He never mentioned anything about having made appointments with his solicitor—or about forgetting to keep them. But then, he rarely told her the details of his daily dealings, and, she realized with a twinge of regret, it was just as rare for her to ask.

"Item one," Mr. Dugro continued. "First and foremost, I commit my soul into the hands of Almighty God our Savior. . ."

Clara blinked. In the two years they had been married, she'd not known Mr. Driscoll to be particularly devout. When pressed, he would admit to leaning toward the Methodist Episcopalian faith, but his attendance at church was sporadic, at best, and even then he viewed it more as a social gesture than a religious event.

"Item two. To Mr. Peter J. Hulse of New York City, my friend and longtime business associate in Empire Properties Incorporated, I hereby acknowledge and honor the terms of our partnership agreement, dated December twenty-first, eighteen seventy-one, including the right of the survivor to all assets and obligations of said partnership in Empire Properties.

"Further, I release to Peter J. Hulse all proprietary interests in Empire Properties that are held by me at the time of my death to be his as sole proprietor. Any business debts that I may so leave behind, I hereby direct Mr. Hulse to pay in full.

"Item three. I hereby give and bequeath to my beloved daughter, Mary Margaret Driscoll of the Sisters of Charity of Convent Station, located in New Brunswick, New Jersey, the sum of five thousand dollars, to be held in trust for her by the legal firm of O'Hara and McAvoy, 157 Sutton Street, New Brunswick, New Jersey, attorneys for St. Peter the Apostle Parish, also in New Brunswick."

Five thousand dollars to a cloistered nun? Clara bit her lower lip. What could a nun who wasn't allowed to have so much as a letter from the outside world do with such a fortune?

"Item four. To my dearest friend . . ." Mr. Dugro paused. Even in the dim light, his discomfort was obvious. After a momentary silence, he resumed. "To my dearest friend, Clara Pierce Wolcott, of Miss Todd's Boardinghouse, 32 Oxford Street, Brooklyn, New York, I hereby bequeath the sum of five hundred dollars, all my personal property, including my jewelry, my rare books and my Egyptian antiquities collections, to do with as she pleases.

"Further, to her sister, Josephine Wolcott, of the same address, I bequeath the sum of two hundred fifty dollars, to be used exclusively for the completion of her art studies at the Art Students' League of New York City."

He rushed on. "Item five. I hereby direct that the remainder of my estate which, at the date of this document, amounts to no less than thirty thousand dollars. . ."

There was a sharp, collective gasp. Clara clutched the arm of her chair, her mouth gone dry.

". . . and includes all my personal bank accounts, stocks and bonds heretofore listed at the conclusion of this document, be given to St. Peter the Apostle Parish in the Diocese of Newark, New Jersey. I hereby direct that these monies are specifically to be used in the building and maintenance of an orphanage and school for impoverished children who . . ."

Clara stopped listening as despair descended over her. He'd promised.

I meant to. I forgot . . .

He'd betrayed her. How could he have forgotten such an important thing as changing his will? She was his wife.

I failed you. I forgot . . .

Her anguish changed abruptly to guilt. If only she'd talked to him, made him explain his plans instead of waiting for him to bring up the subject. She was sick with the realization that she'd simply not paid attention. She'd been so busy pursuing her own interests and insisting he become part of her life, that she'd not bothered to become a part of his.

Thirty thousand dollars! She pulled off her gloves and removed her collar altogether, not caring what any of them thought. Perhaps she'd not heard correctly. Mr. Dugro might have said thirteen thousand. But even at that, she could easily have afforded a large studio with a showroom gallery. She could have formed a cooperative with twenty-five or even fifty rentable spaces for the best young artists in New York. With Mr. Belknap's connections and marketing savvy, the entire lot of them could have made a fortune.

She let out a strangled cry and got to her feet. A church! A church he'd never mentioned, let alone frequented. A church in New Jersey, of all places. Holding onto the back of her chair, she steadied herself before heading to the door. There was much to be done—it was only a matter of figuring out what to do first.

"Excuse me, Mrs. Driscoll." Mr. Dugro looked up from the document. "You can't leave yet. You have papers to sign."

"I need to walk," she said without slowing. "I need to take measure of . . . of my situation."

Mr. Hulse followed her into the hall. "May I be of service, Mrs. Driscoll?"

"No. I need . . . I want to . . ." her voice broke.

Mr. Hulse draped her coat about her shoulders and guided her down the stairs. The moment she stepped onto the pavement, she set off at a fast clip, gulping the freezing March air.

Mr. Hulse called to her, but she dared not stop for fear of breaking down altogether. She broke into a run, taking no notice of the people turning to stare. She needed to keep her thoughts organized. She couldn't afford to dwell on questions that had no answers, just as she couldn't berate herself or Mr. Driscoll for what they had or had not done. She needed only to keep moving forward.

Five hundred dollars.

His antique books and the Egyptian collections would have to go to an auction house that could get the best prices; Mr. Belknap would help find a dealer she could trust. That might cover the funeral expenses and Dr. Hydecker's bill, but there was no way of telling.

When her lungs began to burn, she slowed, her mind cleared of confusion. If they were careful, the money might take them to the end of May, but no longer. Without studio, supplies or gallery, she would need to find work, the sooner the better.

She rounded the corner from Park Place onto Broadway. Mr. Driscoll was a businessman. How could he have left her in such a mess? Was it forgetfulness, or had he resented their chaste arrangement? She shook her head, refusing to believe such a thing; he would not consciously have left them destitute.

It wasn't until she turned down Murray Street that she felt her ultimate refuges of logic and practicality had been restored. They had saved her in the past; they would save her now. She would go back to washing her own laundry. The order for their new afternoon dresses needed to be cancelled. They were well-fixed for warm coats and boots, but she would have to sell her gowns and use the money to buy sturdy skirts, waists and shoes for work.

She could certainly go without breakfast and lunch. The extra seven dollars a week was better spent elsewhere, and she could definitely spare a few pounds. Since she'd been married, she'd indulged herself with three meals a day, plus tea and biscuits before dinner. Her once-lean frame now sported an extra layer of flesh she neither needed nor wanted.

By the time she reached Church Street, she had already determined what prices she could get for the silver samovar and the parlor sofa. When Mr. Hulse caught up with her, he was out of breath, and, she noticed, he'd forgotten to put on his gloves.

"I'm sorry, Mr. Hulse. I didn't mean to run off like that, but vigorous exercise helps clear my mind, especially when I've had a shock."

"Most women faint," he smiled, "but I think I like your method better."

She took his arm. "If you would be so kind as to escort me to Mr. Dugro's office, I'll do what is required of me."

They had gone only a short distance, when Mr. Hulse slowed. "Mrs. Driscoll, I won't pretend to understand why Francis failed to make proper arrangements for you and your sister, but I was aware of his increasing absentmindedness. Still, to leave such an important matter unattended was unconscionable.

"If you will permit, I'll speak to my attorney about how you might enforce your dower rights. I believe New York laws give you the legal right to claim a third of Francis's estate, possibly more. Properly invested, even a third of his estate would leave you financially independent."

She shook her head. "I appreciate your concern, but I shall not challenge Mr. Driscoll's will. Pursuing legal recourse would be a great expense and undoubtedly cause embarrassment in all quarters. *The New York Times* is guaranteed to print some lurid story that will vilify us all and forever tarnish the good names of Wolcott and Driscoll. I'd be condemned as a fortune-seeker for the rest of my days.

"I can already imagine the headline: 'Greedy Widow Steals Food and Shelter From New Jersey Orphans.'"

"I understand how you might feel," he countered, "but for the sake of your sister's and your own wellbeing, you must consider that ten thousand dollars is not an amount to be dismissed so quickly."

"Thank you, sir, but even a fortune such as that isn't worth the misery it would cause my family. I'm sure most people would consider me a fool, but I won't ask my mother and sisters to live with that embarrassment."

"All right," he sighed, "but rest assured that Francis's' funeral and medical expenses, along with any outstanding household expenses, including the money due on your lease, I insist on paying out of the business account as part of his just debts. It isn't much, but I hope it will relieve you of some immediate worry."

Moved by his generosity, she studied the stooped and graying man and wished she'd taken the time to know him. "Your kindness is much appreciated, Mr. Hulse."

He gave her arm a consoling squeeze. "I should have paid more attention. I would have made sure Francis attended to his duties the moment you were married. I'm worried for you. How on earth will you and your sister get by?"

"Don't worry about me, Mr. Hulse. Mr. Driscoll was fond of saying that I was capable of managing even if the sky fell in. I believe his theory is about to be put to the test."

Lenox Hill
March 4, 1892

Wonder of wonders. I've received a note from Clara requesting a meeting. It hasn't even been two weeks since she was widowed. I don't know whether to be appalled by her blatant disregard of the rules of genteel conduct during the mourning period, or shout for joy at the prospect of having her back again—and at such an auspicious time. I've sent word that I'll see her Monday in my office.

Baby Dorothy bears the closest resemblance to me of all my children. If only her eyes were blue instead of brown. Nonetheless, she's a hearty, sweet-natured child.

Burnie outdid himself at Sunday dinner. The children were terrified. I wanted to take the addlepated bully to the cellar and pummel him.

Rather than move to The Briars for the spring season, Louise wants to stay at Lenox Hill until the end of June, so as not to upset Baby Dorothy. I've agreed to wait until the end of April, with a stern warning that she had best have her children and herself ready to go, so that I might tend the gardens.

I suspect her reluctance to accompany me to The Briars has nothing to do with the babe, but rather with my flirtation in Paris. Ever since she caught wind of it through the infernal gossips, she has kept the door between our bedrooms locked and regards me as one might an insect. I will allow some time for her to calm herself, and then I'll assert my rights, even if I have to break down the door to do it. I am sick to death of her sanctimonious attitude.

I went to Stourbridge Furnaces in Queens this morning for my meeting with Arthur Nash, hoping to find this latest batch of glass to be more in line with what I'm looking for. It wasn't anywhere near what I'd asked for.

I smashed the entire lot. Damn the man! I despise being restricted by his traditional approach. This time I have insisted he experiment with free-form glass in all manner and colors. I hope the damned building goes up in flames with him in it!

A brandy and then off to the theater with Stanford White. L.C.T.

~12~

March 7, 1892
Tiffany Glass and Decorating Company

THE FAMILIAR SMELL of Mr. Tiffany's freshly pressed shirts jarred her memory. As implausible as it might seem, Clara realized that she'd missed him, despite his volatile temperament. She didn't even flinch when he took her hands in his, with no apparent intention of releasing them. Certainly some license could be taken for a show of sympathy toward a newly widowed friend.

From under the brim of her hat, she gave him her warmest smile. Her mission, she reminded herself, was to impress without appearing needy, something she hoped to accomplish by countenance alone. Never before had she given so much attention to her appearance. She'd spent the better part of an hour rubbing her hair with silk until it shone, and had even gone so far as to use red crepe paper to apply the faintest touch of color to her lips and cheeks.

Her plum silk dress was the best of those she hadn't sold. Cut to flatter her figure, it was of a shade that few women could have worn so successfully. Alice made over her black taffeta hat by adding netting, and while it wasn't a perfect match for the dress, it was so elegant it didn't matter—the overall effect was fashionable, yet somber enough to be considered proper mourning garb.

"How good it is to see you again, Mrs. Driscoll," Louis said, returning her smile. "Please accept my condolences for your recent loss. Though my acquaintance with Mr. Driscoll was brief, he seemed a fine man. How is your sister, ah . . . ?"

She let him flog his memory for a few seconds before coming to his aid. "Josephine has resumed her studies at the Art Students' League. Mr. Driscoll bequeathed her sufficient funds expressly for that purpose, and—"

She bit the inside of her cheek. The details of what Mr. Driscoll set out in his will were not the sort of thing one discussed with anyone other than a relative or an attorney. "And she's happy to be actively creating again."

Louis clapped his hands. "Creativity! Now that is precisely why I wanted to meet with you today."

Her eyebrow arched delicately. It was she who had proposed the meeting, though she'd been careful to give only the slightest hint she was toying with the idea of a position. She wanted him to think of her as an artist driven by boredom, rather than desperation.

She watched as he began circumnavigating the desk and chairs. He was still trim and impeccably dressed. Had he been only an inch or two taller, women would have thrown themselves at him. But of course they had. The one thing she'd observed about society people was that great wealth made up for any imperfections.

A smile played at the corners of her mouth. Rumor had it that Louis sometimes enjoyed not only the attentions of many young ladies who worked in the theater, but he'd had his way with many society divorcees and wives as well. His recent break with the famous Parisienne courtesan, Leonide LeBlanc, for keeping him waiting in one room, while she bedded her hairdresser in another, was the talk of the town.

She agreed with George that had Louis not been able to buy off the press, his romantic scandals would have long since ruined him.

Pulled from her thoughts, she realized he was concluding his discourse, his expression as serious as if he were pleading his case before a hanging judge.

". . . and I assure you none of them is a small undertaking, Mrs. Driscoll."

She nodded, hoping to be able to pick up the thread of his subject. Whatever it was, he was definitely warmed to it. "I completely understand," she said. "Now, please start again at the beginning, and tell me the details of what you have in mind."

He sat down and once again laid claim to her hands, jouncing them to the rhythm of his words. "Up to the present, I've concentrated on stained-glass windows, mosaics, tiles and glass plaques for architectural detailing. But now, I'm envisioning new horizons for Tiffany's."

"I've started by changing our name to the Tiffany Glass and Decorating Company; I feel that better reflects the company's changing nature. From now on, I want to focus on high quality, handmade goods; one-of-a-kind pieces designed exclusively for our wealthy clients.

"When I received your letter, I had an epiphany. I told the board in no uncertain terms that the idea wasn't up for discussion, but that it only required your approval."

She tilted her head, as if she hadn't heard him correctly. "I don't understand. You need my sanction on your work?"

Hanging onto his lapels, he got to his feet and struck a pose that reminded her of a strutting rooster. "Mrs. Driscoll, I wish to offer you a position, the likes of which does not exist for any woman anywhere else in America."

Suspicion instantly replaced her incredulity. "Go on."

"I've created a department expressly for you. If you agree to my proposal, you'll be the managing director of the women's glass-cutting department." He threw her a quick glance, checking for a reaction. When she didn't immediately respond, he again took up pacing, with renewed vigor. "I plan to assign all my best girls to your department, including Miss Ring, Miss Griffin, and of course, Miss Northrop."

"Mr. Tiffany, I'm not sure I—"

"These girls are good workers. Some need more pushing than others, but under your expert guidance, I expect they will all become proficient at their tasks."

"Mr. Tiffany, I—"

"Granted, much of the design work will be on your shoulders. As usual, I'll supervise the execution of each piece from start to finish. Each day, we'll meet to discuss whatever projects are in the works, and, as in the past, I'll critique what has been done and tell you what changes need be made. Every piece that bears my name has to be perfect."

He looked her square in the eye. "I'm interested in making money, and art is my route to that end. People are in desperate need of beautiful things, and so I shall give them the beauty they crave—at a price."

She remained silent, trying to separate the chaff from the wheat of his list of gifts and commands. The fondness she had felt for him only minutes before began to lose some of its warmth with the memory of his cane destroying months' worth of work.

"You are to play a key part in this, Mrs. Driscoll. I want Tiffany's— you and I—to focus not only on the quality of the work, but also on our individual freedom to be creative."

She cleared her throat. "I'm sorry Mr. Tiffany, but I think I need more—"

"Of course, you will want a salary commensurate with your position as a Tiffany manager." Louis's smile tightened.

In the time it took her to draw her next breath, she understood how desperate he was to retain her. The realization changed everything. Instantly, she began calculating what might be a proper salary to ask for, and whether to set a number or see what he was offering. Mr. Driscoll had always told her that the first person to speak when making a business deal lost the advantage. She decided to let him name the price he was willing to pay for quality designing.

"Yes, of course," she agreed. "What salary are you offering?"

"Well," he began, a little less fire in his voice, "the assistant managers in the men's department start out at fifteen dollars a week. Considering that you've proven yourself in the past to be more than capable, fourteen dollars a week should be an acceptable starting salary." He paused to gauge her reaction, found none, and then went on.

"Initially, I expect the men will be somewhat unnerved at having a women's department on the premises, so I don't think it wise to give them further cause for upset by making your salary any higher than that. I'm sure you'll agree that would not be conducive to an affable working relationship."

She pushed down the impulse to walk away, and instead, counted to ten. "Mr. Tiffany, I'm grateful for your offer, but this is a responsibility that will require a great deal of my time. To be frank, I'm not sure I want to—"

Louis bristled. "The men's department managing director receives twenty-five dollars a week. I wouldn't be able to pay you more than seventeen without going to Mr. Mitchell for his approval. I highly doubt he'll agree to such a wage. It's an unprecedented salary for a woman."

"Mr. Tiffany?" She rose from the chair, pulling on her gloves. "When I agreed to marry Mr. Driscoll, my one and only regret was having to leave my position here," she paused for effect, "working with you.

"Tiffany's is known worldwide for quality and excellence, and I'm proud to have been an integral part of that process. I have a store of design ideas that would go a long way toward making this company even greater than it is now, leaving studios such as J. and R. Lamb and Stillwell's far behind in the minds of the customers."

The mention of his two main competitors made Louis uneasy. "The Lamb Studio? Have you spoken to the Lambs? Has Victor Stillwell made you an offer of employment?"

She walked to the opposite end of his desk and gazed out the window, thankful to Mr. Driscoll and Mr. McBride for giving her lessons in acting, both on stage and in business. "It's a well-known fact you are one of the cleverest businessmen in New York," she said softly. "As such, you should never have to beg anything of anyone who isn't familiar with the labor of art and who doesn't have the slightest ability to tell the difference between artistic perfection and the garish."

"Beg?" Louis frowned. "I beg nothing."

"In that case, the final decision of what you pay your employees, especially an employee who shares your artistic tastes, should be yours and yours, alone." She hoped she'd not overplayed her part. Tiffany was neither gullible nor stupid, especially when it came to money.

"That being said, I'll accept twenty dollars a week to start, plus the contractual promise that my salary will be reviewed once a year and raised on the merit of my work."

He opened his mouth to protest and stopped. From the fact that he was controlling himself, it occurred to her that he was in some kind of a bind and could not afford to lose her, no matter what the cost.

He ran his fingers through his beard. "Twenty dollars a week would certainly be a precedent in the matter of women's pay."

"Isn't it wonderful?" She smiled. "Tiffany's will make news, and, your competitors will be jealous."

"Jealous? More likely, they will think I've lost my mind. I'd be willing to bet my rivals will laugh me down in the streets!"

"Were I a betting woman, Mr. Tiffany, I'd wager that they'll shake in their boots, worrying over what that clever Louis Tiffany has up his sleeve and how he's planning on getting the best of them."

Louis laughed and then immediately sobered. "Twenty dollars a week is a great deal of money, Mrs. Driscoll."

"To some it is," she agreed, "but not to those who are supporting a family and trying to survive in New York City. Nor is it too much to pay for quality and skill.

"As I've said, I have quite a few design ideas already sketched out."

"All right then," Louis sighed, "your salary will be set at twenty dollars a week. Mr. Mitchell will certainly object, but I'll deal with him."

She gave a nod, careful not to let her expression betray her elation. She hoped it wouldn't occur to him that she'd capitulated too easily. "There is one more thing that I—"

"I have a most challenging project that you'll be working on for the next while," he cut in, watching her out of the corner of his eye. "It's an important undertaking for which you'll need to hire more girls."

"I'll have the freedom to pick and choose my own workers?" She could barely believe her luck. On top of no longer having to depend on Mr. Mitchell's approval for every pencil and sliver of glass, it was like a dream come true.

"Yes, and they are your responsibility, so make sure you screen them well. I don't want any low women in here, no matter how good an artist they are. I'll need you to begin tomorrow morning. We can discuss the project that will be your sole focus for the next year."

She took a step toward him. "Mr. Tiffany, please. There is another matter that—"

"You must give me your word that you won't discuss this project with anyone outside the company," he interrupted. "Even those within your family."

"Mr. Tiffany, I—" She faltered, a victim of curiosity. "What manner of project requires such secrecy?"

He led her back to her chair. "Do I have your word you won't repeat this information to anyone?"

"Of course."

"My father and I have both been invited by the directors of the World's Columbian Exposition to create exhibits for the Chicago World's

Fair. I've been given a pavilion in the Manufacturers' and Liberal Arts Building, and I need you to help me."

Goosebumps went up her arms. For more than a year, she'd been following *The New York Times* articles about Daniel Burnham's fantastical White City with great interest.

"The Columbian Exposition! What an honor. What do you have planned?"

Elbows on knees, they sat on the edges of their chairs, their foreheads almost touching.

"The theme of the exhibition is based on the Beaux-Arts principals," Louis said, "namely, European classical architecture. I've decided on a Byzantine-inspired chapel, a neoclassical room with an emphasis on balance and symmetry. It shall be entirely of iridescent tessera."

Her imagination soared with an image of a domed ceiling supported on mosaic columns. She was choosing color gradients of tiles, when she came to her senses.

"Mr. Tiffany, please, before I commit myself to this position, I need to speak to you about another matter."

Louis paused, already wary of what she was about to ask.

She lightly gripped the arms of her chair. "I want my initials engraved on all my designs, and I want my full name printed on the invoices that accompany each of my pieces."

The change in him was instantaneous. "That," he said drawing himself up, "would be impossible. Obviously the excitement of my offer has clouded your judgment. As you are well aware, it is this company's policy that no name other than my own shall appear on the pieces made at Tiffany's. The customers expect to see my signature—*that* is what gives the piece worth. Surely you don't believe that Tiffany customers would pay as much for an item if they thought the design was not mine but that of a woman they'd never heard of?"

She stared at him unblinking. His ill temper no longer had the power over her it once held. This time she would not retreat. "Of course they would, if the work is of excellent quality and the design outstanding. You and I both know I'm capable of that.

"Modern society women like your present wife, champion the advancement of other women; they would most likely find a woman designer much more to their liking, both aesthetically and politically."

"You are correct on that score," he said, his voice losing none of its hard edge. "Except may I remind you that it is their husbands who pay for the goods, and there are few men who would pay the same amount for an object designed by a woman as one designed by a man—especially a man with a famous name."

"Your argument is not without merit," she countered, falling into the spirit of their badinage. It was, she thought, like playing Whist—a bluffing game. For the first time she understood completely Mr. Driscoll's love of bartering and making deals. "However, it's the woman who will have what she wants in the end, and it will be the woman who tells her acquaintances about the wonderful things she bought at Tiffany's and how clever that Mr. Tiffany is to have a woman designer."

He started to object, but stopped. Going to the sidetable where he kept his potted orchids, he feigned sudden deep interest in their stems. "Since it's essential that we begin work without further delay, I'll agree to having your initials inscribed on certain pieces, but not until you have proved to me that you deserve the honor. If, let's say in two years, your designs are selling well, I might be persuaded to allow your initials to go on select items." He looked at her, his face without expression. "Will that satisfy your need for recognition?"

She wasn't fool enough to believe him, but she sensed he'd been pushed as far as he would go. To argue further would only result in some sort of unpleasant scene. Still and all, she had a perverse desire to put up a fight, or take the extreme course and simply walk out with her head held high.

Her practical nature persevered. She could hear both her mother and Mr. Driscoll telling her that patience is a necessary virtue in business. She only had to be patient and wait for the time when he could not refuse.

"Credit where credit is due, Mr. Tiffany. My mother is fond of saying that about both our good and our bad deeds. It's an arrangement that will do for the present, however be advised that I'll bring the matter to your attention in one year."

"Fine, but for now we must begin work. You have much to accomplish in a short time."

She adjusted her hat so that it shaded her eyes. "Tomorrow at eight?"

He looked at his watch, as if calculating the number of hours until they could meet and nodded. "After I show you around the new workshop, we can discuss the work."

"In regard to Mr. Mitchell," she said. "I won't tolerate his constantly looking over my shoulder."

Louis opened the door that still bore the scar from his cane. "Leave Pringle to me," he sighed. "I'll find some way to placate him."

Together they stepped into the hall, where he bowed and kissed her hand.

It was all she could do to keep herself from laughing until after she'd turned the corner.

Noon at Tiffany's
March 17, 1892

Dear Mama et al,

It's the strangest thing to be back at my old work desk. Daniel Bracey, Frank and many of my flock (now known amongst the city's artisans as "The Tiffany Girls") were here to welcome me. Even Mr. Mitchell made a special trip downstairs to greet me, although I don't think he did so of his own volition.

The San Remo manager refused our request to rent one of the servants' rooms. He did, however, offer us jobs at $4 a week. When I begged off, he insisted on three months' rent, paid in advance, "Seeing how youse is a widow now and not as reliable as the mister was." He employed the smug, condescending attitude that well-off and dishonest people often take when dealing with those they consider beneath them. It was precisely that smirk that flung me into action. I gave notice on the spot, and bid adieu to him and his ever-present cloud of cigar smoke.

We have found an affordable boardinghouse at 1135 Madison Avenue, just down the street from Central Park, where the trees are presently budding in that clear, fresh green, so dainty in their newness. Josie will have the convenience of a trolley close by to take her to the Art Students' League.

Our youngest lamb is coming out of mourning. I know this, because I found the new Harper's *tucked inside her sketchbook. She has also taken an apprenticeship with a Mrs. Greenwald who owns a dress shop close by. I have never seen her so happy. If that isn't enough to convince you, just yesterday she gave the Italian vegetable and fruit vendor our only umbrella, so the rain wouldn't spoil his wares. I'm happy to report he returned it at the end of the day, along with four turnips.*

Mama, do not worry over how we shall manage. May I remind you that my sisters and I were raised by a capable woman who taught us how to fend for ourselves?

Emily, do not speak ill of Mr. Driscoll again. His neglect in making arrangements for us wasn't intentional. The sooner this matter is forgotten, the better. It's only when we look behind ourselves that we have a tendency to trip.

I'm more resolute than ever about succeeding in the world, which brings me to your question about why I've agreed to undertake this staggering and monumental task at Tiffany's. In answer, I can only tell you that until I reach my goal, I wouldn't have it any other way.

> *Much love,*
> *Clara P. Driscoll, Manager*
> *Tiffany Women's Glass Cutting Department*

"Twenty dollars a week? Have you lost your mind?" Pringle Mitchell looked up from the employee hire form in disbelief.

Louis leaned back. "Mrs. Driscoll works harder than anyone in the company. In turn, the women work harder to please her."

"But twenty dollars, Louis! The men will—"

"The men will what? Strike? They've been threatening to do that for months. They know I'm under the gun to finish the exhibition chapel, so they think that if they refuse to resume work on the mosaics and windows, I'll give in to the demands of the Lead Glaziers and Glass Cutters Union for higher salaries and reduced working hours."

Louis examined the ash on his cigar. "Which is precisely why I've hired Mrs. Driscoll. She provides us with a workforce that will out-produce the men and do a much better job. Her department will pinch-hit until the men come to their senses."

"But even so, paying her this much will only create resentments among the men."

Louis shrugged. "Initially there might be some hard feelings, but ultimately they'll get used to it. They don't really believe women are capable of replacing them."

"I'm warning you, Louis, the men will make her life miserable."

"Are you worried that they might make her more miserable than you do?" Louis tapped Mitchell's desk and leaned in. "Hear me now, Mitchell, you will lay aside whatever resentments and hostility you're harboring for Mrs. Driscoll. I can't afford to lose her again, nor do I intend to even if I have to give her the moon and the stars. Do I make myself clear?"

Mitchell nodded, though his natural pigheadedness forced him to try for the last word. "Very clear, but I still think you're making a mistake."

"Mrs. Driscoll will prove you wrong." Louis paused, "However, I am curious—why do you harbor such a violent dislike for this woman?"

"She has an unnatural attitude of superiority," Mitchell retorted. "Her type endangers the very fabric of our society. Her belief that she's our equal is offensive. She'll corrupt the younger girls with her insolence, you wait and see."

"I daresay your attitudes about women are a little outdated. I doubt Mrs. Driscoll poses any great danger to Tiffany's, or anyone else, for that matter. Just make sure to keep her salary to yourself. If any of the men ask what she earns, lie. I've got enough on my plate without having tempers stoked."

Louis thought for a moment. "Change the employee hire form to thirteen dollars a week, but make sure her pay envelope contains the extra seven dollars in cash. I don't want any record of that extra money, and I don't want anyone finding out by accident."

"Where's this extra cash to come from? Surely you can't expect me to take that much out of the company cash box every week without someone noticing."

"Take it from my personal account."

"Now I'm certain you've lost your mind. Either that or—" Mitchell stared. "My God, Louis, are you having a dalliance with this woman?"

Louis looked down at his cigar and slowly, deliberately, knocked the ash off onto the desk. Without warning, he grabbed Mitchell by the lapels, jerking him out of his chair. "If I were a less civilized gentleman, Mitchell, I'd bash your damned teeth down your throat." Louis shoved him back into his chair. "You had best be sure to keep that filthy-minded fabrication to yourself, or I promise you'll regret the day you were born."

Shaken, Mitchell smoothed out his jacket. "I meant no disrespect, but surely you must see how it might appear to the men if you continue to indulge her. I know how these men think, Louis. The majority of them are unrefined. They bitterly resent women in positions that rival their own. I tell you that if you continue to favor Mrs. Driscoll's department, there will be trouble. Perhaps not this month, or maybe not for years, but the jealousies are there, and we'll have to deal with them when they've grown into something ugly."

Louis donned his Panama hat. "Nonsense. Sometimes I think you'd see doom in a garden full of roses, Mitchell. Stop worrying about the mundane jealousies that are common to every workplace and try to understand that the monetary benefit to Tiffany's resulting from Mrs. Driscoll's employment will make the extra three hundred and sixty-four dollars a year seem like the best investment since the Dutch purchased Manhattan for twenty-four dollars and a few beads."

Lenox Hill
April 4, 1892

Going against all the rules, the widow Driscoll has thrown herself into her work with utter determination. I can't help but admire her. I've been informed that Driscoll left her with nothing but a few hundred! I'm sorry for her sake, but the circumstances work so well to my purpose, I'm convinced it must be divine providence.

Tiffany's Byzantine Chapel is now guaranteed to win enough awards to put Father's exhibition to shame. Of this I am certain. L.C.T.

1135 Madison Ave.
April 21, 1892

Dear Ones,
You can tell from the beautiful script that Alice is writing this while I rest my poor eyes. The work on the Columbian Exposition installment has everyone involved twelve to fourteen hours a day. The mosaics are beautiful, but the work strains my eyes and challenges my every faculty.
I give my best to each demand Mr. Tiffany makes of me, with the hope that in the future my creative efforts will earn recognition from the public at

large. I want to feel that I have truly earned every penny of my generous salary.

Our new flat has been transformed into a cheerful nest. Alice and the Waldo brothers have freshened up the paint and contributed a few of their own watercolors for our walls. The ceiling in our room is much more interesting than the ceilings at the San Remo. This one has character in the artful way the cracks find their way through the whitewash. The variety of patterns gives my imagination plenty to play with during the long nights I'm unable to sleep.

8 p.m.

I meant to finish this letter with all my petty concerns over the price of shoe repairs and dentists, but now these seem such meaningless complaints, when compared to Mr. and Mrs. Tiffany's misery this day. Henry Belknap came by to inform me that Mr. Tiffany's three-year-old daughter, Annie, died this afternoon of diphtheria, following a bout of scarlet fever. Apparently, Mr. Tiffany is out of his mind with grief. He has locked himself in his studio and will allow no one near him, save for the family dog.

I cannot help but think of Mr. Driscoll, and how different the death of a child is compared to the death of a battle-weary lion. With the ending of a child's life, we each experience a little death of hope.

The best I can do is to take command of the chapel and seek excellence in our work. In the morning, I'll return to the workshop and do what I can. It being Sunday, I'm looking forward to working without interference. It's the least I can do for Mr. Tiffany.

Much love to all, Clara

P.S. Dear Family,

My apprenticeship at Mrs. Greenwald's dress shop has taken an unexpected and happy turn. As it so happens, one of her society ladies saw my spring gown and cape design and insisted that Mrs. Greenwald make it for her. Mrs. Greenwald was so pleased she gave me five dollars! I can attest to the fact it is a wonderful thing to earn money while doing something that brings one joy. If I never achieve another success in my life, I shall die happy.

Your loving daughter and sister,
Josephine Minor Wolcott

1896 ~ 1908

~ 13 ~

April 17, 1896

Dearest Mama, Rev. Cutler, Clara, Kate and Emily,
*   The thought of being separated from you grieves me sorely, but do*
not despair. I derive great happiness from knowing that I will soon be free
of this flawed body.
*   Use the money I've earned at Mrs. Greenwald's to help with expenses.*
You will find these funds, presently totaling $63, in an envelope taped to
the back of George Waldo's portrait. Please, never forget that I love you.

*   Josie*

THE WESTERN UNION TELEGRAPH COMPANY
INCORPORATED
21,000 OFFICES IN AMERICA.
CABLE SERVICE TO ALL THE WORLD

RECEIVED at: Tallmadge, OH at 8:21 a.m.   April 22, 1896
Dated: New York NY

To: MRS. FANNIE WOLCOTT CUTLER
MAMA COME AT ONCE. SITUATION GRAVE . I WILL NOTIFY
EMILY AT SCHOOL URGENT.   CLARA

IT SEEMED TO Clara that days, instead of hours, had passed since they had boarded the westbound train to escort Josie home. She entered the private railcar where her mother and sisters were holding vigil. "The conductor has just informed me that we'll arrive in Tallmadge at seven twenty-two in the morning. Uncle Walter and Reverend Cutler will meet us with the wagons."

Her mother slowly raised her head. The shine of tears had transformed her ashen face into an alabaster mask. It was, Clara thought, the anguished expression any mother might wear when burying her youngest child.

By far the loveliest of the Wolcott daughters, Kate sat at the head of Josie's casket. Serene in her sorrow, she moved her fingers steadily, working an ivory tatting shuttle, weaving white thread into lace. In contrast, Emily sat at the foot of the casket, glaring. With her dark brows and thin line of a mouth that rarely smiled, she was, as Alice was fond of saying, the burr in the Wolcott family shoe.

Emily tapped Clara's arm, "Whatever was wrong with George Waldo at the memorial service this morning? From the way he blubbered on forever like an old woman, you'd think he was related to her."

Clara let out a slow breath and sat next to her mother. Other than as a lesson in patience for the rest of the family, she'd never been able to determine the reasons behind Emily's prickly nature. "George is a sensitive man, Emily. You shouldn't begrudge him his expression of grief. He and Josie were very close. Her death is especially hard for him."

"As if it isn't hard on us?" Emily sniffed. "Why couldn't you have made him sit down or—"

"Josie was so full of joy," Fannie said, putting her hand out, as if to touch Josie through the casket.

Falling silent, they turned to their mother.

"I cannot think of her and shadow together," Fannie continued. "Hers is the one death I shall never feel reconciled to. The only thing that helps to soften this crushing blow is to think of what it would have been like for her had she lived. It's hard to part with my child of the light, but then I realize it would be harder still to watch her perish by inches in suffering."

Clara knelt, taking her mother's hand. "I'm so sorry, Mama. I should have wired you earlier, but I thought she'd rally—she always did."

One of her mother's tears fell on the back of her hand. Clara stared at the glistening drop, and the wall of desolation that she'd held at bay crumbled. She lowered her head onto Fannie's lap and wept.

"She didn't belong to us," Fannie said. "She was just on loan so she could teach the rest of us how to be."

"I hope we didn't disappoint her too much," Kate said.

Emily stood and touched her mother's shoulder. "Come, Mama. You need to rest. You can lie down in the sleeper car. I'll read to you."

When her mother and sister were gone, Clara found herself staring at the narrow casket, unable to imagine Josie shut away forever inside. "It doesn't seem possible she was laughing and designing ladies' summer frocks just a few weeks ago."

"It does to the rest of us," Kate said, her green eyes intent on her work. "You were with her every day; you weren't aware of how much she'd changed over the last year. Mama and I could tell from her letters that she was giving up."

The shuttle slowed and then stopped altogether. "Clara? I hope you don't mind, but I'd like to hear what happened the last few days before she died. I think knowing will help me get through this."

"There isn't much to tell." Clara took up a stray piece of thread and wound it around her finger. "Josie had just finished her spring commissions for Mrs. Greenwald and seemed easier in her mind—in the same way people are relieved when they escape the city during the summer heat. She did seem a little more worn down than usual. I instructed her to see a doctor about getting some tonics to give her some vigor, but she balked."

Clara smiled. "Our little sister had an excuse for everything. The pains in her back she told me were due to hunching over her drawing pad; that hideous rash on her stomach she said was an allergy to cooking oil; the swelling and the nausea was because, I don't know—because the sky was blue."

For a brief instant Clara met Kate's eyes and then looked away. "The night before she died, the Waldos came to call, but Josie excused herself, saying she was going to retire early. I should have known then that something was different, because she loved George's company above all else.

"I retired around midnight and found her restless and complaining of pains in her back and head. I gave her one of Edwin's Chinese sleeping powders, and she slept through the night. She was still asleep when I left for work at seven-thirty, so I asked the housekeeper to wake her in a half hour's time and to make sure she ate something.

"When I arrived at work, Mr. Tiffany was waiting for me with the news that Dr. Mackley had been called to the house to tend to Josie and that I was needed. He insisted on taking me home himself.

"Josie was in a terrible state by the time I got there. She was frightened, fighting for breath. Dr. Mackley told me she'd contracted pneumonia, and there was nothing to be done except to administer laudanum to keep her comfortable."

Clara stopped, waiting for the tightness in her throat to ease. When she felt able, she resumed. "I gave the laudanum to her, Katie. I probably gave her more than I should have, but she was at least peaceful when she slipped away."

She saw the meaning of what she'd just said register on Kate's face. "Don't look at me like that, Katie. The one thing Josie feared above all else was dying in the same agonizing manner as Mr. Driscoll. The physical pain alone would have been unbearable, but worse for Josie would have been the terror of not being able to breathe. I refused to let her suffer in that way. You would have done the same."

Rising from the bench, Clara walked to the far end of the car and sat by a window. Forehead pressed against the cool glass, she watched the half moon race over the open meadows, wishing she were ten again, when she believed they were all immortal. She trusted and loved Kate, but could not bring herself to share Josie's last moments. They were private, just between her and Jo.

She closed her eyes, reliving how she'd wrapped herself around her sister's small body, trying to force the cold out of her flesh. For hours, she recited every poem she could remember, and when the poems ran out, she resorted to telling fairy tales, just as she'd done when they were children.

She was awake when Josie's hand moved over the bedspread, searching for her, her pale lips moving, forming words. Josie's eyes were luminous, the pupils so fully dilated as to leave nothing of the colored irises. Clara brought her ear nearer to her sister's mouth in order to hear the words that were so faint as to seem like puffs of smoke on the wind.

"I'm sorry, Clara. I gave you such little return on your sacrifices."

"That isn't true, Jo. You gave us joy and made us look at the good in everyone."

Josie turned slightly, a smile forming on her lips, her eyes wide. "I wish I could be here to see you win."

"See me win?" She wondered if Josie were falling into the confusion that Dr. Mackley said was common at the end. "What is it you want to see me win, little one?"

Josie did not answer. The marvelous brown eyes closed, and a great peace seemed to have settled over her. For the few seconds her sister hovered between the earthly and spiritual realms, Clara dared not take her eyes away.

There was one long sigh, Josie's hand loosened its grip and she was gone.

Clara had thought herself fully prepared, but she wasn't. Panicked, she rubbed Josie's arms and legs, trying to make them warm again. It wasn't until Alice pulled her away an hour later that she finally let go.

Pushing the memories away, she went to sit at Kate's feet. "I'm wretched."

"I know, dear. We're all wretched. Losing Jo is the worst thing that has happened to us for a long time."

"No, what I mean to say is that I'm a wretched person."

"I doubt anyone who knows you would agree to *that* nonsense."

"After Josie died, there was a moment when I—" She shook her head. "I can't say it. You'll think me a monster."

"Shall I say it for you?"

In the upheaval, she'd forgotten about Kate's uncanny ability to see into people.

"You felt relief," Kate said softly, "and not just because Josie's suffering was ended. You've been worrying over Jo for eight years, caring for her all on your own. To feel some relief is natural. The sacrifices you made were not small." Kate leaned back and smiled. "If you don't believe me, try to imagine Emily making those same sacrifices."

In spite of herself, Clara laughed.

Kate drew her up onto the bench and pulled her close. "Now, tell me about Edwin Waldo."

Clara stared.

"Oh, don't look so flummoxed." Kate resumed tatting. "I know you too well not to have noticed your interest. Does he care for you?"

Clara shrugged. "His moods change so quickly, it's hard to know what he feels. I admit there are times when I don't like him particularly well, but then I see him working at the Settlement, and how he's always striving to help people who are down on their luck, and my feelings change again."

For a time, there was only the sound of the train wheels and the occasional piercing scream of the whistle. To keep herself from dozing off, Clara turned to sorting through the boxes of Josie's belongings, separating clothes that still had good use in them from the shabby ones that would have to be made over into petticoats, aprons and smocks.

She found Josie's sketchpad in the last box. Scanning the sheets with interest, she marveled at the large array of fashion designs, every dress, gown and coat beautifully executed, finely detailed and colored in.

She was about to show them to Kate, when her fingers brushed over a bulge inside the back cover. From the inner part of the cover she pulled several envelopes bunched together and bound with one of Josie's hair ribbons. The top letter was addressed to their mother, Emily, Kate and herself. The second envelope bore George's name, and the third was addressed to her.

April 15, 1896

My Dearest Clara,

I feel blessed to have been granted the pleasure of living with you for all these years. In many ways, I learned from your living example about true determination and courage. It is because of you that I didn't give up, and it is because of you that I did not fail in touching my dream. In short, dear sister, your love and care have kept me alive.

I love you more than I have words or the amount of paper and ink it would take to describe. I don't know when you will read this, or even if you will, but if you do, and I'm no longer with you, know that I love you with all my heart.

I want you to have the pink cameo broach Aunt Josephine gave to me on my sixteenth birthday. It's my most valuable possession, and I cannot think of anyone more deserving to have it than you. Please wear it on occasion and think of me.

Send me a prayer before you sleep. I will always hear you.

My love forever, Josie

~14~

Dearest Robinites,

Last Friday, I attended a reception for Mr. and Mrs. Tiffany at the Majestic Hotel on Central Park West. I was impressively announced as 'Mrs. Clara Driscoll,' and escorted to my table. We ate while Marie Clary sang. Since I last saw her eight years ago, she's added fully two hundred pounds to her frame so that she resembled a tightly stuffed pink and white satin cushion. Isn't it strange how singers always transform into behemoths if they attain any notoriety?

Alice's yellow crepe gown fit me perfectly, and, with yellow roses and yellow feathers in my hair, I was a vision, albeit a canary-like vision, but a vision nonetheless. You might ask about what shoes I wore—please don't.

Mrs. Tiffany was very gracious. She told me I resembled Robert Louis Stevenson closely enough to be his sister and promised to send me a sprig she took from his grave the day he was buried. Mr. Tiffany remained on the other side of the ballroom, and for this I was glad, considering that every time I see him, he has another set of orders for my department.

Please make note of my new address as noted above. Alice, Miss Griffin, and I each have our own room. However, for the $7 a week that we each pay, we agree Mrs. Gordon's Boardinghouse for Ladies should provide better meals.

We are all delighted for George, whose portrait of Madam Helena

Modjeska, the Polish actress, is to be sent to the Chapman Gallery in Stratford, London. He's such a fine artist when he sets his mind to it.

Two of my Tiffany Girls are spending the night, so that we can get an early start for Troy. One of the churches there has windows that we created after we completed the Byzantine Chapel. I feel we deserve to see them in place.

Young Miss Wilhemson (a beautiful, six-foot Swede) is stretched corner-to-corner on my bed. The other is Beatrix Hawthorne, Nathaniel's granddaughter. I like her a great deal, for she's unusual, outspoken and very bright. She and I will squeeze in together on the sofa. I see that Miss Hawthorne is already in her nightgown and staking out her half, so goodnight.

Love, C.W.D.

PS: I've ordered a dozen copies of Josie's photograph ($6.00) and will send them as soon as they are ready. Unbeknownst to any of us, she had this photo taken just a year ago. Taking into account how much she hated to be photographed, she must have guessed how much we would cherish a remembrance.

THE CHURCH WAS divided into even sections by shafts of sunlight coming through the stained glass windows. *Her* windows.

Clara pulled the woolen scarf higher on her neck and sank into the warmth of her coat. She'd never seen her windows in their final resting places. Rarely did she know where they ended up, let alone what they sold for. Henry Belknap once confided that the larger ones went for as much as five to ten thousand dollars, a sum she could hardly imagine.

In the window above her, Christ, surrounded by a bevy of saints, rose on a cloud made up of seven different shades of white glass. The sky into which he floated was of a rare blue that she'd special-ordered from the Corona factory for this sky alone.

The three women moved together to the next window, The Annunciation. Miss Hawthorne pointed to each section of the Virgin's gown. "That piece of glass there is green number twelve, and this one here is red number twenty-one. Remember how Mr. Mitchell insisted red twenty-one was too expensive, because the key ingredient is gold?"

"Didn't you have to go behind Mr. Mitchell's back for that one, Clara?" asked Miss Wilhemson.

"You might say that." Clara smiled. The irony of confessing her small crime in church did not elude her. "After Mr. Mitchell insisted we couldn't afford red twenty-one, I went to the Corona factory and became my own shipping and delivery company. It wasn't easy, carrying three, five pound sheets of glass in one's portfolio case and not breaking anything."

Possessed of a tomboy's sense of mischief, Beatrix Hawthorne perked up noticeably. "You snitched the glass? How did you manage that, with all those men around?"

"Secret artillery."

Miss Hawthorne smiled uncertainly. "What secret artillery?"

"Ice cream," Clara said, moving on to the eight Beatitude windows. To her mind, the Beatitudes were much more interesting and lively than the wearisome and repetitious Stations of the Cross that most churches coveted. She stopped at her favorite, The Meek Inheriting the Earth.

"I don't understand," said Miss Wilhemson. "You gave them ice cream?"

Clara nodded. "I had it delivered a few minutes before I arrived. I believe all parties thought it a fair trade. I'm just thankful the need for red twenty-one came in August and not February."

She stood on tiptoes to examine Jesus's robe more closely, wondering how many eyes missed the intricate embroidery pattern in the hem. It was one of her special details that delighted everyone at Tiffany's, mainly because no other studio could boast such precision.

The priest, a spry man of older years, appeared noiselessly out of the shadows, his hands wrapped inside the cuffs of his robe. There was a pious gravity about him, though it was mixed with a spark of cheerful optimism.

"I see you ladies are admiring our new windows," he said, rocking on his feet. Red number twenty-one reflected off the lenses of his spectacles, giving him a decidedly demonic look.

"Yes," Clara said, "They're—"

"Tiffany windows," he finished for her, smiling wide enough to give them a good view of his dental failings. "Mr. Tiffany worked on them for more than a year."

"Actually, " Clara said, "these ladies and I made them in about six months."

Intent on bragging, the priest failed to take in the meaning of what she'd said. "Mr. Louis Tiffany himself designed them with his own hands, you know."

Miss Hawthorne and Miss Wilhemson glanced at each other and then at her. From their expressions, she saw they were not yet inured to the humiliation of having their talents attributed to someone else. She was embarrassed for having grown so accustomed to it.

"With all due respect, Father," Clara said, "Mr. Tiffany provided the materials and the general idea of what was to be represented in each window. Otherwise, it was these young women and thirty-three others who created the windows in this church."

"Though, Mr. Tiffany does contribute his cane criticisms," Miss Wilhemson added without a trace of humor.

"Mrs. Driscoll is being modest, Father," Miss Hawthorne said. "She's the designer of all of these windows. The rest of us work under her direction as glass selectors and cutters."

The priest adjusted his spectacles to see them more clearly and chuckled, "You ladies are fooling with me."

"I assure you we're quite serious, Father," Clara said. "We're well-acquainted with every inch of these windows. Look here," she pointed to the tight cluster of blossoms, "this is confetti glass, called so because of the way it's made with all little bits of colored glass. And these folds here in Christ's robe? See how the glass folds? That's called drapery glass. We're the only glass studio to use this technique."

The priest lifted his glasses and squinted at the folded glass.

She stepped back and pointed toward the top of the window. "Did you notice the lustrous sheen of the sky? Mr. Arthur Nash formulated that glass. Lovely, isn't it?"

Miss Wilhemson pointed to the borders portraying flowers and vines. "And see how the borders are all in the art nouveau style? That was Mrs. Driscoll's idea."

"Lillian Palmié painted all the faces," Miss Hawthorne said, "and I painted the feet and hands."

The priest stared at them, incredulous. "But you are women!"

"So was the Virgin Mary," Clara remarked drily, "and just think what *she* created."

Still unconvinced, the priest shook his head. "But these windows are signed. It's written right here, see? Tiffany Studios." He looked at them as if this proved everything.

Clara broke into a smile. "Well, Father, just *who* do you think Tiffany Studios *is*?"

December 24, 1896
Norwich, Connecticut

Accompanied by harness bells, the sleigh runners sliced through the snow, making the hollow, high-pitched sound that Clara always found eerie. Mesmerized by the rise and fall of the horses' shadows on the unbroken snowdrifts, she leaned against Edwin, seeking the warmth of his body.

Taking the reins in one hand, he slipped an arm around her. His increasing attentiveness toward her was a welcome change from his usual remoteness, and it made her happy.

"We should have asked the Norwich stationmaster to telegraph word to your mother that we missed the last train and are coming by sleigh without George," she said.

"No time!" Edwin shouted over the noise of the bells. "Anyway, they wouldn't have received the message before we arrived. It's only twenty miles to Danielson. We'll be there in no time."

"But this is the third time in a row George has failed to come along," she argued. "Your mother is sure to suspect something's amiss. Don't you think it's time someone told her about his seizures?"

"That would only serve to upset everyone. I'll tell her that he was obligated to complete an illustration by Monday and couldn't spare the time. She'll believe whatever I tell her."

"I don't know, somehow it doesn't seem fair that your parents know nothing about his illness. Can't you at least inform your father?"

"What would you have me tell them, Clara? That none of the doctors Belknap has hired can find anything wrong? Or, perhaps I should tell them about the last quack who told him to forget art and find a career on the stage, so as to divert his mind to something *useful*."

Both of them collapsed in laughter. Resting her head against his shoulder, Clara gazed up at the halo of purple, orange, and yellow that encircled the moon.

"I'll bet you didn't know that in this region the January moon was called the 'Wolf Moon,' because during the deepest part of winter, starving wolves used to surround the Indian villages and howl." She paused. "Do you ever wonder what the moon is like?"

"It's probably nothing more than rock craters, but that's one mystery that will remain a mystery forever."

"You mean like yourself?"

"You mistake simplicity for secrecy, my dear. What you see is all I am."

"What I see is a complex mystery. I suspect below that simple exterior there are many layers that I know nothing about."

Edwin fell into silence. He wasn't much for chatter, especially when he was the subject of conversation. Nestling close to him, she amused herself with peering inside the farmhouses they passed. Some were dark, but most glowed with the golden light of gas lamps and fireplaces. The thought of families gathered around cozy parlors, sipping mulled cider, made her yearn for a real home of her own, one where she could rise, work, eat and sleep by her own clock and at her own pace.

Her thoughts were interrupted by the sight of a woman's nightgown hanging on a clothesline, flapping in the wind, tossing its arms and hurling itself every which away, so that it looked like a fat old woman giving way to a furious temper. It reminded her of Mr. Tiffany when he was in a mood.

"Mr. Tiffany came down to see me this morning," she said. "He spent an hour going over the list of things he wants designed and finished before next Easter."

She paused, hoping he would comment. When he didn't, she continued. "It's going to mean working all day on Saturdays, and probably every evening, except Sundays."

The sleigh swerved over a large drift, almost throwing them from their seats. Edwin called to the horses and pulled up on the reins. He set the brake and jumped out.

"Is everything all right?" she shouted after him. "Wait a minute while I light the other lantern."

He took the lantern from her and went about checking the team in his thorough, impassive manner. When at last he finished, he came to her, reached up beneath the blankets and caught her roughly under the arms, swinging her to the ground. She marveled at his strength; at five feet eight inches and one hundred forty pounds (if the glass scales in the basement were to be believed), she could not be called a dainty woman.

For a long time he watched her, saying nothing. Eventually his eyes shifted to a nearby copse of pines, his expression unreadable.

She glanced nervously around the desolate countryside, and a wave of fear went through her, though she could not have explained the reason for her alarm. Spears of icy wind tore through her coat, numbing her. "We're going to be late. Your mother will be worried."

"Be quiet and listen," he said, his breath coming in shivery sighs, as if he were having a fit of nerves. "Two months ago I answered an ad in the *Times* for a position as foreman on a coffee plantation in Mexico, inland from Veracruz. The company that owns it has promised to supply me with fifty workers. The plantation house goes with the job."

He took out his handkerchief and blew his nose. "It doesn't start until August, and the salary isn't much, but if I make the production quota for two years running, the company will give me a twenty percent interest in the plantation and the option to buy them out."

She started to shiver, unsure whether it was more from nerves or the cold. "Have you signed a contract?"

He nodded. "When I told them I'd been teaching at the Settlement, they said they'd add a few dollars to my monthly pay if I agree to teach English to the local boys. I thought that since you've been to Mexico, and already know the place, you could do the teaching part."

"I wouldn't go so far as to claim familiarity," she said, jiggling her feet, hoping to bring some feeling back into her toes. "I visited a different part of Mexico for a few weeks. I know nothing about the language except a few basic phrases. I'm sure there are books on how to go about it, but . . ."

Her freezing feet were momentarily forgotten with the sudden realization of what he was getting at. To hide her elation, she buried her face in his heavy coat, breathing in the flowery fragrance of the exotic pipe tobacco supplied to him by the Chinaman who sold him his miraculous headache powders.

"Leave New York and come with me," he whispered. "Just think, no more snow or ice, and you would never again have to deal with the likes of Tiffany. We might even be able to afford that bicycle you want so badly." He pulled her toward him. Kissing her lightly he held her anchored against his chest. "What do you say? Will you marry me and come to Mexico?"

Vivid memories of Mexico's blue sea and exotic plants and flowers instantly came to mind. The image of taking shower baths in the tropical afternoon rain filled her with delight. Even the idea of teaching appealed to her as a challenging adventure.

There would be no end of fascinating things to sketch. She could work in tile, creating mosaics. Surely there would be a market for it someplace in Mexico. She would bring a camera with her. Tiffany might even commission her to design landscape windows or perhaps exotic one-of-a-kind pieces. It wouldn't be as if she were working for him directly, so it wouldn't matter whether she was married or not.

Despite the cold, a drop of perspiration slid down between her breasts under her corset. "Could we . . . could my mother and sisters come in the winter to visit?"

"I suppose," he said carefully. "Once I start making money, you might even be able to visit them in the summer and stay as long as you liked."

She looked at him, thinking of the life they could have. It would be the most reckless thing she'd ever done. The very thought of it made her feel wild and free, and the feeling suited her. "Yes," she said, finally, "I'll marry you and go with you to Mexico."

With a satisfied smile, he lifted her into the sleigh, as if she weighed no more than a child, and hoisted himself up behind her. He took up the reins, and with a quick snap they were under way.

Clara quickly glanced back, wanting to memorize the place where her life changed course.

———§———

Just outside Mr. Tiffany's door, she checked her hairpins and smoothed down the front of her skirt. All morning she'd been jittery, thinking of how best to deliver the news. On the verge of nervous exhaustion, she built up her courage by revisiting thoughts of Mexico and how easy her life would become without the constant pressure Tiffany's served up each day. She would just tell him outright and be done with it, once and for all.

At the sound of men's raised voices coming through his door, she turned to leave, but thought better of it. If she went back to the workroom, the women would assume she'd lost her nerve. It would be better to stay put. Recognizing Henry Belknap's voice, she was drawn closer to the door.

"You simply *must* prohibit Dr. McIlhiney from nosing around Arthur's studio, Louis. Arthur Nash is your master glassmaker, for God's sake, he should be respected as such."

At the mention of Arthur Nash, she pressed her ear to the door, trying not to think of how disappointed her mother would be at her shameless eavesdropping. Mr. Nash was a likeable English gentleman, who had once enjoyed a very brief partnership with Louis in the first glass factory at Corona until it burned down, some said by arson. He also had the distinction of developing some of the most magnificent art glass the world had ever known. Unfortunately, the world knew nothing of Arthur Nash—Louis Tiffany had seen to that.

"Thank you, Mr. Belknap," Mr. Nash's voice was low, but firm. "My son discovered Dr. McIlhiney here rifling through my private notes this morning. When confronted, McIlhiney had the unmitigated gall to try and wheedle the formulas out of *him*—as if my own son would ever give out such information."

"You and your son are imagining things, Arthur," Louis said. "Dr. McIlhiney has no more interest in stealing your formulas than . . ."

"Please sir, do not insult my intelligence," Nash said. "Dr. McIlhiney is an analytical chemist. What else would the man want with my notebooks at six-thirty in the morning? You have already stripped me of my factory, my due, and every penny I owned, Louis. You cannot have my formulas as well."

The pause that followed was so lengthy, she panicked, afraid the door would fly open at any moment. She was about to flee, when Louis's voice boomed through the door.

"What is it you want, Arthur? Another partnership? I'll have my attorneys draw up papers today if that's what you want."

"Oh yes, of course you will." The note of sarcasm in Nash's rising voice could not be missed. "May I inquire whether they'll be the same solicitors who helped your father hornswoggle John LaFarge out of his opalescent glass formula?"

"Now hold on, Arthur," Henry said with the voice of reason. "We need to go at this with equanimity."

"Of course," Mr. Nash agreed, "you're quite right, Belknap. Therefore it is with equanimity that I say if you wish to continue having quality

Favrile and all the other types of glass I invent, keep Dr. McIlhiney out of my workshop."

From the note of finality in Arthur Nash's voice, it was clear the meeting was at an end. In her panic to get away, Clara tripped over her skirts and fell against the door. Making a quick recovery, she knocked just as Dr. McIlhiney stormed out, followed by Arthur Nash.

"Happy New Year's Eve, Mrs. Driscoll," Mr. Nash said. "How lovely to see you."

Returning his greeting, she nodded at Henry and stepped inside the office.

"Close the door please," Louis said, his voice still carrying a fringe of agitation. "How may I help you, Clara?"

She winced. He'd started calling her by her Christian name when they were alone. She hadn't been able to get used to it. It felt too familiar— almost a violation of her person.

"I believe you've met my friend, George Waldo, the freelance illustrator who teaches at the Art Students' League? His brother, Edwin Waldo, has taken a position as manager on a coffee plantation in Mexico and has asked that I accompany him as his wife."

Louis exhaled and covered his face with his hands.

"I'll be leaving at the end of April, after the Easter rush." She dipped her head to try and make out his expression from between his fingers. "I thought it only fair to give you plenty of advance notice."

He took his hands away, his fingers having left impressions where they'd pressed into his flesh. "Why are you doing this to me? Why now?"

"I'm not doing anything *to* you, I'm simply leaving to—"

He brought his fist down hard. "This is nonsense! I thought you'd gotten that marriage lunacy out of your system. You're an artist, not a domestic slave. Marriage is a foolish occupation for young girls, not someone of your talents. Didn't you learn your lesson last time? Your first and only responsibility should be to Tiffany's. I won't have you wasting your life on some man who in the end will only make your life miserable. I . . . ."

He paused in his tirade, seemed to think better of it, and changed tack. "Have you seriously considered what living in Mexico would mean? Life in those filthy places presents all manner of dangers to your person, treacherous snakes and deadly insects, for instance. No one escapes being struck down by malaria, and if Mexico is the same as it was when I visited there last, there won't be a qualified doctor within a hundred miles to help you.

"It's a lawless land; there are savages who roam about looking for people to rob . . . and worse. They have no fear of consequences, because there are none."

It was true that she hadn't fully considered any of the perils he named, but she was certain he was exaggerating. If the plantation was as prosperous as Edwin assured her it was, physicians and supplies wouldn't be far away, and surely there had to be some law and order.

"I appreciate your concerns, but I possess a hardy constitution; and, having been raised on a farm, it will take more than a few snakes and insects to scare me off. As far as bandits, I'm sure we'll have adequate protection."

Louis pushed a hand roughly through his hair—a sign he was working himself into a fit of temper. The unease she felt whenever she found herself on the other end of his displeasure rose up, threatening to undermine her resolve. She shifted on her feet.

He went to her. "After years of cajoling and threatening, I finally obtain permission from the board to give you carte blanche for the lamp designs. My god, I've practically put myself into ruin organizing a foundry and metal shop at the Corona factory, just so you can do as you please." He spoke almost kindly, his expression a little sad. "Do you know what that means, Clara? You can design whatever you want—lamps, deluxe pieces— every idea you've ever had will be produced without interference."

He took her hand. "Please, don't leave me now. We're on the brink of greatness."

It took her a few seconds to fully grasp what he was saying, though she wasn't sure whether or not it was a ploy to get her to stay. "I knew nothing of this. Why didn't you tell me before now?"

"Because the foundry won't be operational for a another month. I wanted to surprise you with the board's approval and the finished foundry at the same time. "

She searched his face and saw that he was telling the truth. The disappointment that comes from lost opportunity welled up inside her, giving rise to fury.

"Once again, Mr. Tiffany, you come to the rescue too late. You should have told me sooner. But then again, you seem to believe that I should never have any kind of life outside of this building and working for you."

Holding onto her last shred of composure, she went to the door. "At least in marriage, whatever art I create will be known as mine."

"Don't you dare walk away from me!" Louis shouted after her.

She stopped, but did not turn around.

"You seem to have overlooked the fact that without me you would no doubt still be in Cleveland designing chairs and tables for farmers. No one would have given you the chances I have."

Eyes narrowed, she swung around to face him. "Perhaps, but it's much more likely I would have gone to J. and R. Lamb, and if they hadn't taken me, Stillwell's would have. *Those* men would have given me the honor of allowing my mark to go on the pieces I design.

"I'll finish the windows I've started and show Miss Griffin how to go about things. Agnes Northrop can handle the rest." A shadow of a smile crossed her lips. "As for the lamps and the deluxe individual pieces, I think the great Louis C. Tiffany should design those—if he can."

"Clara, listen to me, please." Louis ran after her, catching her by the arm. "Don't do this. I'm begging you. Don't go."

Before she knew what he was doing, he pressed his mouth to her palm and kissed it with all the heat of a lover.

She wrenched her hand away and cradled it against her chest as if she'd been burned. "I've given my notice," she said. "We have nothing more to discuss."

Clara checked her watch. Alice and Henry were both late. She was sure Henry said they were to meet at the Fifth Avenue and Forty-Second Street corner of the Croton Egyptian Reservoir. Shivering, she decided rather than end up with frostbitten toes while she waited, she'd take a quick turn around the rim of the fortress-like structure for a bird's-eye view of the city. Just as she finished one circuit and was about to begin another, she saw both of them hurrying toward her.

Without so much as a hello, Henry grabbed their hands and sprinted toward Fifth Avenue. "Come on, I've hired a private cab to take us to the Empire Hotel. I'm treating us to dinner."

"What are we celebrating?" Alice inquired, after the cab was under way.

"I've given Tiffany notice that I'll be taking a leave of absence for six months starting in May," Henry said. "Mother has arranged a trip to the Italian Riviera then and insists George and I accompany her. I'm sure she'd settled for just George, but she's too afraid of the gossip it would generate."

"Perhaps we should have coordinated our timing," Clara said. "I also gave him notice for the end of April. He'll undoubtedly think we've conspired against him."

"Or that we're eloping," Henry added.

They looked at one another and laughed.

"How did Mr. Tiffany receive the news of your engagement *this* time?" Alice asked.

"As you would expect," Clara shrugged. "He listed all the things that could, and probably would, kill me while living in Mexico. He made it sound more like a safari to an unknown continent than the land just south of California."

"While we're on the subject of lost continents, Alice," Henry said, trying to appear serious, "what exactly is all that business on your hat?"

"All what business?" Alice's hand shot up to her hat—a complex affair of pinecones, pheasant feathers and what appeared to be a battalion of miniature snowmen standing at attention around the rim.

Clara squinted at the ersatz snowmen. "I'm not sure I understand what you're trying to achieve there. It looks like you've gotten into some dust balls."

Alice regarded them sourly. "Obviously, neither of you knows the first thing about millinery fashion." She fixed Clara with a stern look. "What in the blazes has come over you? For as long as I've known you, which is to say all my life, you've steadfastly claimed to anyone who would listen that your life is devoted to art. Suddenly you can hardly wait to give up your work and go off to some jungle to teach English to children. You hate teaching, and I'm not so sure you're all that fond of children either."

Hurt, Clara looked out the cab window. "My life will always be about creating art. As my dearest friend, you should know that. The simple truth is that I'm tired of working day to day to make Mr. Tiffany wealthy. From now on I'll let Agnes Northrop do that, considering how she's so fond of saying that she wants to work for him until her dying day.

"I'm no longer happy being just another cog in the Tiffany Company wheel. I long to wake up each morning happy to be alive and eager to work for *myself*. More than that, at the end of the day I want to be able to claim that whatever I've done is mine. Most of all, I want a new life, and I don't care if it *does* include malaria and snakes."

"It's not so much the malaria or the snakes that worry me," Alice said, her voice losing some of its it's severity. "You have to admit this business of Mr. Waldo asking you to marry him in order that he might drag you off to some primitive, unknown land is frightening to those of us who care for you."

The blood rushed to Clara's face. "I'm quite aware that none of you like Edwin, but it's only because you haven't taken the time to know him."

"That isn't true!" Alice protested. "We've all made the effort to know this man."

"I have to agree with Alice," Henry said. "It's Edwin who is unreceptive to being known. He's guarded to the point that one has to wonder what he's hiding. He's polite about it, but he disregards people, except for you and George."

"I'll be blunt," Alice said. "Edwin is handsome, a talented artist and well educated, but if he has more positive attributes than that, he hides them from us."

"He rarely keeps his engagements with you," Henry said, picking up where Alice left off, "and if the man is actually taken ill as often as he says he is, he should be in a sanatorium. He never laughs, and his moods have little range beyond various levels of pique. To tell the truth, were he not George's brother and so close to your heart, I would have no association with him."

She opened her mouth to argue when Alice leaned forward and grasped both her hands. "Nothing I can see in his demeanor suggests that Edwin Waldo is a man basking in the glow of love. Help us understand what drives you to a man who is so unworthy of you."

Lost for an answer, Clara closed her eyes. His good works for the Settlement had initially drawn her, but after she'd had a chance to observe him at his occupation, she soon realized that his generosity and kindness were not so much for the benefit of those he served as for securing glory for himself.

His artistic skill had initially impressed her, until she took a closer look at the things he created and realized his artwork lacked the essential passion that makes art come alive. As the months wore on, it became clear to anyone paying attention that he had no real interest in art at all.

She could not deny that he had the appearance of a scholar, but she soon perceived this façade was, in fact, created by a certain amount of cleverness rather than possession of any real intellect. His eloquence when explaining his theories kept her interest, though more and more he'd begun to sound like someone reciting from memory rather than one who believed in the substance of his words. As of late he seemed less interested in conversing with her, which made her think he'd either run out of things to say, or couldn't keep up with her.

She couldn't even claim lustful desire as a reason for marrying him. He was, as Alice pointed out, a handsome man, but she didn't feel any different on the occasions he'd kissed her, than from the instances she'd kissed the chimney sweep for good luck.

Once she'd peeled away the layers of pretense, she recognized the core truth—Edwin was simply her bridge from the endless drudgery of Tiffany's to an adventurous and exciting new life. That he had no fear of venturing into the unknown aroused her far more than any physical passion.

At length, she raised her eyes to Alice and Henry doubting she could ever make them understand. Instead, she gave them the answer she thought they wanted to hear. "I'm sure that with time and patience, Edwin will grow to be a loving husband on whom I can depend."

"Is that so?" Alice said, settling back in her seat. "In that case, my friend, I'm afraid you're in for a terrible surprise."

Tiffany's
January 7, 1897

Dear Ones,

Last week's trip to the Waldos' in Danielson was not as exciting as I would have liked, although it was such a relief to get away. I wouldn't have cared where I went, just as long as it was away from Tiffany's.

For the entirety of the trip, George was about twice as crazy as usual, owing to his anxiety over an impending interview to teach mechanical drawing, a subject he knows not a whit about. Edwin remained calm, quietly reading an article on sociology, while brother George buckled and unbuckled his satchel, jumping about and talking for what seemed like a few thousand miles until I was nearly insane myself. At my urging, Edwin finally gave George one of his magic powders, and he slept like a baby for the remainder of the trip.

Edwin and I spoke of our favorite books and the various artists we like. We have much in common including our views on women's rights and politics (Hooray for McKinley!).

I finally met Irenie, the Waldos' beautiful cousin (the one Mrs. Waldo hoped George would marry). She wore a short-waist, square-neck gown that made her look like a tall flower. George says this is the new 'slinky' style of dress. (Slinky! Isn't that the most wonderful word?). George's attentiveness to his cousin is strictly cousinly, as he is much more interested in himself than in her. On the other hand, Edwin seemed quite absorbed by her beauty and wit—a difficult thing to witness for poor Clara with no slinky dresses or brilliant repartee. Still, even Irenie is no match for Mrs. Waldo, upon whom both sons dote.

If I am to be honest, I don't find Mrs. Waldo particularly interesting. Her ideas are very old-fashioned. When I mentioned that I was saving up to buy a wheel, she thought I meant a spinning wheel instead of a bicycle. She was scandalized at the very idea of a woman in a bicycle suit.

All my love, Clara

Ming's Dream Palace

Mott and Pell Streets, Chinatown

Fan Li Ming took Edwin's dollar and bowed, backing away. The Chinaman placed two pipes on the ornate table in the middle of the room and began rolling a sticky clump of black resin into pills.

Edwin pressed against the woman lying next to him. Ming's rule of one smoker per crib was relaxed for him and Sophie. They were his best customers, and lately business was slow due to the increasing frequency of police raids.

"Next time get one of them lower bunks," Sophie said, fussing with her skirts, "so I don't gotta worry 'bout fallin' out an' breakin' my head open."

"The lower bunks cost more," Edwin replied, shifting his body so they were facing each other. "I need to save money for now."

"Save money? You never done that before, Eddie. What gives? You thinkin' of buyin' me one of them fancy diamond engagement rings or somethin'?"

Ming approached with the pipes, each bowl holding a precious ball of opium. Edwin pointed to his watch and held up a hand, fingers spread. "You come back in five minutes. The lady and I make talky-talky first. Understand?"

The Chinaman bowed and disappeared behind a curtain of glass beads.

Sophie rose up on her elbow to stare at him. "You're scarin' me, Eddie. You don't never wanna talk. What's a matter? You gonna skip out on me or somethin'? Found yourself another girl?"

Glancing around to make sure the other smokers were insensible, Edwin dangled his legs over the side of the bunk. "I've got a plan, Sophie, but you have to promise not to breathe a word to anyone, not even to the police if they come around asking questions."

"You know me, Eddie, I'd never say nothin' if you don't me want to." Sophie shrugged. "Hell, half the dandies in New York would be in jail if I ever opened my mouth 'bout some of the things they told me, 'specially them married ones."

She patted at a clump of frizzy hair, bleached and hot-ironed into straw. "Besides, you're the only one I love. Them others don't mean nothin' to me. You know that."

"I do, but now you have to listen to everything I say." He paused, picking his words carefully. "You remember I told you about my brother George and his—?"

She sat up so fast, she all but knocked him off the mattress. "You mean the nellie? The one that's got fits?" She shook her head and began pulling on her jacket. "Oh no you don't. I don't care if he is your brother, Eddie, I ain't gonna fool around with no nellie. It ain't natural. He'd probably have a fit before he could even—"

"For God's sake, be quiet!" Edwin jerked the jacket out of her hands. "I'm not asking you to be with my—"

"If it's 'bout posin' nekked for them artist friends of his, I don't do no posin' for less than five dollars, an' I get paid *before* I take off my clothes."

"It's not about nude posing. Now listen, my brother has a friend, a widow by the name of Mrs. Driscoll."

"You mean the artist lady that has them art swarees you go to? You're thick as thieves with them people, ain't you?"

"I wouldn't say thick, but I like to keep ties with people who might be useful to me someday. I think that someday has come."

"You mean they're gonna sell them art pictures you made?"

"Better than that." He drew up his legs and leaned back. "After old man Driscoll died, I ran into a clerk who used to work for his accountant, and he told me Driscoll was worth a fortune. That got my curiosity up, because his widow was living in a second-rate boardinghouse and working six days a week. I thought I might show a little interest in her, you know, to see what the real story was, and well, she took a shine to me."

"Hey, wait a minute. Is this widow lady a looker?" Sophie put her hands on her hips. "You steppin' out with her?"

"Let me finish."

Pouting, she fell to picking at a green ribbon that laced the bodice of her dress.

"A few months ago, I found the opportunity of a lifetime—a company in San Francisco is wanting to sell a Mexican coffee plantation. They've agreed to let me buy the place a little at a time after an initial down payment of a thousand dollars. The place is going to make thousands. I mean, everybody drinks coffee, right? I figure I'll pay a little each month while I'm working the plantation. When the money starts rolling in, I can pay off the other four thousand, and the rest is mine. Maybe after a couple of years, I'll sell it for two, three times what I paid for it."

Sophie eyed him suspiciously. "Wait a minute, what's the widow lady got to do with all this?"

He tried to gauge how she might react to his next piece of news. Other than a rare temper tantrum, she was a trouble-free companion. He figured she was the only woman he would ever be able to tolerate for longer than an hour at a time.

When she'd first come to the Settlement begging for help for her sick child, the depth of her trust in him had touched him. At his own expense, he'd taken the baby to a reputable doctor, but it did no good. After the child died, she'd gone mad with grief, refusing to eat or drink until she was on the brink of death herself. He'd stayed with her then, bathed and fed her until she came out of her misery.

And then, he'd introduced her to opium.

"You won't like this much, Sophie, but I've asked her to marry me."

Eyes wide with reproach, she opened her mouth to protest when he put a finger to her lips. "I wouldn't be telling you any of this if there wasn't something in it for you.

"Here's how I'm going to work it: after the widow and I are married, I'll convince her to put down the thousand dollars, and the first year's operating costs. When the money starts rolling in and I know I'm in the clear, I'll divorce her and send for you.

"You'll take over managing the household, while I work on the plantation. We'll be just like a regular married couple. You'd like that, wouldn't you?"

Brooding, Sophie shrugged. "How long do I gotta wait?"

"A year, maybe less. I'll meet you in San Francisco, you'll like it there. Frisco dream palaces have private rooms draped in satin and lace, and the customers are waited on hand and foot. The pipes are made of jade encrusted with jewels. They'll make Ming's look like a chicken coop."

"I guess I like the part about San Francisco and Mexico," Sophie said, "but I don't much like you goin' off and marryin' the widow. What makes you so sure she's gonna just give over her money to you?"

"She'll give it to me because she's loyal and she loves me, and because she's an educated woman who was raised like a lady. Women like that don't go back on their word."

"But it still don't make no sense, Eddie. How come she works if she's so smart an' rich? Why don't she spend the money on nice things and stay home?"

Edwin rubbed his fingers across his stubble of a beard. It was the one thing he hadn't figured out yet. He was sure she had it, but Clara never talked to anyone about her money. A couple of times he'd managed to steer her to the edge of the subject, but she'd veered away, leaving him no wiser as to what she'd done with it.

"I'm pretty sure she has it stuffed away in some bank, saving it up to buy a studio downtown."

"I'll be old and wrinkled before you get rid of her," Sophie stuck out her lower lip. "I don't wanna wait so long."

He pulled her close. "Think of the wait as the priming of a water pump—you've got to put in a little before you get a lot back. While you're waiting you can spend your time imagining yourself as the lady of a big hacienda out on the side of a mountain with servants at your beck and call. When you get to San Francisco, I'll buy you some fancy new dresses—

respectable, quality dresses with pretty shoes and hats to match."

At the promise of a new wardrobe, Sophie perked up. "Would you buy me a real wedding ring? One with diamonds and rubies?"

He heard the acquiescence in her voice and smiled. "If all goes according to my plan, I'll buy you a ring for every finger."

She threw her arms around his neck, but he pushed her off. "First, you have to promise on your babe's soul that you will never whisper one word of this to anyone, not even the police."

"Not my baby, Eddie. It'll send his little soul straight to Hell if I slip. I couldn't stand that. I'll promise on my soul."

Edwin shook his head. "Not good enough. You and I are already damned. Swear on the babe's soul. That way you'll be sure to keep your word."

Nodding, Sophie dropped her head into her hands and cried softly.

Edwin waved to the Chinaman, signaling that they were ready.

With a long needle, Ming skewered one of the opium pills and heated it over the special lamp. The smell of burnt flowers filled the air, prompting Edwin to lie on his side. He pulled Sophie down next to him.

Ming placed the pill inside the pipe bowl and handed it to Edwin who touched the mouthpiece to Sophie's lips.

Eagerly she pulled in the first long draw and held it. Her lids fluttered slightly as her eyes rolled back into her head and the smoke escaped from between her parted lips.

Edwin accepted his own pipe, taking only a short draw at first, wanting to make the pleasure last as long as possible. The sharp bitterness filled his mouth. A faint smile came to his lips as he recalled how the taste made him sick his first time. Now he relished it the same way some gentlemen savored their soup.

With some effort he raised his head to get a glimpse of Sophie. Eyes glassy, she lay perfectly still, lost in her dream. He took another, longer pull, until he felt himself begin to float. His life was going to be perfect. His mother and father would be upset when they learned of his plans to leave for Mexico, but that couldn't be helped.

As for Clara, she could take care of herself. She wasn't using the money, so why not put it to good purpose? After the coffee money started coming in, he might even repay her.

He smiled. He was going to be rich.

From somewhere far off he thought he heard a man's laughter. It sounded like his, but he couldn't be sure. With his last bit of consciousness he watched the tail of smoke rise from the opium pill, curling and swirling lazily toward Heaven.

———§———

"It's up to you to persuade her," Louis said. "She'll hear no more from me."

Pringle Mitchell looked doubtful. "Mrs. Driscoll neither likes nor trusts me. Have Belknap appeal to her—she'll listen to him."

"I've already asked him. He actually had the cheek to say she was better off in Mexico." Louis fell exhausted into a chair. "Damn it, Mitchell, I give her a man's salary, and she chooses to squander her life in some godforsaken jungle?"

Mitchell gave him a sidelong glance. "Well, she did produce a good amount of work. She was at least partially responsible for making the Columbian Exhibition Chapel the success it was. You walked away with the lion's share of the awards. How many was it? Fifty-four? And the Glass Gas Tower? Didn't she help with that design as well?"

Louis stared at him. "*You* defending *Mrs. Driscoll?*"

"The woman is insufferable and insolent," Mitchell said," and she goes over budget, but I can't deny that the quality and volume of her work are good. Our sales have doubled."

"Then convince her to stay on."

"Even if she would listen to me—which she won't—how would you have me entice her?"

"Appeal to her on behalf of the Tiffany Girls. Tell her she'll be letting them down. Tell her she can have the foundry at her beck and call. Tell her anything you think she wants to hear."

"All right," Mitchell sighed, "I suppose I can approach it from the standpoint of saving some poor soul from a life of being married to her."

468 West 57th St.
January 27, 1897

Dearest Family,

I've just come from witnessing a most amazing spectacle and must write it down while it's still fresh in my mind's eye.

Seven thousand people crowded into Madison Square Garden tonight to view the unveiling of the Tiffany Gas Tower, which Consolidated Gas paid Mr. Tiffany $10,000 to build. People thronged every street for blocks. Alice and I were jostled and pushed so violently that we soon lost sight of each other. The last I saw of Alice, she was several feet off the ground, being carried along in the crush. She seemed to be enjoying herself immensely.

I kept my purse under my skirts and my eyes on the piece of magic towering above me. When the silk veiling fell away, cries of awe went through the crowd like a tide. What a marvelous wonder to behold! Imagine, Mama, a tower of glass sixty feet high, covered inside and out with 2,939 lights that illuminated the sprays of water cascading over long strings of sparkling glass jewels.

Nearly every person at Tiffany's had a hand in the tower, from Mr. Tiffany right down to the basement men. The pride in their faces and their best clothes on their backs, they were a radiant sight. Mr. Mitchell came up and shook my hand quite cordially and then gave a long sermon on why I should not leave Tiffany's. I had no rescuers, and my girls are shy of getting in his way. My knight in shining armor was Mr. Bracey, who excused me to Mr. Mitchell, picked me up bodily, and carried me on his back up to 26th Ave. where I caught the trolley.

Emily, I'm sorry to hear about your stay in the college infirmary. What treatment does melancholia require? Perhaps you should read something other than physics books. Just be sure to stay away from Anna Karenina.

I grow more excited by the day about our plans for Mexico. I've planned out our house and garden to the smallest detail. I have foregone having an engagement ring since Edwin believes our money will be better spent on things we might need, like furniture.

Enclosed you will find a photograph of Edwin. He hates having his photograph made, but in light of the week's events, he's glad these were taken when they were. As the story goes, Monday evening he failed to attend our charade party, and it wasn't until the next afternoon I received word that Edwin had been injured when he attempted to break up a fight between two Chinamen squabbling over a woman.

I found him at the Settlement, a sight to behold. He has a deep cut from the corner of one eye to his jaw; the rest of his face was purple and swollen. He was in no pain, however, having taken one of his magic Chinese powders.

I told Alice she was not to go overboard on my wedding hat—no birds or little people playing lawn croquet on the brim.

Love, Clara

P.S. Kate: I've begun studying Spanish from a book and practice by speaking the language to the pigeons that congregate outside my window. Fewer of them return each day.

~ 15 ~

Tallmadge
April 14, 1897

Dearest Clara,
    I am pleased with the photo of your beloved. I trust he is as good as he looks. I hope I'm still alive by the time you arrive in May, as I'd like to see him in person and judge for myself.

Love, Grandma

The Briars
May 6, 1897

    All bids for Clara and Belknap lost. Clara to Ohio to prepare for the folly of marriage, Belknap to set sail for Europe. This comedy is not without irony, for Belknap's companion is none other than the brother of Clara's betrothed. It would seem there is a conspiracy of Waldos out to ruin me.
    Miss Northrop has brought it to my attention that Clara's intended remains here and the wedding date is left open. It provided the incentive to hire Pinkerton's to gather information about the hesitant bridegroom.
    Louise too involved in the Infirmary for Women and Children for my liking. Being a trustee wasn't enough—thanks to Jacob Riis and his social reform ideas that feed on women's tender natures, she now insists on going with the nurses and doctors into the disease-ridden rats' nests of the rabble, coloreds and Jews alike. I forbade her to do so, but she defies my

order. God knows what contagion she might bring home to my children. I reminded her that our Annie died of two such blights. Hopefully she will come to her senses before I'm forced to take more drastic measures.

   She continues to shirk her social duties. It has been months since she has accompanied me to any social events or the theater. I deplore this aspect of her and have told her that, as the wife of Louis C. Tiffany, she has an obligation to be seen in the right society. Her affections for the riffraff are most unnatural for a woman of her station.

   Here comes little Dorothy to lead me to the garden. A sunny child, but needy. L.C.T.

The Diary of Kate Eloise Wolcott

   May 9: Rev. Cutler brought Clara home from the station. She appears to be fine but isn't. Her first words were: "You see, Katie, I've come home early so that you might have a chance to rescue me." What am I to make of *this*? K.W.

   May 22: Edwin's first letter arrived. Clara read it to us as we embroidered undergarments for her trousseau. He writes that he has been busy with meetings at the Allied Political Clubs and is uncertain as to the date of his arrival. The absence of declarations of affection was noted. K.W.

   May 30: Another letter from Edwin. He claims he has been asked to run for State Assembly, but he isn't sure about having to be in Albany 3-4 days a week. No word whatsoever regarding his date of arrival or the wedding. Clara pretended to ignore the omissions, and instead made a fuss over his political prowess. K.W.

   June 1: Received Edwin's rambling letter about his Citizens' Union Meeting speech, the striking tailors, and the Cooper Union Meeting. Some of it did not make sense, and the writing is almost illegible. Not one tender or personal word to be found among all those empty sentences. K.W.

   June 6: No letter from Edwin. Perhaps we should knit him some socks for those cold feet. We keep Clara occupied with calling on neighbors and expanding her trousseau. She won't have to purchase another undergarment for the rest of her life. K.W.

June 6, 1897
University Settlement
26 Delancey Street

L OUIS CLIMBED THE narrow stairs to the third floor, a handkerchief held to his nose to ward off the unpleasant smell of cooked cabbage and onions. He made his way slowly down the dark hall, pausing at each door, using his pince nez to make out the faded numbers. He tapped lightly on the door without any number at all.

A man in topcoat and gloves answered at once, as if he'd been expecting him.

Louis raised his hat. "I'm looking for Mr. Edwin Waldo."

"You've found him," Edwin snapped. Sophie was waiting for him at Ming's, and he was already late. "What is it you want?"

Louis glanced around. "I have business with you, sir, that requires privacy. May we use your room for further conversation?" He saw Edwin's hesitation and added, "Or, if you wish, we can speak out on the street, although the weather is not particularly favorable this evening. Either way, I assure you, you won't regret sparing me a few moments of your time."

Edwin's gaze wandered over the man's clothes. The ease with which his visitor wore the expensive garb marked him as a gentleman of means. Still, Edwin was disinclined to admit a stranger to his room. These days, one could not discount villainy, even in gentlemen.

"Oh, come now, Mr. Waldo," Louis said in a mildly condescending tone. "Don't hesitate too long, or I shall leave and take opportunity with me."

Reluctantly, Edwin allowed him inside. "Make it quick. I was just about to go out."

Louis removed his hat, taking in the small room at a glance. There was an uncomfortable-looking cot, a writing desk, and a cheap armoire missing its door. In the far corner, the wallpaper was blackened with years of smoke and grease from the iron brazier on the floor. The one small window above the desk was bare of screen or curtain.

"Well?" Edwin barked impatiently. "Who are you and what business is so important that you seek me out in the dead of night?"

Louis did not answer immediately, but rather studied Edwin's face with interest. Dark circles ringed his sunken eyes, and an angry red scar ran the length of his face. Under the man's surface was a sinister current that made Louis want to be done with the matter and away from him. "I'm Louis Tiffany, and I've come to make you a generous offer."

Edwin's eyes widened then, just as quickly, narrowed. "Shall I assume your offer is somehow related to Mrs. Driscoll?"

"It is," Louis replied. "I'm here to make certain you break your engagement, for I have no doubt that you mean to do her a number of injustices and bring her good reputation to ruin."

"How dare you accuse me of such a thing?" Edwin hissed. "I'm a Christian scholar and an honorable man. I work for the good of the poor and the disadvantaged."

"And I am a man of the world, Mr. Waldo. As such, I've met all manner of scoundrels in my day, and the one thing I know for certain is that unscrupulous men frequently seek employment and education in fields that are the opposite of their true nature. You, sir, are one of them."

Edwin pushed past him and wrenched open the door. "Get out! I've heard enough of your claptrap. You've wasted my time and made me late for an important meeting."

Louis's laughter contained no humor. "I'm sure a girl like Sophie won't mind if you arrive at Ming's a little late. Aren't you her best-paying patron, or is it opium she takes in trade for her services these days?"

Edwin's expression changed from one of annoyance to one of menacing anger.

Louis had no doubt that Edwin was perfectly capable of violence. He firmed his grip on the cane and used it to push the door closed. "I can't help but wonder what Clara might do if she knew the man she's engaged to is an opium addict and keeps a whore."

"Why don't you ask her?" Edwin stepped closer, fists clenched. "Better yet, have your detective tell her everything himself. She won't believe a word of it. She knows you'd stop at nothing to have her back."

"Clara is correct on that last point." Louis tugged at his collar. The air in the room pressed in on him, stale and hot. Feigning indifference, he stepped to the window, happy to put distance between Edwin and himself. "I've come to the conclusion, Mr. Waldo, that you must be a clever man to have deceived her so completely. I don't know what evil you're planning in this Mexico scheme of yours, but first hear my proposition."

His interest piqued, Edwin paused. "All right, but be quick about it."

"I'm prepared to offer you a generous amount of money to break your engagement."

"How generous?"

"Five hundred dollars."

"Five hundred dollars?" Edwin sneered. "You insult me. I've visited your showroom, and I'm well aware that one of your—excuse me—one of Clara's windows sells for ten times that much." He slouched against the door. "I have some knowledge of the way you run your business, sir. It's no secret to me how much you have profited from Clara's sweat."

"You know nothing of my business," Louis said brusquely. "For every dollar received, I spend two in production costs."

Edwin didn't miss the change in Tiffany's tone or the way those gloved hands tightened over the gold handle of the walking stick. He pushed himself away from the door. "Unless you're prepared to make a serious offer, I insist you leave at once."

"One thousand," Louis said through clenched teeth. It pained him to think of giving the worthless miscreant a nickel, let alone a small fortune. "That's my final offer."

Edwin's mind raced. A thousand dollars would insure the down payment on the plantation with some left over for opium. He studied Tiffany for a moment, wondering how far he could be pushed. Normally, he was good at reading people and knowing how to get them to do what he wanted, but Tiffany was not an easy study; wealthy men rarely were.

There was risk in bargaining, but Tiffany was desperate, that much was clear just from the man's presence. "Make it two thousand, and I'll do as you ask."

"You've lost your senses!" Louis bawled. "You're no better than a common thief."

Edwin's lips curled into a contemptuous smile. "Tell me, Tiffany, is a blackmailer better or worse than a common thief?"

Louis grabbed the man's overcoat and pushed him roughly against the wall. He saw the fear come into Edwin's eyes and quickly let go. He would have to treat the devil the same way he would treat any man who was a threat to his business. He again surveyed the shabby room and considered the poor quality of the man's clothes and knew that to a man like this a thousand dollars was a king's ransom.

"Twelve hundred," he said with finality. "But I warn you, if you try for more you'll get nothing." He rested a hand on the door. "Yes or no? Be quick. I've wasted enough of my time with you."

Edwin had a brief impulse to try for more, but something in the man's eyes told him to accept the offer. "Very well. Twelve hundred."

Satisfied, Louis nodded. "You will do as I tell you. If there is one deviation from my directions, you'll get nothing. Is that clear?"

"Go on."

"First, you will never mention this meeting to another living soul, not to your family, your whore, or your degenerate friends. Secondly, you are to immediately conclude whatever business you have in the city in a manner that won't invite question.

"When you're finished here, go to Tallmadge and, with as much gentility as you can dredge up, break off your engagement to Clara. Your reasoning shall indicate only that you are in some way faulty and not worthy of her hand. Make sure that she and her family are left spotless and do it in a manner that does not assign them any blame whatsoever.

"After that, go as far from Clara and New York as you can. Make sure you have your harlot under control—you never know when she might grow tired of her trade and take up blackmail. If you don't adhere to this course to the letter, I'll see to it your life is visited by such misery, you and your family will wish you'd never been born."

Edwin grasped Louis's arm. "What about the money?"

Louis clapped a gloved hand over Edwin's and threw it off as if it were a piece of gutter soil. "After you've broken the engagement, send a note letting me know where you want it wired."

"How can I be sure you'll keep your end of the bargain?"

"Because, Mr. Waldo, the money is my one insurance against your ever coming back."

Lenox Hill
June 7, 1897

Home to a hot bath and a bottle of my best brandy. I feel tainted by that creature. God forbid Clara should be further corrupted by him. I cannot bear to think that she may have allowed him to take liberties. Just the thought of his filthy hands touching her flesh leaves me violent.

I feel no shame. He undoubtedly would have ruined her. I've rescued the woman from a fate worse than death and my business from certain collapse. $1200 is a small price to pay for so much. *L.C.T.*

<u>The Diary of Kate Eloise Wolcott:</u>

June 19: Rev. Cutler and Clara are off to Kent to bring back her dear Edwin. *K.W.*

June 21: Clara, Edwin and I took the cart to Fenn's Grove for a picnic. Emily couldn't be persuaded to go, even with promises of pickled beets and fresh clotted crème.

Edwin told stories of his work at the Settlement and read to us from scriptures. Clara and I pretended interest. *K.W.*

June 25: Edwin, Clara and I to Kent to shop for the pre-wedding trip to Chicago. Again, Emily resists our company. She has made it clear (as only Emily can) that she finds Edwin's company repellent.

I, too, have caught glimpses of him that disturb. He's nervous at times, rushing here and there and doing errands and chores that sometimes would best be left undone or at least done in a more serene manner. Other times he seems drained of all liveliness, his eyes half-cast and his tongue clumsy. *K.W.*

June 26: Mama is fretful that Clara hasn't set a date for the wedding. Clara jokes that it will probably take place on her way to the barn to milk the cows. I pray she isn't thinking of elopement—that would hurt us all. *K.W.*

June 28: After dinner Edwin, boasting of his excellence at Seminary College, engaged Rev. Cutler in a long discussion on doctrine and scripture. Being a fine theologian, the Reverend caught him at every vagary and flimsy assertion. Poor Clara blushed to her roots, but said nothing. *K.W.*

July 1: Rev. Cutler and I took Clara and Edwin to the train. They travel first to Cleveland to visit Aunt Kate and Uncle David. After that they'll take a short sightseeing trip to Lake Geneva and then home to Tallmadge, though still no date has been set for the wedding.

The moment Edwin was out of sight, the sky brightened as if a dark cloud had lifted. There is something false about him. His eyes are too close, and they dart about in a suspicious manner, as though searching for an escape route. I see no warmth between him and Clara, let alone fire. We all quietly despair. K.W.

Lake Geneva, Wisconsin

Clara believed the trouble started the moment they stepped off the train. By all appearances it didn't seem possible that any sort of problem could exist, it being one of Lake Geneva's blue-sky days, when everything is possible and life is lived in the moment. Beautiful in their white linen finery, they drew smiles from the people they passed. From the way he nervously played with his watch fob when asking for separate rooms, one might have concluded they were newly wed, were it not for his unhappy countenance.

Clara retired to her room, while they waited for the porter to deliver their luggage. An hour later, she was roused from her nap by the sound of a heavy fist assaulting the door. In the hall she found Edwin in a sweat-soaked undershirt, gripping the arm of a young Negro porter.

"Tell her!" Edwin roughly shook the boy. "Tell her at once, or I'll whip your hide!"

"Yers an' da Mistah's bags dey gone on the train, Ma'am."

She looked from Edwin to the porter. "Our trunks are gone? Where?"

"Yas'm," the porter nodded, "Dey gone to Chicaga. The bag car man, he clean fergit to puts 'em on the platform. Owie! Youse hurtin' mah arm, mistah."

"Let him go, Edwin," Clara said wearily. "It isn't his fault and abusing the child isn't going to help anything."

She looked down at the boy. "When will our trunks be delivered?"

"Maybe tomarra." The porter gave Edwin a sidelong glance. "An' if ah don' git back right away an' tell 'em to wire Chicaga, maybe not then neither."

Edwin yanked the boy off his feet and shook him until his head wobbled on his thin stalk of a neck. "Don't you get sassy with us, you insolent good-for-nothing. I want our bags delivered within the next hour or I'll . . . I'll call the police. I'll have the whole damned lot of you arrested for robbery!"

"Stop it, Edwin!" Clara pulled at his arm. "Didn't you hear what the child said? There's nothing to be done about it until they get word to the trainmaster. We'll just have to make do in the meantime."

She dug in her pocket and handed the porter a quarter. "Thank you for letting us know. Now run back and tell the stationmaster to wire ahead. Can you do that?"

The boy wiggled free of Edwin's grip. "Yas'm, ah do it right away."

Edwin collapsed in on himself with a cry of misery. "My powders and tonics are in the trunk. I can't get by without them. I'll be sick."

"Surely the chemist here can supply you with similar remedies, at least enough to get you through until your trunk arrives."

"No drugstore will have what I need," Edwin said, his jaw twitching spasmodically. Without another word, he went into his room and slammed the door behind him.

An hour later, Clara found him on his knees retching and shivering. He was deathly pale and soaked in sweat. He refused to talk to her except to ask for more blankets and a damp cloth. She stood by helpless until she couldn't stand it any longer and reached for the bell pull. "I'm going to send for a doctor, Edwin. You're beginning to frighten me."

Eyes blazing, he turned on her in a fury. "Don't you dare call anyone! The last thing I need is some pompous charlatan prodding and poking about my person. Just leave me alone. I can't—" He doubled over, choking.

She rushed to him, but he pushed her away. "You can't help."

"But there must be something I can do," she cried. "You don't realize the seriousness of your own situation. If you won't let me call the doctor, then at least let me run a hot bath for you."

Without waiting for his consent, she stepped into the bathroom and filled the tub. She rummaged through the cabinets until she found a tin of bath salts and emptied the contents into the steaming water. When she returned, Edwin was sitting on the edge of his bed, crying.

"Take your bath," she said in a voice that left no room for argument.

"Come to my room when you've finished. I'll leave my door ajar. If you need help, call out. I'll hear you."

She returned to her room and tried to read, but her mind kept wandering back to his first few days Tallmadge. He had grown so strange. It was more than prenuptial jitters. There had been times when she thought he might have been having some sort of mental collapse.

He was suddenly standing in the doorway, his skin still red from the near-scalding water. Handsome, aloof, he leaned against the door staring back at her with steady eyes.

"You're right about finding what I need at the chemist's. I thought I'd take a stroll through town and check in at the drugstore."

She rose, her book falling to the floor. "Give me a moment to change into a fresh jacket and button up my shoes. We still have a few hours before dinner, and I could use a good walk. We'll both need toothbrushes and toothpowder, but—"

"No! You stay here in case there's news of our trunks. I'll buy what we need."

"But the boy said—"

"I know what the boy said!" Edwin barked. "I prefer you stay here. Please don't argue with me on every little point. It grates on my nerves."

Beads of perspiration stood out on his forehead, and the idea crossed her mind that he was on the brink of delirium. She opened her arms to him. "Please dearest, let me come with you. You aren't yourself."

He surprised her by falling into her embrace and burying his face in her neck. She could feel his thin body shaking under his coat. She held him as she would a wounded child and stroked his hair. "You're going to be fine, darling," she murmured. "You're under great strain, what with the wedding and beginning a new business venture. Try to think of good things. After we're married, we'll be free to . . ."

He pulled out of her arms and shoved past her into the hall. "I'm going to find a chemist. I'll be back soon."

Before she could utter another word, he raised his hand in farewell and was gone.

She noted the time. If he had not returned in an hour, she'd go searching for him.

And search she did—down every street and alleyway and every inch of lakeshore that was accessible by foot. She urged herself to keep going through the night and into the next morning, until her feet felt like two blocks of wood. If the opportunity had presented itself, she would have sold her soul for a bicycle and the ability to ride it.

When she finally dragged herself up the hotel steps and into the lobby, people turned to stare at the disheveled woman splattered with mud, who bore the appearance of one not quite sound of mind.

<u>*The Diary of Kate Eloise Wolcott:*</u>

<u>July 13</u>: Received a telegram from Clara. Edwin was taken ill at Lake Geneva with a severe disorder of the nerves and has 'disappeared.' Emily cannot travel, due to her hypochondriacal obsession with her bowels, and I've been ordered to stay and care for her (what joy) and the farm. Rev. Cutler must remain with his congregation, so it's left to Mama to take the train to Wisconsin first thing tomorrow morning. This event comes as no surprise to any of us. I admit to expecting worse. K.W.

Lake Geneva's Constable Pratt was a big man with receding, wavy hair and a face that fit the image of the naval officer he claimed to have once been. "My search party has been at this now for four days, ladies," he said, clasping his hands behind his back as he gazed out the window. He seemed to have trouble looking at Clara or Fannie, preferring instead to address distant space. "Short of dragging the lake, we've done about everything we can."

"Yes, Mr. Pratt you have," Clara said. "And I'm grateful for the time and effort you and your men have spent searching for Mr. Waldo. If only we could have gotten an earlier start."

She bit her lip, remembering the hours they'd wasted interrogating her. When she first went to them, the constable and his men showed no interest whatsoever in Edwin or his perplexing behavior. Their only concern was in knowing why an unmarried woman was traveling unchaperoned with a man who wasn't her husband or a blood relative. When she didn't answer to their satisfaction, they automatically assumed foul play and asked her point blank if she had reason to want Mr. Waldo 'out of the way.'

She'd protested, but they'd kept at her for hours. As far as she could tell, their main objective was to create a scandal or a sensational tale of murder to thrill the townsfolk and bring in more tourist trade. It wasn't until she threatened to have Mr. Tiffany contact his good friend, Wisconsin's Governor Scofield, that they began their lackluster search for Edwin.

The young officer standing by the door came to his superior's defense. "I hope you appreciate, ma'am that it's impossible to drag a lake that has over twenty miles of shoreline and is one hundred thirty-six feet deep."

"I would never have requested that the lake be dragged," Clara said, raising an eyebrow. "Mr. Waldo is much too self-absorbed to even think of destroying himself."

The two men exchanged glances that indicated they were just as sure he was not.

Fannie coughed and rose gracefully from her chair. Everything about her spoke of her genial nature; she could have been at a garden party instead of in a cheerless police station surrounded by disagreeable and incompetent men.

"I do hope we haven't stepped too far out of line, Mr. Pratt, but my daughter sent a telegram to Pinkerton's Detective headquarters in Chicago yesterday asking for assistance in finding Mr. Waldo. They have already dispatched one of their detectives, so if you would be so kind as to return our photograph of Mr. Waldo, I will arrange to have copies made."

Mr. Pratt gave a stiff nod to the young officer. Within seconds, the officer returned with the photograph and handed it to Fannie. Unable to look at the likeness of the man who had betrayed her daughter, she dropped it into her purse.

"You're wasting your money hiring private detectives, Ma'am," Pratt said. "They aren't going to do anything different than we did."

"Perhaps," Clara said, "but while you're waiting for Mr. Waldo to surface, so to speak, kindly supply the Pinkerton's detective with any information you've collected thus far. Hopefully, he'll find a lead."

At the station door, Mr. Pratt stared hard at the street as if checking for criminals who might be lying in wait. "You shouldn't allow yourself to hold out much hope, Mrs. Driscoll. I've seen this before in young fellas. They get themselves all wound up and ask some gal to marry 'em then they fall to nerves and . . . and . . . then they—"

". . .Throw themselves in the lake?" Clara took her mother's arm. "That might be true for some, but as I've said, Mr. Waldo would never do that, considering he doesn't know how to swim."

The Diary of Kate Eloise Wolcott:

July 19: No word of Edwin. Mama and Clara will arrive in Chicago tomorrow. They plan on staying in Oak Park with Rev. Cutler's sister, where they'll wait for the detective to contact them. K.W.
July 26: No word. K.W.
August 1: Clara's telegram arrived. Edwin traced to Dubuque, Iowa, where he bought a pair of shoes—hopefully ones he can run in. K.W.

The hammock swayed as Clara stared through the branches of the oak trees. From the kitchen, the sound of her mother and Susie Cutler putting up green tomatoes provided a momentary distraction from the barbed thoughts that left her without sleep or appetite.

It was the matter of Edwin's trunk that upset her. Each night she'd lain awake staring at it as if she half expected it to tell her the reasons for his desperate flight. Several times she'd gotten out of bed to circle the thing, her desire to know what was inside battling with her moral code. In the end, it wasn't much of a fight—her need for the truth outweighed her anxiety about actually finding it.

Her hatpin was handy in springing the lock. As the trunk swung open, the queer smell of his Chinese pipe tobacco assaulted her nose. His shirts and collars were in perfect order, as were his shoes and extra pair of linen trousers.

The shiny brass pull knobs on the four small compartments proved too enticing. She pulled open the top drawer and found an uninteresting pair of gold cufflinks and an inexpensive watch fob. The second was crammed with vials of black pills that she assumed were the ones he took to calm himself. She hesitated before opening the third drawer, wondered what her mother would think if she were to discover her firstborn involved in such a nefarious task, then slid it open.

Instead of socks and garters, she found three jars of white powder. On top lay a lock of hair bound by a green ribbon. Gingerly, she picked it up between two fingers and examined it. It was too blonde and over-treated to be his mother's or his cousin Irenie's. She sniffed it and wrinkled her nose—it reeked of cheap perfume. She dropped the thing back into the drawer and slammed it shut. Whatever was in the fourth drawer no longer mattered. She reset the lock and the next morning sent the trunk on to his parents.

Fannie came out to the porch carrying a tray of lemonade and cookies. "Come have some lemonade, dear. Susie is going upstairs to take a short nap, so it's just us."

Clara climbed the veranda steps and plunked herself down in a green wicker chair that squealed under her weight. "How could he have done this, Mama?"

Fannie handed her a glass of lemonade. "Obviously, Mr. Waldo was stricken down by some sort of brain fever, since no one in his right mind disappears without leaving a note. I honestly can't imagine what could have gotten into the man to do such a thing to his family. His poor mother must be beside herself."

Clara jiggled her glass, making the chipped ice clink against the sides. "I don't know how I'm going to face anyone ever again."

"When you overcome the shock of this calamity, you'll be surprised at how warmly your friends will receive you. I'm sorry, dear, but you must have noticed that your betrothal to this man was met with less than enthusiasm."

"I thought you were happy for me."

"I was only happy because you were, but in my heart I'm glad the thing has turned out as it has. I never believed you and Edwin were meant to be husband and wife. He didn't seem to be an elastic being who could throw off cares or be buoyant. He seemed more the type of man who would settle gravely down and allow the worries of life to encrust him with so thick a covering that he'd lose interest in the active world. I feared he'd soon fall victim to depression and erratic behaviors that would vex you."

Fannie lightly patted her hand. "I doubt Mr. Waldo would have provided you with one moment's joy or peace. You would have spent the rest of your life constantly wanting of him that which he was unable to give. Why, even Emily thought he was—"

Clara slapped the table. "I don't care what Emily thinks. Emily doesn't like anybody." She covered her face as misery seized her. "I'm sorry. It's just that I feel like such a fool."

"You'll survive," Fannie absently stirred her lemonade. "Mr. Waldo isn't the end of your world, nor is this the end of your loving soul."

Clara shook her head. "I'll never again place my trust in any man."

"You mustn't limit yourself in that way, Clara. There are good men who can and will be as devoted as your . . ."

Clara silenced her mother with a look. "If you mean to use my father as an example of devotion and love, please don't. He was the worst disappointment of all."

Fannie drew back, "How can you say such a thing?"

"Because it's the truth. He was an impenetrable man, who paid little attention to his daughters except to scorn them."

Fannie started to protest, but Clara shook her head. "The night Josie was born, Kate and I were in the barn hayloft making straw necklaces for you when father and Uncle Walter came in, I suppose seeking refuge from the houseful of women.

"We thought it would be great fun to eavesdrop, but instead of happy talk about the new baby, father was full of complaints about being saddled with useless girls. If I recall, his actual words were: 'If a man's life is measured by his issue, then I'm a failure.'

"Those words changed my life; I was determined to make him proud of me. I always worked twice as hard at everything I did, even after he died."

Despite her mood, Clara suddenly laughed. "Do you remember how you always hung my drawings in your sewing room? Every poor soul who called was ushered into 'Clara's Gallery.' If they didn't respond enthusiastically enough, you'd prompt them until they did."

"Not much prompting was ever needed. You were accomplished even then."

Fannie took Clara's hand in hers. "You shouldn't judge your father so harshly, dear. It's true that he wasn't generous with his affections, and perhaps he didn't give praise as often as he should have, but he did love you in his own way."

Clara was about to ask what way that might have been, when Susie Cutler stepped onto the porch waving a Western Union telegram.

The Diary of Kate Eloise Wolcott:

August 9: Clara has called off the search. The Pinkerton detective confirmed that Edwin boarded a westbound train at Council Bluffs, Iowa. Mama and Clara arrive home tomorrow. K.W.

August 11: We received a letter from Alice saying that the Waldos believe Edwin is dead despite Pinkerton reports. George sailing home from Italy. K.W.

August 12: Clara arrived home thinner, but no worse for wear. She seems not so much heartbroken as suffering from hurt pride. Her anger will save her in the end. Mama keeps us busy with errands. K.W

August 25: No further news on Edwin. No one has mentioned his name. The newspapers are reporting him dead. Just as well. K.W.

August 26: Rev. Cutler and Clara to Akron to shop and talk. She returned much cheered and more like our old Clara. Rev. Cutler is a marvel at making people see their follies for what they are—learning opportunities in life's classroom. K.W.

September 6: Clara made watermelon pickles and then went out to dwell on where to put the new driveway. We paid a moonlight call on cousin Annis, who was already in her nightdress, but we threw pebbles at her window until she came out. We talked and giggled like schoolgirls until well after midnight. K.W.

September 18: We put Clara on the train for New York this morning. I prefer to think of this farce in a positive way—as if she's been in a sanitarium and miraculously cured of a life-threatening illness. K.W.

San Francisco, California
September 25, 1897

Mr. Tiffany:

Your lost bird is free. How you manage to get her back into your cage is your concern. Wire reward posthaste to: Stockton Street Western Union Office, Union Square, San Francisco.

According to the newspapers, I've met my end. I prefer to keep it that way.

E. W.

Lenox Hill
November 22, 1897

I have arranged for my 'lost bird' to pick up where she left off. I shall say nothing more about it. Belknap is due to return to work next week as well. Strange coincidence.

Father has once again shown his true colors. Mother has not been in her grave a full week, and he has already turned Burnie and our spinster sister out of the house. L.C.T.

~ 16 ~

Dearest Mama et al,

I devoured the robin while having breakfast, and what a magnificent bird she was! No, there has been no word on Edwin. I have all but forgotten about that unfortunate incident, and I hope you will follow my example in this matter. It seems so long ago that I stepped off the ferry at Christopher Street, worn and heart-weary, amazed at how much bigger and busier New York was than any other place on earth. But now I'm back in the flow of work and the loving embrace of my New York family.

I was flabbergasted at Mr. Mitchell's kind letter asking me to return to Tiffany's, and then, to find everything just as it was when I left—as if everyone knew I'd return.

The best prize of all was to find my own dear Alice hired on as my assistant! Mr. Tiffany likes her work, and the Tiffany Girls have taken to her like ducks to water.

Please send cherry and apple blossoms and primroses the moment they're in bloom. I need them to make studies of the colors and veining for my lampshade designs. I have so many ideas for lamps that I can barely get one drawn before another is crowding my brain. Mr. Tiffany is still reluctant to put the finished samples in the showroom, but I'm hoping he'll soon overcome his fears and get on with it.

You can see from the above address that there's been another change.

Last Monday, our landlady gave Alice and me the bad news (not quite as bad as Tammany Hall being elected, however) that either we sign a year's lease or vacate. We found Miss Owens's Boardinghouse the same day. It's a first-class house with all the modern improvements—electric fixtures, hot and cold water, baths, furnace, etc. The rooms are clean and airy. The owner, Miss Mary Owens, seems a practical, capable woman who has excellent sense about varying and adapting her table to the weather. Best of all, most of her boarders are artists of one persuasion or another, with a few schoolteachers and businessmen thrown in as stabilizing influences on the more passionate artistic temperaments.

On the evening we visited the house, several of the boarders were rehearsing a play one of them had written, while others were reading Jane Austen's Emma *aloud. That alone decided us. This and three meals a day comes at a cost of $50 a month. Yes, expensive, but worth it. The house is surrounded by parks—Union Square, Madison, Gramercy and Stuyvesant. Before long, I'll have enough money to buy a bicycle, and then I shall be free to visit every park in the city at my leisure.*

Mama, you needn't worry over my going about unchaperoned. New York is the safest place I can imagine, with all these masses of people milling about every moment of the day and night.

I've joined the Town and Country Club for $10 a month. It's a place where I can go for a hot lunch each day and lie down to rest my eyes. I also subscribed to The Nation, *($3) which comes once a week and gives me the best articles from the daily papers.*

Henry Belknap found extra work for George at Georges Glaenzer Decorating for $3 a week. If he works out, he'll be sent to Hyde Park to help decorate the new Vanderbilt mansion. He found a doctor here, who recommended some sort of elixir to treat his fits, but he discovered it was made from lizard droppings so into the East River it went.

One of Miss Owens's boarders, Mr. Bainbridge, is a stage manager. He asked me to read for one of the roles. I was all nerves, but my love for theatricals came to my aid. Mr. Bainbridge was quite impressed with my memory for lines. When I told him I harbored a secret desire to be on the stage, he replied that he hoped I would continue to resist the temptation.

Love, Clara

P.S. Kate: I sympathize with you about hats. Milliners must all possess wicked natures. How provoking that purchasing headwear should cause such anguish of spirit.

June 13, 1898

CLARA FOUND MR. TIFFANY in Mr. Mitchell's office contemplating her most recent lamp. Above a base of intricately detailed copper that mimicked a twisting grapevine hung a dome of purple and red glass grapes inset with opalescent pieces meant to soften the overall effect.

"Mr. Mitchell might be delayed," Louis said, "There was a problem with one of the furnaces at the Corona factory. It blew up several thousand dollars worth of vases last night. I sent him to assess the—"

A rumpled Pringle Mitchell dragged himself across the threshold, his summer frockcoat slung over his shoulder. He dropped into a chair mopping his face and neck. "It's only the middle of June, and it's already hotter than blazes. There's got to be a half-dozen horses dead in the streets between here and the station."

"It's too hot, Pringle. Let's get on with the discussion about placing the lamps in the showroom."

"I still don't like that grape lamp," Mitchell grumbled. "It's too large. You need to make it smaller and of calmer colors . . . white and green perhaps."

Suffering beneath three layers of heavy skirts, Clara groaned. Just the thought of having to undo what took her and the other women weeks of hard work to accomplish made her tired.

"I wouldn't think of having it changed," Louis said. "It's perfect as it stands."

"Then I'll repeat what I've said all along," Mitchell said. "These things will never sell except as novelty items. We should leave them to the street peddlers."

Annoyed, Clara stamped her foot. "They will sell, and not only that, they'll sell for top price."

"They most certainly will not!" Mitchell countered. "All the time and money you've spent over these gewgaws has been a waste. We'll never earn it back."

Resisting the temptation to argue, she began again. "I tell you what, Mr. Mitchell. I'll wager my week's salary that this lamp will sell within seven days. Not only that, but with Mr. Tiffany's permission, I'll add the poppy table lamp into the bargain. Both lamps must sell within a week, or you can keep my wages."

Mitchell's face lit up with a flash of genuine glee. "I accept your wager, and because I am so sure these glass follies of yours won't sell, I'll sweeten the stakes for you. If they both sell within the week, I'll personally double your next paycheck. We can place them in the showroom today, if you like."

"Well then," Clara said, rising from her chair. "I say we adjourn to the showroom. What say you, Mr. Tiffany?"

Louis glanced from Mitchell to Clara. "Have you two taken leave of your wits? Surely you don't mean to put them in the showroom *now*?"

"What better time than the present?" Clara said. "Mr. Mitchell? Are you with me, or have you already decided to back down?"

Pringle Mitchell donned his coat. Together they looked at Louis.

Laughing in spite of himself, Louis picked up his cane. "All right, then. Let's go."

To make sure the lamps received the benefit of full light, Clara chose a display table near the showroom window. When she was satisfied the lamps were displayed to their best advantage, she and the men retreated to a side room where they could judge the customers' initial reactions.

No sooner had they settled in than a handsome matron in mourning dress and with the bearing of an empress entered the showroom. At her side was a striking woman of perhaps twenty, her shining black hair tucked under a hat of pink rosebuds and white feathers. A tasteful rope of pearls hung low across her bosom. Neither woman appeared to have been affected by the killing heat.

With a sharp intake of breath, Louis turned away, pretending to inspect a vase. "Good God, it's Mrs. and Miss Goelet!"

Clara had no idea who the Goelets were, but it didn't take much to conclude the women were from money, and a great deal of it at that. "Who are they?"

"Widow of Ogden Goelet," Louis whispered. "Vast real estate

investments. Founded the Metropolitan Opera. Next to the Astors and the Morgans, they're among the stars of New York society." He shoved her toward the showroom. "Go! Don't let them out of your sight until you've sold them something."

When she stepped into the showroom, the women were turned away, examining a gilded mirror. Using a childhood trick Kate taught her, she stared hard at the backs of their heads, willing them to turn their attention to the lamps.

Searching the room for the force that summoned them, the women were all at once gliding toward the lamps. Clara heard their intake of breath and then Miss Goelet's urgent exclamation.

"Oh Mother, look here!"

Their excited murmurs drew her and Mr. Mitchell across the room like puppets on invisible strings.

The young woman was touching the poppy lamp. " . . . so unusual, we *must* have them, Mother. I want this one for my writing desk and the grape will go perfectly in the first floor library."

Clara inched closer, Mr. Mitchell on her heels. Mrs. Goelet beckoned her with a bejeweled finger. "You there, excuse me."

"Yes, Madam, how may I help you?" Amused that she had suddenly adopted a slight British accent, Clara bowed in imitation of the Tiffany showroom salesclerks.

"These lamps are not priced," said Mrs. Goelet.

"I apologize, Madam, but that's because they were placed in the showroom only moments ago. You are the first to view these magnificent works of art."

Mr. Mitchell nudged her. Out of the corner of her eye she saw his highly arched eyebrow making her think perhaps Mr. Bainbridge was correct in discouraging her longings to be an actress.

The young woman smiled, revealing even, white teeth that perfectly matched her pearls. "Do you know the price?"

"Of course. The grapevine table lamp is . . ." she could feel Mr. Tiffany and Mr. Mitchell tense, ". . .three hundred and fifty dollars, and the poppy desk lamp is three hundred."

Behind her, Mr. Mitchell let out a faint gasp. Clara took a quick glance over Mrs. Goelet's shoulder at Mr. Tiffany, who was standing stock still, his mouth fallen open.

Mrs. Goelet appeared doubtful.

Clara stepped in front of Mr. Mitchell, blocking him completely from Mrs. Goelet's view. "I am sure you will agree, Madam, that these two unique and extraordinarily beautiful pieces are well worth the price. They are works of art, worthy of placement in any fine European gallery."

"She's right, Mother," Miss Goelet said." They are unusual, and so perfectly suited to our décor."

Mrs. Goelet sighed. "You're the one with the eye for art, my dear, and there is no denying they are beautiful."

She took a gilt-edged card from her purse and handed it to Clara. "Have them crated and delivered today to this address. Make sure they are accompanied by trusted men who can place them for us."

Appearing as if by magic, Louis swooped down, plucked the card out of Clara's fingers and bowed.

Mrs. Goelet offered him her hand. "Ah, Mr. Tiffany, I see you have added yet another stunning jewel to your collection of masterpieces."

"Mother is much too modest with her praise, Mr. Tiffany," Miss Goelet said. "These lamps are exquisite, and such a clever idea. Who is the artist behind these magnificent pieces?"

Clara felt her heart pounding in her throat. It was the moment she had waited for all her life. From this time forward her name would be linked with creations of beauty. She dried her hand against her skirt in anticipation of the women's praise and extended it, a bashful smile on her lips.

Louis moved in front of her. "They are the first of a new line I'm designing," he said without any hesitation. "There are soon to be many more, all made with Tiffany glass in unique motifs from nature."

Stinging disappointment and humiliation left her mute. She buried her hand in her skirt pocket and bit her lip to keep herself from saying something, or screaming, or worse yet, breaking down in tears.

Mr. Mitchell stepped closer and gave her a swift, commiserating pat on the shoulder. The small gesture helped eased her anguish. By the time she could breathe normally, she'd numbed herself to the pain of Mr. Tiffany's betrayal with reassurances that it was only her first triumph— there would be more.

Certainly Mr. Tiffany couldn't take credit for *all* of her work.

——§——

On the walk back to Mr. Mitchell's office, Mr. Tiffany had not stopped talking. Any attempt on Clara's part to voice her thoughts about the sale of the lamps was thwarted.

Louis rubbed his hands together after the fashion of a man who has just discovered a gold mine. "I want you to direct all your energy into designing lamps. Have your girls start making copies of the two we've just sold. I'll have Mr. Mitchell include them in our next catalog. Show me the sketches you brought of the new models."

When they reached Mr. Mitchell's office, Clara rummaged through the pile of designs until she found the ones she liked best and placed them before Louis. "This wisteria motif is more complicated, but if you like it well enough, I could begin working on it at once. The base would be a bronze imitation of a wisteria trunk with roots fanning out on the bottom. You can see here . . ." she pointed with the end of her pencil ". . . the branching laterals support the pendulous clusters of purple and blue flowers against a background of opalescent glass. I've replaced the usual straight bottom rim with irregular shapes like clusters of hanging flowers."

She chose another design. "This is my evening primrose and butterfly lamp. The shade is made up of clouds of yellow butterflies, each butterfly set in a network of gold wire in graceful waving lines—like the lines of smoke."

Louis studied both sketches. "Where did these ideas come from?"

"We have a wisteria arbor at home, and next to our farm is a field of primroses. As a child, I'd sit all day in that field and make believe I was in Heaven. I have so many ideas crowding my head they wake me in the middle of the night. I have to keep my sketchbook next to my bed."

Louis pulled the pencil out of her hand began sketching haphazardly over her design. His erratic pencil strokes grew more spasmodic with his increasing frustration until the lines made no sense. "Never mind. Work out whatever ideas you want. I suspect Mrs. Goelet and her daughter will be our best advertisers. Miss Goelet has already gained a reputation as a discerning collector. This sale is going to set off an explosion of interest."

He studied the wisteria design again. "I don't want you wasting your time making molds. Have the men in the plaster room make the casts from your drawings and instructions. I want you to keep your mind on the designs and the color selections."

She brought out several more drawings, one a watercolor showing a dome of gold petals. "This is the laburnum library lamp, and this one here is my lotus design. I thought having hanging lotus blossoms inside an outer shade was a unique idea. Also, I haven't sketched it out yet, but I have an idea about using a moth motif for a desk lamp. I'm just waiting until they invade my clothes again to make studies."

"Moths?" Louis slipped down into a chair, his fingers tented under his chin. "I'm having a hard time envisioning moths as a lamp, although the idea is intriguing."

Mr. Mitchell entered his office, hands held up in surrender. "Don't start crowing over your victory, Mrs. Driscoll. I want to go on record as saying that watching you hoodwink the Goelets into purchasing the lamps for those preposterous prices was almost worth losing the wager."

He threw himself into a chair opposite Louis. "Those women must have been addled by the heat."

She laughed in spite of herself and glanced around his gloomy office. "I noticed you don't have a shade for your gas globe, Mr. Mitchell. I was thinking that if you had one of my shades, you might come to appreciate them more. Besides giving your eyes a rest, it would be an A-one advertisement for the lamps. Tell me which flowers you like, and I'll design a motif just for you."

Pringle Mitchell stared at the bare globe, deliberating. "I like autumn leaves," he said quietly. "I find the colors soothing, especially the reds, but the oranges and yellows are pretty, too. They remind me of happier times—when I was a schoolboy."

Clara and Louis exchanged glances. Never would she have guessed the man had a sensitive, color-conscious thought in his head.

Catching the look, Mr. Mitchell smiled. "You both think I'm a lump of coal, but I assure you I was once a passionate and wild young man."

"Well then," Clara said carefully, "I think autumn leaves would make a lovely design. If you and Mr. Tiffany like it, perhaps we'll make several more for the fall display. We'll call it 'Mr. Mitchell's Autumn Lamp.'"

"Most generous of you, Mrs. Driscoll," Louis said, "but I want that primrose butterfly lamp done first, and then the lotus."

She gathered up her drawings. "I should get back to the workshop, so I can warn the women of the impending storm. If it's agreeable to Mr. Mitchell, I'd like to take on three extra cutters and two more selectors."

Mr. Mitchell fanned himself with a newspaper. "I can't fight the two of you. Do as you wish, but I suspect the board may have something to say about the extra expense. I don't even want to think about how the men's department is going to take this."

Louis took an envelope from his breast pocket and handed it to her. "I almost forgot. Mrs. Tiffany and I are having a reception tomorrow night from five until eight. We'd like you to attend."

Instantly, Clara's mind got tangled in all the things she needed to finish at work and then the complications of going home, dressing her hair, changing into a nice gown, and making her way to Lenox Hill. Furthermore, Wednesdays were always her busiest day, with the rush of repairing Mr. Tiffany's cane criticisms and now, there would be chaos getting out his newest flood of orders. A social visit was completely and utterly out of the question. She would simply have to refuse.

"That would be lovely," she said, not quite believing the words coming out of her mouth. "I look forward to it."

———§———

Clara approached the Lenox Hill Tiffany Mansion at a turtle's pace, the heat having made her feel stupid and slow. She'd had to work straight through the dinner hour in order to catch up, so there'd been no time to brush her hair, let alone have a change of dress. She hoped she could slip through the crowd, say hello and thank you, and then slip out.

As she was ushered up the grand stairway from the dark entry hall toward the cascades of light at the top, her head swam with the intoxicating scent of gardenias and roses. The spacious marble reception hall, resplendent with flowers of every color and description, left her staring in wide-eyed wonder.

Mrs. Tiffany greeted her warmly and introduced her to Louis's two oldest daughters, Hilda and May-May, and then to the eleven-year-old twins, Comfort and Julia. At the far end of the hall, she caught sight of Mr. Tiffany, engaged in animated conversation with a man whose close-cropped red hair and bushy eyebrows competed for attention with his absurdly large mustache.

For the next ten minutes, Clara and Mrs. Tiffany managed to plow through a range of small talk—flowers, the reception hall, Mrs. Tiffany's work at the Women's Infirmary, the weather, and the success of the lamps. When she caught herself repeating for the third time how lovely the flowers were, she excused herself and made her way toward her employer.

Halfway across the hall, she became suddenly aware of the stares from the sea of stylish *beau monde* surrounding her. They stepped away, clearing a path as if she were some creature who had wandered up from the coal cellar. She looked down at her shabby work clothes and scuffed boots and went scarlet with mortification. She wanted to kick herself for not making even the slightest effort to be presentable. Fighting the urge to turn and run, she presented herself to Mr. Tiffany.

Louis bowed deeply, making a show of kissing her hand. From his bloodshot eyes, and the smell of spirits, she surmised he was tipsy, if not fully inebriated.

"Mrs. Driscoll, how good it is to see you. Let me present my friend, Mr. Stanford White. Stanny, this is my dear Mrs. Driscoll."

She half-smiled at his introduction, wondering if he referred to her as "my dear Mrs. Driscoll" to all his acquaintances.

Executing a theatrical bow, Mr. White kissed her hand. His eyes wandered over her in a slow, salacious manner that made her feel he was physically violating her. A wave of revulsion caused her to draw back.

"So, this is your lovely Mrs. Driscoll," Mr. White grinned. "A very pretty piece of merchandise. I can see why you prize her, Louis."

She froze at the base meaning behind his words. Jerking her hand out of his, she stared at him in disgust.

"Mr. White is an outstanding architect," Louis said. "He has—"

"Yes, I know," she said stiffly. "Mr. White designed Madison Square Garden and the Washington Square Arch. I've read about his work . . ." she hesitated ". . . and his reputation."

Mr. White's lips snaked upward in a predatory grin. "And I've heard about *your* work, and *your* reputation, Mrs. Driscoll."

"I find that difficult to believe, Mr. White, since unlike yourself, I have no celebrity, and neither my accomplishments nor my foibles have been printed for all the world to know."

"In that case, Mrs. Driscoll, let me offer you the opportunity to make certain that at least your foibles are widely known and step out with me some evening." He winked. "I assure you the journalists will take notice. Within hours, your name will be linked with mine in every major newspaper in the country and abroad."

"If I may be frank, Mr. White, in the interest of preserving whatever reputation I may own at present, and, in the name of decency at large, I enthusiastically decline your offer."

Louis guffawed, and finished off the rest of his brandy in one swig.

Seemingly impervious to insult, Mr. White gave her another suggestive once-over, before glancing at his watch. "I'd like to continue this pleasant repartee, Mrs. Driscoll, but I'm already late for another appointment with a young lady who has no decency whatsoever." He leaned close. "I shall make it my business to make sure we meet again."

She forced a smile. "And I shall make it mine that we do not."

"We'll see about that." Stanford White tipped his hat and walked away, a pronounced swagger in his stride.

She turned to Louis. "I apologize for arriving in such a sorry state, Mr. Tiffany, but I didn't have time to prepare."

"It wouldn't matter if you were dressed in rags," he said, taking her hands. "You are always lovely to me."

She stared at his hands holding hers and nervously glanced to the other end of the hall. She couldn't be sure, but Mrs. Tiffany's attention seemed to be focused on them.

"I'm late because the men decided to move the Bodine Memorial window downstairs." She eased her hands out of his. "It took six of them to carry each of the four easels. You would have enjoyed seeing the girls tiptoeing anxiously at the rear of the procession, in case some of the heavier pieces should fall."

"Did anything perish?"

"Two pieces from Christ's robe, but Frank managed to catch them. Once it was safe, I went back to working on the primrose lamp and lost track of time."

"Well, you're here now and that's what counts." His hand slid up her arm, pulling her after him. "Let me show you the library."

Not daring to check and see if Mrs. Tiffany were still watching, she allowed him to guide her through a set of mahogany doors into a room that was at least two stories high. Soft-colored lights set in such positions as not to stab the eye, illuminated walls lined with books and rich tapestries.

Her eyes roamed the room, while she memorized as many details as she could. She paused at a table holding dozens of framed photographs, mostly portraits of Louis as a young man, the present Mrs. Tiffany holding the twins, and a myriad of others she guessed must be ancestors of one stripe or another. She was about to move on, when her gaze fell on a photograph set inconspicuously in the center of all the rest.

She picked the frame off the table, baffled that he had obtained a photograph of her. The gown wasn't familiar, and as far as she knew, she'd not had a photograph made of herself since she was thirteen.

"That's my first wife, May," he said, coming up behind her.

"But she looks just like—" Before she could finish her thought, he had her hand and was again rushing through doorways and halls into countless palatial rooms, lavishly furnished. At the top of an odd, winding stairway, he pushed open a carved double door and led the way inside.

The splendor of the room was unlike anything she'd ever seen. Every element conceivable had been enlisted to contribute to an exotic atmosphere for the senses. A profusion of hothouse plants perfumed the air, while music seemed to float down from the ceiling. In the center was a sculptural, four-hearth fireplace that rose from the mosaic-tiled floors.

"It is a work of art," she whispered. "You've juxtaposed old and new, rich and plain, and created something magnificent. I'm in awe."

"Now you know how I feel when I see your designs," he said, not taking his eyes off hers.

She searched his face. "Are you mocking me, sir?"

"Not at all. The greatest art is accomplished by having an ideal and a desire to attain it. I see that genius in your work. It's evident to anyone with an appreciation of fine art."

He bent to kiss her hand, and without thinking, she lightly touched his hair, surprised to find it so soft.

He looked at her questioningly and slipped his arm about her waist.

"Papa?"

In one seamless movement, Louis released her and stepped away. "Ah, my little Dorothy. Come here and meet Mrs. Driscoll. She's Papa's best worker."

The girl politely held out her hand. "How do you do? My name is Miss Dorothy Tiffany, but everyone calls me Dorothy. What's your name?"

Clara knelt so they were eye level. "I'm Clara Driscoll. How old are you?"

"I'll be seven on October eleventh, and I'm going to be a doctor and a musician when I grow up."

"In that case, I'm sure your patients will find you highly entertaining,"

Dorothy squinted, tilting her head side to side. Breaking into a delighted smile, she patted Clara's face. "You look just like a pretty daffodil."

They were still laughing when the nurse found them and took Dorothy back to the nursery.

Clara sat in the shadows of the Madison Avenue car, turning Mr. Tiffany's words over in her mind until an irrepressible resolve to do her best work welled up in her; she would create designs so unique and fine, that not even Louis Tiffany would have the temerity to claim them as his own. At some point, he would have to let her put her mark on her work.

The fantastical sights and sounds of the Tiffany mansion continued to glow in her memory long after she climbed into bed. The experience gave rise to so many new ideas that she was forced, time and again, to rise and commit them to paper. As she sketched, her thoughts wandered from the photograph of May Tiffany, to the insanity of touching Mr. Tiffany's hair and then to the way he'd looked at her.

Shaking off the embarrassment, she tiptoed to the washstand mirror and surveyed her features, looking for the daffodil.

Lenox Hill
June 15, 1898

Louise overheard Mrs. Mellon talking about the "exciting new Tiffany lamps" at tonight's reception. Word will soon reach Mrs. Astor and quickly trickle down her list of 400. Soon, the Vanderbilts will want them for the Hyde Park place, and that will put me at the top. I've already decided to price the next few pieces between $400 and $600. The lotus lamp may go even higher. What a coup—Father proven wrong, and I to be rewarded for my perseverance.

Clara's idea about producing smaller items of high quality: pen trays, clocks, and pin boxes, that could be priced to accommodate less advantaged buyers, seems sound, although I don't see where the money is in this. I'll reconsider once the lamps are in full production.

Louise questioned my motives for inviting Clara to an event where she was clearly out of place. I explained that it was necessary to expose her to the level of society she is designing for. I did not, however, waste my energy explaining to a woman unfamiliar with the mechanics of a profit-seeking business how it serves the company's purposes to keep Mrs. Driscoll humble.

Clara's disappointment at not being introduced to the Goelets in the showroom yesterday could not be helped. I already fear that with this new triumph, she'll soon be clambering for recognition and, God forbid, a substantial increase in salary. I hope this glimpse at the grand scale of society will put an end to her unrealistic longings and make her understand that the entitled class would find accepting a common woman as artistic genius an impossible chasm to cross.

As for myself, I can claim no such hauteur; I was deeply affected by her presence in my private studio. I imagined her working with me side-by-side for the rest of our days. The feel of her slim waist still has me in a state of excitement.

Dr. McIlhiney made another attempt at obtaining Nash's formula books, but without luck. Not that it would have done much good since Nash still refuses to give up his damned formula codes.

I must attend to Lou. She gave me such a look when I returned to the hall with Clara. It makes me shudder to think she may have guessed my thoughts. L.C.T.

Noon at Tiffany's
June 20, 1898

Dearest Family,

With the crush-rush at Tiffany's, these short notes are going to be the best I can do for some time. All this designing is a fine thing for me right now, which makes me think I ought not take any vacation this year. I must do especially well at my work now, as I refuse to fail at building my reputation as a topnotch designer.

The city has cleared out for the summer, and there are only 9 of us left in the house. The brutal heat drove Alice and me to make a sitting/ sleeping area on the roof. It's the only place one can hope to find a breath of cool air.

We have a new boarder, Edward Booth. He's taken the room directly below mine, and so far I've not had any complaints about my heavy step. He is either exceedingly polite, or a sound sleeper.

Last week, George suffered another of his fainting spells, so we submerged him in a cold bath, where he revived nicely. I gave him my wrappers to wear, and of course he couldn't resist showing off. He did look funny—so like a girl, and yet like himself, and, in association with my dress—like me!

Mr. McBride took me to the theater on Friday to see 'The Fortune Teller," starring Alice Nielsen. I wore my black silk with white chiffon around a square collar and my black velvet hat with the white feathers. I was picturesque against all odds.

My tall Swede, Miss Wilhemson, is to be married in early September to a butcher who has a chance in Texas. She asked me for a letter of recommendation, in case she should need work there. She's sad to be leaving, as she is quite fond of Mr. Tiffany, even though she mimics his lisp and other of his personal particulars that I shall not mention here, lest I upset Grandmother.

Must leave off here. Mr. Tiffany wants me in his office immediately to go over my cobweb library lamp. He wants a limited number of this one as he plans on charging a fortune for it. He won't tell me how much.

Love, Clara

P.S. Emily: I'm glad you enjoy teaching your young ladies. Your stories about your 'problem parents' are enough to make me wonder what the world is coming to. However, I'm going to cultivate your calm disregard for the feelings of individuals and let great laws, such as survival of the fittest, work themselves out.

Clara knew it was going to be an uphill day from the moment she stepped outside and saw that New York looked like a deserted brick oven.

By eleven, the temperatures hovered at 101 degrees. Despite the bank of electric fans and the girls' frequent visits to the buckets of cold water and rubbing alcohol, Mr. Bracey was forced to close the shades. Fifteen minutes later, her cutters began complaining that they couldn't see and had to have the electric light, which in turn, spoiled the daylight for the glass selectors. Quarrels broke out and at eleven twenty, the resilient Mr. Bracey said he couldn't see to work for the sweat stinging his eyes.

Miss Lillian Palmié fainted at eleven twenty-five, and one minute later, her twin, Marion, followed suit.

It was eleven-thirty when Clara finally marched to Mr. Mitchell's office, made a few minutes of amiable conversation about his lovely autumn lampshade, and then demanded the shop be closed. To her amazement, he readily agreed.

She and Alice practically fell over each other getting back to Irving Place, where they were out of their corsets and into cold baths before anyone could ask what happened. Rebellion being the order of the day, Clara refused to get back into her corset and skirts. From the back shelf of her wardrobe she brought out a flat gift box and read the card.

> *For Clara: the only respectable corset-hating free spirit to be born in captivity. Wear this when you're feeling adventurous and wish to fly without restriction.*
>
> *With loving affection, Kate*

She pulled on the silk skirt that had been made over into a pair of billowy ankle-length pants and completed the ensemble with a gauzy summer waist and a loose-fitting artist's smock. At dinner, little was made over her outfit, other than Alice and Miss Owens vowing to make similar costumes for themselves.

What did pull the boarders' attention was her discussion with Alice about the design for the moth lamp. Mr. Bainbridge misunderstood completely and thought they meant to encase real moths in glass, while Miss Owens questioned how they would go about getting all the moths to stick to the shade and not fall off.

Afterwards, she and Alice carried their sketchbooks and a pitcher of lemonade to the roof, where they listened to the sounds of children playing in the street below.

"I was thinking about your Deep Sea lamp and how nice it would look with a circle of brass shells around the base," Alice said.

Clara began sketching. "That's perfect. To that I think I'll add a series of clear glass beads rising upward from the mouth of each fish and have them ring the top opening of the shade, like air bubbles. I've talked to the Corona men and Mr. Nash about making glass that mimics underwater reflections. They said they'd work on it. "

The door to the roof squeaked open, and Edward Booth appeared, looking cool and refreshed in his spotless white linen suit. He carried a thick book under one arm and a leather case in each hand. Despite his burden, there was lightness to his step.

He set the cases next to Clara's chair. "I beg your pardon ladies, but I wonder if I might join you?"

Alice motioned for him to sit down. "Have a seat and enjoy the ability to breathe again. Clara and I were just going over lamp designs."

"Actually, it's your lamps I've come to discuss. I found the dinner conversation about your moth lamp fascinating."

"Are you an artist, Mr. Booth?" Clara asked. "I was under the impression you were one of Miss Owens's stalwart businessmen, meant to keep her artistic boarders behaving properly."

"I don't know how stalwart the superintendent of an importing firm can claim to be, but I do enjoy viewing good art, even though I personally have no artistic talent."

The fair skin of his neck, barely discernible from the white of his collar, blushed red. "When I visit museums, I might not recognize the artists' names, but there are certain paintings that make an impression." He lifted one of the cases onto his lap.

"I have something here that I think might be of service to you. I collect butterflies and other winged insects. These are my mounted specimens, and this book here . . ." he handed it to Alice, "contains enlarged photographs of flowers. I'd be happy to lend them to you." He opened the case and placed it on the table between them. The array of richly colored specimens caused the two women to make identical sounds of astonishment.

"You mentioned your primrose and butterfly lamp," Mr. Booth continued, "and I thought these fine fellows could be the specimens you're searching for." He tapped the glass over two small butterflies, one of yellow and the other, orange. "Clouded yellow and orange-barred sulphurs—they're quite the dandies."

He pointed next to an iridescent blue dragonfly. "It's just a suggestion, but I thought you might like to use this Blue Dasher as your motif instead of a moth. The wings resemble lace, which might work out well in stained glass."

Clara looked from the butterflies to him. The lines around his mouth suggested he had laughed a great deal in his time, and there was a passion behind his eyes that told her he would be a good person to know. "I'm overwhelmed by your generosity," she stammered. "I hardly know what to say."

"That statement in and of itself is fairly overwhelming," Alice said. "Mrs. Driscoll is so rarely at a loss for words."

Ignoring Alice's remark, Clara continued: "These specimens would be of inestimable value in the work we're doing. I would never be able to thank you enough. The way it stands now, I have to depend on my family to send specimens. I'm still waiting for my box of primroses, and the moths they sent were no more than a small pile of dust by the time they arrived."

Mr. Booth suddenly got to his feet. "I've just had a brilliant idea! Are either of you ladies in possession of a wheel?"

"I'm saving up to purchase one," Clara said. "Of course, I'll have to learn how to ride, but considering that thousands of women are bicycling all over New York every day, I doubt my natural clumsiness will hold me back."

"It's ever so easy to learn," Mr. Booth said with growing excitement. "Once you're up and rolling, I'd be delighted to show you some rides that would take us into the Hudson Valley. There are hundreds of varieties of wildflowers and plants you could choose for your work, not to mention that it's an entomologist's paradise. I've been meaning to go there to collect more specimens."

Alice fanned herself with the cover of her sketchpad. "Susan B. Anthony believes that bicycling has done more to emancipate women than anything else. She thinks it gives women a sense of freedom and self-reliance."

"That would be right up your alley, Mrs. Driscoll," Edward said, eyeing her outfit. "I see you already have your trousers."

~ 17 ~

Dearest Clara,

 I am 89 years old—not dead. I want to hear all about Mr. Tiffany's "personal particulars." Feel free to send them on to me in a private note separate from the robin—no sense educating Katie or Emily on these matters. Enclosed is a dollar. Spend it on what you want.

          Love, Grandma

44 Irving Place
July 10, 1898

ATTENTION ROUND ROBINITES! On July 7th, 1898, I purchased my very own Yukon Ladies' Bicycle from a man whose wife tried riding it once. He didn't charge for the lamp, the bell, or the touring case, but judging from the relief on his face when I wheeled the bicycle away, I believe he would have gladly given me the whole kit and caboodle for free, had it not been for his wife's doctor bills.

 My desire for admiration gave me confidence and greatly assisted me in learning how to ride in a remarkably short time. I sallied forth in my new bicycle suit and fancy straw hat with a cornhusk top and wobbled up *and down the street, but was unable to turn around gracefully, so that I had to get off every time.*

Finally, with Mr. Booth's encouragement, I ventured as far as Gramercy Park. The following day, we rode up Madison Avenue and through the park to 72^{nd,} and up Central Park West to 110th. Several twists and turns later, we took our places alongside the two hundred other riders cycling up and down Riverside Drive.

To answer your questions, Mr. Edward Booth is six feet tall, English, and of athletic build. He has a beautiful voice and pronunciation, and is most agreeable. We get on quite well as <u>friends</u>. He came to America five years ago and thought it an awful place compared with London, but now he says nothing would make him go back to England.

I'm working on a secret project for Mr. Tiffany, which necessitates that I stay after closing. It's a one-of-a-kind, never-to-be-reproduced, centerpiece table lamp, done in a peacock feather motif. The shade is in tones of royal blue and gold. The bronze base is an ornate swirling water pattern inset with iridescent tiles. Incorporated into the pattern are places for six Favrile glass cups of the most delicate blue. It's so exquisite as to take my breath away.

Mr. Tiffany is paying me privately ($25!). Were this lamp to be sold, he could easily ask $1,000 for it. I can only guess that it's meant as a special gift for his wife, although he has not said as much, and I don't like to ask.

Alice and I are doing piecework for Mr. Tiffany's father, Mr. Charles Tiffany. So far, he has commissioned me to design a silver cover for his personal diary and a brooch and necklace for his shop. Alice is working on an earbob and pendant set.

Difficult to believe Mrs. Price allowed herself to die. I was sure she would outlast us all. It shouldn't surprise anyone that Miss Violet Price immediately accepted Mr. Talbot's proposal.

I have it on good authority that a new type of S-curve corset is in the making. It forces the upper spine forward and pushes the hips backward. The overall effect (other than bending one into a pretzel) is to make the hips, behind, and bosom protrude (the latter into what is called a "pigeon-pouter" bosom). It is said to crush the lungs and be more harmful to a woman's spine and innards than all the other current fashion contraptions combined.

I decided I'd had enough, and in the names of comfort and health, I'm taking up freer clothing. It's a change I've dreamed of making, but haven't had the courage to carry through until now. Don't worry Mama, I'll be decent and not give in entirely to eccentric behavior.

My love always, Clara

P.S. Henry and I went to see "The Royal Box." It's one of those rousing musicals that never fail to make me picture myself as the leading lady, admired by all. Then I come home and sing to myself in the mirror, and the spell is broken.

September 7, 1898

CLARA GLANCED UP from her work and was rendered momentarily mute. Her newest girl stood in the doorway, wringing her hands. Barely fifteen, the child wore a brown brocade dress sporting puffs of pink silk at the shoulders and hem. Her pink hat, adorned with ostrich feathers, was set at a rakish angle on her small, neat head.

The girl curtsied, causing Clara to bite her tongue so as not to guffaw outright. "A man stopped me as I was coming in, ma'am, and he told me—"

"That was Mr. Bracey," Clara said. Daniel must have thought the girl had mistaken the building for a fancy hotel.

"No ma'am." She curtsied again. "He said his name was Mr. Mitchell. He told me to tell you that Mr. Tiffany wants to see you right away."

As the girl began backing away, Clara held up a finger. "Before you go, if I may make a few suggestions?"

"Yes, ma'am?" Another curtsy.

Clara removed her apron and smoothed down her skirts. "First, no one in this department calls me 'ma'am.' The title ages me, and I already feel much older than my actual age. Please call me Mrs. Driscoll, or even Clara, it's shorter."

The girl curtsied.

"Secondly, you must not curtsy. It's bad for the knees, and, though I would like to think so at times, I am *not* the Queen.

And last, while your gown is quite lovely, you mustn't wear your good dresses to work, because by the end of the day they will be ruined beyond repair." She handed over her apron and a smock. "Wear these today, and tomorrow wear an everyday skirt and waist, the more worn, the better."

The girl began to curtsy, remembered herself and backed out of the room.

"Well, what do you think?" Louis asked, watching her closely.

Clara dared not touch the lustrous yellow sheet of glass through which multicolored glass filaments had been threaded.

"It's . . .wonderful," she breathed. "Did Mr. Nash make this?"

"*He* supplied the formula," Tiffany replied tartly. "*I* supplied the materials, the factory, the manpower, and the money to make it a reality. It's costly to make—about ten dollars a pound. This is the only sheet of its kind in existence. I want you to utilize it to best advantage in a design of your making. Just make sure you're both selector and cutter—it's too rare to entrust to anyone else."

He wandered over to his orchids, pinched off a dead leaf and let it fall to the carpet. "The primrose lamp sold the first day, so I'll want three more of them, along with another three of the cherry blossom lamp. We've had quite a few requests for more of the lotus leaf design, too. In fact, I'll have Mr. Mitchell make a list of the designs that have sold well and have you repeat them."

He glanced at her. "It's already September. If you're to get all this done before the holiday rush, you'll need to step up production. I want everything done and in the showrooms no later than November first."

An uneasy feeling in the pit of her stomach worked its way into her temples. It would be humanly impossible to make that many lamps in such a short time. What further worried her was the way Tiffany wouldn't look at her. She knew him—he had more to demand of her, and it was something she wasn't going to like.

"About my idea for small novelty items," he began, "I've decided they might prove lucrative if we can make enough."

She started to point out that the novelty items were her idea, but thought better of it. It wasn't worth the risk of inciting his anger; with Mr. Tiffany, she knew to choose her battles carefully.

"I was thinking we could introduce these things slowly," he continued, "perhaps two styles of ink trays, several types of small boxes and three or four different tea screens. After the first of the year, I want you to start working on making fancy clocks."

He left his orchids and faced her. "As always, your designs for these items should reflect my belief that art can be found even in everyday things."

She tapped her notebook with her pencil. "While I'm busy doing all that, who will work on the windows and mosaics?"

He seemed genuinely surprised by the question. "You and your girls. You know as well as I do that the mosaics and windows can't be ignored, even for a day. I have customers who expect their things to be finished on time—which brings me to my next bit of news."

He paused while she braced herself.

"I'm putting Alice Gouvy in charge of the women's department at the Corona factory designing Favrile vases and glassware. I'm—"

Fury, born of bitter disappointment, lifted her to her feet before he could finish. "You must not do that, Mr. Tiffany! Alice is the one artist I trust implicitly. If you take her from me, there's no way we could possibly complete all these things by the time you want them."

"You didn't let me finish," Tiffany said gruffly. "I'm assigning Joseph Briggs as your new assistant. He'll be completely under your direction. Being one of Queen Victoria's subjects, he doesn't seem to mind following a woman's orders as much as our men do. He's the finest mosaicist in England, and I daresay in America as well. He'll be most beneficial as a liaison among your department, the men's department, and the foundry. However, as Mr. Briggs won't be able to start work until January, I'm letting you keep Miss Gouvy until then."

The misery over losing Alice settled in her chest, making it difficult to talk. She wanted to cry almost as much as she wanted to walk away. "I'll need to hire more women," she said finally. "Even then, it's going to mean working ten or twelve hours each day, including Saturdays. The women aren't going to like that. They already work more hours than they're paid for."

Louis struck a condescending pose. It was one of his attitudes she hated most. "If they don't want to work, they can leave my employ. Hire on as many extra girls as you need, but make sure everything is done to my standards of quality."

"Please, Mr. Tiffany, try to see reason. Even with the extra women working twelve hours a day, we can't complete all this work in so short a time."

"Yes, you can."

"No, we cannot. You ask too much. I can't do this."

"You can." He stared across the desk. "You can, because, my dear Clara, you're the only one who *could*. You are by far the best artisan in the field. The men's department could never do what you and the Tiffany Girls accomplish."

She was unable to respond, until, in a flash of brilliance, she grasped the opportunity, opened her sketchbook and placed it on his desk. "If you truly believe what you've just said, then you should have no objection to this."

Louis adjusted his pince-nez and studied her drawing of a circle in which a delicate vine twined in and around stylized letters. He looked up, his expression blank. "What is it?"

"Don't you see?" She leaned forward and traced the ornate C. and the W. "It's my mark, the one I'd like engraved on each of my designs."

"No!"

"I thought since the lamps were such a success—"

"No." Louis shook his head. "It's too early to tell how long that success will last."

"But if we—"

"I said no, I mean no. I'll reconsider when I'm assured the lamps and novelties will continue to sell after the initial enthusiasm has died down."

"But you promised!"

He slapped his desk. "Enough! We have more important things to deal with than your mark. You need to step lively. Make sure your girls enter into the spirit of things."

He strode to the door with purpose, picking up his cane on the way. "I'm taking the stairs down to speak to the men about preparing for the onslaught of work that you'll be bringing them." He gave her one of his imperious smiles. "However, in the interest of saving time, I suggest *you* take the lift."

Tiffany's
September 13, 1898

Dearest Family,

I have only ten minutes in which to eat my dinner—a buttered roll and hot coffee, which was all the vendor had left after the noon rush. The spills and smears of food may be unsightly, but they do prove that I am receiving nourishment.

These are troubled times into which your robin flew this morning. Do you remember my tall Swedish girl, Miss Wilhemson, who left to be married? Yesterday morning, the newspaper criers were shouting from every corner, and, thinking it was another Tammany Hall murder, I went down to get a paper. Instead it was an illustrated account of how Miss Wilhemson had been found dead in an alley, an empty bottle of carbolic acid by her side. My recommendation letter was in her pocket, along with a letter from her fiancé saying he never intended to marry her. I immediately went to the tenement house where her family lives. They were in a terrible state, both terrified and hysterical. They had no idea what to do, so it fell to me to send for the undertaker. Every penny of their lifesavings went for a pine box and a small stone marker.

Everyone in my department has been deeply affected. The girls can hardly keep their minds on their work. Thursday, I am taking them all to the funeral. It is the least we can do.

I'm at my wit's end over the burden being heaped on me at Tiffany's. I must refuse all invitations to go anywhere or do anything. I give my callers a book to read and go on working. Mr. Tiffany seems particularly inspired to have <u>all</u> my designs made, and so this makes for a lively time for tired old Clara. Added to this is more thumb-screwing from Mr. Mitchell, who insists I take on the bookkeeping for my department. (Emily, if I am not here when you visit at Christmas, you'll find me in the nearest sanatorium for the insane).

I'm designing from 7 a.m. to 7 p.m., and then spending the rest of my evening getting up a new system of books for estimates of costs and what is charged me for labor and expenses. Mr. Booth is quite efficient at these things and is willing to help. I shall come out all right, but the amount of detail is appalling, and it's something I know nothing about.

I must stop here, as I have to run (literally) to Stern's for fabric with which to make over the worn hems of my work skirts. Mr. Mitchell's observation that I have been dressing rather low these last weeks made an impression.

Love, Clara

P.S. Kate: Your first days in Cleveland's art salons as portrait maker remind me so much of my first days at Tiffany's. Remember, flattery pays well; second chins and wrinkles do not.

October 16, 1898
44 Irving Place

"You can't possibly be serious about going into Tiffany's today." Alice put down her tea. "It's Sunday. You have to rest sometime, Clara. You haven't eaten or slept properly in weeks." She looked from Dudley to George to Henry. "Can't one of you please talk sense into her?"

They watched Clara fumble with her hatpin, her face pinched with fatigue.

"It's a lost cause," Dudley said. "I detect that stubborn determination in her eyes. It's a stronger force than any or all of us could fight."

George elbowed Henry in the ribs. "You're one of the Tiffany Powers—do something. Convince her to go with us to Prospect Park instead of that slave mill. I can't stand the idea of her missing a scrumptious picnic lunch."

"I've tried," Henry sighed. "I've even asked Mr. Tiffany to let her take a few days away, but he's driving himself as hard as she is herself. He's probably at his desk this very moment, slaving over lists of new things for her to work on."

"Just keep talking amongst yourselves as though I'm not here," Clara said, pulling on her gloves. "But I would appreciate it if you wouldn't go on about what a glorious day you're going to have until after I've gone. I'm already about as low-spirited as a snake, and so tired that I barely had the energy to lift a fork to my mouth."

Edward Booth appeared in the doorway looking both jaunty and elegant in his bicycle breeches. "Hello there. I say, is anyone up for a ride to the country? Clara? Alice? How about you, George? Dudley? It's a lovely day. I don't think we'll get many more like it before the snow flies. What say? Anyone willing to have a go?"

"Sorry," Alice said, "I've already thrown my lot in with these gentlemen. Perhaps next week?"

"I'm just a penniless artist," Dudley said. "I can't afford the price of a streetcar, let alone a wheel."

"I'd like to go with you some other time," Henry said, "but I don't think we have that much ambition today."

George raised his chin to show contempt for the idea. "Really, Mr. Booth, I doubt anyone here would be even remotely interested in wasting the day getting sweaty and dirty. As far as I'm concerned, the country is a place best visited while looking out the window of a train dining car."

"I'd love to go."

They turned in unison to stare at Clara.

Alice frowned. "But only a minute ago you said you couldn't even lift a fork, you were so tired."

"You didn't offer a bicycle ride into the country, now, did you?" She removed her hat and brushed a wave of dark hair from her eyes. "If you can wait five minutes, Mr. Booth, I'll change into my bicycle suit and hat."

"I was thinking of riding along the Hudson River past Yonkers," Edward called after her retreating figure. "It should be about a 70-mile trip, and some of the going will be fairly strenuous. Do you think you're up to it?"

"If Annie Londonderry can go around the world on a bicycle," Clara called cheerily over her shoulder, "I figure I can do a piddling 70 miles without much complaint."

They passed the aqueduct through which the city water flowed and six miles later began the long climb up Mount Saint Vincent. Clara's eyes were in constant motion, taking in the Hudson and the perpendicular blue hills beyond. At the summit, the world spread out below her like a map. The blue rivers and the sound were dotted with boats and little towns, pink and white among the great general green. A breeze came off the river, filling her nostrils with the scents of the Hudson Valley countryside.

Pulling off her hat, she let her hair fall around her shoulders, hairpins dropping to the ground like metal rain. In the thicket of sweet grass, the warmth of the sun embraced her, as she marveled at the world. She closed her eyes and lay back. When she opened them again, Edward was sprawled beside her, watching her curiously.

"What were you thinking right then?" he asked.

"I'm not thinking at all. Experiencing with my senses would be more like it."

She rolled over onto her stomach. "I see the way the afternoon sun slants through the trees and then across the goldenrod in yellow bands. Just when you asked, I was smelling the sweet grass and envisioning the wild carrot in a design." She sat up and slipped off a boot. The sight of her large toe sticking through a hole in her stocking set them off laughing. She got to her hands and knees to search for the fallen hairpins.

The thought of what she must look like to him—a disheveled woman without shoes, holes in her stockings, hair blowing in every direction—brought home the discovery that it wasn't easy being a companion to the immaculate Mr. Booth, whose hat and bicycle suit were luminous with cleanliness. Unlike her, he wore his clothes with ease, appearing elegant without seeming contrived.

"I am afraid, Mr. Booth, you are witnessing me in my untamed animal state. I hope I haven't frightened you."

"On the contrary, I enjoy your spirit a great deal. Are your sisters as lively?"

"Not quite," Clara laughed, thinking of how mortified Emily would be to see her in her present state. "Emily and Kate are much less barbarian than I. What about your siblings?"

"I have quite a few brothers," he said, smiling. "And I don't believe they would find you barbaric either. William works in the city as an editor at Macmillan Publishers. He's just married Mary Brewster, one of the nurses who founded the Henry Street Settlement House. Cecil is an inventor in London. He's recently finished a machine that sucks dirt from floors and carpets. He calls the contraption a 'Puffing Billy,' but my brother Seymour, who is Cecil's technical advisor, thinks it should be called a 'vacuum cleaner.' Fredrick, the youngest, is still at university."

"So you are a family of scholars?"

"Not all of us. My interests lie in nature and the outdoors. I prefer exploring places in person, rather than reading about them. I mostly read about flora and fauna and the occasional instruction manual."

When she said nothing, he added, "I might not be as well-read as my brothers, Mrs. Driscoll, but I do know every foot of every road from Sag Harbor to Schenectady. If you ever get away from Tiffany's long enough, I'll show you places that are beautiful beyond description."

"I'd like that," she said pinning her hair into place. She turned and studied him for a moment. "I'm glad you've become part of our circle, Mr. Booth."

"I'm not sure Mr. Waldo would agree with you on that account," he laughed.

"Pay no mind to George, he'll warm to you eventually. It's just that he's so vain at times he can't get out of his own way. The only reason he's so full of nettles right now is because the attention isn't fully on him. Give him time."

She got to her feet. "I'm so famished, I could eat a goat, fur and all."

"Well then, I suppose I'd best take you to Madame Coutant, the finest cook in all of New York. She owns an inn three miles from here."

"Point the way," she said, pulling her wheel onto the path. "Just make sure it's downhill."

Never in her life had food tasted so good. After savory soup, clams roasted in the shell, green beans with hot peppers, and chopped steak with onions, they ate their dessert on the veranda. Cozy in the cushioned wicker chair, she fell into a stuporous doze, in the manner of an anaconda after feasting.

Mr. Booth coughed politely. "You'll have to postpone that nap, if we're to catch the 9:20 train out of Bronxville into Grand Central."

They had mounted their bikes and were about to start off, when Clara gave him a grateful smile. "I'm glad I came out with you."

"Me too, except next time I'd really enjoy seeing you eat a goat, fur and all."

Noon at Tiffany's
November 8, 1898

Darlings,
I left work at 9 p.m. last night and went with my Irving Place family
to see the returns. It was a wonderful conglomeration of human noise
and excitement. Miss Nye (our newest boarder, a kindergarten teacher
who is pretty and reasonably interesting) and I elbowed our way through
the crowds, shouting with the best of them, as it became more and more
evident that Teddy Roosevelt was our new governor.
We wiggled ourselves back to 23rd Street for the fireworks in Madison
Square. The smoke transformed the trees, fountain and buildings into a
misty and illuminated vision out of a fairy tale. From the Fifth Avenue
Hotel steps, with the searchlight in Madison Square Tower flashing in all
directions, we could just about see forever.
Love, Clara

Henry stepped into her office and closed the door behind him. "Are
you free to accompany me to the opera tomorrow? It's opening night."

She shook her head. "Thank you, but I can't possibly take the time.
I'm hoping to get this jewelry box done before then, and I still have the
two tea screens to work out. Can't George attend?"

"My dear woman, haven't you figured out by now that half the pleasure
in listening to fine music is being with someone who appreciates it?"

"I'd love to, but . . ." She waved a hand over the half-finished lamps
on her worktable. "As you can see, it isn't possible."

He plopped himself down in the chair next to hers. "We sold the first
butterfly lamp today."

"Good, because I've made eight more in slightly different ways."

A worried expression crossed Henry's face.

"Are you afraid they won't sell?" she asked.

"They'll sell, but I'll have to price them at $400 each if we're to make
anything on them. It becomes a question of whether people want to pay
that much for an oil lamp."

"So, have the men change them over to electric. It won't affect the designs."

"What I'm saying, Clara, is that we have to think about the costs."

She sat back. "My God, Henry, you sound like Mr. Mitchell."

"Tiffany is nervous," he said. "He's down in the showroom every day, hiding out behind the statuary, listening to customers' comments and coaching the salesclerks. He wants every piece sold or it's my neck—and yours. You need to think of Louis in terms of King Henry the Eighth."

She arched her back and stretched her arms over her head. "We've already sold the majority of the lamps and deluxe pieces, and my mosaic ink trays sold out the first day. You know as well as I that people will pay anything for what they like."

Her eyes went to the wild-carrot jewelry box sample. "Mr. Tiffany isn't the only one watching the sales, you know. If everything goes well, I'll want an increase in salary and the right to put my mark on my designs."

"Don't get your hopes too high on *that* account," Henry said. "I think you'd have a better chance at flying." He drummed his fingers on her desk and resorted to staring out the window.

"What's on your mind, Henry? You didn't come down here just to tell me you're worried about lamp sales. Out with it."

He shifted his gaze back to her. "I managed to arrange a consultation for George with Dr. Hughlings Jackson, the world's foremost expert on epilepsy. At the end of the exam, he gave us all the whys and wherefores of epilepsy, leaving us little wiser than when we arrived. Yesterday, he scheduled a private meeting, in which he told me George's case was hopeless.

"He said the seizures will come more frequently, each one leaving George weaker. The longer it goes on, the more erratic George's behavior will become. At some point, he'll have a prolonged seizure that will strain his heart, and he'll die.

"I haven't told George; I see nothing to be gained from that."

"How long before this might happen?"

Henry tucked his hands tight in his armpits. "It could be months or decades. It's a hideous thing. There's no effective medicine, diet or treatment—nothing."

"Perhaps this isn't such bad news," she said finally.

"How can you say such a thing?"

"Look at it from the viewpoint that George isn't a man to restrict himself. He can barely sleep longer than four hours at a time, because he hates being cooped up in bed, and honestly, can you imagine our George on a restrictive diet?"

They smiled at the thought.

"Weaning George off his beloved sweets and hearty meals," she said, "would be tantamount to death by torture."

Henry groaned. "But surely we have to do something?"

"We will do something, " she said. "We'll love and care for him as we always have, and then deal with what is to come when it gets here."

44 Irving Place
November 24, 1898

Dearest Family,

I refused all invitations to dinner and spent my Thanksgiving being a woman instead of a businessman. So far, I've mended my shirtwaists and stockings and treated my hair. This evening all of us 'holiday orphans' went to Miss Nye's room for cake and tea and took turns reading "Cyrano de Bergerac," the new play that has excited so much comment here and abroad.

Last week, Miss Nye confided that she wishes to go out with Mr. Booth, but didn't want to ask him herself. I thought he might like that, so I brought it about last Saturday evening. I was to act as chaperone while they attended an Italian puppet show, but then Mr. Booth sent word he couldn't leave his work. He has shown no interest in renewing his offer, which is a shame, for they are well suited to one another.

George is here talking to the back of my head so that I can't concentrate. I'll finish this when I'm caught up at Tiffany's.

I love you all, Clara

P.S. Mama: Alice and I had a good laugh over your comment that when we're on our bicycles we must represent 'grace of motion.' We each looked at the other to see if we could discover it. What we found instead were the many scrapes and bruises that—

She threw down her pen and glared at George, who was pacing about the room wringing his hands. "What are you on about now?"

Full of drama, he flung himself onto the couch. "Haven't you been listening? I said that every time I visit, I find Mr. Booth hanging around like a piece of furniture. We never go out sketching anymore, because Mr. Booth doesn't sketch. No one ever has time to model for me, because everyone is bicycling with Mr. Booth, or out to dinner with him, or calling on *his* friends."

"George, you exaggerate. You know that isn't true."

"Yes it is!" he stamped his foot. "We don't have our private salons like we used to, and even when we are all together no one pays the slightest attention to me. Like right now, I can tell you'd rather be writing your round robin or with Booth or that Miss Nye creature. You hang on their every word like they're the prophets of the Bible!"

"Stop!" Clara shouted. "I can't stand anymore of this senseless whining. You're such a dreary companion when you get into these fits of hating people. The only reason you don't like Mr. Booth is because he isn't exactly like yourself. What's worse is you denounce him to anyone who is foolish enough to listen, saying he's dull-witted and not worthy of our company, simply because he's unable to distinguish Early from Late Greek art!

"No one else feels these things about him." She poked him in the chest. "This is the sort of thing that makes people unhappy with you. And now you're going after Miss Nye, whose only crime seems to be that she doesn't laugh at your jokes."

"A lamppost has more animation than that woman," George sniffed.

"You are so exasperating! This is the same egregious behavior you displayed toward Miss Hicks last year."

"That Hicks creature deserved it. She's dirty and queer."

"How dare you say that about one of the sweetest, cleanest young women in the entire house! What could possibly make you say such a damning thing?"

"Have you forgotten about the tea she gave in September? She purposely gave me a sandwich with a hair in it. In the name of genteel manners, I was obliged to swallow the disgusting thing." He shuddered. "It made me sick for days. It's a wonder I didn't die."

"Miss Hicks did no such thing! It was an unintentional oversight, for which you condemned the poor woman with the same rabid veracity one might use against a murderer of children. Really, George, you sound like a madman."

"I knew it!" he sobbed. "You hate me! I'm not a madman, I'm . . . I'm lost."

"Oh, George," she dropped down next to him. "I don't hate you. I love you, but sometimes you push the limits of patience. I'm afraid one of these days you'll fall over dead in a fit of pique over some inconsequential thing."

"They all hate me," he said, wiping his eyes. "Even Henry. Sometimes I catch him watching me with such an unhappy expression. It makes me shiver to think what he must be feeling."

"No one hates you, least of all Henry. Even Mr. Booth tells everyone you're a tiptop chap, despite your dislike of him."

"Booth said that? That I'm a tiptop chap?"

She nodded. "You have no cause to be jealous of Mr. Booth or anyone. You're one of a kind, darling. No one could ever replace you in our hearts. Besides, who else can we count on to expertly decorate our rooms, make us crazy and laugh all at the same time?" She handed him a handkerchief.

"I'm sorry," he said, blowing his nose. "I don't know what comes over me. It's only that I never seem to get anywhere. I'm tired of wasting my life doing silly illustrations for magazines and penny romances. I've accomplished nothing."

"Oh, I don't know about that. Alice, Dudley, Mr. McBride and I don't have our work hanging in a London gallery, and none of us has ever exhibited in the Salon de Champ de Mars. For God's sake, you took honors at the Académie Julian and studied under Jean Paul Laurens!" She took him by the shoulders. "Look at me."

When he brought his eyes level with hers, she saw a great tiredness in him that no amount of sleep was ever going to fix. "No one can illustrate as well as you do, and few have your talent for interior decoration. For goodness sake, George, you're decorating the Vanderbilt mansion!"

He sighed and attempted a smile. "I am, aren't I?"

"Do you think I, or Mr. Booth, or even Alice could do that?"

He shook his head violently. "It makes me shudder just to *think* about it." Idly, he popped a lemon candy into his mouth and stared off into the far distance. A second later, he bolted upright, visibly paled. "My God, can you imagine? You'd all be installing puce carpets and yellow drapes in no time."

44 Irving Place
December 21, 1898

Mother and Kate, et al:

Clara is prostrate with a sick headache, so I'm commandeering the robin until she's well. I arrived safely in NY, even though George stood in the wrong place and Clara was busy petting a cat at the baggage counter, so that I nearly missed them. Sister's room is cozy, but she's rarely home long enough to enjoy it.

Everyone here considers this Tiffany scheme a low trick by which the firm slides out of a lot of work and responsibility and duty to its employees by putting it off on Clara. Unlike my own fragile constitution, she is strong, and from the way she took to sliding downhill yesterday, standing up on the sled on one foot, I don't think she'll have nervous prostration right away. The only way she and Alice stand the strain of Tiffany's is the good food served by Miss Owens. It's hot and substantial and on time.

Here is Mr. McBride and Mr. Booth, come to hear me play the zither. I'll continue at a more opportune time. E.W.

Christmas Eve, 1898

I went to Tiffany's today. Clara's daffodil shade is lovely. It's as large around as our butter board and in beautiful green and yellow colors. I also saw some brass boxes covered with wavering lines, which she made with Favrile glass. I can't bring myself to tell you the prices these things command, except to say we could live nicely for a year or longer on the sale of just one of sister's lamps.

Emily Wolcott

Lenox Hill
December 31, 1898

Mitchell's yearly tallies show that the sales on the lamps and deluxe individual pieces have brought us even with the expenditures. Father made it a point to remind me that the Tiffany Glass Company has never shown a profit, thus, he crows about how I have not lived up to the Tiffany imperative. I once again explained that, unlike him, I will always put quality above profit. He went so far as to say I ran my business in effect as a mission. To this I responded: "Yes, but a mission which teaches the gospel of good taste at cost."

We are off to the Goelets' for the New Year festivities and midnight dinner. I understand my lamps are so well liked, there is one in every room. As in past years, we were left off the list of those invited to the Astors' New Year's Ball. I've heard that when my name came up as a possible guest, Mrs. Astor made the comment: "Just because I purchase my lamps from the man doesn't mean I have to invite him in to enjoy them." It is well known she hates anyone in the trades. To the Devil with her! As long as she keeps spending money in my showroom, I don't give a damn.

I'm increasing the number of pieces for the 1900 Paris Exposition. I sent photographs of the lamps to Maison de l'Art Nouveau in Paris, so that Siegfried Bing might see for himself how beautiful they are. He wrote back immediately, calling the lampshades "glowing fantasies" and agreed to be Tiffany's exclusive European distributor.

Julia announced at the breakfast table that she wants to become a physician. A woman doctor! Louise immediately led May-May and Hilda in giving the child words of encouragement to pursue this absurd notion. I let them all know in no uncertain terms that I would never allow any of my children to enter such a degrading profession.

Louise and her cronies at Stuyvesant Square Infirmary have filled the children's heads with this rubbish. This is the trouble with marrying an intellectual woman. Over Louise's objections, I sent them all to their rooms. It's quite enough for this family that my son will soon be graduated from Yale with honors. No daughters of mine will be traipsing off to college to fill their heads with ideas that will turn them strange.

We are again fodder for the gossips in the New York Times. *One of the servants at the Irvington-on-Hudson house saw Burnie raise his fist against Father and found it too exciting a morsel to keep to herself.*

Louise has descended the stairs in her newest gown and headdress; both worth a small fortune in material alone.   L.C.T.

Clara rested her forehead against the ferry window as threads of rain slid across the glass. In the distance, the Manhattan shore slithered by like a long, spiny snake. She smoothed a piece of writing paper over the top of her sketchpad and began her New Year's round robin.

December 31, 1898

Dearest family,

I'm on the return ferry from escorting Emily as far as the Jersey City station, and have just finished reading the last robin. It nearly made me weep to think of how nice my own family thinks I am. I only hope that when you are undeceived, you will love me just the same. I do not recognize myself at all in this person you praise as going on from strength to strength.

To myself, I seem an ineffective creature, who always falls short of doing what another in my place, with a little more gray matter and strength of will, would easily accomplish. I'm always having opportunities that I'm not quite agile enough to catch and take advantage of.

She absently tapped her pencil against the paper, debating whether or not to include the incident of a drunken Stanford White coming to Irving Place and forcing himself on her in full view of Emily. Her grandmother would enjoy her description of how Mr. Booth picked the miscreant off his feet and pitched him headlong down the steps. She decided against it since Emily would most assuredly describe the whole incident in lurid detail, complete with illustrations, the moment she arrived in Tallmadge.

She wet the tip of her pencil and resumed writing.

After this last barrage of work at Tiffany's, I feel a great need to restore myself.

I must stop here. Chambers Street is the next stop, and with the New Year's crush, I must be ready to disembark. I will then hurry home, where I shall take a hot bath and fall into a deep, Rip VanWinkleian sleep, from which I shall emerge sometime in 1899.

Love to all, Clara

P.S. My flock gave me a Tiffany vase made of Mr. Nash's Favrile glass. I'm going to place it under Josie's photograph and make sure it's always filled with flowers.

~ **18** ~

CLARA READ OVER the list of Mr. Tiffany's orders for a third time. Whether from disappointment or exhaustion, she didn't feel tied to her body, but rather trapped inside a recurring nightmare.

"You want to *increase* production of the lamps," she said flatly, "make more of the individual deluxe items, plus design two or three windows for the Paris Exposition, plus make fancy mantle clocks for our showroom and your father's store, and design lamps for the London galleries exhibit this June? All this on top of our regular orders for windows and mosaics?"

Without bothering to reply, Louis continued writing in his notebook. She imagined he was busy planning how he was going to fill her life with unending work.

He snapped the notebook shut with a theatrical conclusion, and sat back in his chair. "That's exactly what I want. The six clocks should be finished by the middle of March—three for me, three for my father's studio. As far as the lamps go, I want at least six new designs. Don't be afraid to abandon conventionality. People prefer the art nouveau style now. Expand on that. Invent an exotic and unique Tiffany style. At least three of the new lamps must leave for the London Grafton Galleries exhibit no later than May."

He tapped his pen on the blotter. "The lamps and windows for the Paris Exposition will be your first priority. I've already provided you with the Four Seasons design; I leave it to you to design a companion window, but it has to be submitted before the end of this month, let's say no later than January twentieth. For every piece you design, you need to be thinking not only of the London exhibit and the Paris jury, but of the entire European market."

Clara felt the walls close in around her like a prison. "You ask too much. We'll never get all this finished in time."

His eyes fixed on her with an easy, approving familiarity that, while meant to convey assurance, only added to her frustration. "No excuses. How many girls do you have at present?"

"Thirty-one. It's not enough."

"Nonsense. I would think that's more than a sufficient number of workers, considering that you know how to rally them to the cause. You've done it before, and you will do it now."

"But I have all the bookkeeping, all the designing, all the managerial duties, and . . ." She trailed off. "I must speak plainly. I'm tired, and my department is tired. We've run ourselves ragged over the last five months trying to meet your demands for the Christmas rush. I didn't ask to meet with you this morning so that you could heap more work onto the department. I came here to tell you that I need time away. I need rest."

"Don't be foolish," Louis chided in a tone one might use with a petulant child. "You've got more pluck than that. I have it on good authority that you work twice as efficiently and three times as fast as the men."

"Which is precisely why I need time to rest. I've worked twelve hours a day for months. Getting ready for the season and having to do all the bookkeeping has brought me to the brink of physical prostration."

He heaved a weary sigh. "Oh, very well. How much time do you require?"

"One week to visit my family in Tallmadge, plus two extra days for travel. My last visit to my mother was so long ago that I don't even remember what she looks like."

Louis shook his head. "Out of the question. You may have the next two Saturdays off. That's all I can spare you. You have to get these things started. I can't have you going off on vacation every time you feel a bit weary. Can you imagine the men taking time off whenever they felt like it? My business would fail inside a month."

She regarded the man who sat in constant judgment of her—a man who more than likely had never known a hard day of work in his life—and wanted to scream out of sheer frustration and resentment. With his increasing edicts and demands, he was becoming more like a draconian workhouse overseer than a purveyor of fine art glass.

Anger boiled up inside her. His refusal to let her go felt as though he were locking a prison gate, closing out everything she found bright and joyful.

"No," she said resolutely, "I can't do it again, not without rest. Give the designs to Miss Northrop or Miss Griffin, if you're so eager to enter into another anxiety-ridden rush. You can't push my department and me again and expect us to produce anything of value. None of us can continue working at such a pace. It's inhumane."

Wearily, she got to her feet. "If this makes me somehow faulty in your estimate, then do as you wish. I'll return on January twelfth. In the meantime, my girls have plenty to work on with finishing the deluxe orders and the last two primrose lamps. Mr. Bracey and Miss Northrop can give them guidance should they need it, though I doubt they'll need much.

"Don't bother calling Mr. Mitchell. I'll tell him of my plans on my way downstairs." She hesitated, "Unless, of course, you wish to have me dismissed. To be perfectly honest, I'm so tired of this constant work, that at this point I don't much care if you do."

Halfway down the hall, she remembered her last order of business and hurried back to his office, where Tiffany was already attempting to raise someone by telephone.

"While you're alerting Mr. Mitchell of my arrival," she said, "please inform him that I won't return to work until I'm assured in writing that my salary has been raised to twenty-five dollars a week starting immediately. Seeing how the men's managers received year-end bonuses and I did not, I'm sure you'll agree this is a fair request.

"And stop looking so glum, Mr. Tiffany. Try to concentrate on all the glory and fortune you'll have in return for a little patience."

Noon at Tiffany's
March 14, 1899

Dear Ones,

Received the robin this morning and savored each sentence as one does the first juicy peach of July. What tries me now is the no-let-upness of Tiffany's. If it were not for Mr. Booth's help with the bookkeeping and finished contracts, I would surely lose my mind.

Last night Mr. Booth took Alice and me to the corner of Broadway and 27ᵗʰ Street to see the Holland Brother's kinetiscope parlor. While I found the concept of moving pictures exciting, I can't say that watching dogs and monkeys doing tricks and people flapping their arms about like asylum escapees was particularly stimulating. Here in New York, all I have to do is look out the window, and I can see the same thing in color, and with sound, any time day or night, for free.

We have added another worthy soul to our Irving Place family: Mr. Thomas Yorke, who works at the same firm as Mr. Booth and is quite knowledgeable about a great many subjects. Even you *might find him agreeable, Emily. Mr. Yorke and Mr. Bainbridge have adapted* Alice's Adventures in Wonderland *into a play for the other boarders. We're having auditions this week.*

The work at Hyde Park agrees with George. His salary has increased to $12 a week, so at last he feels he is worthy.

I visited Alice at the Corona factory yesterday. The furnaces felt especially comfortable, coming in out of the damp wintry weather. They're in an immense, scalding hot brick room, with great shafts of golden light pouring from the open doors. Dark and evil-looking men wearing few clothes were rushing around with long red-hot pokers. I do enjoy going over there.

My new assistant, Mr. Joseph Briggs, is a nice Englishman with a great deal of good sense, since he seems to favor everything that I do—a good start to an effective working relationship. Of course, he's a full six inches shorter and a good twenty pounds lighter than I, which makes it even more likely that he would agree with me.

He's a little mysterious about himself, but he did tell me that when he first came to America, he worked in the Wild West shows, holding out playing cards for the sharp shooters to shoot out of his hand! Lucky for us nobody missed the target, for he has a keen sense of beauty and is a master mosaicist, which eases our workload considerably.

I must return to work. Today I'm designing a set of glass water lily screens for Mrs. Astor's shower room.

Love always, Clara

P.S. Purchased my first store-made shirtwaist at Wanamaker's for $1.95. It's pink with white stripes. Imagine—it was ready to take off the shelf and wear. Clever!

Mr. Bainbridge clapped his hands. "Miss Owens has graciously allowed us to use the dining room for a limited time, so we must make this dress rehearsal count. I don't need to remind you there are only two weeks left to opening night. As I call first scene characters, please line up stage left. Alice of Wonderland?"

Amid cheers and whistles, Clara stepped forth, wearing a pinafore, white stockings and black slippers.

"Mad Hatter!'

Laughter broke out as George swept off his top hat and made a flourishing bow with all the exuberance of the Mad Hatter.

From the back of the room, Emily Wolcott spoke up in a voice that demanded attention. "Since I'm a frequent visitor here, I have pledged my assistance in the direction and critique of this play. Thus said, I strongly recommend that we wait a few moments until the men return from Dudley's studio with the backdrops. As I'm sure Mr. Bainbridge will agree, thespians do much better when the scene is set properly."

"I agree," George said. "Let's have a round of refreshments while we're waiting,"

Emily glowered at his straining waistcoat. "Control yourself, Mr. Waldo. We took tea no more than twenty minutes ago. If I didn't know you better, I'd say you'd sent away for one of those disgusting weight loss tapeworms Sears and Roebuck advertises in their catalogs."

The doorbell rang twice and then again.

"That will be the backdrops now," Clara said, heading for the foyer. "Come on, Alice, they're going to need help carrying them." She swung open the door and went still at the sight of Louis Tiffany, hat and cane in hand.

Louis nodded. "Miss Gouvy. Mrs. Driscoll. I see that I've interrupted something. . .a masquerade ball, perhaps?"

"We're rehearsing a play," Alice said, quickly pulling off her Cheshire Cat ears. "We were expecting the men with the backdrops."

"*Alice in Wonderland*," Clara added for want of something better to say. Remembering her manners, she opened the door wide. "Please, won't you come in?"

Tiffany stepped into the hall and presented her with a leather portfolio case. "I'm sorry to just drop by like this, especially on a Sunday, but I've suddenly been called away, and I didn't want you to wait until I returned to begin work on the *River of Life* window. I've noted my changes on the sketches and thought I'd deliver them on my way out."

She was barely listening, her mind momentarily occupied by a mortifying awareness of her humble accommodations. The clean and cozy home, of which she'd always been proud, now seemed no more than a hovel made up of cracked plaster, worn carpets, and offensive cooking smells.

"Since you're here, Mr. Tiffany, you should have Clara show you her new lamp ideas." Alice touched her arm. "We insist, don't we, Clara?"

Clara gave Alice a look that, if looks alone had power to harm, would have dealt her best friend a heavy blow indeed. "I'm sure Mr. Tiffany has better things to do than to waste his time with preliminary sketches."

"On the contrary," Louis said. "If these are lamps for Paris, I should view them now rather than later—that is, if you don't object."

She wanted to say that she did object, but Louis Tiffany would not be deterred so easily. When it came to her new designs, he was like a bloodhound on the scent—nothing stood in his way.

He was barely through the door of her room when she shoved the first sketch into his hands. "This is my electric dragonfly lamp. As you can see, the eyes will be cut beads and their wings very finely veined, like lace. When finished, this base . . ." she took a stray hairpin off the writing desk and circled the parts, ". . . will be of iridescent mosaic tiles in a design of ascending dragonflies from a field of arrowhead flowers."

He studied the drawing. "The way you've inverted the dragonflies around the bottom rim and have them in flight on the base is precisely the sort of thing I want."

She handed him the second sketch and watched as a fan of wrinkles spread out at the corners of his eyes. The lamp was just as it had been presented to her in the dream, its canopy a maze of spider webs, each section in a different colored glass. Thin strips of metal, made to resemble spider threads, hung from the edges of the shade's rim, anchoring it to a base of mosaic narcissus.

Louis looked from the sketches to their creator in wonder. "These are exquisite. Put your other work aside and make three variations of each of these. I want one of each for my father, the exposition, and myself. After that, I'll want another half dozen for the showroom. Both lamps are going to sell very well."

"I'm glad you like them," she said, placing the sketches facedown on the desk. "I'll start on them tomorrow. Thank you so much for stopping by." The look she gave Alice was clear enough.

Following the silent command, Alice discreetly herded their employer to the door. "Nice to see you, Mr. Tiffany. We hope you have a pleasant journey to . . . well, to wherever it is you're going."

They'd successfully driven him to the foyer, when the doorbell rang again. Emily stepped out of the dining room at the same time Messrs. Booth, Yorke and Belknap barged through the door struggling under two bolts of canvas backdrops.

Mr. Booth nodded to Louis. "I say old chap, clear out of the way, would you? These things weigh more than a team of dead horses."

Pushing himself flat against the wall, Louis caught sight of Henry. "Belknap! Whatever are you doing here?"

Straining to keep the bolts balanced, Henry lifted his chin. "Hello, Louis. Sorry I can't talk right now; we need to hang these backdrops in a hurry."

At the sight of Emily standing with her hands on her hips and staring hard at Louis, Clara felt a spasm of alarm. Given Emily's acerbic tirades against the 'Despot Tiffany,' she knew her sister's righteous indignation was about to be made known to all within shouting distance. Panicked, Clara shoved her employer to the outer door, but not quite soon enough.

Emily barreled toward them, an accusing finger pointed at Tiffany. Her shrill, scolding voice cut the air like a sword. "Is that Mr. Louis C. Tiffany?"

Confused by the sight of the formidable woman coming at him, Louis half smiled. "Why yes, I'm Mr. Tiffany." Chuckling, he leaned toward Clara and whispered, "She must be the Queen of Hearts, or is she one of Macbeth's witches? Either role suits her perfectly."

Emily arched one of her thick eyebrows and gave him the same look she might give an incubus. "I wish to have a few words with you, Mr. Tiffany. I'd like to know just what sort of presumptuous, inconsiderate halfwit forces his employees to work like slaves while he robs them of—"

Clara grabbed Louis's hand, and with strength she was not aware she possessed, yanked him out the door and onto the stoop, calling out behind her, "Mr. Tiffany is in a hurry, Miss . . . Miss Smith. His car is waiting so he must be on his way—immediately."

She gave a bewildered Louis one last nudge to keep him moving down the stairs. "Thank you so much for stopping in. Have a good trip."

When Clara returned to the house, she found Emily and Alice in the hall, looking dumbstruck. "Oh for God's sake," she snorted, hurrying past them, "don't just stand there like ninnies. We've got to get to the Mad Hatter's tea party before dinner."

April 3, 1899

Mother, Kate, Rev. Cutler,

Mr. Belknap and Clara are attending Spring Opera at the Philharmonic to hear Mme. Schumann-Heinck sing. Last week it was to hear 'Gotterdammerung,' next week it will be 'Tanhauser,' with Emma Eames. It's beyond me how she stands all that yodel-screeching. It's enough to cause damage to the ears, if not the whole intestinal system.

Mr. Booth kept me company until past midnight. I suspect he's sweet on Clara, but he is a true gentleman and would never be so bold as to actually tell her so, rather like the men in the Midwest. Unfortunately for him, Clara takes men's devotions entirely for granted, so she may never notice.

Clara took me to Tiffany's to see the St. John on the Isle of Patmos window. I swear the figures are alive and breathing.

Emily Wolcott

Tiffany Hall, Irvington-On-Hudson
April 3, 1899

Why Father has called me to this drafty old ruin to discuss his will is a mystery, for he neither needs nor values my opinions. Burnie, of course, did not honor the patriarchal summons, nor did he bother to send excuses. So much the worse for him.

My impromptu visit to Clara was rewarding. Without a doubt, I shall enter the dragonfly lamp in the exposition.

The lady was charming in her costume, And all that beautiful hair held back from her face by girlish ribbons, the rest to hang loose in long curls. As I was being rushed out, several strands brushed my fingers, twining around them like living rings. I wanted to throw her down and possess her then and there. It made for a most uncomfortable ride to Tiffany Hall.

I must remember to ask Belknap about that queer Miss Smith who was ranting in the hall as I was leaving.

The dinner bell has rung. I wonder—would Father still use the switch on me if I dared to be late? L.C.T.

June 22, 1899

Clara faced the assembled company of her department and was overcome with pride. To her way of thinking, each of them was a true artist in her or his own right.

"As you are all aware, Mr. Tiffany and Mr. Belknap will be sailing for Europe on July twenty-seventh to meet with Siegfried Bing. Mr. Tiffany has presented me with a long list of the things he wants designed and finished before he goes."

Out of the corner of her eye, she saw Miss Griffin break with her normally upright stance and slump at the shoulders in anticipation of what was to come. "But that's only five weeks away," Miss Griffin said, "and we already have so much to do. There's no way we could take on more."

Mr. Bracey bobbed his head in agreement. "His Highness is gettin' mighty greedy, ain't he? He'll work us to death at this rate."

"I suppose," Clara said, "but our things are very popular with the customers right now, so we must feed the fires to keep them hot. You know Mr. Tiffany's motto: 'Gain we must'!"

"Except it isn't 'we' who are gaining," said Miss Hawthorne.

The Palmié twins raised their hands. "Why doesn't he lock the doors," Marion began, ". . . and let us all go home for the summer?" Lillian finished.

"Yes, that would be lovely," Clara said, "but it's not to be. I'll tell you now, so there will be no surprises or great disappointments later—it's going to be uphill work from now until December. It's not . . ."

She hesitated, unsure about telling them everything all at once.

"Go on, Mrs. Driscoll," Joe Briggs prompted. "No sense sparing the whip in the middle of the beating, you know."

"Thank you, Mr. Briggs." She cleared her throat. "It's not yet been accepted, but Mr. Tiffany has put in a bid for a ten foot by thirty foot mosaic panel of the Virtues."

Their groans of protest made her wretched, though she tried not to show it. "If we are awarded the job, and depending on how soon Mr. Tiffany wants it completed, we may be thrown into another mad rush. In light of this, I want to share with you a thought that came to me in the middle of the night, while I lay worrying about getting things done on time: If, for some reason, the work started slowing down and we were left twiddling our thumbs, wouldn't we all wish we were back in the whirl?"

She could see from their expressions that the thought struck them as the truth of the matter. "Knowing this about ourselves, we should be grateful to be so busy. I expect that Mr. Tiffany will be looking over your shoulders. Try not to be nervous, and under no circumstances are you to take his critiques or his destructions personally. Remember, it's not your fault. It's simply a matter of . . ."

". . . of a man who has too much money for his own good." Marion Palmié finished for her.

She let the ensuing laughter lull her into what she knew was a false sense of well-being.

July 27, 1899

Bent over her newest lamp design, Clara was absorbed by Mr. Briggs's latest tales about his ill-natured wife. Her atrocious behavior at times seemed so far-fetched as to be fictional, though he didn't appear to be the type of man to invent such stories.

He was recounting an amusing story involving a frying pan and his head, when she sensed someone standing in the doorway. It wouldn't be like her girls or Mr. Bracey to eavesdrop. Mr. Tiffany and Henry were on a steamship bound for Europe, and none from the men's department would lower themselves to enter the women's department.

"What can we do for you, Mr. Mitchell?" she asked without looking up.

Embarrassed at having been caught spying, Mr. Mitchell waved a hand around the room. "What is all this you're working on?"

"You know perfectly well these are the lamp designs that Mr. Tiffany wants done before he returns. He specifically told me to have at least ten finished."

"That's all well and good, Mrs. Driscoll, except Mr. Tiffany isn't here now, and I've had an inspiration."

There was something about his smile that made her stomach flip.

He clasped his hands behind his back. "I think you and your girls should take time off. All you women are looking peaked lately. Have yourselves a nice rest. Go to the seashore and frolic . . . or whatever it is you do in those sorts of places." He glanced at her out of the corner of his eye. "How would that suit you?"

She could just imagine Mr. Tiffany returning to find his lamps unfinished and the Virtues mosaic in the same state as when he left. His rage would know no bounds, and the blame would be placed on her.

"It doesn't suit me at all," she said, keeping her voice steady. "While I appreciate your kind consideration of our health, I'm afraid we have too much to do to go gallivanting about. "

"Oh, don't worry about that." He gave her an ingratiating smile. "I'll make sure everything is taken care of in your absence. The men's department can easily finish up whatever it is Tiffany wants."

"The men don't have the skills to complete what has to be done," Mr. Briggs said bluntly. "What about the lamps and the mosaics? It isn't fair to Mrs. Driscoll's department. Tiffany will fire the lot of us."

"It's fair if I say it is," Mr. Mitchell said, heading out the door. "As of noon, I want every woman gone from the workroom. Mrs. Driscoll, I want you to stay on and give the men's department directions as to what Tiffany wants done. Mr. Briggs, you and Daniel Bracey are to stay on. Just make sure the workroom is ready for occupancy by the men."

After he was gone, she turned to Joseph. "What are we going to do now?"

Mr. Briggs broke into a smile. "I think our best bet would be to introduce Mr. Mitchell to Mrs. Briggs on one of her snappish days."

Alice shook her. "Wake up! There's a call for you."

Bounding out of bed, Clara searched blindly for her wrapper. "What's happened?"

"I don't know. Miss Owens said there's a gentleman on the telephone who wants to speak with you urgently."

Anxiety propelled her down the stairs. The prospect of hearing bad news delivered in such a cold and direct way as a telephone seemed heinous; telegrams were so much gentler. One could take one's time with a telegram. Trembling, she picked up the dangling earpiece. "Hello? This is Clara Driscoll speaking."

"Clara? This is Henry."

The voice was Henry's, but she could make no sense of it. Henry Belknap was on a ship somewhere in the middle of the Atlantic Ocean on his way to Paris. "Where are you?"

"I'll explain later. I've sent a private cab for you and Alice. We need both of you to come right away."

Before she could ask what was wrong, she heard several clicks then a sound like that of wind blowing through an endless tunnel.

44 Irving Place
August 3, 1899

Dear Ones,

George has typhoid. Take care not to mention this in your letters to Mrs. Waldo. One son is as good as dead to her; she couldn't bear the thought of losing the other.

The day Henry Belknap was to sail with Mr. Tiffany to Europe, George was brought home from Hyde Park with a high fever. He was then struck down by several hard seizures in a row, and was only half-conscious. Refusing to abandon his friend, Henry sent word to Mr. Tiffany to go on without him.

Alice and I, Dudley and Mr. McBride were summoned late that night to Henry's apartment, where I set up nursing duties. Dudley and Henry took turns changing George's bed linens and making him drink water, Alice and I bathed him with cold water mixed with witch hazel every half hour, and Mr. McBride was left to do the pacing for all of us.

The next morning, a doctor was summoned, who insisted George be taken to a hospital. The men carried him to the carriage and laid him flat. They raced up 5th Avenue to Presbyterian Hospital, while the doctor alternately took George's pulse and administered whiskey followed by sniffs of ammonia and cocaine.

When we arrived back at Irving Place, Saint Edward had saved breakfast for us, and made sure we had a full pot of hot coffee. We could not have borne another hard day at Tiffany's without it, for my brain is already numbed with constant work and worry.

One good thing that has come out of this is that Henry has canceled Mr. Mitchell's orders. Mr. Tiffany means to win at the Paris Exposition at all costs, and my department is the only way he'll ever manage to do that.

Love, Clara

P.S. St. Vincent's Hospital has its first horseless ambulance this week. I'm told it can race at a speed of 30 miles an hour! How I would love to try my hand at driving at such a dizzying speed.

~ **19** ~

December 14, 1899

Dearest Ones,

Tomorrow I turn 38. How did I get so old without noticing? The days are short, and my last few hours here are in the dark, which is bad for mosaic work, the color being different by artificial light. In spite of that, the Virtues panels go well—all 300 square feet of them. There is some satisfaction to be had in knowing I'm one of a handful who is able to do this kind of work.

I've also designed a new pen tray, where each end is a scarlet poppy with black centers, so that whichever way you lay the pen, the inky part rests on the black centers. I would love to own one of these, but alas, I can't afford it.

The fates are again against me as to time. I wish I could have balance in this matter—to have some of the time full and running over, so that you leap from one thing to another in such a manner that you feel the exhilaration of accomplishment. The rest of the time, I would wish to feel the luxury of repose and, when I wish to think at all, have only pleasant unhurried thoughts.

George's health continues to worry us, and although he says he's never felt better, I don't think he has ever fully recovered from the typhoid fever. He doesn't allow himself to rest, but I shall refrain from throwing stones from my glass tower.

Miss Griffin has taken the room across from mine. She is efficiency in motion, and I love seeing her all curled up on my sofa with a book. She's an intelligent, free-spirited little bird-like woman, who has blended into our circle without a ripple. She and Mr. Yorke get along splendidly, but a romance might be too much to hope for.

There is much excitement in the department these days. Tiffany's exposition windows have been chosen to flank the entrance to the American Arts pavilion.

Love, Clara

P.S. Kate: What is it exactly that you want to know about opera? I can sum them all up in two words: everybody dies.

T HE TIFFANY GIRLS were lined up straight as soldiers. Like a general at inspection, Clara went down the line, smiling at each woman, straightening a crooked collar here, tapping a slouched shoulder there.

Joe Briggs walked calmly at her side, though she knew he was far from relaxed. A sensitive man, he'd not yet grown used to the nature of Mr. Tiffany's rough-and-tumble critiques. For her part, she was sick to death of Louis's tyrannical intimidation. She'd lost too many fine artisans to his bullying, and spent far too much time putting to right those things he'd spoiled.

"Since Mr. Tiffany is delayed, I wish to take this opportunity to again thank you for your hard work and dedication. I also want to say that I've never received a better birthday surprise than the one you have given me today. To be met with cake and coffee was rather wonderful in and of itself, but to be given such a magnificent and special gift is sublime."

She turned to admire the desk lamp proudly displayed on the table outside her workroom. It was a beautiful piece, made all the more precious by the knowledge they'd all had a hand in the making of it. The women and Mr. Bracey used her clematis design for the shade, while Alice, Mr. Briggs and the foundry men created a base of bronze stems rising up around bubbles of jade milk glass.

"I'll make this lamp the centerpiece of my home no matter where I live, be it a palace, or my cell at the Tombs."

While they laughed, she checked her watch. Louis Tiffany was late by twelve minutes. Reading her thoughts, Joseph touched her elbow. "Perhaps his automobile has broken down."

"Either that," said Miss Ring, "or he's been delayed at the livery, where the smithy is reinforcing his cane with iron."

Their giggles were cut short when Louis barged through the door. From the set of his jaw and the poisonous gleam in his eyes, it was clear he was already on a rampage. Greeting no one, he glared at the *Four Seasons* window, slapping his cane menacingly against the palm of his hand.

Clara prayed that whatever put him in his fractious state of mind wouldn't taint his artistic judgment.

Louis rested his cane against the section entitled *Spring*. Every eye in the room was glued to the point where the tip touched the glass. "The yellow you've chosen for this part of the window is too bright."

"*You* chose this particular glass yourself, Mr. Tiffany," she said in a neutral tone, hoping the women were remembering to breathe. Anyone who fainted now would be left where she fell until after he was finished.

He leaned forward scrutinizing the rest of the window's sections. At last he stood back. "The only segment I am fully satisfied with is *Winter*. However, seeing as it's too late now to change things, it will have to do."

She almost laughed. *Winter* was the only section she disliked. On more than one occasion, she'd tried persuading him to change his initial pattern, but he'd held fast. She knew he'd meant it to represent snow-capped mountains and pine boughs, but no matter how much she squinted, to her eyes, it still resembled a large white crab claw at the end of a stick.

He moved on to the *River of Life* window, his cane now threatening the ribbon of blue that represented the river. "This blue isn't right, damn it! There's no balance between this blue here . . ." his stick came up for the strike, "and this blue here!"

With a cry, she seized the cane before it could connect with the glass. "No! Not this time. I won't let you!"

For a brief moment, there ensued an inelegant tug of war, her strength matching his. "You aren't thinking!" Her voice went high and shrill. "This is the blue we agreed balances the other colors."

He threw his full weight against her. "I said . . . it . . . isn't . . . right!"

Wrenching the cane out of her hands, he stumbled backward, the stick making an arch and coming down squarely on her birthday lamp. Through the yelling and cries of dismay, she heard the unmistakable sound of splintering glass, and then a terrible shriek, like that of a badly injured horse.

She looked wildly about, trying to locate the source of the hideous shrieks, when Joseph touched her arm and pointed to where Tiffany was doubled over, both hands tightly cupped over his right eye. Screaming, he threw his head back and forth, stumbling about the room as if possessed.

In the ambulance, he gripped her hand and begged her not to leave him. Until the moment he was wheeled through the surgery doors, he refused to let go of her.

An hour later, the doctor found her waiting in the hall. In the grave manner common to surgeons, he handed her a small envelope containing the fragment of jade milk glass removed from Louis Tiffany's eye.

"Is this Clara Driscoll?" The voice on the other end of the line was faint, as if the speaker was a long distance from the mouthpiece.

Turning so she wouldn't have to look at Mr. Mitchell's reproachful frown, she pressed the receiver anxiously to her ear. She couldn't imagine what call could be so important that Mr. Mitchell would personally summon her to his office and allow her to speak on his private telephone. "Yes, this is Mrs. Driscoll. Who's calling, please?"

"Don't you know me? This is Miss Dorothy Tiffany. I'm Papa's youngest girl, except I'm eight now, so I'm not so young anymore."

"Of course, I remember you," Clara laughed. "How are you, dear?"

"Fine, but Papa told me to call you and tell you to come to Lenox Hill right away, because he wants to talk to you about business. He said to bring your drawing pad and colored pencils and . . ." The small voice hesitated and then resumed, ". . . and he said to bring some colored pencils for me, too."

An hour later, a parlor maid, dressed in black poplin, crisp white collar and a pert lace cap, opened the door to the Tiffany mansion. Clara announced herself and reluctantly allowed the maid to collect her coat. A *frileuse* by nature, she would have preferred keeping it on, but did not want to appear unsophisticated. She was about to inquire as to the state of Mr. Tiffany's health, when Dorothy popped out from behind the maid's skirts and grinned.

The girl pulled her toward the grand staircase at a run. "I'll announce Mrs. Driscoll to Papa," Dorothy called back to the maid. "Please tell cook to make a pot of hot cocoa and send it, along with two cups, to the sewing room."

On the landing, Clara brought out a package and handed it to her. "Your colored pencils."

Dorothy examined the contents and looked up at Clara smiling. "Would you like to see my artwork? We could go to the sewing room, and I'll show you."

"I would love to see what you've done, but your papa won't like it if I'm late."

The corners of Dorothy's mouth turned down. "Papa hates for us to be late, too. He punishes us for one second lateness." She pinched her fingers together to demonstrate the tiniest sliver of time and glanced up from under a wrinkled brow. "He has a temper, you know."

"I certainly do," Clara said, "which is why we'd better hurry."

Dorothy whisked her through the reception hall and library, then into a grand room with an open fire under an ornate mantle. Everywhere Clara looked, her eyes fell on large Favrile vases filled with roses of every color.

A flutter of movement drew her attention to an enormous four-poster bed at the far end of the room. Looking small and wizened between mountains of fine linen sheets, Louis Tiffany lay still, his head swathed in a turban of bandages.

"Clara, my dear, come here and sit by me." He patted the bed.

Disconcerted by the lack of chairs, she gingerly lowered herself to the corner of the bed nearest his feet.

Dorothy crawled onto the bed and ducked under Clara's arm. "Papa, can Mrs. Driscoll come upstairs to the sewing room and see my artwork?"

"Not now." He did not take his eyes off Clara. "Mrs. Driscoll and I have work to discuss, and we're not to be disturbed. You may wait quietly in the hall for her to come out."

Dorothy tugged at Clara's sleeve. "Promise you won't leave without letting me show you my pictures?"

She gave Dorothy's hand a squeeze. "I promise. I want to see your entire collection."

Louis propped himself up against the dozen or so pillows that lined the head of the bed. "Now, tell me about everything going on at the company. You're the only one I can trust to tell me the truth. I haven't stopped worrying. Of all the times for me to be away, I can't think of a worst time than this."

"If you don't mind my saying so, Mr. Tiffany, I don't think it's healthy for you to have your work so much on your mind. You've sustained a serious injury. You should try and rest. Perhaps your older children could read to you?"

"I assure you my children would not spare me the time." His smile faded, and in his voice she heard bitterness laced with sorrow. He reached out and found her hand. "You *are* a sight for sore eyes . . . or eye, as the case may be. I feel stronger just seeing you."

Their close proximity, the dim lighting and the fact she was in his bedroom, on his bed, made her squirm. She quailed at the thought that one of his older children or, God forbid, Mrs. Tiffany, might enter at any moment, but for the life of her, could not think of a tactful way to disengage her hand and rise from the bed without giving offense.

"Everyone sends his regards," she said. "Daniel and Mrs. Bracey are having masses said for your quick recovery, and the girls insist on daily reports as to how your eye is healing. You can rest assured we're holding strong in your absence. All the pieces are coming to completion beautifully."

"What about the Paris window?" he asked, "I've not dared ask anyone else. Is it . . . did I . . .?"

"You harmed nothing but your eye. The glass splinter came from a lamp that was perfectly restored by the time I returned from the hospital."

"Tell me the truth—do you think I have a chance at winning the exposition?"

Until that moment she hadn't been sure, but now she knew without doubt they would capture the show. "Definitely. The windows are exquisite, and there's nothing in the world to compare with the lamps and Favrile glassware."

With a sigh of relief he fell back into his pillow, and immediately sat up again. "I want to see them."

"See what?"

"The windows. I want to see them."

"You will, as soon as you're healed and feeling up to it."

"No," he said stubbornly, "I want to see them now, within the hour."

Her shoulders tightened, rising toward her ears. "You're unwell, Mr. Tiffany. You shouldn't get out of bed; you might do permanent damage to your eye, and then what would become of us?"

He reached behind the massive headboard and gave the bell pull a tug. "I'll have Belknap send them up; I'll be able to view them in the main reception room at my leisure."

She wondered if his eye surgery might have affected his mind. The task of moving the windows from the workshop to Lenox Hill was monumental. To move them when the streets were covered with snow and ice was insane.

Stooped with arthritis, a graying man in valet attire slowly shuffled his way across the room. He stared into the middle distance, seemingly not noticing her at all.

"Simpkins, ring up Mr. Belknap, and tell him I want my two exposition windows brought to the house immediately. Tell him at least six men are to accompany each window, and it will be his neck should there be any accidents."

Simpkins made a noise of assent and was halfway to the door, when Louis called him back. Without losing momentum, the valet pivoted on his heel and shuffled back to the bed.

"Since you're here, Simpkins, perhaps you could bring me another of my medicinal brandies. I'll need a bracer for this event."

The wrinkled corners of Simpkins's mouth twitched. The voice that came out was dusty and ancient like the man himself. "Sorry sir, but you have already taken your morning brandy. The doctor has specified only one serving of spirits before lunch and one before dinner."

"Hang it, Simpkins! I'll have my dinner brandy early."

Simpkins was unmoved. "I am sorry sir, but Mrs. Tiffany has the brandy and all other spirits under lock and key."

Louis pursed his lips. "All right, never mind. Just go call Mr. Belknap."

Simpkins bowed again and slipped as noiselessly from the room as he'd entered. No sooner did the door close, than Louis, dressed only in a loose nightshirt, shot out of bed and made a beeline for the bookcase. Reaching behind the books, he brought out a crystal decanter with an inch or two of brandy at the bottom. He dumped the contents of his water glass into a vase and returned to bed with his prize.

Pouring out a healthy measure, he drank it down in two swallows, poured another and handed it to her, his disposition greatly improved.

"Won't you join me? Brandy is an excellent restorative, you know."

"No, thank you." She pushed the glass back into his hand. "I'll be working on the dragonfly lamp this afternoon, and I wouldn't want to drop anything."

Fixing her with a look she did not know how to interpret, Louis drank off the rest of his bracer and poured another, before tossing the empty decanter off the side of the bed. "Do you think my employees like me, Clara?"

"Of course they do, although some of the younger girls find you frightening at times."

"And what about you?"

She felt the blood rush to her face. "My loyalties are with Tiffany's."

"It isn't your loyalty I'm questioning." He swirled his brandy around the glass. "I want to know if you have feelings for me."

Slowly, she rose to her feet. Pretending to admire a bouquet of yellow roses, she stalled for time, while thinking of an answer that was both prudent and neutral. "You are my employer, Mr. Tiffany," she said finally. "I like everyone at Tiffany's in the general sense. I'm even fond of Monsieur Rigaud, our workroom cat."

He caught her hand and held it, his fingers closing around hers for one brief moment, before letting go. "Do you have any idea how much I care for you, Clara?"

She moved further away, out of his reach. "It means a great deal to me that you admire my work, Mr. Tiffany. I—"

"You know very well that isn't what I'm saying. There are times when I'm near you that I can hardly keep from touching you. I have dreams about—"

She whirled around, her skirts almost knocking over a delicate vase. "You must not say these things, Mr. Tiffany, I don't want to hear them." She stooped to pick up her sketchpad and backed toward the door. "You're my employer, and that's all. It's not right that you should feel that way."

"Clara, please allow me to tell you how I—."

"I'm sorry," she rushed on, "I'm afraid I've tired you. We'll go over my new designs when you return to work." She yanked open the door and was free.

The moment she stepped into the hall, Dorothy latched onto her wrist and took off at a run.

Dorothy pointed to the garden fairies window. "Mama said you made that before I was born. It's my favorite window in the whole house. I like to make believe I'm the fairy in the green dress and can fly away anytime I need to."

Hearing despair behind the words, Clara looked into the child's sweet face and found staring back at her a lonely and wounded soul. It pained her to think of the child surrounded by so much wealth and yet not having the one thing she needed most.

The ghostly Simpkins materialized at the top of the attic stairs with a tray bearing cups and a blue and white ceramic pot. Taking no notice of either her or Dorothy, he placed the tray on the table, poured out two cups of the steaming chocolate, and then slipped away without a word.

"Nurse lets me have as much hot cocoa as I want," Dorothy said, taking a dainty sip. "Especially on the days my mother is at the 'firmery with all the sick mothers and babies." She shot Clara a quick glance. "Papa doesn't like her to go there. He yells and throws things, but my mother goes anyway. I heard Nurse tell the maid that Papa got glass in his eye because he was angry at Mother for not staying home."

Dorothy looked at her with a depth of concern that Clara found unsettling in a face so young. "Does Papa yell at you, too?"

"No," Clara said, then, "well, maybe a little."

Dorothy lifted Clara's arm and wrapped it around herself, briefly resting her head against Clara's shoulder. Touched, Clara leaned down and tenderly kissed the top of her head, taking in the salty sweet scent that belonged only to children.

"I have to go back to work now, but before I go I'd like to see your artwork."

Springing up, Dorothy grabbed a handful of drawings from a battered toy box and placed them in Clara's lap. "I'd like a crick . . . crickeek . . ."

"A critique of your work?"

"Yes, one of those. Papa's always too busy, and Mama only likes to look at phototototography."

Clara carefully examined the watercolor drawings of lions, flowers, and horses, until she came to the one that gave her pause. The scene was of a golden meadow dotted with specks of red flowers. Beyond was a hill and beyond that, a sea of blue with white-peaked waves. A girl stood at the top of the hill, her face turned toward the sun.

"This is the best of your work. Your choice of color is excellent, and the balance of all the things in here is perfect."

Dorothy put her finger on the girl. "That's me making a wish."

She couldn't help herself; she had to ask. "And what were you wishing for?"

Dorothy looked surprised, as if the answer were evident. "I was wishing for a friend like you to come and take me away from here."

January 4, 1900

The moment he entered his office, Louis sensed something was out of order. Halfway to his desk, he saw the empty gap where the dragonfly lamp had been only a half hour before. He searched the room frantically, and, finding nothing, hurried to Pringle Mitchell's office.

"What's wrong?" Mitchell put down the newspaper he'd been reading. "You look like you've seen a ghost."

"The dragonfly lamp—the one with the squat base of arrowhead flowers and dragonflies in mosaics and gold. It's gone! Someone has stolen it from my office! Call the police; tell them we've been robbed. Tell them—"

"Oh, *that*," Mitchell relaxed. "I took it down to the showroom. The clerk called saying a woman was in the store, insisting on having one of the dragonfly lamps at any cost. The others were sold, and I'd seen the sample on your desk, so I assumed—"

"You idiot! That was the premier lamp for the Paris Exposition. When did you take it down?"

Realizing the enormity of his mistake, Mitchell's face drained of color. "About fifteen minutes ago. I quoted her a price of five hundred, and she didn't even blink. I thought you'd be pleased. We sold the other dragonfly lamps for three-fifty."

Louis's feet barely touched the stairs as he flew down the four flights to the showroom, arriving just as a rotund dowager was leaving. Trailing behind her was a uniformed chauffer carrying a large box bearing the Tiffany label.

Louis almost choked on the thick miasma of perfume that surrounded the woman like a widow's veil. He cut her off at the door and bowed stiffly. "Excuse me, Madam, I am Louis Tiffany. I understand you have just now purchased one of my dragonfly lamps from our showroom?"

"I have," she trilled, her ample jowls jiggling with her excitement. "Mrs. Astor has one in her drawing room. The moment I saw it, I knew I had to have one." She laid a plump, gloved hand on his arm. "You are a marvel, Mr. Tiffany. Everyone is talking about your wonderful lamps. Only yesterday, Mrs. Vanderbilt told me she was going to install four of them in her library and another two in the front hall."

"I'm glad the lamps please you, Madam. Nevertheless, a terrible mistake has been made." He dabbed at his forehead. "You see, Madam, the lamp you have just purchased is not for sale."

The woman broke into girlish laughter. "Of course, it isn't for sale, you silly man. It's mine—I just purchased it."

"I'm afraid you don't understand," he said gravely, reaching for the box. "I must take the lamp back. However, I shall personally see to it that you receive another lamp that is as beautiful. If you tell the clerk what color scheme you wish to have, I'll make sure—"

The dowager's hands landed on the box at the same time as his. Wrenching it out of her chauffer's grasp, she pulled the parcel against her ample bosom and wrapped her arms proprietarily around it. "You can't have it." Her voice rose. "It's mine! My money is as good as anyone's."

"Yes, of course it is." He bowed again. "But this lamp is . . ." Louis paused to consider. The old cow had high connections. He would have to proceed with extreme care. He knew well the power society women's talk had in building or destroying the reputation of men far greater than he.

"This lamp is a second-rate version of the dragonfly lamp, meant for sale to our less—how shall I say it?— our less discerning customers. When my assistant told me that you were a lady of obvious high standards, I hastened downstairs to save you from making a terrible blunder. As I am sure you are aware, Tiffany's is dedicated to preserving the sterling reputations of its customers."

A smidgen of doubt crept into the woman's defiance. Scowling, she glanced at the box, and then at him. "But I want one of the dragonfly lamps, and I must have *this* one."

"And you shall have a dragonfly lamp," Louis smiled. "Except you will have one that will make this lamp seem drab by comparison. I give you my word; I'll personally see to it that you receive a lamp of the highest quality, an absolute diamond among lamps." He tried again to remove the box from her grip and was aggrieved to find a last vestige of resistance.

He steered her away from the chauffer, employing an air of conspiracy. "Be assured the lamp you receive in exchange is worth five times what you paid for this one. Consider it my personal gift, my way of showing my gratitude for your patience and gracious understanding in this unfortunate matter."

He tried again to pull the box away and found her grasp significantly loosened. "I must insist, however, that you do not disclose to anyone how cleverly you managed to come away from Tiffany's with such a bargain. If word ever got out, I would be besieged. I wholeheartedly ascribe to the old adage that the best way to keep a secret is without help."

Affronted, the dowager took one hand off the box to pinch at the copious amount of flesh that cushioned her neck. "I beg your pardon, but I am not the sort of woman who prattles gossip and tells secrets!"

"Excellent practice, Madam." Louis tightened his grip. "You're a shining example of womanhood."

Blushing, she giggled like a schoolgirl. "Well, I suppose it might be all right, especially if I have your personal guarantee, Mr. Tiffany."

Seeing his chance, Louis tugged at the box, and the lamp was his.

Lenox Hill
February 12, 1900

The exposition pieces are on their way to Paris. Father and I are to have our exhibits adjacent to each other in the American Industrial Arts building—his leather, stationery, damasking, gems and metals against my blown glass, enamels, lamps, mosaics and windows. Now we shall see.

Once again I've had to speak to Louise about a wife's duty. Her reluctance to share my bed is in blatant violation of the marriage contract. We are healthy, and while another confinement is out of the question, it seems perverse to deprive me of my conjugal rights. I've insisted she seek the counsel of Pastor Osgood. I'll speak with him privately first thing tomorrow to make sure he and I are of the same mind on this issue.

The land adjacent to The Briars has drawn my interest as the ideal site for building my masterpiece. The main parcel overlooks a natural cove in Cold Spring Harbor, but is presently occupied by the Laurelton Hall Hotel and the public picnic grounds. The owner has informed my agent that he will never sell to me specifically and will go to great lengths to prohibit me from ever obtaining the parcel. He should spare himself the trouble, for I mean to have his land and all the land around it. L.C.T.

April 25, 1900

My darling Clara,

It is three years to the day since we brought Josephine's body home. The night is as it was then—soft and warm, doors open, and frogs singing. I have been looking over the box with her picture and the lock of her beautiful hair. There are no apple and cherry blossoms now, but when there are, we will cover her grave again.

Take what is yours, Clara. When summer comes you must accept the Palmié twins' invitation to their house by the seashore. Do not let your (and I dare say, Mr. Tiffany's!) desire for money and fame rob you of your life.

Stay well, my darling girl.

Love, Mama

A June rainstorm was brewing, and more than anything, Clara longed to be out in it and away from the crowd gathered in her room. The endless games of Whist were beginning to wear on her nerves.

She slipped into Alice's room to change, and then made her way to her bicycle. Riding off in no one's direction but her own, she removed her hat and let the wind tear at her hair. Drunk on freedom and daring, she was euphoric as streetcars and horseless carriages zigzagged around her like evil spirits. At Church Street, where the roads turned to cobblestone, her lantern sputtered and went out.

The moment she turned onto West Broadway, the rains came, soaking through her clothes to her skin. She ducked into a side street and then another, until she came to an enclave of narrow lanes and alleys that were protected from the storm. Illuminated by the flaring torches and red lanterns, groups of sweating men and scantily clad woman emerged from the shadows. They passed her with curious looks that made her feel as if she'd dropped out of the world as she knew it, and onto some other planet.

A fleshy woman wearing no more than a gauze shift grabbed at her bicycle skirt, holding it out. "Ooo, lookie here," she jeered, "it's her Lady La-di-dah come callin' on us wicked, shameless folk."

The man on whose lap she'd been sitting, stopped swigging from a bottle and gave her a lecherous look. "Or maybe she's come lookin' for a job. Come over here lady, I'll give ya a job."

A chorus of laughter came from a dozen dark corners.

Clara kept her pace, looking straight ahead, though she would have liked nothing better than to talk to them to get a sense of how they lived day to day. She wondered if they ever felt the hopelessness of their lives, or if they were content with their lot.

By the time the rain stopped, she was pedaling down Spring Street, and then Prince. She changed direction again, and raced down unfamiliar alleyways and through parks. The church bells ringing ten startled her, and suddenly Washington Square lay before her. Somehow, without trying, she'd found her way back to her own country.

As she passed through Union Square Park, she thought she heard her name. Through the fog she could just make out three men on wheels. Dudley's gangling legs, Edward Booth's tall frame and Mr. Yorke's distinct Boston accent couldn't be mistaken.

Her initial resentment at being searched out like a child collided with her pleasure over their concern. After a moment of watching their misty silhouettes weave among the trees, she gave in and let herself be captured.

July 2, 1900

Louis entered her workroom without knocking, but instead of giving her a list of new things to be done, he stood perfectly still, gazing about him like a man lost. "I'm leaving for the Paris Exposition on Friday and taking Mr. Belknap with me."

"Mr. Belknap?" she looked up in surprise. "But I thought Mr. Mitchell was going with you."

He dropped into the chair beside her desk. "Mr. Mitchell isn't going to Paris or anywhere. My sister sent word that he died this morning from typhoid." Louis tapped his chest. "Something went wrong with his heart."

The news took her breath away. The man had been a thorn in her side, but the memory of him telling her that bright autumn leaves made him happy brought with it a deep sadness that she could not explain.

"He was only forty-one, Clara, a young man. I don't understand. It was so fast." He looked to her, his eyes pleading for some explanation.

The thought crossed her mind that the strain of working under the direction of Louis Tiffany might have contributed to whatever killed Mr. Mitchell, but she immediately abandoned the notion as too cruel. "I don't think there's any rhyme or reason when it comes to death's choices," she said glumly. "As for those of us left standing, it's all a matter of luck."

Paris, France

Louis strode across the parquet floor to where the two American judges on the Jury of Awards sat waiting behind an elaborate desk.

Judge Riordan looked up. "Mr. Louis Tiffany?"

Louis bowed with the military precision he'd perfected during his years at Eagleswood Academy. Only the continuous rubbing together of the forefinger and thumb of his right hand gave away the true state of his nerves.

Riordan shifted his attention to Henry and motioned him forward. I take it you are Mr. Belknap, the art director at Tiffany Glass and Decorating?

"Yes, sir," Henry replied, taking his place alongside Louis.

Judge Getz cleared his throat. "Mr. Tiffany, we are not here to question the quality of the fine works of art that you've presented to the exposition— that much is evident in light of your overwhelming success." He shuffled through a stack of papers, selected two sheets from the bottom and read:

"Louis Comfort Tiffany has been awarded three grand prix, ten gold medals, ten silver, six bronze and . . ." Getz brought the paper closer as if not believing his eyes, ". . . and you have been named Chevalier de la Légion d'Honneur for your Favrile glass." He put the paper aside, clearing his throat. "I am sure it was only an oversight on your part, Mr. Tiffany, but where it asks for the names of your collaborators—"

Judge Riordan interrupted. "That was the question about collaborators who deserve recognition for services rendered in the design and making of the individual pieces? In that space, Mr. Tiffany, you entered your name and the name of your company.

"We mean no disrespect, but we must have the specific name of each designer."

Louis looked from one judge to the other, his expression changed to one of confused concern. "Specific name? I'm not sure I understand the inquiry."

The two judges leaned close together, conferring in low whispers. From where he stood, Henry could make out a word or two of the muffled discussion, 'reputation' and 'honor' being the most alarming.

"Mr. Tiffany," Riordan said finally, "the rules of entry clearly state that you are obliged to reveal the full names of your collaborators—the individual creators of the pieces. Considering the great number of items entered by your company, are we to believe that you alone designed every piece in your catalogue?"

With growing apprehension, Henry watched Louis's smile pull down into an expression of haughty indignation.

"You may believe what you wish," Tiffany said, "but I tell you plainly that I am the designer of all—"

Henry leapt toward the judge's table, shouting loud enough to drown out the rest of Louis's declaration. "Excuse me, gentlemen. I think I can explain. The oversight is mine.

"While Mr. Tiffany is the sole designer of a few pieces in the collection, there are, as you correctly presumed, a number of other individuals who designed the bulk of the winning works." He glanced at Louis whose face was frozen in outraged shock, and quickly looked away.

"Of course, all these collaborators work for Tiffany Glass and Decorating Company under the direct supervision of Louis Tiffany. In my haste to make sure the forms were submitted on time, I'm afraid I didn't fully understand what was required. However, now that we know what is needed, Mr. Tiffany and I will gladly supply the names of all the collaborators and a list of the pieces they each designed."

Judge Riordan smiled. "In that case, gentlemen, *le polémique* has been solved."

Henry turned in time to see the fury come to his employer's face. As Louis opened his mouth to begin his tirade, Henry shot him a warning look fierce enough to make him snap it shut.

"I am curious about the windows at the entry of the American pavilion," Getz said, "Are they both your designs, Mr. Tiffany?"

"I designed the *Four Seasons* window," Louis answered tersely. "The other was designed under my personal supervision by one of my employees, although I did most of the—"

Henry interrupted. "*The River of Life* window was designed by the same woman who designed the dragonfly lamp, your Honor."

Riordan's eyes lit up. "Ah, the exquisite dragonfly lamp. What is the woman's name?"

Filled with a sense that justice was being served, Henry responded at once. "Mrs. Clara Driscoll, with Miss Alice Gouvy as her collaborator. I'm certain you'll be hearing more about these two artisans in the future."

Judge Getz gathered his pile of papers and tapped them straight. "Thank you, gentlemen. If you will deliver the list to the clerk at the Jury of Awards office by the end of the day, I'm sure this omission can be overlooked."

Hotel Continental, Paris

Henry waited until Louis was fixed with his brandy and cigar before attempting to break through the wall of silence he'd built between them.

"You are a success, Louis. You've come away with more honors than many of the other exhibitors, including your father. Isn't that reward enough?"

Louis stared out over the Rue de Castiglione without responding.

"People are thronging to see your exhibit, and there's talk of a reception in your honor."

When there still was no reply, Henry dropped all pretenses. "Louis, be reasonable. You have done the honorable thing by giving the names of all your artisans."

"Damn the honorable thing!" Louis swiveled and threw his glass across the room, where it shattered against the corner of a mirror. Brandy and broken glass ran down the maroon wallpaper, leaving long spears of stain.

The vein in his forehead stood out, pulsing with rage. "How dare you!" he yelled, spittle flying with the force of his words. "Your interferenth threatens to ruin me! Once word is out that I'm not the sole designer at Tiffany's, people will thtop . . . stop buying. Siegfried Bing might decide to cancel our contract. I'll be left without a European gallery."

"You have an exaggerated sense of your own fame, Louis. If you're that desperate for praise, then take it for a fact that you have an eye for recognizing and hiring talented artisans."

Louis poured another brandy, drained it, and quickly poured another. "I have a notion to fire you, Belknap. Were it not for your mother's busy mouth and my father's willing ear, I wouldn't hesitate."

"Do as you wish." Henry picked up his hat. "I'm going out to send a wire to Clara and Mr. Nash. They'll be thrilled to know they've won recognition from the Paris jury."

When he thought back on it later, Henry would marvel over how nimbly—how *fast*—Tiffany hurtled across the room and grabbed hold of him.

"Are you out of your mind, Belknap? I forbid you to tell them anything. With Mitchell gone, we have no one there to keep them in line. God only knows what ideas they might have if they think they've won recognition. We could lose them to other companies."

"Not tell them?" Appalled, he shrugged out of Tiffany's grasp, bile rising to the back of his throat. "You would withhold news of their triumphs from them? What about the newspapers? Surely you can't keep news like this from the American press?"

Louis straightened his jacket and pretended to study the glowing end of his cigar. "Don't you worry about the press. I'll make sure the reporters are given all they need to know for now. I'll tell the collaborators about their awards—later."

Henry felt tired, as if he'd been in an overlong fisticuffs match and was losing the round. "What do you plan on telling the reporters?"

"Exactly what I want them to print—that Louis C. Tiffany won many awards and was named Chevalier de la Légion d'Honneur."

———§———

August 26, 1900
44 Irving Place

Hair tucked neatly under their scarves, Clara and Alice moved about on their knees polishing the furniture legs. They were still in the dog days of summer, but according to Alice, there was no reason they should put fall cleaning off until autumn.

"You have to see Point Pleasant seashore," Clara said. "My time at Mrs. Palmié's guesthouse was wonderful." She hesitated. "Well, almost wonderful."

"There was a pea under your mattress?"

"A pea in the form of a five-year-old known as 'Mommy's little buttercup.' By someone's evil design, this child was my across-ways tablemate for the full five days. She had the perverse habit of grinning at me, while patting any piece of food she liked particularly well with the palm of her hand before swallowing it whole."

She waited a moment, then gave Alice a sideways glance. "Actually, I liked the place so much that I inquired about renting one of the cabins for next summer. It would be easy to ferry over to Point Pleasant on Saturday afternoons and return Monday mornings. It really isn't that far from here, and we could be back in the city in no time. Mrs. Palmié said the nicer cabins rent for about twenty dollars a month. I thought that if everyone contributed, we could rent one for a couple of months next summer."

"Why not four months, or even the whole season?" Alice grabbed paper and pencil from the desk. "We'd have a base group of six—you, Edward, Miss Griffin, Miss Nye, Mr. Yorke and I. If we took a place for four months, that's eighty dollars, which comes to just thirteen dollars and some cents each. That's less than four dollars a month."

"Then there would be the regular *sometimes* people," Clara added, her excitement growing, "Henry and George, Mr. McBride, Emily and at least four or five once-in-a-while visitors. We could charge them a dollar each to stay for the weekend."

Clara rested her back against the sofa leg and wrapped her arms around her knees. "We'll have a weekly artists' salon."

"Mr. Yorke and Mr. Booth both know how to fish," Alice said. "That would help lower our food expenses. We could have cook-outs every evening on the beach, and when we didn't want to cook, we could have our meals at Palmié's guesthouse."

At the knock, they looked up to find Mr. Booth and Mr. Yorke standing in the open doorway. "Tell us, gentlemen," Clara said, "just what sort of landlords do you think you'll make?"

October 16, 1900

Lost in concentration, Joseph Briggs was setting mosaic tiles when Clara arrived. He flinched at the sound of the door closing behind her.

"Sorry, didn't mean to scare you," she said, unpinning her hat in front of the mirror. "You must have been up late reading *Frankenstein* again; that sort of book always makes me jumpy. The first time I read it, I couldn't sleep for days. I—" Catching sight of his reflection she whirled around. One side of his face was covered in dark bruises, his eye swollen closed. The lump on the side of his head was so large as to make his hair stick straight out. "Joseph! What happened?"

"Mrs. Briggs." He could barely move his lips, the bottom one being split. "She got into a snit."

"This looks more like a war than a snit. What possible cause could she have had to do this to you?"

"I was late coming home from work. One of the children was sick. She thought I was shirking my duties. She thought I'd been . . ." He waved a hand, "It doesn't matter."

"What about your eye? Have you been to a doctor?"

When he didn't answer, she sighed. "This is your vision; it's essential to your work. You have to see an oculist immediately."

She wrote something on the back of her calling card. "Take a cab to this address, and see Dr. Anderson. Don't come back until you've been treated. If he tells you to rest your eyes, then you must. I'll manage without you."

Joseph shook his head, "We're too busy. Mr. Tiffany has already been in once this morning looking for you, and he didn't seem happy."

"Mr. Tiffany is rarely happy unless he's torturing me. Go see Dr. Anderson." She handed him his hat and pushed him toward the door. "When you return, we'll decide what to do."

Hours later, she was preoccupied with putting the finishing touches to a mosaic mantle clock, when Tiffany entered and placed a flat box and a large envelope on her desk without comment. She searched his face for some indication of what might be in them, got none, and opened the box first. On a bed of red velvet, two bronze medals lay side by side. Depicted on the face of each was the winged figure of Victory, holding a palm branch and laurel wreath and carrying the winner on her back. Circling the image was inscribed, 'Exposition Universelle Internationale 1900.' Underneath was her name in raised letters.

The envelope held the two official diplomas from the Jury of Awards: one for the work she'd done for Charles Tiffany, and one for the dragonfly lamp.

"I prefer you not display these," Tiffany said flatly. "Take them to your boardinghouse. Better yet, send them to your mother."

"But what about the rest of my department? It would mean so much to them to have these in the workroom. They deserve to see these and be proud of what they've done."

"No. It will only cause trouble and resentments—mostly aimed at you."

"That's an absurd assumption. The Tiffany Girls aren't . . . " She meant to say her women weren't a petty, spiteful bunch like the men, but thought better of it. "My girls are a fair-minded and decent lot. They don't harbor jealousies or resentments."

"You are far too sentimental about your workers. Take care not to place too much confidence in them, lest you invite dishonesty and bring heartache to yourself."

"It's my confidence in them that insures their loyalty," she said defiantly. "I wouldn't think of treating them in any other way."

"I don't give a fig for their loyalty," he snarled. "These things are not to be shown about anywhere in this building! Do you understand?"

She wheeled on him, eyes burning. "You mean unlike your medals? The ones on display in the showroom?"

He jabbed a finger at her, his eyes narrowed. "You go too far. I don't like disrespect in a woman, and I find it particularly unbecoming in you!"

When he was gone, she sat for a spell, watching the women as they arrived for work in their usual clusters of two and three. Listening to their laughter and good-natured teasing, she realized how much she'd grown to love them. Her respect for them and how hard they worked at times meant more to her than the work itself.

Rebellion seeped into every part of her. With resolve, she pulled her jacket from the rack and went in search of the nearest street vendor.

Gramercy Park

The Tiffany Girls, Mr. Briggs, Mr. Bracey and Frank sat under the chestnut trees enjoying their catered lunch of coffee, hot buttered corn, baked potatoes and sausage.

Their pleasure at being treated to a hot meal away from the workroom was well worth the price she'd paid the vendor. When the last morsel was consumed, she brought out the medals and diplomas and passed them around.

"We should hang the diplomas over the door of the workroom," Miss Hawthorne suggested. "We can build the frames, and picture glass costs nothing."

Miss Griffin raised her hand. "While we're at it, we can make a glass display case for the medals and put it on the cup shelf by the door so it's the first thing a person sees when they come in."

"These fine awards won't be sharin' no shelf with anythin' else," Mr. Bracey said. "Ya can be sure I'll be buildin' them medals their own pedestal."

There were murmurs of approval.

Steeling herself, Clara held up a hand. "More than anything, I wish we could do those things in celebration of our work. Unfortunately, the Tiffany Powers That Be have requested we not make a show of our awards. In fact, they've made it an order. I was told not to show these even to you, but as we're not on Tiffany property, I doubt there's much they can do about it."

A profound silence fell over the women; the only sounds to be heard were the birds and the rustle of fallen leaves in the wind.

Miss Griffin broke the silence, "What earthly reason could they possibly have to deny us this small pleasure?"

Their chorus of unhappy protests made her heart ache. At a loss, she sank onto the bench. "If it's any comfort, I'm sure Mr. Nash, Miss Gouvy and the men's department are all being given the same edict."

Joseph, his bandages replaced by a distinguished black patch, rose from the bench and removed his hat. "Instead of grieving over closeted medals and such like, we should instead dwell on the fact that fifty million people saw and appreciated the things we made. A panel of the most astute judges thought our work worthy of worldwide recognition.

"There can be no doubt that we've accomplished something extraordinary. Let Tiffany and his toadies hide our medals—no one can take away our pride of accomplishment."

Cheering, the women crowded around to shake his hand, inadvertently forming a canopy of feathered hats over his head.

Noon at Tiffany's
October 25, 1900

Dear Fellow Robinites,

Forgive me for not keeping our robin looking round and stuffed. We are once more up to our necks in the holiday rush. I manage to hold on to my sanity by taking my bicycle out whenever the chance arises.

In an interesting twist of events, Henry introduced me to Mr. Tiffany's competitor, Richard Lamb of R. & J. Lamb Studios. We were invited to his studios and shown everything they had. I could see right away that their things lacked quality and imagination, so perhaps he intends to make me an offer. If he does, I may take it, though I don't like their shop nearly as well as ours.

I have received the two bronze medals from the Paris Exposition. Miss Owens looked properly impressed when she saw the diplomas and asked if I would frame them for the wall. I told her that I was going to keep them under my bed, and when people called who didn't think much of me, I'd bring them out and show them around.

Many of the others won medals as well: Miss Northrop (1 silver), Arthur Nash (3 silver); but best of all, our own sweet Alice won a bronze under Louis

Tiffany's banner, and a silver under the senior Mr. Tiffany's banner.

I'm having my old black coat cleaned and pressed, and my nearly ragged black skirt and flyaway jacket are to be made over one last weary time by Alice. These will all go toward making a decent suit. My straw hat will look new after a few drops of oxalic acid for the rain spots and a new black ribbon. I found a wing feather in the park and will add that for a touch of whimsy. God knows I need whimsy.

These days, it's a choice between new clothes or finding less expensive lodgings and eating less. If I could earn more money, I would begin plans for my own business. Mr. Tiffany must intuit this, which would explain his reluctance to raise my salary.

I went to Vantine's to buy material for the cat costume I'm making for the Tiffany costume ball. We couldn't get waited on, so went to Wanamaker's instead. I made an all-black velveteen suit that covers me from my ankles to under my chin. For my headpiece, I've sewn together a cat head with green-jeweled eyes, a red sealing wax tongue and two whiskery ears. The tail is long and black, and I shall switch it back and forth when bothered. This arduous project has taught me that I cannot do ANY outside work as long as my work at Tiffany's is so taxing.

Now that Mr. Mitchell is departed, Mr. John Cheney Platt (Treasurer) and Mr. Bond Thomas (General Manager) are having more of a presence around Tiffany's. Mr. Platt likes me and my designs especially well—a lucky thing for me.

Sunday, Henry and I took a train to Yonkers, biked to the Palisades, and then ferried over to Tarrytown through Sleepy Hollow and up the river to Mr. Rockefeller's home at Pocantico Hills. The man who has charge of the place, Mr. Hawks, knows Henry, so showed us all around the place.

When I returned home, I found that Mr. Booth had filled my room with vases of bittersweet, and on my desk he'd left a beautiful hornet's nest. Hopefully there was no underlying meaning to his gifts.

September 29ᵗʰ

I danced holes through my cat feet slippers at the Tiffany ball. Mr. Platt came out of his box and had three dances with me, but I most enjoyed dancing with the boy who dusts the lamps in the stockroom. There were no signs of apron and dusters or servility about him. Slim and young and agile as a monkey, he spun around the floor like a piece of thistledown, conversing meanwhile with the grace and ease (though not the grammar or punctuation) of an ambassador.

Sorry for the delay in sending this off, but I wanted to include details of the ball.

Love, Clara

Lenox Hill
November 18, 1900

Most men my age are settled and content with their lot by now—I am neither. It is an evil flaw that despite all that I have, I cannot find lasting satisfaction in any of it. Even when I am in my garden, some force within me bars tranquility. Then again, perhaps Stanford White is correct when he says there will be plenty of rest once we are dead, so one might as well live to the hilt now.

Louise and I have made a pact: I am to give up drink and in exchange I may reclaim my conjugal rights. She believes this is a fair trade. On my part, it seems a harsh bargain.

Father is not well. As always, I am split between the fear of losing him and the desire to be free of his hold over me.

With Laurelton Hotel burned to the ground, I have finally crushed all opposition and purchased 580 acres of land on Cold Spring Harbor. The plans for my masterpiece are nearly complete. It shall be a synthesis nonpareil of fine, decorative and industrial arts—a showplace and my legacy. L.C.T.

~20~

February 5, 1902

Dearest Ones,

You can imagine how surprised Rev. Cutler and I were to read in the daily news how Edwin Waldo, supposed dead these last four and a half years, was found alive and well in San Francisco. Only for the sake of his poor mother am I glad of this news. We are curious to know details and are surprised that there was no mention in your last letter, considering that the story has been printed in every newspaper in the country.

Kate is home from Academy so that we might try and cure her of these troublesome stomach pains. The doctor is to see her on Tuesday. She is weak and quite changed in appearance, but with our care, our prayers, and wholesome food she will soon be well. Rev. Cutler and I took her to see Sir Henry Irving and Ellen Terry perform in "The Merchant of Venice," to occupy her mind. It did her good.

Love, Mama

Tiffany's
February 12, 1902

Dearest Family,

I didn't write about Mr. Waldo, because I wanted to be sure of my details, which I have only now had from George.

Dr. Dickenson, a family friend of the Waldos, was in San Francisco and ran into Edwin on the street quite by chance. When pressed to explain himself, Edwin gave the following story: In brief, he claims to have come to consciousness down on the Mississippi, below the point to which the detectives had traced him in early September 1897, having no recollection of events after November of 1896. This seems incredible, for we were with him before Election Day and after, and there was no chain of thought that was fractured or forgotten.

When he came to himself he claimed he could only do the simplest manual labor and felt in this condition he might better be dead to his family and friends. He worked where he could, and finally enlisted in the Army, going to Manila (under an assumed name), and was transported to California. He gained in health and then took a job in a copper mine in Northern California, where he is now employed pleasantly and profitably, although he claims to be intent on joining the ministry.

How much of this is true, we will probably never know. In his present condition, no one would have a right to confine him in an asylum— unfortunately. This has all told on George, who feels the responsibility and disgrace to his core. I'm grateful that the newspapers referred to me only as a 'former fiancé' and did not drag our good family name through the mud.

My feeling in this matter is wholly of sympathy for George. Anything more than that ended for me years ago. My personal feeling could not be anything but that of deepest gratitude that I escaped. Rest assured, I shall never again entangle myself in such folly. I'm quite settled on that score, Mama, so you must place your hopes for grandchildren solely on Kate, as Emily seems to be married to her studies and I to my work at Tiffany's.

I've negotiated my salary with Mr. Tiffany and Mr. Platt to $5.80 per day, or, $35 per week. The best thing is that I'm no longer restricted to hours, but to a definite result, so that I can go and come as I please. Mr. Tiffany *continues to expect the unusual and dramatic from me without any reference to cost. It's perhaps just as well that Mr. Mitchell is no longer with us.*

As with the Paris Exposition debacle, Mr. Tiffany has been working us day and night on the pieces for the International Exhibition in Turin, Italy, which is based on 'Art in Useful Things.' My wisteria and pond lily lamps are to be entered in the competition. The pond lily lamp is fast becoming Tiffany's biggest seller. If this success keeps up, I may have to buy larger hats for my swollen head—won't the evil milliners love that?

Presently, I'm working on the butterfly candle shade and milkweed powder box in silver. If truth be told, nearly every Tiffany piece you see around is something I've designed.

I'm sending a hot water bottle and some abdominal support bandages to help relieve Kate's discomfort. I'm also sending a hand-colored photo of Mr. Briggs and me hard at work in my studio.

Henry has finally quit Tiffany's for good and is now fully occupied by his venture with Joseph Taft in opening the Taft and Belknap Gallery. I'm green with envy.

On a happy note, we have all agreed to rent a cabin in Point Pleasant for the whole season—a bargain at $75.

Love, Clara

P.S. I have decided to rent out my bathing costume for $1.00 per use.

T○ BREAK UP the monotony of her work, Mr. Booth instituted a monthly ritual of escorting Clara to places she'd never been. That a foreigner knew the city better than she put her off at first, but she soon found herself eagerly looking forward to the adventures.

It was a beautiful moonlit night, perfect, Edward said, for taking their wheels over to the St. Nicholas artificial indoor skating rink on Sixty-sixth Street, where they could watch the graceful young men of St. Nicholas and Brooklyn Skating Clubs battle it out for control of the puck.

The moment the agile heroes of the ice were gone, hundreds of spectators poured onto the ice like so much smooth-flowing lava. Organ music filled the air, as pretty girls in bicycle costumes and handsome men in thick sweaters skated effortlessly over the ice.

"Are you ready?" Edward touched her shoulder.

"Can't we stay a while longer?" Clara pleaded, not taking her eyes off the skaters. "It's fascinating the way they make all this elegant fluidity seem effortless. I want to see how they do it."

"I intend that you shall see exactly how they do it, Mrs. Driscoll. I didn't mean that we should leave, I'm asking if you're ready to go out on the ice."

She turned to find a pair of black skates dangling from his fingers.

"I had to rent a men's size for you, but I dare say it's better to be embarrassed and comfortable, than socially correct and have your toes broken."

"I don't know how to skate." She looked from him to the skaters. "I could never do that."

"You can, and you will," Edward said, leading her to a bench. "I'll teach you to skate in the same manner as I've taught hundreds of others. There's nothing to it; if you can walk, you can skate."

She let him lace up her skates, listening to his detailed instructions on keeping her balance and controlling her ankles. Seconds later he led her out to the middle of the rink, where she at once began floundering in a ridiculous manner, while a procession of lithe youths and maidens swept around her like fairies floating on air.

"Don't look at your feet!" Edward barked, struggling to keep them both upright. "Don't stick your stomach out like that! Lean forward and look graceful! For God's sake, can't you see how these other people do it?"

Her mouth puckered with annoyance. "Don't you yell at me! Is this how you teach people to skate? By bullying them? I do see how the others do it, but if I manage to stay in an upright position, it's a cause for celebration, not criticism!"

His arm around her waist, Edward pushed her forward. "Stop wobbling! Pick up your foot and push yourself forward with your other foot. Take it slow and easy. No hurry. Just glide like a swan, smooth and . . ."

She was suddenly moving forward much faster than she wanted. All around her the skaters were like demons, whizzing by at alarming rates of speed. She looked down and lost her balance, pulling Edward almost off his skates. For a few seconds, they did a mad dance with tottering legs and arms flung haphazardly about.

"I told you," he growled, "never look down at your feet! My God, you look slender, and you walk and ride with a certain amount of grace, so that I supposed you'd be light on your feet, but I swear Clara, you must weigh five hundred pounds!"

She twisted away from the arm steadying her, shouting above the music, "You are quite unfair, Mr. Booth! You brought me here to humiliate me, and I won't have it!"

Picking up her feet, she skated against the circling crowd, successfully weaving around the other skaters, only faintly cognizant of a sensation that was akin to flying downhill on her bicycle. As she reached the railing and was about to step off the ice, she was staggered by the sudden realization that she'd skated a quarter of the way around the rink without losing her balance.

Over her shoulder she saw Edward standing in the middle of the circling crowd applauding, his approving grin directed at her.

Clara flicked the snow off her gloves. "You seem to have undertaken my physical training, Mr. Booth. First, the bicycle, and now, skating. All my various sides will be developed by the time you're done with me." She stooped to pry her feet out of her boots.

"We'll have you training in fisticuffs next," Edward teased. "That might come in particularly handy when dealing with the characters at Tiffany's. When you've finished with that, we'll look into diving and kite flying."

Someone flung open the foyer door, knocking her off her feet. She would have gone headfirst into the wall, had Edward not caught her.

She brushed herself off. "For goodness sakes, watch how you come into a place! You could have killed—"

The man removed his hat, and the reproach died on her tongue. It was the most amazing face she'd ever seen. His jaw, straight nose and strikingly sensuous mouth were so artistically without flaw that she was tempted to touch him to make sure he was real.

"I do apologize," he said. "It was thoughtless of me to have charged in like that." He helped her to her feet with an elegant movement. He was lean, and taller than she by several inches. "I hope I haven't caused any permanent damage."

She shook her head, staring at him, the power of speech having abandoned her.

Puzzled, he looked to Edward who, in turn, looked at Clara.

When she still didn't respond, he extended his hand. "I'm Philip Loring Allen. I've just moved in."

Introducing himself, Edward shook the offered hand. Both men turned to her. Vaguely aware something was expected of her, she looked to Edward for assistance.

"This is Mrs. Clara Driscoll," Edward said, giving her a quizzical glance. "We've just come from the skating rink where she's in training."

Mr. Allen shook her hand looking faintly amused. "Are you thinking of joining up with the hockey leagues, Mrs. Driscoll?"

Collecting her wits, she gave him her brightest smile. "Not unless the rules change to include playing the game on all fours," she replied. "I believe what Mr. Booth euphemistically calls my training is another way of saying that he pushes me around the rink, rather like a perambulator or an invalid's chair."

She couldn't recall which man suggested they sit in the parlor and share a pot of tea, but she was glad for it. As Mr. Allen spoke of his journey from the University of Wisconsin to New York, he impressed her as a marvelous speaker who knew how to phrase things to make everything seem new and interesting. He was obviously well-read, for he knew a fair amount about every subject they touched on.

Edward brought in a second pot of tea and refilled their cups. "Mr. Allen, you must tell us all about the position that so completely occupies your time that none of us has met you before this."

"I'm a journalist and a writer," Philip replied. "I started at the *Evening Post* as a reporter, and then went on to be exchange editor and Washington correspondent. I mostly do political writing, but I also write stories with a social conscience for *Scribner's*."

He moved forward in his chair, the light of the flames falling softly on his face as he turned toward her. She caught the scent of his shaving soap—bay rum—and breathed it in as deeply as she could without being obvious. When she dared to look directly into his eyes, a wave of heat began in her thighs and traveled up her body into her throat, where it gained a voice in the form of a quiet moan. Whatever emotion he'd touched in her was not one with which she was familiar.

"I understand you're an artist, Mrs. Driscoll?"

Pulling herself up straight she coughed, willing herself to say something that would demonstrate that she was a sensible woman and not some young ninny taken in by his good looks. "I'm an artist of sorts," she said, blushing furiously. "I design things."

"Clara's modesty only extends as far as first introductions," Edward said good-naturedly. "Don't let her fool you, Mr. Allen; her designs are what keep Louis Tiffany's company alive. Her work has won awards at the Paris Exposition, and I'm sure she'll take the upcoming Turin exhibition, as well."

"I admit that I already knew about your triumphs in Paris," Philip said. "I wanted to find out if *you* did."

She drew back to see if he was teasing. "How could you possibly have known that? I don't believe my name was ever mentioned in the newspapers."

For an instant, Mr. Allen seemed unsure of himself. He looked briefly at his long fingers twined together in his lap. "I'm a journalist, Mrs. Driscoll. It's my business to know what goes on in the world. Actually, if you don't mind, I'd like to hear about your work. I greatly admire those whose talents are in the visual arts."

He listened with rapt attention as she spoke of patterns and cartoons, molds and cames, and how the glass was selected and cut. When she finished, she looked up to find him staring. She thought of her rough, too-large hands and her inelegant clothes and burned with embarrassment.

Edward looked at his pocket watch, yawned and rose from the settee. "Isn't anyone else tired? It's nearly midnight."

Disbelieving, Clara glanced at the mantle clock; it felt like only minutes since they'd met in the foyer. "I'd like to spend the rest of the night in conversation," she said rising. "Unfortunately, Mr. Tiffany expects me at seven tomorrow morning to go over the final entries for his Turin exhibit."

"I don't think you'll need worry about being on time." Mr. Allen shrugged into his overcoat. "Mr. Charles Tiffany is in a bad way and not expected to live out the weekend."

She stared at him. "Are you sure? Mr. Tiffany gave no indication that his father was ill."

"I received word from one of the Tiffany staff last night." He wrapped his scarf about his neck. "I should have been at my office an hour ago writing up an account of Mr. Tiffany's life, so it will be ready for print as soon as he passes."

"You're going to your office now? In the middle of the night?"

"This is the best time to write, when it's still and the only things I have to contend with are my own thoughts. It's similar to how your work is best done in natural light."

Edward cleared his throat. "Well, sir, I wish you a good night and good writing."

Afraid he might vanish and she would never see him again, Clara followed Mr. Allen to the door. "If you can find the time, please consider yourself welcome to join our group. Most of us are on the second and third floors at the front. My room is the usual gathering place. I can't tell you exactly what it is we talk about or what adventures we have, but I can guarantee that whatever we say or do is usually pretty lively."

"If you get lost," Edward said, "Ask anyone you see to direct you to Clara Driscoll's Impromptu Salon for Lively Dilettantes."

She could not sleep for thoughts of Mr. Allen. Tossing about, first too hot, then too cold, Clara finally gave in and called to mind every line of his face, every gesture, every word spoken. She luxuriated in the memory of his voice and the scent of bay rum, until she remembered how she'd stumbled over introducing herself.

Her embarrassment deepened when she realized that, as a journalist, Mr. Allen might know the details of the Edwin Waldo story. The humiliation of it drove her out of bed. Crossing her arms over her flannel nightgown, she paced about the room, hoping to exhaust herself enough to sleep.

Philip Loring Allen. She liked the way the names rolled off her tongue, round and smooth. He'd charmed her, frightened her and made her laugh. His fire and his intelligence intrigued her.

Bone weary, she climbed back into bed and tried not to think about him. She couldn't let herself be drawn in; she had work to do and a reputation to maintain. Romance was a sticky wicket—it had failed her in the past, or, more than likely, she had failed romance. Either way, she was better off remaining a widow.

Determined not to give the man another thought, she fell asleep an hour before she had to rise, her dreams betraying her with visions of Philip Allen.

Lenox Hill
February 18, 1902

Father dead this day, my fifty-fourth birthday. I am released from the
Reign of the Iron Hand. My sisters and I are handsomely rewarded for our
forbearance. From this day forward, I shall have complete control of both
Tiffany and Company and Tiffany Glass and Decorating, and run them as
I please. My restaurants will be four-star, my railroad cars private, and my
hotel and liner suites, imperial.

But most importantly, without that controlling, strangling hand, I am
now free to spend all I like on creating beautiful things for the world to
enjoy. That, I solemnly promise. L.C.T.

Noon at Tiffany's
March 26, 1902

Dearest Family,

Emily, we all read your story, 'Poppa's Mistake,' in The Century. *I'm*
so proud of you. Even Mr. Tiffany read and liked it. Our resident writer,
Mr. Philip Allen, (In my mind I think of him as Philip the Fair, after King
Philip IV of France) said it was well done; he ought to know: besides
his reporting for the Evening Post, *his stories and political commentaries*
have appeared in Leslie's Magazine, Scribner's, Saturday Evening Post,
Harper's, The Century, *and* The Black Cat.

Kate, I'm so sorry about your hair. Miss Griffin suggests rubbing
Vaseline into your scalp twice a day. Once this peritonitis is cleared up, I'm
sure you'll grow it all back. It's encouraging that you're only sometimes in
pain and can sit up. My doctor has prescribed quinine and whiskey for my
headaches. Perhaps this will work for your stomach pain as well.

Please come to Point Pleasant this summer. I'll teach you how to
swim. You'll be restored to health before you know it. I'll send the wallpaper
stencils next week to keep you occupied for the time being.

Mr. Platt is having one of my novelty inkbottle and pen tray sets manufactured by the hundreds. They sell for $10 each. The inkbottle is a poppy blossom of red glass, and the stopper is of black and purple in the form of the center stamen and seedpod. It makes for a lovely gift.

Mama, Mr. Booth has gone over your contract for the oil furnace with an attorney, and they both think it's a swindle. He says he can get a hot water furnace for much less and that they are better for your health than hot air.

We have another challenging play from Mr. Yorke. A Chinese play— in Chinese. Mr. Allen, who has had theatrical training at the University of Wisconsin, will be directing. He is brilliant!

With Love, Clara

P.S. George's illustrations for 'The Mountain Matchmaker' in The Century *will be published sometime between May and October. I was the model for 'the girl,' but I don't think it looks one bit like me.*

July 6, 1902
Point Pleasant Seashore, NJ

The summer cast a tranquil spell over their world, making simple pleasures all that was required to make life complete. Their cabin and the Palmié guesthouse were filled to capacity. The women slept two to a bed upstairs, while the men slept downstairs and on whatever available space they could find. Edward set up a hammock in the kitchen, so as not to disturb anyone when he rose at five a.m. to catch the fish for their morning meal.

By the end of their first day, they'd voted five to one to have Mr. Yorke as Point Pleasant General Manager instead of Edward, their complaint being that Edward was too task-oriented and not enough pleasure-bent to allow them time for quiet reading and long naps.

He didn't object to having his title seized, but soon found it difficult to sit idle and let Mr. Yorke and the others do all the work, the worst of it being that he wasn't allowed to tell the men *how* to do it. Taking pity, they agreed to let Edward catch breakfast, lunch and dinner. At once

Philip volunteered to accompany him to give instructions on the scientific approach to fishing.

Clara tagged along to watch the competition and play referee, should one be necessary. For two hours, she listened to their boasting about how one had caught more fish than the other had ever seen. Philip repeatedly threw out his line, discoursing all the while on the art of fishing *scientifically*, while Edward caught two flounders and three bucktail flukes.

Back on shore, Edward gave Philip careful instruction on the scientific way to gut and clean a fish.

After lunch, they all adjourned to the beach where Alice, her luxuriant black hair freshly washed, sat in a scarlet kimono reading a volume of Henry James. At her feet, Philip rubbed lemon juice into his hands to rid them of the fish odor, at the same time having a rousing debate with Miss Nye about women's right to vote; he being for the idea, while Miss Nye held that most women would not be able to cope with the responsibility of political decision.

Clara unfolded the latest round robin and commenced to read Kate's part.

. . . *According to the doctor, there are so many other worse diseases I could have had, that I consider myself lucky to just have peritonitis. Clara, you're so good to send money for our new furnace, and we're grateful to Mr. Booth, et al, for assistance in avoiding a swindle. Mama says his letters are the most enjoyable part of her week. He does make us laugh with his stories. I hope—*

A shadow came between her and the sun. Clara looked up to find Mrs. Palmié, a tall, robust woman, standing over her, looking as though the family dog had died. As the capable proprietress of a busy guesthouse, this woman wasn't often given to fits of worry. She put down the letter, endeavoring to remain calm.

"I'm sorry Clara, but Mr. Tiffany called. He asked me to tell you and Alice that it's of the utmost importance that you return to work immediately. He wants both of you and someone by the name of Miss Northrop in his office tomorrow at nine sharp. He was adamant that you be on time. He kept repeating, 'Nine a.m. sharp! Do you understand? Nine a.m. sharp!'"

"What could Tiffany be thinking?" Philip said, after the initial groans of protests had died away. "Wasn't it his decision to give you the week off? Perhaps he meant next Monday."

"No, he was quite clear," Mrs. Palmié said. "He wants them in there tomorrow morning."

"Did he sound. . ." Clara stopped herself before she could say 'drunk'. It was, after all, only one in the afternoon. "Reasonable?"

Mrs. Palmié paused. "Reasonable?"

"What Clara means to ask," Alice said, shielding her eyes from the sun, "is, did Mr. Tiffany sound as though he'd breakfasted with the brandy bottle?"

Mrs. Palmié thought for a moment. "No. As a matter of fact, he sounded more like he *needed* a drink."

Clara began gathering up her things. "I'll take the next ferry. Something serious must have happened at the factory or the shop. He promised he wouldn't call unless it was a matter of life and death."

Philip briefly touched the small of her back. Without thinking, she pushed against him so his arm slipped around her waist. "There isn't any reason to go in now. You and Alice can return with me first thing in the morning. We'll arrive at Miss Owens's in plenty of time."

Lillian Palmié looked up from her embroidery hoop. "Anyhow, you can't leave; you're the only one brave enough to lead us in the discussion on *Dorian Gray*, and how it pertains to the current state of society."

"If you go now," Philip said, "you'll miss Mr. Yorke's sailing lesson and my tutorial on how to fish scientifically."

"I agree with all arguments," Alice said. "There's nothing to be gained by our going into the city today, so we may as well have one more afternoon and evening of relaxation. I'm sure whatever the problem is, we'll be there in plenty of time to save Mr. Tiffany and his company from ruin, just as we have so many times before. Finish your letter. We can worry about what Master Legree has in store for us tomorrow."

They were again drawn back to the beach, this time to watch the full moon rise out over the water like a great gold ball. Mr. Yorke softly played the harmonica, while Marion Palmié read aloud the last few chapters of *Dorian Gray*.

Just as Dorian plunged the knife into his portrait, Philip pulled Clara to her feet and danced her down to the beach. They strolled barefoot in the surf, held spellbound by the silver moonglade cutting across the water.

"What do you think Louis wants of you this time?"

She shrugged, concentrating on the moon and the sound of the waves instead of his physical proximity. "It could be anything. Mr. Tiffany is a man of many surprises. Whatever it is that he wants, it's going to be a challenge. Chaos is what drives him, and because of that, he believes it should drive everyone, especially me."

"And, what exactly *does* drive you, Mrs. Driscoll?"

"Nature," she answered in earnest, "and making beautiful things."

Philip swung her around to face him. "If you weren't dependent on your salary, and if Mr. Tiffany were not so dependent upon you, would you still work yourself to exhaustion to make these beautiful things? Surely you'd follow more pleasurable pastimes?"

"Tell me, Philip, why do you write about social activism?"

"Because I have to—it's my passion."

She went ahead of him. "Then we understand each other. Were I as wealthy as Mr. Tiffany, I would still work at my art—it's what I was meant to do."

"Clara?"

She heard his intent, and her skin pebbled with gooseflesh.

His maneuvering brought her around so that she was again facing him. In the moonlight, he seemed dream-like. "You are like no other woman I have ever met."

There were a hundred clever things she could have said that would break the tension of the moment and deflect his attentions, but she could not make herself form the words.

He entwined his fingers with hers and brought her hand to his lips. "I want to spend time with you alone, away from the others."

"I don't think that's wise. You need to concentrate on your writing, and I need to continue with my work."

He embraced her, and for a brief moment she gave in, letting her body relax against his. His warmth and the strength of his arms as they enclosed her in an embrace felt strangely like a home she'd searched for all her life.

"I want to know who you are," he whispered. "I want to be more to you than just one of the group."

She fought the desire to let him kiss her. "Don't do this." She pulled away. "I don't trust myself with romance. You scare me—my feelings for you scare me. I find myself thinking of you when I should only be thinking of my work. I shouldn't even be with you now. It's—"

His eyes suddenly focused on something behind her.

She turned in time to see a man loom out of the darkness walking his bicycle. His shirt and hair were soaked with sweat, and he looked on the brink of exhaustion, as if he'd come a long way. He raised a work-roughened hand in greeting. "I hear there's a county fair somewhere hereabouts."

"About a mile that way." Philip pointed in the direction of the town. "Follow the path along the shoreline."

The man tipped his hat murmuring his thanks, and then whistled three times. From the bushes came a raggedy barefoot boy of about twelve. "Come on," the man called, mounting his wheel. The boy, tipping his cap at them, ran after the bicycle, whooping and waving his hands as he went.

Grateful for the interruption and inspired by the child's spirit, Clara snatched Philip's handkerchief from his waistcoat and twisted around in the sand. "Come on," she said, already running in the direction of the group. "Let's see if you can catch me."

———§———

At precisely nine a.m. the following morning, Clara, Alice and Agnes Northrop filed into Mr. Tiffany's office. Messrs. Platt and Thomas sat casually chatting, while Louis paced, hands clasped behind him.

They'd barely taken their seats, when Louis began. "I apologize for calling you back from your vacations, ladies, but we're faced with an urgent situation that requires your assistance. Tiffany's has received a request from the Astors for six landscape windows. I know each of you understands how important it is that we give them exactly what they want."

Clara tilted her head in concern—the landscape windows were the exclusive domain of the men's department.

"What Mr. Tiffany is getting at, ladies," Mr. Platt said, rising from his chair, "is that we've run into some trouble with the men's department."

"They won't take on the job." Louis bristled, as if still unable to believe they'd refused him. "They insist it's not possible."

"Not possible?" Miss Northrop frowned.

"That's absurd," Alice said derisively. "Six landscape windows are a simple, straightforward task."

"Unless," Clara said, "there are extenuating circumstances such as . . ." She looked from Louis to Mr. Platt ". . .time restraints? How many weeks do we have?"

"Not weeks—six *days*," Mr. Thomas said.

Incredulous, Miss Northrop shook her head, the vein in the middle of her forehead visibly throbbing. "Six windows in six days? The men are correct. It cannot be done."

The heavy silence that followed was broken when Clara pushed back her chair and stood. "We accept the assignment. You shall have your six windows six days from today."

Mouths agape, Alice and Agnes stared at her.

"By God, Mrs. Driscoll!" Louis hooted, "I knew you'd rise to it!" He turned to the men. "What did I tell you? The woman is a marvel!"

Clara raised her voice above his. "Before you get too far in your praises, Mr. Tiffany, my department will agree to this challenge only if the following conditions are met."

Quickly calculating what she could ask for in this careful game of give and take, she held up a hand and ticked off her demands, one per finger.

"First, Miss Gouvy, Miss Northrop, Mr. Briggs, and I are to work together in making the designs without any oversight or cane criticisms from you.

"Second, every person in my department who works on this project must receive an extra ten cents an hour for every hour they work in the next six days.

"Third, lunch and coffee are to be provided for every person in my department each day including today, so that we don't have to stop what we're doing in order to hunt up sustenance. Taking into account that the men's department is given free beer every day, it seems only fair.

"Last, once we've completed the assignment, we are to have the following two Saturdays off. You may call them congratulatory holidays or whatever you please, but my girls must have time to recuperate."

The outraged refusal on the tip of his tongue, Tiffany opened his mouth to let fly, when Mr. Platt held up a hand.

"That sounds entirely reasonable to me, Mrs. Driscoll. You give us our six windows in six days, and I and Mr. Tiffany will personally see to it all your demands are fully met."

Beaming with satisfaction, Mr. Platt shook hands with the three women, never once giving Louis Tiffany so much as a glance.

Clara told her department about the extra benefits before telling them about what Alice officially dubbed the 'Six in Six Project.'

"It will mean working twelve full hours each day. I know you're apprehensive, but—"

"Scared out of our wits is more like it," shouted one of the girls at the back of the room.

When their nervous twittering ceased, Clara resumed, "It will be an onerous task, and we *are* taking a risk. However, if we meet this challenge, it will be a shining accomplishment. The men insist the project is not possible. The fact of the matter is that it's not possible for *them*. It *is* possible for *us*. To date, we've met all of Mr. Tiffany's challenges and come out ahead."

The women began to applaud, but she held up a hand. "Keep in mind that the reason we've won out over every arduous, maddening task is that Tiffany's Women's Department and the Tiffany Girls are the best."

This time when they cheered, she didn't stop them.

It wasn't ten minutes later that Mr. Bracey and Joseph tracked her to the glass racks, where she was selecting the pieces they would need. The moment she saw them, she knew the trouble had already started.

Joseph spoke first. "It's the men's manager, Mr. Fitzgerald. He must have known something was afoot, when he saw the three of you come in this morning."

"Yes," she said, trying to ignore the ache behind her eyes. "He came into the workroom while I was explaining what we're up against."

"Aye," Mr. Bracey said, "I saw him leave. Ya could see the steam risin' off the top of his head."

She removed her spectacles and rubbed her eyes. "He's been sore about the women's department since the day it opened. Mr. Mitchell once said he blames me personally for everything that goes wrong with the company. However, for now, we need to concentrate on the job at hand and regard Mr. Fitzgerald and his bullies as harmless garter snakes and continue walking forward."

Mr. Bracey scratched under his cap. "Ya can be thinkin' what ya please, Miss, but if ya don't mind, I'll be sendin' up a prayer that the serpent don't come round to strike ya in the back."

August 2, 1902

Edward removed his shoes and noiselessly crossed the darkened room. "I've come from the chemist," he whispered. "He gave me aspirin powder; he said it's much more effective at curing headaches than quinine and whiskey. Miss Owens mixed it with lemonade to make it easier to swallow.

"If you like, I can read London's *Son of the Wolf* until you fall asleep."

She swallowed the too sweet concoction and lay back. "I don't think I'm up for a book, but perhaps you could just talk for a bit."

"That's easy enough." Edward settled himself on an ottoman next to her. "I've received news from London about my brother, Cecil, and his vacuum cleaning machine. It seems that King Edward and Queen Alexandra heard about the miraculous powers of his invention and invited him to give them a demonstration at Buckingham Palace."

She sat up. "King Albert Edward the Seventh. . .of *England?*"

"Is there another?" Edward smiled. "According to Cecil, the king is quite a jolly fellow, and Queen Alexandra is a most attractive woman. The real news is that they were so impressed by what they saw, they commissioned him to clean the coronation carpets in Westminster Abbey for the crowning next week, and purchased two of his machines for permanent use at Buckingham Palace and Windsor Castle."

Edward shook his head. "Who would have thought little Cecil would be invited to tea by the King and Queen of England?"

"You must be so proud of him." She swung her legs over the side of the couch. "I'm proud of him, and I've never even met him. We'll have a celebration party. We should tell Miss Owens. You know what a zealous Anglophile she is; she'll be sure to make a special dinner."

Philip rapped on the open door. "Miss Owens informs me you're ill with another Tiffany headache, but I've come to say you have to abandon your ills for now."

She let go of Edward's hands. "I'm feeling much better since hearing Edward's wonderful news about his brother. It seems that King—"

Philip clapped Edward on the back. "Sorry, old man, I don't mean to steal your thunder, but Mrs. Driscoll has great cause for a celebration of her own." He took Clara by the shoulders, holding her in a firm, proprietary manner that annoyed and thrilled her at the same time. "It took some doing, but I've ferreted out information from one of our men in Turin."

At the mention of Turin, she went still.

"Your wisteria and the pond lily lamps won gold medals. They're the talk of the exposition."

Flooded with exhilaration, she sucked in her breath. "Gold medals? For both? Are you sure?"

"I'm sure," Philip laughed. "The European papers are describing them as 'unique and revolutionary.'"

"Has Mr. Tiffany received the news?" she asked eagerly. "Has he been told?"

"Months ago." Philip reclaimed her hands. "He was notified in June."

Hurt, and then anger clotted in her throat like an iron ball. She closed her eyes, willing herself not to cry.

"You've won the gold." Edward patted her gently on the back. "Don't pay the spiteful old humbug any mind, he's jealous is all. Your lamps inspire people. For an artist, it doesn't come finer than that."

She pushed a few stray tendrils away from her face. "Of course, you're right," she said, reclaiming her elation. "It's a night for celebration all the way around, but right now I'm going to run my wheel down the longest hill I can find with my feet off the pedals."

Tiffany's
December 17, 1902

Dearest Family,

I can't leave until the late train on Wednesday, as my girls and I were stuck with yet another batch of windows that Mr. Tiffany withdrew from the men's department. He feels we do a better job, which is nice, but at the same time adds to our already stretched time budget. Worse, it fuels the men's resentments against my department. Ever since we triumphed on the 'Six in Six Project,' relations between our departments have been strained. One of the men called out an offensive word the other morning as I arrived. It left me feeling low all day.

It's only because Christmas comes on Thursday that I feel I can sneak off to Tallmadge at all. I can work night and day afterward to make up for it—I do that anyway, but never mind. Last month we received an order for 40 dragonfly and 20 wisteria table lamps. Immediately following that was another for 20 conventional peony globes, with each one going for $250 to $750—a fortune in sales.

Mr. Platt asked me to make a watch chain using the sand flea as a model. It's so detailed that it nearly ruined my eyes, but he's very pleased with it, and he is the one person I enjoy pleasing. Added to this, I have to make statistical reports for the 1903 lampshades, besides modeling a $200 inkwell so it can go into the works before I leave.

The last few nights Philip has been coming to my room to play the mandolin and discuss the plots for some stories he's writing. Last night, he remained until after 1 a.m., so I am befuddle-headed today.

I've hired on five more people. The new deaf boy and the pretty Cuban girl do such beautiful, careful work. Our new Italian boy doesn't eat at lunchtime, but instead reads books—he's thin, but smart.

Frank and the new deaf boy have joined in continuing my education in sign language and the alphabet. They have insisted on teaching me phrases that they assure me are the most useful: 'Another beer, please,' 'I want to eat now,' 'Help me get up.' and 'Help! I see a bear coming.'

Kate, when I get home, I'll teach you exercises that may help you stand straight without causing further pain.

I attended the Taft and Belknap gallery opening at 41 E 20th Street with Dudley and Mr. McBride. Henry is so much happier since he left Tiffany's—something I completely understand.

I hear Mr. Tiffany bellowing nearby. He's pushing for more of my designs, and I feel my brain is gradually turning to putty or some equally unproductive substance.

Love to all, Clara

P.S. No, Emily, your 'superior knowledge' doesn't impress (or oppress) me. We all know as much as you, but in subjects other than Latin and mathematics. Our interests lean more toward <u>useful</u> knowledge.

Lenox Hill
December 26, 1902

Construction of Laurelton Hall coming along as well as can be expected during winter. It shall be magnificent— more breathtaking than anything ever built on American soil.

Louise maintains she will never live there, insisting that she prefers the simplicity of The Briars for her summer residence. I've explained the difference between simplicity and unexceptional from an artistic point of view, but to no avail. She does not understand the concept of our station in life. I'm hoping that when she's done with these endless complaints of stomach pain, she'll see reason.

Ensconced in all their petty jealousies over my acquisition of all the lands around Laurelton Hall, the rabble at Oyster Bay continue their dispute over my rights to the five underwater acres at Cold Spring Harbor. Their attempts to thwart my plans for building a seawall and breakwater in order to enlarge my private sand beach below the house will assuredly fail. With some persuading the courts will rule in my favor. Let's see how the scum like that. L.C.T.

~ 21 ~

January 19, 1903

Dear Katie,

    I received your card at the breakfast table today and have made up my mind to come home February 1ˢᵗ. It isn't foolish at all—the Wolcott girls don't have abdominal surgery every day. I'll be there when the doctor takes you into surgery on the 2ⁿᵈ. You may not need my moral support, but you'll enjoy it just the same.

    I'll bring all the carpet and drapery samples that George chose for the parlor. I'm sending on several silk scarves from Vantine's that you can wear until your hair grows out. Let me know if you need anything else. Chin up, dearest; you'll be fit as a fiddle before you know it.

Love, Clara

PS: Remind me to tell you about the American Sculptor's dinner at Madison Square. There were over 10,000 candles burning all at once. Breathtaking!

Tallmadge
January 30, 1903

Clara: Come home at once!

Emily

February 15, 1903

Dearest Clara,

　I expect to rise to the situation gradually, but at present I cannot write much. It was a trial for me, that as good and capable as Kate was, her life seemed humble. You and Emily so easily gathered the renown for brilliance, but Kate served with calm and wisdom. Do you remember how wide open and surprised her eyes were in the moment of death? I think she saw beyond this terrible storm to the land of summer.

　After you left, I went into the parlor and sat in front of her picture, feeling shaken and alone. And yet grievous as our loss is, it would have been worse for her if you had died, than it is for you to lose her. Her life lay largely in you. She was always planning for you, for the times when you were home. Your loss would have made a void in her simple life that nothing could fill.

　Her strength and ability made it easy for me to lie on my oars, but now we must go on as she would have wanted us to.

Love, Mama

Noon at Tiffany's
February 20, 1903

Dear Mama,

　Today for the first time, my mind seems to have adjusted to our loss. We must go on. It occurs to me that people's lives are composed of two great elements, love and work, and through these two expressions of ourselves, we influence others. The reason that Kate's life left such a beautiful impression behind is that she loved spontaneously and unselfishly, creating beauty and peace wherever she went.

　We will continue her work. She loved her home and never tired of making it a beautiful, restful place. Let's keep it so and consider it our tribute to what she was to us. Nothing else we could do would be more pleasing to her.

All my love, Clara

April 6, 1903

CLARA APPROACHED TIFFANY'S dreading the mountain of work that needed to be done, yet knowing that being idle would be worse. She'd always dealt well with tragedy while it was upon her; it was only afterward that the emotions and nerves came crashing down. In the two months since Kate's death, every day seemed a pointless struggle merely to get out of bed. She had lost weight until her face was hollow, and what little sleep did come, was short and fraught with nightmares.

She kept everyone at arm's length. Her door was now kept closed. Whether out of respect for her grief or their discomfort with the stranger she'd become, no one dared to trespass.

Alice slipped daily notes of love and condolence under her door, while Edward left a flower each night. Philip serenaded her from the hallway once a week, and Henry sent a pot of tulips and a copy of *Past and Present*. George came by several times, talking to her through the keyhole until he got tired—or hungry—and went away.

Eventually, Alice managed to get her to a doctor, who diagnosed her with acute melancholia and prescribed she go into seclusion at the Town and Country Club every noon hour, and drink two ounces of whiskey followed by a one-hour nap.

The Tiffany Girls built an invisible shield around her, shouldering and solving all the problems that normally fell to her. At Mr. Platt's suggestion, she hired on Miss Frances, an instructor from the Art Students' League, to work alongside her half days. Once she supplied the designs, Miss Francis was able to lay out the lampshades almost as well as she. When the whiskey-induced headaches proved too painful, Miss Francis suggested she give up the liquor and visit the animals in the park instead.

The ostrich and the camel captivated her. She wasn't clear on why she found such comfort in those two creatures in particular, but Miss Francis suspected it had something to do with the serenity in their eyes.

Occupied by thoughts of zoo animals, she almost missed the four rough-looking men slouched near a corner of the Tiffany building. Their caps were pulled low over their eyes, but she still recognized them as the Union men whose job it was to torment anyone who the Union bosses felt were a threat.

One man pushed himself away from the wall and blocked her path. "Where do ya think yer goin', Clara Driscoll?"

The other men crowded around, their eyes like those of predatory animals on the scent. She straightened her shoulders and glared. If they expected her to run, they would be greatly disappointed—grief had made her immune to fear. "Once you move out of my way, I'll be going in to an honest job, which is more than I can say for you and your bunch."

"Oh don't ya be worryin' none 'bout us, Mrs. Driscoll. We'll be goin' to work, but I ain't so sure 'bout you an' the girls. Won't be long now, you 'n yer bunch'll all be out on the street where ya belong."

Her eyes flicked to the front of the building where Mr. Tiffany and Mr. Platt were walking up the steps. Fighting down the urge to scream, she brought her eyes back to the man slapping his fist against his palm.

"I don't know what you're talking about, and I don't think you do either, so if you'd please move aside and allow me to go on about my business, I'll continue on with my day as if your attempt to delay me never took place."

She stepped to the man's left and was blocked by another, who smelled of beer.

"Go home and leave the honest work to the men, lady. You ain't needed here."

"Get out of my way," she said, making another attempt to step around them.

They closed in on her, one of them kicking at her shins until his boot got tangled in her skirts. Another caught her arm and pushed her face-first into a lamppost. Her spectacles skittered across the sidewalk into the gutter.

Falling to her knees, she grabbed for her glasses and brought her arms up over her head to protect her face. When no blows fell, she opened her eyes and discovered the men were turned away, their attention on an enraged Louis Tiffany charging toward them, his cane slashing the air as he ran. They scattered like cockroaches.

Agile as a cat, Louis cracked two of them across the back. "Filthy scoundrels! Attacking a woman? If you lay another hand on any of my employees again, I'll hunt you down and shoot you myself!"

He helped her to her feet, searching for injury. "Have they hurt you?"

She brushed off her skirt and attempted a smile. "I'm all right, thank you. I think they were only trying to scare me." She let him help her across the street, praying none of the girls had witnessed what happened; it would upset them, and that would require her to spend precious time in calming them down—there was too much work to be done for that.

"They said I no longer had a job. What were they talking about?"

Louis hurried her along. "I should have warned you."

"Warned me?" she pulled back. "Then what they said is true?"

Louis glanced around nervously, "We don't want to discuss this here. These mongrels have spies everywhere. Come upstairs."

The moment they were inside his office, she insisted on an explanation.

"The Glass Cutters Union has issued a demand that your department stop making windows, effective immediately," Tiffany said. "To prove they mean what they say, the large landscape window your department is currently working on was dismantled late last night and moved to the men's department."

"What else? You're keeping something from me. I can see it in your face."

"They want your department shut down altogether. Mr. Platt and I told them we'd rather see every man out of a job for a year than to have that happen."

They were interrupted by a knock. Louis opened the door to find Joseph and Mr. Bracey wearing identical expressions, a sense of urgency wrapped tightly about them.

Before they could tell her what happened, Clara was on her feet and running.

————§————

The workroom was in ruins; tables overturned, easels smashed, glass splintered into thousands of pieces. The worst of the destruction had been reserved for her room, where hate was made visible in the broken windows and the torn sketches scattered over the floor.

At the sight of her flock huddled together, each face pale with the barbarity of the men's show of hatred, something inside her broke. Fleeing the building, she didn't stop running until she reached the safety of Irving Place. She had no conception of time—it might have been hours or maybe only minutes, when someone sat next to her on the couch and started making comforting sounds one might make to a fretful child.

"We'll get through this, Clara," Joe Briggs' voice was choked with emotion. "We can't let them get the upper hand; we need all our strength to fight."

"Did you see what they did?" She pressed the heels of both hands against her temples, the tears sliding down her face. "They destroyed it all. Thousands of dollars worth of glass. All our beautiful lamps, the samples, my designs—everything gone.

"Did Mr. Tiffany and Mr. Platt see what those . . . those depraved creatures did?"

"Yes, and Mr. Thomas, too. Mr. Platt was irate. Mr. Tiffany seemed bereft of reason," Joseph paused, "but not so much that he didn't have the sense to order the girls and Mr. Bracey to start setting things right. He sent for two of the company cleaning ladies and then sent me here to fetch you. He warned me not to return without you."

He stopped her before she could protest. "You know about getting back on the horse that throws you? Mr. Tiffany and Mr. Platt know nothing about how to run your department, and I would never presume to attempt such a task. You have to pull yourself together—the department will only be as strong as you are."

She shook her head. "I can't. I'm worn down. First there was Katie's death, and now *this*? It's more than I can bear."

"No, it isn't." Joseph pulled her to her feet. "I'm sorry for the loss of your sister, but you have to put that behind you for now and think of the living who depend on you."

He led her to the washbasin and handed her a dampened cloth. She held the cool cloth to her swollen eyes and thought of how strongly her mother would agree with Joseph. Everyone, especially her girls, would be disappointed if she didn't rise to the occasion.

The haggard woman in the mirror bore little resemblance to the sensible and resilient person she'd once been. Until she found that woman again, she would have to play the role.

"Wash your face," he prompted. "I'll arrange your hair. Half of it has fallen out of its pins."

Despite her misery, she gave him a puzzled look.

"Yes," he sighed, "Mrs. Briggs says pinning up her hair tires her arms, so she's made an expert hairdresser of me."

44 Irving Place
May 21, 1903

Dear Mama and Emily,

I'm not myself as of late, and I'm hoping another season at Point Pleasant will put me right. The cabin is far from my everyday life, and the only rest I have. I beg both of you to come and stay. Katie's death has made us all in need of a break from hard life. I want to have you close while Mr. Tiffany is in such a demanding spirit—having me do twenty of the same thing instead of four. Sometimes I think he means to squeeze as much out of us as he can, before the men's union shuts us down for good.

Now that we've been relieved of the windows, I've been making lamp designs, until there seems to be no end of them. I'm not sure if my department will survive, but I won't give up on it until I am forced. Every difficulty we've ever been in before has opened out into something bigger and more advantageous to us.

I've stopped going to see the animals. It seems so wicked to capture those beautiful creatures and keep them with all their wonderful lithe strength and grace eternally pacing up and down in a small prison with no variety or change, until their entire lives become only eating and sleeping.

We've had gusting winds for three days. One woman was blown off the sidewalk near the Flatiron Building, while others held onto lampposts until the police could help them out of the vicinity.

Don't worry about money, Emily, I'll send you $50 now and more in a few weeks. Buy a new pair of spectacles and extra coal and some new arctics and flannel undergarments while they are cheap. Your health isn't worth sacrificing for the sake of saving money.

I must go. Here are the Palmié ladies looking so pretty and twinny and becomingly dressed to take drab old Clara to dinner at that German restaurant over on Third Avenue. Afterward, Philip is taking us to hear Felix Adler speak.

Love, Clara

P.S. Yes, Mama, I promise to have my photo taken when I've gained back some of the weight I've lost. Mr. Tiffany referred me to a photographer who, he assures me, is one of the best in New York. She takes 'artistic' photos that will make me look glamorous and totally unlike myself.

P.P.S. No, Emily, I don't see marriage as a solution to any of our troubles.

Pt. Pleasant, N.J
August 1, 1903

From the top of the dune, Clara could see her mother and Edward, heads bent together, strolling on the shore below. No doubt they were plotting strategies regarding the men's strike.

The men's strike. It ate at her like a disease. She dreaded going into work each day, anxious over what cruelties the men would subject them to next. Some days it was nothing more than the men lined up on either side of the hallway, waiting for her and her girls to run the gantlet of taunts and insults. Of late, there had been kicks and pinches.

Mr. Tiffany had been forced to employ private police to guard the building, but otherwise, negotiations lagged.

Seeing her, Fannie beckoned to her to join them. Linking arms, mother and daughter walked on, Edward trailing close behind.

"I've come to hear what you two are planning for me," Clara said.

"You always were a perceptive child," Fannie laughed. "Mr. Booth and I have come to the conclusion that you need to reset your mind about this men's department business."

"Reset my mind?" Clara put her hands on her hips. "Just what does that mean?"

Edward coughed politely. "If you'll excuse me ladies, I'll put myself to use in fixing the cabin's water pump that seems to have pumped its last drop."

"Such a nice man," Fannie said, watching after him.

"Such a coward is more like it," Clara muttered. "This resetting of my mind must be a troublesome undertaking. Edward is usually at his happiest when he's telling people what to do."

They sat on a rock, letting their bare feet dangle in the water. "So, Mama, how could I possibly reset my mind, when I have such hate for these men?"

Fannie looked at her in surprise. "Hate? I thought these men were once your friends."

"They were, and that is precisely what hurts most. Our two departments have worked amicably for years. I can't stand that they've turned on us with such loathing!"

Covering her face, she waited for the lump in her throat to ease enough to allow her to speak. "I have less than four weeks before I'm to plead my case in front of the Tiffany board of directors. If I fail to convince them, they'll side with the men. I don't mind so much for myself, but many of my girls have families who depend on them for their survival." She picked up a stone and violently threw it into the water. "It's too much! I hate this worrying day after day!" Furious with herself, she broke into sobs.

Her mother held her until she cried herself out. "You're all bogged down in the muck. You've let them pull you to the level of unenlightened men, and they've blinded you to the obvious solution."

"Obvious solution? You mean gather them in a large burlap sack and drown them?"

"In a way, yes. Drown the misguided hatred inside them. That can only be done with all the compassion and joy you and your women have to give these poor creatures."

"That's preposterous! You're suggesting we use kindness with the same people who would just as soon see me and my girls begging on the street—or dead."

"Yes," Fannie smiled, "although I don't believe they wish to cause you such severe harm as you believe. These men have wives, sisters, mothers and daughters. I doubt there is one man among them who doesn't think of his loved ones and feel ashamed of himself even while he's persecuting you. They won't change their behavior, so you must change your reaction to that behavior. Don't you see? It's your negative reaction they seek. They *want* to distress you and make you retaliate because that gives them justification for their own poor behavior.

"They might easily act badly toward a frowning, angry woman who threatens them, but not to one who is smiling and wishing them well. With that in mind, I suggest that you and your women forego your rancor and act kindly toward them—send them gifts."

"Gifts?" She looked at her mother, certain she was suffering from sunstroke. "I'll do no such thing! The very idea makes me want to spit."

"It can't hurt to try, my dear. Smiles and kind words cost nothing, and a few pennies spent on rounds of cheese and good bread will be worth every bit if it softens the heart of only one man. If you treat them cordially, they will respond in kind."

Peals of women's laughter were carried to them on a breeze that smelled of fresh-baked pie. The stubborn resistance that proved both friend and enemy in her life reared its head. "What about the meeting with Mr. Tiffany and the board? Shall I bring them cheese and bread too?"

Fannie pressed Clara's hand to her lips. "Do you remember what I used to say each time you and Emily engaged in one of your battles of the will?"

The entire scrapbook of their childhood skirmishes opened in Clara's memory. Without hesitation, she lifted her head and recited: 'It's the soft tongue that breaks the bone.'"

"Precisely!" Fannie smiled. "I would suggest, my dear, that you face Mr. Tiffany and his board with an eye toward breaking bones."

The Briars
August 27, 1903

Louise is out of sorts. The quacks have told her she suffers from bowel cancer and that it's hopeless. I don't believe it's more than some sort of intestinal parasite she picked up in one of those filthy places she visited during her lunacy at the Women's Infirmary. She has moved into her own rooms, where a good deal of moaning goes on. I bring her little bouquets of flowers each day, as this is what she prefers to all other gifts.

Mr. Thomas is busy convincing the board we can get more out of Clara for much less—a dangerous assumption. How is it that, after all these years, the men still don't see how much more creative and able the women are at making beautiful art? I've warned them that they're playing with fire.

The rabble at Cold Spring persists in questioning my rights to what they are saying has always been 'their' beach. All this with an eye toward building public bathhouses directly on my land! Over my dead body will I allow them to pollute my property with their noise and filth! L.C.T.

September 3, 1903

Right from the start, the thing that made the meeting distinct from any other, the thing that would be joked about in board meetings throughout the city for years to come, were the heaping bowls of ice cream. For the first twenty minutes, the only sounds inside Tiffany's meeting room were of spoons clinking against the bowls.

If the ploy worked on the factory men, Clara thought, it might be successful with this crowd, too. She'd adopted Fannie's other advice, as well, and showered the men's department with bread and cheese, and notes of appreciation. Though not all her girls fully grasped the reasoning behind their actions, they learned to greet the men with cheer and good will, no matter what foul words or stones were thrown in return.

By the time the last gift basket was sent, only Mr. Fitzgerald and his Union bosses remained staunchly loyal to the cause against them.

John Dufais, Tiffany's secretary, indicated with a nod they should begin.

Mr. Thomas cleared his throat. "As you are aware, Mrs. Driscoll, Mr. Tiffany is not partial to long, drawn-out meetings, so I'll get straight to the point.

"The union stands firm in their demands that the women's department be shut down, the women got rid of, and all commissions for windows, lamps, and mosaics be handed over to the men's department.

"At present, your department is made up of thirty-five women, four boys, Mr. Briggs and Mr. Bracey. The men's union wants all of the women let go, excepting you and Miss Northrop. Mr. Briggs would be given his own Mosaic Department with Mr. Bracey as his assistant. The four boys would also be his, plus ten new men he could hire at his discretion.

"Moreover, Mrs. Driscoll, the men insist your salary be reduced from thirty-five dollars a week—an amount perceived by Mr. Fitzgerald and his men as something of a personal affront—to fifteen dollars a week." Mr. Thomas reddened and looked away.

Clara didn't wonder that he couldn't look at her—his own wife having committed suicide after being unfairly demoted from her position by an employer jealous of her superior skills.

"You and Miss Northrop will be strictly limited to lampshade design," he continued. "All other work will be taken on by the men's department.

The men and their two managers are also demanding raises. They've insisted on having their daily beer restored, with the added demand that a supply of comestibles be brought in with—"

Mr. Schmidt, another of Tiffany's board, cleared his throat. "I think, Mr. Thomas, what the men are asking for themselves is none of Mrs. Driscoll's concern. Suffice to say, the men have threatened to strike if the women's department isn't closed down. "

"Let's not waste time." Louis got to his feet and faced her. "Mrs. Driscoll, I regret to say that the general feeling of the board is that we should accept their demands and do as the union has asked."

Clara was relieved that her mother and Edward forewarned her of the possibility this would be their decision. Yet, even with the knowledge they were only testing her, it hurt to think that the entire board would go against her.

She glanced from one face to the next, noting their expensive clothes and jewelry, absolutely sure that her designs helped pay for every stitch and bauble. Considering that not one of them was able to meet her gaze, she suspected they were aware of the same. Going completely against what she was feeling at the moment, she smiled as if she'd been awarded ten thousand dollars and a new wardrobe.

"First, I would like to thank you for asking me here today. I also want to thank Mr. Tiffany for giving me the opportunity to put my artistic talents to use, and for the chance to see how much the world appreciates what I create—as is evidenced by the profits and awards my work has amassed for his company."

She paused, letting her words sink in.

"Too, I am thankful for the experience of managing a large department. No one has thirty or more workers to manage without some serious trials." Her smile held, confident. "Therefore, I am of the opinion that in order to keep the men's department happy, Tiffany's Women's Department *should* fold."

Clearly shocked, the men turned to look at one another.

"You see, gentlemen, my mother taught us that when one door closes, many others open. Thus, if my department is closed, and my women fired, I will, at that time, explore the opportunities that will certainly be opened to me."

With a weary sigh, Mr. Thomas sank down into his chair.

"Opportunities, Mrs. Driscoll?" Mr. Platt asked, eyebrows raised.

"Yes, opportunities, Mr. Platt. When I first understood that the men wanted to get rid of my department, I began peeking behind some of those other doors I'm sure will open to me. At first I was attracted to the idea of learning how to blow glass at the Corona factory and—"

The men burst into laughter, as if she'd made an excellent joke. She laughed too, but at them, for the idea *had* enormously appealed to her.

"I'm sure it must seem beneficial for Tiffany's to dispense with my full salary and the salaries of my girls. However, as you are aware, I have been in charge of keeping the books for my department for some years, and therefore, I know exactly how much profit there is to be made from the women's department's efforts.

"All being fair in love and war—and I must stress that the men's demands do feel like war—I took the liberty of meeting with the owners of a glass studio here in New York, who have expressed great interest in my work and have made quite an attractive offer."

She gave them a few seconds before continuing with the part of her announcement that, while not being entirely true at the moment, would be true once she gave Henry permission to send out word of her availability.

"I have also received word of another proposal from a gentleman who is interested in helping me open my own studio. I'd be designing lampshades and deluxe individual pieces under my own name. He's already found a small factory situated in the countryside."

She fixed Louis with one of her sweetest smiles, "As Mr. Tiffany knows only too well, there's nothing like nature for healthy inspiration." Pausing, she readied herself for the coup de grâce.

"In regard to the Tiffany Girls, it will be an easy matter to get them placed in other quality studios, seeing how they are some of the finest selectors and cutters in the country. I have no fear these women will be able to command wages that are commensurate with their skills."

Clara waited for someone to respond. When it was clear there would be no further argument, she smiled dazzlingly at no one in particular. "More ice cream, gentlemen?"

——§——

September 17, 1903

Louis surveyed the faces of the two men on the other side of the table. How right Clara had been in thinking of the situation as a war. Mr. Parks, the head boss for the Glass Cutters Union, and Mr. Fitzgerald looked like a couple of bloodthirsty soldiers ready for a brawl.

Mr. Parks, a squat man with a thick neck and pale hair cut close to the scalp, tapped his pen irritably on the table. "The Glass Cutters Union rejects all your adjustments and amendments to our original demands. Further, we reject your amendments to raise the men's salaries in yearly increments. We also want our daily beer rations restored, and lunch provided."

In his usual agreeable manner, Mr. Platt nodded. "When laid out like that, Mr. Parks, it sounds rather greedy. What are your grounds for such demands?"

"The women are given all the important work, and according to Mr. Fitzgerald here, a total of some thirty-eight windows were taken away from the men last year and given to the women's department. This resulted in five men—"

"That's five men with families to feed, mind ya," interjected Mr. Fitzgerald, his eyes flashing.

Mr. Parks gave Fitzgerald a warning look. "That action resulted in five men being laid off. Meanwhile, twelve extra women were hired by the Driscoll woman for her department."

"How many men do you have now, Mr. Fitzgerald?" Mr. Platt inquired.

"Thirty-one, not including me or my assistant manager. We used to have forty, until the women's department came in and stole our livelihoods away from us."

"At present, Tiffany's Women's Department has thirty-five women employed," Mr. Parks said. "Mrs. Driscoll's exorbitant salary of thirty-five dollars per week is a disgrace." He pounded his fist on the table, setting his jowls wobbling. "That alone is a slight to every honest working man in this city."

"Thirty-five is how much *I* get!" Mr. Fitzgerald chimed in, "Me! The manager of Tiffany's Men's Department. The men were like to riot when they was told what she gets."

Louis rose, his eyes hard as steel. "She has more workers than I do.

She gets more money than I," he mocked in the voice of a petulant child. "For God's sake, you sound like my daughters arguing over who has the most dresses. I'm sick of listening to this nonsense, so I'll expedite matters by enlightening you as to how things are going to be around here."

Mr. Thomas raised a finger. "Mr. Tiffany? I don't think you should—"

"I should and I *will*, Mr. Thomas."

Mr. Schmidt cleared his throat. "Louis, you're being too hasty. We shouldn't. . ."

"I don't need anymore people telling me what I should or shouldn't do in my own company!" Louis shouted. "I had enough of that while my father was alive. I'm the head of this business now, and what I say is damn well the way it will be."

"Louis, please," Mr. Platt said. "We need—"

"We need guts and honesty for once, and that's just what I'm going to give these swindlers right now—pure honesty. Do you recall, Mr. Fitzgerald, telling me it was impossible for your department to do those six landscape windows for the Astors? You said you couldn't have your men working long hours, and you didn't feel it could be done in six days. Remember?"

Fitzgerald screwed up his mouth. "Sure I remember, but—"

"The women took on that 'impossible' job and did it perfectly in the time given them. As a matter of fact, you consistently take twice as long as the women, and the results are never as satisfactory.

"The reason that Mrs. Driscoll makes as much money as you do is that, besides working longer hours, and giving more of her energy to designs that make yours look like the messes they are, she and her girls do better work."

Mr. Fitzgerald opened his mouth to argue, but Louis pointed a finger, his eyes narrowed. "You keep your mouth shut while I'm speaking, or I'll have you thrown out on your ear."

His eyes returned to Parks. "Granted, the women lack mechanical genius on the more symmetrical designs, but they have marked decorative instinct; their eyes are more sensitive to nuances of shading, their fingers more nimble, and, they have a superior sense of color. Most important, they pay attention to what I want. They're as fanatical about detail as I am. We never have returns on their account, whereas with the men's department, there are at least three returns a month.

"Therefore, gentlemen, none of your outrageous demands will be met. I have no intention of shutting down Mrs. Driscoll's department. Those women have as much right to their jobs as the men. You'll receive your usual yearly raises in increments, and if you want beer and a free lunch, go to a bar and buy them yourselves."

He waved a hand at the door. "This meeting is over. When you want to negotiate reasonably, notify Mr. Thomas or Mr. Schmidt, and we'll set up another meeting."

Mr. Parks pointed a finger at him. "I warn you, Tiffany, you won't get away with this. We'll strike and shut you down for good."

"Go ahead," Louis said. "There are plenty of able-bodied men willing to take your place, men who will be glad of working as hard as the women and will be grateful for the pay.

"One more thing Parks—if any of my women are harassed by your thugs, or if you so much as step foot within fifty yards of this building, I'll see to it you and your entire organization are put behind bars."

Louis hooked his cane over his arm and headed for the door. "You can all sit there and jack-jaw for the rest of the day for all I care, but I have a business to run. Good day, gentlemen. Notify me when you've come to your senses."

October 1, 1903

Enormously satisfied after three helpings of Miss Owens's mulberry pie, George had not ceased talking about his favorite topic: 'Desserts I Have Loved.'

Alice and Dudley, having both stopped listening sometime after Corn Pudding, but before Baked Brown Betty, returned to sketching the unusual scene before them.

Edward, Mr. Yorke, Philip and Miss Griffin were crowded around Clara's naked feet, studying them with the same concentration they might have given some rare Egyptian artifact. Miss Griffin, following Philip's directions on the most scientifically efficacious way to do things, applied half a jar of petroleum jelly to the bottom surfaces of the exposed trotters.

Clara freed her ankles from Mr. Yorke's grip and sat up. "Do you honestly think this will work?"

"Certainly," Edward said. "If we can get a decent mold of your feet, Mr. Bracey will be able to pour the metal for the inserts. This is exactly the best thing for people with broken-down insteps. Once I get them into your shoes, I doubt you'll ever have an aching back or feet again."

He nodded at Philip. "Mr. Allen, if you would, please pour the plaster to a level of about five centimeters. I believe Mrs. Driscoll is ready to have her feet immortalized."

"Wherever did you find the boxes to fit her?" George asked.

"It wasn't easy," Edward said, smoothing out the plaster as it oozed into the boxes. "I had to settle for breaking down crates and making them myself."

"I happen to be very fond of my feet," Clara said, "so stop talking about them as though they're carnival sideshow oddities."

Philip helped her place her feet into the plaster. "That should do it, although. . . hello?"

Mr. Thomas stood in the doorway looking decidedly ill at ease.

Clara waved to him. "Mr. Thomas. Come in and have a seat. I'm having plaster molds made of my feet."

Hesitant, he glanced around the room as if looking for hidden assassins. Clara wasn't sure if he were simply overwhelmed at their number all crowded into the small room, or appalled by the familiarity with which they treated each other. At least, she thought, they weren't in their wrappers and rolled up shirtsleeves, which was the case more often than not.

George gave up his chair, and Mr. Thomas sat down gingerly, his discomfort palpable. "Mr. Tiffany asked that I stop by to give you the news about the men's strike, but perhaps I should wait until tomorrow, when I can give you all the details."

"You may as well tell me now. Misses Griffin and Gouvy here are directly affected by the news, and the rest of these people are my family. Whatever has been decided affects us all in one way or another."

Mr. Thomas was not a smiler. In his serious, restrained manner, he took a folded paper from his coat pocket and handed it to her. "The strike is ended. These are the terms that have been agreed to by both sides."

She put the paper back in his hand. "I'm afraid I've left my spectacles in my room. I'd be obliged if you'd be so kind as to just tell me what's been decided."

He rattled off the terms in a monotone, without once looking at the paper. "The union has agreed to let your department make windows, shades and mosaics just as you have done in the past except . . ." Mr. Thomas paused and again settled his gaze on her partially submerged feet, " . . . except you won't be allowed to increase your present number of workers."

A sigh of relief escaped her. It was just as well to keep the number of girls to a minimum—it might stop Mr. Tiffany from forcing huge volumes of work on her department, and insure they would produce work of the finest quality.

"It has also been decided that the women's department out at Corona . . ." he nodded to Alice, "will continue on as before, with the exception that they will no longer be allowed to have any hand in the design of the lampshades. You, Mrs. Driscoll, are to be in charge of all the designing."

He stood, allowing his eyes to wander once more to the freakish arrangement of her feet. "You will need to come to my office tomorrow and look over the contract before signing."

She thanked him and offered a cup of tea she knew he would refuse.

Halfway to the door he turned. "Mr. Tiffany put the entire company at risk in order to keep you and your department intact, Mrs. Driscoll. I hope you appreciate that."

"Oh, I do, Mr. Thomas," she said, smiling, "just as much as Mr. Tiffany appreciates those of us who make his company worth risking."

Noon at Tiffany's
November 4th, 1903

Dear family,

The overwhelming victory of Tammany Hall has left us down as dogs. New York shall once again be at the mercy of the Bosses' corruption.

Worse yet, Mr. Tiffany's personal battles with President Roosevelt seem to have pushed him unfavorably into the public eye. Philip informed us that Roosevelt's summer residence, Sagamore Hill, is in Oyster Bay, next door to Cold Spring Harbor, where Mr. Tiffany is currently building his palace. He has publicly denounced Mr. Tiffany as an immoral man for his egregious actions against the people of Oyster Bay and for 'laying hands on other men's wives.'

*According to Philip, it's rumored that if reelected, Roosevelt has
promised to have Mr. Tiffany's glass screen that is presently installed on
the first floor of the White House, removed and 'smashed into small pieces.'
I don't know how Philip can stand to be involved in such things every day.
I can barely tolerate a little strike.*

Joseph Briggs and the Palmié twosome just now send their regards.

Love, Clara

*P.S. Mr. McBride is taking me to see Enrico Caruso make his debut in
the New York opera in "Rigoletto" at the end of the month. I've heard his
voice is so powerful it makes women faint. If this turns out to be the case,
I've instructed Mr. McBride to move their silly bodies out of the way so
they won't obstruct our view.*

December 8, 1903
The Gertrude Käsebier Studio
273 Fifth Avenue

Work on the Garden of Paradise mosaic panel was not going well.
The gold tiles chipped easily in the cutting, so that only one in three could
be used. Clara had been forced to take all her cutters and selectors off lamp
production and put them on the panel, which, as a result, left them behind
schedule on both projects.

The grippe hit next, claiming Frank as its first victim, and then within
the hour, three of the women. No sooner had they left, than Miss Hawthorne
got a piece of glass in her thumb, which couldn't be removed without
considerable difficulty and much blood. The Palmié twins, sensitive to the
sight of blood, grew faint and were forced to lie down.

It wasn't the best day to have her photograph made, but the
appointment with Madam Käsebier had been arranged three months in
advance. Since she didn't intend on having another photograph taken until
she was seventy, and as Mrs. Käsebier was much in demand, she had no
choice but to go.

She hurried toward Fifth Avenue, stopping by Miss Owens's only
long enough to change into her black evening dress that displayed her

arms and upper chest to advantage.

Inside the Käsebier studio, she found the usual frightening paraphernalia of a photographer's gallery replaced with tasteful drapes, a fireplace, full bookcases, and vases of exotic flowers. She was inspecting a display of avant-garde photographs of women and children, when a middle-aged woman in a mauve kimono and funny black-rimmed spectacles entered the room with a flourish. Clara liked her on sight.

Madam Käsebier squinted behind her spectacles, while using Clara's chin to move her head in every direction. "Your face is most interesting, Mrs. Driscoll—a perfect study for an artist." She examined Clara's hands. "What is it you do for work?"

Clara told her.

"I knew it!" Mrs. Käsebier snapped her fingers. "I can always tell an artist by their hands and the sensuousness of the mouth. Come with me, dear. Let me immortalize your beauty for all time."

Leading her to a model stand mounted on rollers, the photographer ordered her to relax and 'be herself.' Clara was thinking of what 'being herself' might look like when Mrs. Käsebier commenced to rolling the stand about the room, moving her in all directions, gauging the effects of different light on her face. When she found the light she liked best, she rolled the camera and scrim over and placed them where she wanted them.

"The rollers are a great help in getting different effects," Mrs. Käsebier said, ducking under the focus cloth. "I once had a piano in here, but I sent it away because I couldn't keep from moving it around. I was afraid I was going to injure myself."

Clara laughed, and the first photograph was taken.

"Do you see that piece of thirteenth century Italian pottery on the mantel?" Mrs. Käsebier asked, still under the cloth. "Have you ever seen anything more charming in color and form?"

Clara was searching for the piece when Mrs. Käsebier shouted, "There! Keep your head that way and don't change your expression."

A dozen or so photographs later, Mrs. Käsebier handed her a wide-brimmed hat. "Put this on, but don't pull down the veil, let me do that."

Clara politely handed the hat back to her. "I don't like hats in photographs. They went out of style long ago. It would look absurd."

"Ordinary hats, yes," Mrs. Käsebier pinned the hat to Clara's head at a provocative angle. "But not picture hats like this one. I don't treat a hat as a hat, Mrs. Driscoll, but as an art object." Squinting, the photographer tilted her head, set the hat at the opposite angle, and pulled the black veil part way over her face.

"I never wear veils," Clara protested. "They're passé."

"This isn't veils," Mrs. Käsebier sighed. "This is lines and shadows. You should never allow the conventions of your sex and the times you live in to inhibit you in anything. There will be plenty of other women who will do that. As an artist, you must learn to live without confines."

"But I—"

Head thrown back, eyes nearly squinted shut, Mrs. Käsebier clasped her hands. "Stunning! Stunning! It's a regular Rembrandt! It will be more or less solid black and may not look anything like you, but I don't care. It's a work of art."

"But my poor family," Clara mewled. "These photographs are for those who care more about me than they do Rembrandt."

"These are for me, dear. I want them for my window display. You'll have plenty more to choose from that your family will want." Mrs. Käsebier disappeared under the focus cloth and then reappeared. "Now tell me—how do you like working for Louis Tiffany?" She readjusted the hat and veil.

"I like the designing, but I'd rather not manage."

"Or *be* managed?" Mrs. Käsebier gave her a sly wink. "I expect Mr. Tiffany is a hard taskmaster. When I photographed his wife and daughters, they could not relax if he were in the room. Only when he left us to ourselves was I able to get them to unclench.

"Mrs. Tiffany was quite progressive in her thinking. She gave me permission to photograph the youngest girl, Dorothy, in a pose no etiquette book would have advised: sitting sideways in an old ladderback chair, facing the camera, her chin pressed against the head of her dolly. I liked it so well, I've made it part of my regular collection." She paused, and then added, "Mr. Tiffany didn't care for it. He thought it too simple—not enough grandeur."

"Consider yourself fortunate your photographs aren't made of glass," Clara said. "He's in the habit of destroying what he doesn't like."

"That doesn't surprise me in the least," Mrs. Käsebier said. "One of the things that makes my work superior is that I try to be sensitive to my subjects' inner workings—who they are as sentient beings. I'm good at detecting what a subject's deepest feelings are.

"The Tiffany family was exceptionally interesting in that way. Those children's eyes held such sorrow." Mrs. Käsebier's voice softened. "I believe Mr. Tiffany's darker nature is reflected in every one of their faces."

It was too late to return to Tiffany's by the time she left Madam Käsebier's. The photographer's vitality and honesty made her the most interesting woman Clara had met in some time. To have been so clever and sensible as to have found a way to apply her art in the manner she chose, and, at the same time make an ample living and a name for herself, was no less than genius. The woman was living proof that starting her own company with the backing of those who believed in her might be possible.

She was crossing Fifth Avenue, when Philip Allen suddenly appeared at her shoulder. In his Chesterfield coat, he was so handsome that for a moment she was too stunned to move.

He tipped his hat and tucked her arm under his. "What a stroke of luck. Not only have I received good news from my publisher, I have the fortune of running into the woman of my dreams. Let me take you to dinner. I can't think of anyone with whom I'd rather celebrate."

She started to give him one of her standard excuses as to why it was impossible, but hesitated. It was time to stop thinking in terms of the impossible and believe as Mrs. Käsebier did—that everything is possible.

They went to Child's, where, without asking, he ordered her favorite meal of boiled cod and baked potatoes. When coffee was served, he held her hand under the table, and she let him. In his eyes she saw excitement and something that made her want to crawl inside him and stay forever.

"What are we celebrating, exactly?"

"My publisher has decided to publish the book I've been writing, *America's Awakening*, about the moral awakening of the American populace in opposition to the corrupt bosses who run this country. I'm highlighting Roosevelt as one of our guiding lights in all this mess we're living in now."

"Have you ever thought of running for office?"

"Of course not," he huffed, looking genuinely offended. "I consider myself an honest man."

Later, strolling leisurely toward Irving Place, they passed a drugstore, where an ad for an elixir claiming to grow luxurious hair caught their attention. In the photograph, a young woman in the bloom of health ran her brush through a mane of wavy hair that reached to the floor. The caption under her dainty young feet read: 'Danderine grew this hair and we can prove it!'

Philip looked at Clara's wispy tresses, and then raised his hat to show off his own slightly receding hairline. "We should have ourselves photographed and then change the words to read: 'Danderine grew *this* hair, too, and we can prove it!'"

They broke into laughter. Without quite knowing how it came about, she was in his arms, his mouth fully on hers. Her desire for him was so powerful she feared it might kill her on the spot.

They didn't hear the approaching steps until the last second. Philip disengaged himself first, though he never took his eyes off hers. Surprised by the abrupt loss of him, she pressed her fingers to her chest, feeling the lingering heat from his body.

Alice and Edward, each carrying several small cartons of ice cream, stood staring at them. "Have you been running?" Alice' asked, her gaze settling on Clara's hat, which had been knocked crooked.

Breathless, Clara pointed to the drugstore window. "We were just having a laugh over the Danderine advertisement."

Edward looked blankly at the ad, then back to them. "Well then, since you both seem so easily entertained, you might want to come back to the house. We're having ice cream and getting up a game of Whist. Hopefully the hilarity of that won't prove so overwhelming."

—————§—————

She stood before the mirror trying to see if she were changed. Other than a lingering glow, she was still the Clara she had been yesterday, but changed in some essential, though invisible way. She remained whole and pure. . .well, perhaps not so pure, but what did that matter in a city like New York and in times like these?

Lightly touching her lips, she marveled over her desire for him, and her blatant lack of shame. Apparently, Mrs. Käsebier's words about not allowing the conventions of her sex and the times she lived in to inhibit her had made more of an impression than she thought. The only damper to her exuberance came when she recalled Edward's forlorn expression, and the way he kept sneaking glances at her and Philip all night—as if he knew what she was feeling.

"Impossible," she said, climbing into bed. Edward hadn't shown the least bit of *that* sort of interest in her. Dismissing the thought, she rolled over and tried to sleep.

~22~

44 Irving Place
January 31, 1904

Dear Family,

I meant to write earlier, but Philip took me out for breakfast at the Ashland House on 24th St. and 4th, where we gorged ourselves on milk and new onions, eel with cream dressing and creamed potatoes. We waddled back to my room, where I found George lying in wait.

He was talking in his usual torrent of words and pacing like a tiger until I made him sit down. Next, in came Mr. Yorke, looking lonely and despondent. To get him out of himself, I made him explain the Marconi System to George. Ten minutes later, Alice came in with her face all swollen with neuralgia and looking for solace.

No sooner was the word solace uttered, than Philip, Edward and Dudley all piled in on a mad search for diversion. Alice being my main concern, I darkened the room and made everyone remain quiet. One by one, they all left except Edward, who is now quietly massaging Alice's hands while telling her Sherlock Holmes stories from memory.

Love to all, Clara

P.S. Emily: I'm sorry you're feeling so low. I haven't heard of Dr. Herdman or his electric shock treatments, but it sounds painful, and you don't know what effect it will have on your superior brain in the future. Come spend this summer at Point Pleasant with us instead. We'll shock you without charge—no pun intended.

April 17, 1904
44 Irving Place

M ISS OWENS HANDED Clara the *New York Daily News.* "Did you see this?"

Staring up at her was a detailed sketch of her dragonfly lamp. The caption read: *'Mrs. Driscoll's Paris Prize Dragon Fly Lamp.'*

She dropped her fork, her eyes going over words several times. There was no mistake—it was *her* name on *her* work. Trembling with excitement, she came out of her seat, and, unsure of where she was going, sat back down.

Miss Nye snatched the paper from her hands and waved it over her head. "Look everyone! It's a picture of Clara's lamp."

The boarders crowded around, as the paper was passed from hand to hand.

Incredulous, Philip took the paper from Miss Nye. "How, in God's name did you manage *that*? I thought Tiffany had everyone in his pocket. He'll be fit to be tied when he sees this!"

Clara swiveled in her chair, wearing a puzzled smile. "In his pocket? What do you mean?"

Philip colored, fumbling for words. "I only meant that I've never seen any name other than his and his board of directors mentioned in association with his merchandise before, and certainly not in print."

"But what did you mean about having everyone in his pocket?"

Before he could answer, Alice rushed into the room with another copy of the paper. "Clara, you're famous! We'll have to buy a dozen copies and send them to everyone in Tallmadge."

"Better famous than infamous," Edward said, finishing off the last of his poached eggs. "We must be careful Mrs. Driscoll doesn't get a swelled head, or she'll be wanting a framed copy hung in the parlor."

"Actually, I was thinking of hanging it on the front door," Clara said. "More people would see it that way."

Alice took the last of the toast from the platter. "You mean more than the five hundred thousand who will see it today?"

Laughing, Clara turned back to question Philip again about his comment, just in time to see him slip out the front door. She started after him, but was stopped by the boarders' rousing chorus of *For She's a Jolly Good Fellow.*

—§—

May 7, 1904
Manhattan

Clara was more than halfway home, when someone called her name. In the voice was a tone of desperation. She swiveled around and was startled to see Mr. Tiffany running to catch up with her.

When he finally caught up to her, he hesitated, as if he'd forgotten why he'd run after her. "I was wondering if you would accompany me?"

Her first thought was that she'd missed a meeting, and he'd come to escort her back to his office, but on closer inspection, the lined face and red-rimmed eyes gave evidence of some deep torment. "Of course," she said, "where are we going?"

He shrugged, and, without looking at her, began walking toward Madison Square. "Talk to me, Clara. Talk to me as if I were one of your friends at the boardinghouse. Tell me about your life there."

It was a peculiar request, but she recognized it at once as a desperate need for distraction from pain. "The Irving Place group is like my family," she began, in the tone of a storyteller. "If we aren't out and about on our bicycles or at the theater, you might find us at home playing Whist or discussing literature, politics, and art. Of course, you already know about our parlor plays."

"I remember," he said, "*Alice in Wonderland.* You were dressed as Alice."

Both flattered and embarrassed that he'd remembered, she blushed. "Yes, well, we've expanded our territory and now, each spring, we all chip in and rent a cabin at Point Pleasant Seashore. One of our borders, Mr. Yorke, is teaching me how to sail, and Mr. Booth, our naturalist, taught us how to survive in the woods with nothing more than a pocketknife."

He stopped abruptly and faced her. "How do you go on when a terrible circumstance is thrust upon you? I've seen you pull yourself out of grief and go on. How do you manage the pain?"

She didn't think that explaining her theories about the uncertainty of life and death and personal introspection would help him much—his pain was too new. "You may recall that my sister Kate died last year. Her death knocked me as low as I've ever been. I don't know what I would have done without hearing the Tiffany Girls' everyday chatter. I let myself be absorbed by it, so I wouldn't have to swallow the pain in such large doses.

"I think talking about it helps. I'm a good and willing ear, and you know you can rely on my discretion. Won't you tell me what's troubling you?"

He shook his head. "The only thing that can help me now is the comfort I find in your company and hearing you speak of your everyday affairs."

"If it's simple talk that soothes you, Mr. Tiffany, sit in a corner of my workroom with my girls for a few hours, and I promise you your mind will be rendered numb with silliness."

Louis laughed, and then looked startled. "My god, I was sure nothing could make me smile today."

"That's a relief," she said. "I thought for sure I was going to have to tell you the story of how I once put on *King Lear* for my family, using the barn cats in the roles of Lear's daughters and the goat as King Lear."

When she'd worn him out with her talk, some of it bordering on the inane, she accompanied him to his car. Although she refused his offer of a lift to Irving Place, it did occur to her that she should have asked him to let her try her hand at driving. *That,* she was sure, would have been more than enough to take his mind off any troubles he thought he was having.

May 8, 1904

Miss Owens leaned close to Clara's ear and whispered, "A young lady wishes to speak to you in the parlor. She's quite upset."

Young Miss Barnes immediately jumped to mind. The girl had gotten herself mixed up in a tempestuous romance with a French sailor, whom she foolishly intended on marrying—a union that could only end badly. All her girls came to her for advice or a comforting word when their romances went astray. She was becoming so proficient at providing guidance, she was sorry there wasn't some sort of salaried position where all she had to do was to look understanding while she listened to people's sad tales about their entanglements.

She was barely into the room when the girl launched off the settee and threw herself into her arms, sobbing.

"I'm sorry, Mrs. Driscoll, I don't mean to disturb your Sunday morning, but I had to see you."

Clara held the girl away and looked into the face of a pretty, brown-eyed version of Louis Tiffany. "Dorothy! What's happened?"

"Mother died this morning, and Father has locked himself in his study to drink. No one would talk to me. You told me I could always call on you. I didn't have anyone else to go to, I'm sorry."

"Don't be sorry. I'm glad you've come to me. Does your father know where you are?"

"He doesn't care where I am. He's too drunk. He doesn't care about anyone but himself." The words were so filled with hate that Clara flinched.

She held Dorothy, rocking her until she felt her calm down. "All right, let's go to my room. I'll make tea, and we can talk in private without being disturbed."

She made the girl drink a cup of chamomile tea, though it did nothing to calm her.

"Mama endured!" Dorothy wept. "She endured *him*. When she got sick, he didn't stay with her; he spent all his time at work. All he cared about was making more money! My mother was the one who made him be nice to us, and now she's dead and I'm afraid, because I don't have anyone who really cares about me."

She looked up, pleading. "My father thinks just because I'll be thirteen, I should be able to take this in stride. He doesn't care that my mother meant everything to me. He doesn't even care she's dead!" Her last word was drawn out on a wail of pain.

Clara rocked her, letting her cry herself out until the girl fell into an exhausted sleep. For a long time, she watched Dorothy sleeping, hoping that when the girl woke it might be possible to give her the same nourishing meal of compassion that Fannie Wolcott had so often served.

Tiffany's
June 15, 1904

Dearest Mama and sister Emily,

Today all of New York is under a funeral pall with this morning's news of the General Slocum Ferry disaster in the East River. Of the 1,300 women and children aboard, over 1,020 perished when the boat caught fire. Many succumbed to fire, some were crushed when the floors of the overloaded ferry collapsed. Because of their long skirts and the social dictates against women learning how to swim, most of the women drowned along with their children.

Philip Allen came to say that the shores of North Brother Island were three deep in bodies. He said that when the mothers threw the faulty life preservers to their children, the preservers crumbled like crackers.

Following this news, hysteria broke out in the workroom, and it fell to me and Mr. Bracey to escort all the Tiffany Girls who had friends or relatives on the boat to the morgues.

When I returned to Irving Place, I sat for a long time thinking of death and of how my own life is passing rapidly enough. Because this day has shown us once again that life is fragile, it seems urgent that I should tell you again how much I love you. In truth, when all is said and done, it is our ability to give and accept love that matters most in life. It is what makes us human.

Love, Clara

July 8, 1904
Pt. Pleasant, N.J.

Luckily for Clara, Mr. Yorke proved to be a patient instructor, since she found learning to sail similar to patting her head and rubbing her stomach at the same time. With the aid of diagrams and long hours of trial and error, she eventually got the hang of it. On the days she needed solitude, she took the dinghy to Gull Island or Fisherman's Cove, where she could lose herself for hours in a book or in making sketches of the wildlife that surrounded her.

With a sandwich and a jug of water secured in her knapsack, Clara removed her shoes, tied her wide straw hat to her head, and set about pushing the beached dinghy toward the water.

"May I offer assistance?" Philip came into view, his shirtsleeves rolled part way up to reveal tanned and muscular forearms. Just the sight of him made it impossible for her to move with any grace at all. "I can manage all right, thank you," she said. "I've done this hundreds of times on my own."

He stepped away, watching as she struggled at pulling the deceptively heavy craft across the wet sand. Only inches from the water, her foot came down on a broken shell. Yelping in pain, she hopped about in a circle.

At once he was kneeling, inspecting the bottom of her foot, his hand around her ankle. Every nerve in her body came alive as he kissed the arch of her foot then rose to embrace her, holding her tight against him.

"Let me go with you," he whispered urgently. "We'll go to Gull Island and have the whole day alone."

She nodded and together they quickly pushed the boat into the water.

They weren't a hundred yards out, when she heard the cries. On the shore, Edward waved his arms, motioning them back in, shouting words that were lost on the wind.

"Ignore him and keep on course," Philip directed. "It's probably Tiffany on the telephone wanting you to come in to work on some infernal project. He can wait."

She slacked off the sails, unsure of what to do. There was something about the way Edward waved and the timbre of his cries that spoke of something far more serious than a summons from Tiffany's. She forced the images of her dying mother or a mortally ill Emily from her mind and strained to hear what he was saying.

"What if it isn't Tiffany?" she said. "What if something awful has happened?"

"Bad news doesn't spoil, Clara. It will keep no matter how bad it is."

She looked into the deep blue eyes that captivated her, and back at Edward who now stood silent, watching them, his arms hanging loosely at his sides. "You're only half right, Philip," she sighed, pushing the helm over and slacking the sheet. "Bad news may keep, but it can't be ignored."

Turning her back to him, she set sail for shore, where Edward pulled them in and helped Clara out of the dinghy.

"You need to go to the cabin," he said without looking at her. "Everyone is gathered there."

She waited until he met her gaze. The raw misery she found there sent her hurrying over the sand, her skirts pulled up to her knees.

July 14, 1904

Dear Family,

    I couldn't bring myself to write earlier, but as Philip says, bad news doesn't spoil.

    George died last Friday morning after a prolonged epileptic seizure. It's impossible to imagine all that life and energy has gone out. Yet, I can't help but be thankful it's over. His only pleasures in life consisted of working hard, eating, and being in the city among his friends. Over this last year, this hateful illness has kept him from these things. At times he reminded me of a bird beating itself against the bars of a cage.

    The memorial was held in Danielson, but I could not rise to the task. Henry is inconsolable and will see no one. Everyone else is about as low as I have ever seen them. Dudley weeps unashamed, and even Alice's kind ministrations do not soothe him.

    However, there was a little reprieve from the sorrow, when three days after George died, a cardinal appeared and perched on the back of George's favorite canvas chair. All day, he flew between chair and kitchen window, chattering and whistling at us for attention. I put out bits of suet and peanuts, but he would have nothing to do with them. Nonetheless, last night he ate a slice of blueberry pie that Alice forgot to take inside. We found him this morning perched on the edge of the outdoor table looking stunned, his belly swollen.

    I shouted when the obvious dawned on me: "My God, Alice, it's George!"

    We spent the next three hours talking to it as if it <u>were</u> George. He seemed to enjoy the attention and chirped back at us in George's excited way. We've not seen him since, but I feel so much better now about George's passing.

    All my love, Clara

P.S. Mr. Booth read us Philip's new story, 'Bird or Devil,' in the August Scribner's. *It's wonderful, rather like its author.*

P.P.S. The cabin's owner has agreed to cover the expense of materials for the construction of a screened-in sitting porch at the back of her cabin. The men have decided to wait until mid-September to build, so as not to interfere with our activities while we're in the thick of the season.

September 17, 1904, 12:45 p.m.

Storming about her kitchen, Miss Owens alternated between bouts of tears and fury, while the kitchen maids nimbly scurried around her with trays of dirty dishes.

"I'll kill the man with my own bare hands! He's trying to ruin me!" She clasped her head. "How could he have done this to me? I'm the best customer he's got, and he gives me spoiled sausages to poison my tenants?"

She grabbed Clara by the arm. "Thank God you didn't eat any of the vile stuff. But poor Miss Alice and Miss Griffin, both of them so small and sensitive."

Clara jumped out of the way of a housemaid rushing by with large bottles of Coke Syrup. "Tell me what I can do to help."

Miss Owens handed her a bottle of the elixir. "Make sure Alice and Miss Griffin take their Coke Syrup. Doctor Sherman swears by it for food poisoning."

Upstairs, Miss Griffin and Alice lay side by side on Miss Griffin's couch. Alice, looking white and fragile, raised her head and waved.

"How are you?" Clara whispered, handing her a small glass of the syrup.

Miss Griffin groaned and tossed onto her side.

"I'm faring better than most. I only ate a small bite and thought it tasted funny, so left the rest on my plate. Mr. Yorke and Mr. Bainbridge got the worst of it."

Alice sipped the potion and made a face. "This is almost as bad as the sausage."

"Miss Owens is on the warpath," Clara laughed. "She's vowing to kill the butcher with one of his own knives."

Alice sat up, careful not to disturb the gently snoring Miss Griffin. "Better yet, she should force him to eat one of his deadly sausages. I was so looking forward to getting over to Point Pleasant today to help with the sitting porch, but I suppose next weekend will be—" A look of alarm crossed her face. "Oh no! What about the wood and screening? Mr. Yorke is supposed to meet the delivery at the Point Pleasant docks at four today! We've already arranged for the cart."

Miss Griffin bolted upright and scrambled over Alice. At the door she collided with Philip Allen, bounced off, and continued running for the bathroom both hands held tightly over her mouth.

"I'll meet the delivery," Philip said from the doorway, his eyes locking on Clara's. "Clara can come with me. I'll need her help putting the wood in the shed."

"Is that wise?" Alice asked. "What about Dudley or Edward? Can't one of them go instead?"

Clara shook her head. "Dudley is with Mr. McBride in Boston for the Fall Art Show, and Edward is having to work all day. Everyone else has either fallen victim to the evil sausages, or is out of town."

Alice looked from Clara to Philip. "But you can't go there, just the two of you alone. What I mean is, Clara can't—shouldn't be doing heavy work. You'll strain yourself. You should wait until the other men can help."

"You apparently have never seen me move an eight-foot by four-foot leaded window by myself. Mr. Briggs is convinced Fannie kidnapped me from the Amazons." Clara got to her feet, careful not to look at Philip. "Don't worry about us. We'll be fine."

"But you can't just go off without the rest of us."

Clara pushed Philip into the hallway ahead of her. "Of course I can. Don't be such a ninny. Get some sleep and drink the rest of your medicine. I'll check on you when I return tomorrow night."

6:40 p.m.

Edward had never felt so tired in his life. Rows of numbers still swam before his eyes, as he put up his bicycle and entered the boardinghouse. The bookkeeping had been especially complicated, and for once, he fully understood what Clara meant when she complained about her eyes feeling like they might fall out after a hard day at Tiffany's.

"Ah, there you are, Mr. Booth," Miss Owens said, bustling through the dining room door with a tray of teacups and plates of dry toast. "I'm so glad you weren't one of those struck down this morning."

"Struck down?" He relieved her of the heavy tray. "Was there another runaway streetcar?"

"The breakfast sausage was bad. About half the boarders were taken ill. We've been running up and down stairs with Coke Syrup all day. We're encouraging those who can stomach it to take some hot tea and a little toast, but there are others who still can't hold down the Coke Syrup. However, for those of you who escaped, dinner will be clear soup, chicken croquettes, mushrooms and French peas, and apple turnovers for dessert."

"Exactly who succumbed to this bad sausage?" Edward asked, moving toward the stairs.

Miss Owens put a finger to her chin and thought for a moment. "The casualties from your group were Alice, Miss Griffin, Mr. Yorke, Mr. Bainbridge, and Miss Nye."

He smiled to himself. Wasn't it just like Clara to be the one left standing after the battle? "I'll go up and see what I can do to help," he said, moving up the stairs. "Where shall I land this tray?"

"Take it to the servants in Clara's room. They've made their headquarters there. It makes it easier to tend to the ones who still need immediate assistance to and from the bathrooms."

Edward chuckled. "I've always said Clara would make a good nurse. I'm sure she's got everything set up and running better than one of Nightingale's infirmaries."

"I am sure she would," Miss Owens said, ". . . if she were here."

He felt a pinprick of apprehension at the base of his skull. "Not here? Don't tell me she's still at Tiffany's? I'll go and drag her back here for dinner. It isn't healthy for her to miss so many of your lovely meals."

"She isn't at Tiffany's," Miss Owens said. "She and Mr. Allen went to Point Pleasant to take delivery of the supplies for the sitting-in porch. They planned on having their dinner up there and coming home in the morning. They—"

He didn't wait to hear the rest, because he was already up the stairs and walking as fast as the teacups would allow without breaking. In Clara's room, he gave the tray to the house servants and glanced around. The corner that was home to Clara's valise was empty.

He stepped across the hall to Miss Griffin's room, where Alice sat crocheting, and peered in. "Excuse me, Alice, but do you know where—"

At the sound of his voice, Alice looked up, her expression a mixture of worry and relief. "Go!" she said, as if any further explanation was unnecessary.

"When did they—?"

"They were to receive the lumber delivery at four, and then take the cart to the cabin." She glanced at the mantle clock. "The last ferry leaves in fifteen minutes. You'll have to hurry."

8:10 p.m.

To look at her leisurely sketching the man playing the mandolin, no one would have suspected she was hardly able to think a clear thought. For her, the day was a series of moments when their hands touched and their eyes met. They said little over dinner, their meals going uneaten, as if they were preparing for a long swim.

When the winds picked up, Philip cleaned out the fireplace and built a fire that would have been more appropriate for a winter blizzard than an autumn squall.

She studied her sketch, wishing she could have a photograph of them as they were now — radiant in love. She was surprised at her lack of shame, though she justified it by telling herself it was the dawning of a new age; the rigid rules that once governed women's social behavior were now a thing of the past. Women were no longer required to deny themselves the pleasures that were once the private domain of men.

Philip's mandolin went silent, and his chair scraped back. He came to stand behind her, letting his hand caress the back of her neck as he leaned over to kiss her temple.

A jolt of sensual pleasure shot through her. Mirrored in his face she saw her own longing. His eyes never left hers, as he pulled her out of her chair and kissed her as if he meant to devour her.

She left his mouth long enough to shake her hair free of pins and combs, letting it fall in waves around her shoulders. He buried his face in her neck, his hands traveling over her shoulders and breasts to her waist.

Her desire emerged as a soft moan while they moved together in their sensual dance.

8:34 p.m.

A mile from the cabin, his lamp spit once, flickered, and then plunged him into darkness. Edward cursed himself for not packing extra oil, but in his blind panic to get to the ferry, he hadn't been thinking. As it was, he'd arrived at the dock just as the gangway was being hauled up. It was strictly by chance that the captain heard his shouts, and recognizing him as a regular passenger, allowed him to board.

The wind howled as it came off the water, announcing the imminent arrival of a storm. Shifting his rucksack onto his back, he lowered himself closer to the handlebars and averted his face to shield his eyes from the wind.

He caught sight of someone in the distance trudging along the footpath. Through the dark he could just make out the figure of a woman built tall and slender like Clara, pushing against the wind. He peddled faster, until he thought his leg muscles would tear apart. When he was fifteen yards away, he slowed, not wanting to scare her. "Hello! Who goes there on a night like this?"

The woman spun around so fast she nearly lost her balance. "Why, Mr. Booth!" Mrs. Palmié flattened her hat to her head. "What on earth are you doing out in this weather at a this time of night?"

Struck by equal measures of disappointment and renewed urgency, Edward cast about for an adequate answer. "I caught the last ferry. Thought I'd get an early start tomorrow on the new porch." His laugh was forced and hollow. "Clara and Philip are probably thinking I fell overboard."

Mrs. Palmié raised her voice over the wind. "They joined us at the house for dinner, though between them they hardly ate a mouthful. I invited them to accompany me to my sister's for the evening, but the poor things were tired from unloading the cart. They missed a good evening. My sister can be most entertaining when she gets to talking about—"

"You'll have to forgive me for not offering to escort you home, Mrs. Palmié, but I have to hurry before the rain comes. The blueprints for the porch are in my rucksack, and it's important they stay dry. Besides, I don't want to worry Clara and Mr. Allen. I'm already hours late."

Mrs. Palmié waved him on. "Oh don't you worry about me. I've walked this path a thousand times in much worse weather than this. I'm like the cows at milking time: I always find my way back to the barn."

Needing no further urging, Edward made so quick a start, the bicycle slid out from under him.

8:38 p.m.

Lost in him, she had no awareness of the storm raging on around them. She raised her hand to his face to tell him she loved him, when the window above the couch blew open, showering them with cold rain.

Philip scrambled to his feet, pulling her up with him. As he secured the window, there came a crash from upstairs. She rushed up the stairs and padded quickly through the puddle that had formed beneath the windows. Happy to see none of the glass had been broken, she was fastening the locks when she noticed the shed door banging in the wind.

Hurrying downstairs, she stuck her head into the front room. "I'm going to close the shed door. It's blown open, and the tools and wood are getting wet."

"They'll be fine," he said, drawing her into an embrace. "It's wood. It's meant to withstand the elements." He kissed her, leading her back to the couch. "I'll wipe the tools down in the morning with kerosene."

Clara broke away. "We have to change into dry clothes anyway, so I may as well get entirely soaked first." Before he could stop her, she was out the door and sprinting across the yard, her wind-whipped skirts tangling around her ankles. As she worked to secure the rusted hasp, a sensual memory of Philip's soft mouth made her take in a sharp breath.

She watched him through the window until she was sure of what she wanted, then walked toward him with purpose.

8:40 p.m.

Edward lay in the ditch, cold needles of rain stinging his face. He recalled the dozens of times his mother had warned him about the danger of stormy weather 'widow-makers.' Had it not been for the pain in his ribs, he might have had a laugh over it; but at the moment, laughing was the last thing he felt like doing.

He tentatively probed the stinging flesh above his eye, his fingers coming away dark with blood. With a grunt he picked himself up and kicked at the 'widow-making' branch that had fallen across the path. In light of the fact he was at his top speed when he hit it, he was amazed it hadn't killed him.

He found his bicycle ten feet away, looking like some dead animal torn apart by wolves. He picked up the twisted wheel, quickly dropping it as the pain tore through his ribs. Kicking the ruined bike into the ditch, he began to run, the mud sucking at his shoes.

8:45 p.m.

Clara hurriedly changed out of the wet blouse and skirts that were the last vestiges of her armor, and into her pale green kimono. When she returned to him, Philip was standing by the fire staring into the flames.

He looked up, eyes shining. "Come here, Clara. Let me love you."

8:47 p.m.

Edward almost shouted for joy at the first whiff of wood smoke. Thirty yards away, he could see the glow from the fireplace flickering orange and yellow on the cabin walls. The lace curtains were drawn in a futile attempt to create an illusion of privacy for those inside.

He hesitated below the porch steps trying to remember which was the creaking board. Unwilling to take a chance, he cautiously walked around to the parlor window, where, summoning all his courage, he looked inside.

Silhouetted against the flames Clara and Philip were locked in an embrace, their kiss frenzied, almost violent in its intensity. In their passion, Clara's kimono slipped, revealing the smooth skin of her bare shoulder.

He staggered backward, feeling as if he'd been kicked in the heart. Wild with hurt, he ran like a madman across the yard, stumbled over a rake left lying under a pile of leaves, and sprawled headlong into the garden.

For the second time that night, he lay in the mud, his emotional torment eclipsing any physical pain he may have felt. How could she have chosen *him*—a man who had no other choice except to eventually abandon her? He pressed his fists against his eyes, as if to erase the image of her bare shoulder from his memory. She would ruin herself this night, and there would be no way for her to hide it.

He hauled himself to his feet. He'd allowed his life to twine around hers the way a vine crawled toward the sun. It was her vitality and resilience that drew him; her loving nature left him no choice but to love her. Was that not reason enough to save her? He would do no less for any other woman. Even if he had to force her, he could not allow her to marry a lifetime of disgrace for a momentary pleasure. If she hated him for it, so be it.

Picking up his rucksack and hat, he climbed onto the porch, knocking the mud from his shoes against the one squealing board. He rattled the handle and shoved the door open, let it slam, then slammed it again for good measure. "Hello? Clara? Philip? I'm late, but I'm here. What a storm! I say you two, where are you hiding? I hope there's hot tea."

Delaying the moment as long as he could, he took a breath and stepped smiling into the parlor.

——§——

Years later, when she saw her first Keystone Cops film, Clara would recall the night Edward Booth rescued her from her own foolishness. The sound of footsteps heavy and solid on the porch sent her and Philip scrambling off the sofa like it was a hot griddle.

Frantically rearranging their clothes while grabbing at hair combs, sketchpad and book, they made a mad dash to the safety of separation — she, throwing herself into her chair, and Philip reclining on the couch, pretending to be engrossed in his book.

In a desperate attempt to appear calm, she bent over her sketchpad so Edward might not see the flush of excitement that lingered.

"Hello, Edward," she called in a voice that sounded forced. "We're in the front room."

Edward set down his rucksack. "Sorry I'm late, but the ferry was delayed, and then I had a bit of a mishap with my wheel, so I had to walk the last mile." He took off his hat, revealing the gash on his forehead. "I'm afraid I had a bit of a row with a tree. I think I need your expert nursing, Clara."

She examined the cut to his forehead, and went to the kitchen in search of the medicine kit. Through the door she could hear the men's voices low and serious, with no hint of the usual lighthearted banter that was their custom.

Edward's voice suddenly rose to a sharp pitch, and then just as quickly subsided. She thought she heard him say, 'Not here!' or maybe it was, 'Not her!' She sidled closer to the door, straining to hear more, but their voices dwindled to a faint series of murmurs.

When she reentered the room, the two men were staring at one another, the tension thick as pudding. For an instant, Philip met her eyes and withdrew into himself. She longed to reassure him, to tell him she loved him and that there would be another time.

She cleaned and bandaged Edward's wound, easing the strained silence with a stream of chatter that sounded inane even to her. The moment she was finished, Edward yawned, wincing as he did so.

"Shall I make you something to eat? You must be famished."

Edward shook his head, his eyes wandering everywhere but to her. His gaze came to rest on her hair combs that lay next to the couch, and for a moment his face filled with disgust. "Don't bother; I'll make a cup of tea and set up the hammock in the kitchen. We all need to get some sleep. I expect Mr. Yorke will be up on the early morning ferry. If we're to have this porch done by next week, we'll need to hop to."

Halfway to the kitchen, he reached over the back of the couch and turned Philip's book right side up. "Easier reading that way, old chap."

Sleepless, she lay balled up inside her quilt, interpreting every sound. She willed herself to relax, but her thoughts refused to be corralled. Deceit was not in her nature, and the thought that honest, sweet Edward might know what she and Philip were up to, made her insides wither.

She turned over, impatiently plucking at the tangle of her nightgown. What *were* they up to? Love? Passion? She couldn't get beyond the wanting of him, to be sure.

Alternately cringing and exulting over the events of the evening, she found herself analyzing Edward's every word and nuance of expression. What if he *had* guessed, or even worse—what if he'd *seen*? She shook her head and rubbed at her eyes, scratchy from lack of sleep. He couldn't have known, but why else wouldn't he look at her?

Suddenly furious, she sat up, hands clenched. What business was it of Edward's, or any of them, for that matter? Was she not allowed to have her own private life?

She threw off the covers and got out of bed. What did she care what they thought? She rested her head against the window, her breath fogging the pane, and then clearing. Wrapping her arms about herself, she watched the storm exhaust itself and die away.

In the first gray light of morning, she crawled back under the covers and lay still, eyes on the bare rafters. From below came the quick, successive *thunks* of Edward splitting wood for the kitchen stove.

Exhausted, she closed her eyes and waited for sleep to take her.

Noon at Tiffany's
November 10, 1904

Dearest Ones,

We are fretfully busy at work on the new Fire Worshipper panels and all the lamps and deluxe individual pieces for the oncoming holiday season. In all honesty, I would rather be digging potatoes than making $500 lamps.

We have just now come from our first ride on the Subway that opened a week ago. This wonderful modern marvel took us from 14th Street and shot up to 125th, only 3 minutes from the Fort Lee Ferry. In the past this trip has taken a full hour by horsecar and cost 10 cents. Now it costs a nickel and takes 15 minutes.

You don't realize how fast you're going, because you can't see anything but an occasional station flash by. The white posts on the sides of the tracks are trying to my eyes, but I try not to look. The stations reminded me of expensive, freshly scrubbed bathrooms, with their clean green and white tiles. Another wonderful thing about the cars is the quickness with which they get up speed after stopping—much different from a railroad train.

On Election Day, the Irving Place family hiked to a great flat rock overlooking the Hudson and all New York. We broiled steaks on long, forked sticks over a fire. Around nine, we crawled up Broadway, watching the Times searchlight indicating a majority for Roosevelt. By eleven, it was evident it was a Roosevelt victory.

When I opened my eyes this morning, they were greeted by a splendid patch of sunlight splashed across the yellow chrysanthemums my dear Philip brought last night. I've been light as a feather all day just for the thought of them waiting for me in my cozy room.

I purchased a lovely blue and white lawn dress on sale at Wannamaker's, and my gray silk waist and my black skirt have been satisfactorily altered and mended to look brand new, so I'm set until next year.

Alice and Mr. Booth send their love. Me too. Clara

~23~

Dear Ones,

   Mr. Booth has graciously offered to give up his hand at the Whist table to write for me while I rest my eyes. I'm lying on Miss Griffin's couch with Muggs (our new house cat), asleep on my chest. Across the room, Miss Nye is reading Plato's Apology of Socrates to the Whisters.

   Not much news except that Mr. Tiffany flirts with disaster by taking a major Easter window away from the men and giving it to my department. This on the heels of giving us the Rose window for Mr. Thomas's sister at Bryn Mawr. As I walk by the men's department now, I am a model of contriteness.

   Our own workroom windows are being replaced, and it's so cold, the girls get up and dance every half hour to keep their blood from freezing. They're enjoying these little flights of exercise so much, we may keep up the practice until summer.

   If you haven't seen it in the papers, Mr. Tiffany gave $300,000 to the Infirmary for Women and Children. I am quite sure I helped make a large part of that contribution.

   Emily, sir: I'm sorry I haven't executed your list of orders as swiftly as you commanded, but I've been so miserable with work, I've yet to answer my Christmas mail. I haven't had time to have my hair treated or *even combed properly. I look such a fright, small children flee in terror at my approach.*

Honestly, Em, isn't it about time you dispensed with the electric shock treatments? In case no one has mentioned it, it hasn't improved your disposition one iota.

The aftermath of last week's ice storm was a sight to behold. In the bright sun, the trees were a mass of glittering diamonds. Even with my eyes, as poor as they are—

Miss Griffin craned her neck over her cards, looking into the hall. "Clara! A man just went into your room."

Clara sent Muggs to the floor and hurried across the hall where Joseph Briggs stood in the middle of her room looking lost, his eyes full of worry.

"Joseph?"

He grasped her hands. "I'm sorry, but I've got to resign my post at Tiffany's, immediately."

She sank into a chair. Losing Joseph would mean she would have to take on all the mosaic work herself. It would never do. She'd either go mad or die—probably both. She searched his face for signs of drunkenness or any hint that he might be playing a joke, and found neither.

"You are not leaving. Unless you've committed murder, I won't let you give up your position at Tiffany's and let us all down." She paused, then, "You haven't have you? Committed murder, I mean."

He shook his head. "It's my wife. She's gone mad with jealousy."

Clara regarded her assistant's weak chin and bulging forehead, and could not imagine what it was about him that might incite such feelings in a woman.

He caught her expression. "I know it's hard to believe, but last week a couple of the girls and I were walking to the trolley together after work when Mrs. Briggs came out of nowhere and charged the girls with a knife. I held her back while the girls escaped, but now she's intent on going to Mr. Tiffany directly and accusing him of running some sort of a bawdy house.

"The thing of it is, my wife is colored. I've heard enough of Tiffany's diatribes about Jews and Negros to know he'd fire me on the spot should he find out."

Clara was trying to imagine how Mr. Tiffany might react to a ranting, crazy, colored woman wielding a knife, when a thought struck her. She turned in her seat to face him. "Let me go with you now to see if I can talk some sense into her."

Joseph looked doubtful. "We live in the colored part of town. I don't think you'd like it much."

"I assure you, I've been in worse places," she said getting to her feet. "Besides, it's better than bloodshed, don't you think?" She hesitated. "To be on the safe side, I'll ask Mr. Allen to accompany us. Wait here."

Half asleep, Philip cracked open his door and squinted into the hall light. He pulled her into his arms, kissing her as he kicked the door shut behind them.

She pushed him away and quickly related Joseph's dilemma.

"Why are you telling me this?" he asked sourly.

"I'm going to speak with Mrs. Briggs. Tonight. At their home. I want you to come with me."

"Oh, for God's sake Clara, the man is a toad. Why would you put yourself into such danger?"

"He is hardly a toad. His pride in his work and his perception of what is beautiful are more than admirable. I can't afford to lose him."

"He wasn't keen enough to have avoided marrying a colored woman."

Ignoring the barbed comment she started for the door. "Will you accompany us or not?"

"I won't, and you won't either. You don't know how dangerous this woman is. She might try to kill you. I won't allow you to take the chance."

She fixed her eyes on him. "You won't *allow* me? I wasn't aware you were in charge of what I do."

"That isn't what I meant."

"I know exactly what you meant, and I *am* going, whether you come along or not."

"Don't be a fool! Going off to talk reason to some irate lunatic makes you seem as insane as she is. Why must you always pry into messes that don't concern you? Involving yourself with your female workers is bad enough, but now you must get entangled with your assistant, too?"

She couldn't have felt any more insulted if he'd struck her. "You're forgetting yourself, Philip!"

"I think you're forgetting *your*self, Clara." He turned his back on her.

"Stay home. Let him go back to whatever rat's nest he came from. His marital problems are none of your business. You have to think about—"

Before he could finish telling her what she had to be thinking about, she slipped into the hall, where Edward was just coming up the stairs.

"Ah, there you are," he said. "Mr. Briggs has told me everything. If we're going to prevent disaster, we'll need to hurry."

The Briggs family occupied two airless overheated rooms that smelled of rancid cooking fat. Three young children, dressed only in gray shirts to the waist and nothing more, lay asleep on a soiled couch. Their legs and ankles were covered with sores—whether from fleas or rats, Clara couldn't be sure.

A young woman in a faded work dress came in from the room that served as both a kitchen and bedroom and introduced herself as Mrs. Briggs's sister. "She's gone to find the girls," she said. "She was like a wildcat when she left."

Joseph gave a sudden nervous snicker.

Edward crossed the room and jerked him to his feet. "Do you think this is humorous, Briggs?" He gestured toward the children. "This is an appalling way to live. Look at your children, man; for God's sake, barn animals are kept better. Where's your sense of decency? You make a good wage, take your family out of this hellhole and bring them to a respectable place."

"You don't understand," Joseph pleaded, "My wife is a madwoman. Her jealousies have driven me to desperate measures. I need to have a clean start somewhere else."

Edward shook him like a misbehaved puppy. "Stop this sniveling about running away and stand up to it like a gentleman. You can't live in terror of being found out for the rest of your life. Tell the truth, and let people think what they may."

Clara could not take her eyes off Edward. Next to Mr. Briggs, he looked preternaturally large and healthy, his life untouched by such troubles. The Edward she knew as an amiable and placid individual was miraculously transformed into a man of strength and command. She marveled at the way he'd taken all the twisty wickedness out of the situation and made it clean and straight.

"Your sympathies are wrongly placed," Joseph protested. "You don't know what I've had to live with."

"Sully the woman all you like, Briggs, but my sympathies don't lie with you. You may be innocent with these girls, but you *have* wronged your wife just the same by keeping her hidden in this filthy pigsty. Where's your pride, man?"

A woman with fine skin and dark, almond eyes barged into the room. Her shoddy attire and wild, uncombed hair did little to conceal the fact she had once been beautiful. She threw herself at Edward's feet, sobbing.

"Everything you've said is true, sir," Mrs. Briggs wailed. "He shuns me and his children and leaves us here in this horrible place. When I saw him walking with those young girls, I lost my head."

Edward lifted her up with an easy courtesy. "Mr. Briggs has treated you and your children shamefully, Madam, and I do not for one moment wonder that you feel as you do, but it isn't other women who make him act poorly, but rather his own bad judgment of his situation.

"I can see that you have been badly used, and I'll see to it that your husband does better by you and finds a decent home that's clean and proper."

"All I've ever wanted is for him to love me," she lamented, giving them an imploring look before bursting into tears and throwing herself once again at Edward's feet.

In response to his wife's dramatic outburst, Joseph rolled his eyes.

Edward seized him. "You meeching scoundrel! Tell her you'll take better care of her and the children."

Joseph cowered.

"Stop that!" Edward shook him, this time hard enough to rattle Joseph's teeth. "Tell her! Now!"

"All right, I'll try, but she must give up her threats and her dagger."

"Your husband has proposed a fair deal," Edward said, holding out his hand. "Give your weapon to me."

An hour later, with promises made and the dagger securely concealed inside Clara's purse, she and Edward started for home, reveling in the fresh, cold air.

"I'm ashamed of him," Edward said finally. "What a mess he's made for himself."

"Yes, he has," she agreed wearily, "however, he is indispensible to me and my department. There is no other mosaicist in the world who is as good."

She took Edward's arm, glad for the comfort he afforded her. "To be honest, I feel sorry for Mrs. Briggs—away from her country and her family and among people who hate her for her color."

"I wouldn't pity her too much," Edward said, "With Mrs. Briggs's talent for melodrama, she could very well be the next star of the stage."

March 4, 1905

Dear Clara,

Your late night escapade with Joe Briggs keeps growing on me. How <u>could</u> you think of going into that horrid, dirty place to meet a woman crazed by injured feelings and jealousy? I am so thankful for the noble Mr. Booth, I could embrace him.

What an awful thing for Mr. Briggs to live with a wife he does not love. Use your influence on him so that he will at least take his family to a nicer place.

I'm still trembling at the thought of what may have happened to you.

Love, Mama

Baltimore, MD
March 7, 1905

Sister: I feel so sorry for Mr. Briggs that I can hardly sleep for thinking of him and the horror he must live through each day with that woman. I know it's best that he stay with her, at least for the children's sake, but what a shame to be saddled like that.

Mr. Booth is good-looking, kind, intelligent, practical and chivalrous— all in one man. If you can't find a use for him, please, send him on to me.

Emily

Tiffany's
March 9, 1905

Dear Ones,

I'm afraid I've stirred your sympathies too much. Not to worry over Joe Briggs! All is jogging along for him, as it has for many weary years. If you have pity to spare, give it to me instead—my work at Tiffany's is without end. Philip is taking me to Still's Oyster House for dinner and then to the theater. I would much rather just sit and listen to him talk, for I find the man far more fascinating than any play.

Love, Clara

P.S. Seriously, Emily, you should rethink these electric treatments. Consider how electricity turns the insides of light bulbs all dark and broken-down looking.

April 10, 1905

"Henry Belknap!" Clara set down her packages and ran to embrace him. "I haven't seen you since before George died."

He clasped her in his arms, and then held her away while they looked each other over. It was easy to see the grief that marked him. The face she once considered as having an almost juvenile mien was now lined and careworn.

"You are ageless," he said. "It's a miracle that even Louis hasn't managed to wear you down."

"But he's trying very hard," she smiled. "I've made over the wisteria lamp so many times the poor old patterns are worn out. Only yesterday he sent me a note demanding I design twenty new clocks. He's obsessed with them this year."

"Why do stay with him?" Henry asked. "I've never understood that."

She didn't answer right away, but unpinned her hat, giving it a shake before placing it on the sidetable. "I've come to the realization that the art and beauty of the things I create take on an importance that is far greater than the constant aggravation Mr. Tiffany inflicts on me."

"And the fact that he's still putting his name on your work?"

Clara shrugged. "I'll never give up trying to convince Mr. Tiffany that my name should be on what I create, but I find great solace in the fact that people see something in my work that gives them pleasure. That in and of itself is almost enough."

He pointed a finger at her. "I see something else in your eyes. If I had to guess, I'd say you're in love."

The blood rushed to her face. "If I'm in love, I certainly have no business being so."

"You're quite wrong on that, my dear. When people say they have no business being in love is precisely when they should fall in love. You're too young and alive to remain a widow. Do I know him?"

She nodded. "I believe the others suspect, but he and I have so little time together, they aren't sure, although I have noticed that Edward has taken to watching us like a hawk."

"No doubt, because Edward is in love with you himself."

"Not likely." She made a sour face. "Edward and I are both too dictatorial, he more than I, if that's even possible."

"So?" Henry leaned close. "Who is the lucky fellow?"

"Mr. Allen."

Henry sat back, his smile gone. "*Philip* Allen?"

"Of course, Philip Allen. Why are you looking like that?"

"I thought Mr. Allen was . . ." he broke off and shrugged. "I thought he'd gone back to his Washington post. I wasn't aware he was in New York again."

She saw the lie but didn't push. If Philip were guilty of past misdemeanors, what of it? Everyone had his or her little peccadilloes. She knew all she needed to know about Philip and loved him for it. She didn't need to know every dark corner of his past.

"You must stay for dinner," she said, leaping to a safer subject. "I'll ask Miss Owens to set another place. Everyone will be glad to see you. Dudley is coming by with Mr. McBride. It will be like old times. We want you back with us again, Henry. We've missed you."

"I can't," he said. "Not yet. Actually, I've come to tell you that I'm leaving New York. My mother's doctor has convinced her she'd be better off in a less demanding city. She's purchased a grand country house in

Salem." He shoved his hands into his pockets. "I think I might take up writing, or perhaps I'll try to market my photography."

"But what about the gallery? What about all of us?"

"I can't stay here, Clara. Every street and building holds memories for me. It only serves to remind me of how lonely I am. I think I might have a better chance at a new beginning in Massachusetts." He glanced at his watch. "I have to go. Mother expected me an hour ago."

They said their goodbyes with promises of frequent visits. Watching him descend the stairs, she could not stop the feeling that her life was diminishing bit by bit.

——§——

June 14, 1905

Still inside the remnants of a dream, Clara raised her arms and slipped them around the man's neck to return his gentle kiss.

"Would you like to ride away with me today to parts unknown?"

The whisper was all too real, each puff of breath tickling her nose. She opened her eyes to find Philip's face above hers. Confused, she lay still, trying to decide whether or not she was still dreaming.

The sharp rap at her door was real enough. She made a mad dash across the room and threw her weight against the door. "Yes, what is it?"

"It's Bernice, Miss Clara. Miss Owens sent me up to tell you and Miss Alice that breakfast will be served in the small dining room this morning 'cause there ain't hardly nobody here."

Clara glanced at the mantle clock and groaned. She'd overslept and would have to hurry to make it to Tiffany's on time. She wheeled on Philip, who was sitting on her bed, grinning like a fool. Instead of his city suit, he was wearing his bicycle clothes.

"What are you doing here?" she whispered. "Have you gone mad? What if Alice or someone else comes in and finds you here? They'll think we . . . we . . ."

"Let them," Philip said, gathering himself up. "Did you know that I love the way you look when you sleep?"

She pushed him toward the door. "You have to leave! I've got to get ready for work."

He caught her by the waist. "It's the perfect morning for an adventure. Take the day off. Ring up Tiffany's and tell them you have the grippe. We'll ask Miss Owens to pack a lunch, and then we can ride out of the city and have a picnic in the hills."

She wiggled out of his grip and brushed past him, seeking the safety of her dressing screen. "I can't. I have a meeting with Mr. Tiffany and his cronies first thing this morning about how to get around the Union contract and hire on more people. I have to be there."

"But it's my only day off for weeks," he complained. "We aren't going to have another chance for ages."

She paused over the buttons on her skirt. It wasn't as if Mr. Tiffany and his board couldn't figure it out for themselves. She opened her mouth to tell him yes, but snapped it shut. With their minds always on schemes to save money, there was the danger the Tiffany Powers That Be might come up with a plan that would put her department at a disadvantage. Her input would be essential. If things fell apart because she'd shirked her responsibility, she wouldn't be able to live with herself.

"The temptation is great," she said, pinning up her hair, "but go I must. They expect me, and if I'm not there, they'll find a way to muck it up, and then my girls and I will have to live with whatever cockamamie plan they come up with."

She emerged from behind the screen and held the door open for him. "I can't be late."

"All right," he teased, "but you'll be sorry."

She sighed. "Believe me, I already am."

For the better part of two hours, the three of them waited in Mr. Platt's office for the tardy Mr. Tiffany. Glad to have brought her sketchbook along, Clara worked out several designs, while Mr. Thomas and Mr. Platt could talk of nothing else except Christy Mathewson pitching a no-hitter the day before, giving the Giants a victory over the Cubs.

Simpkins telephoned several times to report on Mr. Tiffany's progress. In the first call, the valet explained in his understated monotone that Mr. Tiffany was on his way and they were to stay put. A half-hour later, Simpkins reported there was car trouble. In his third call, Simpkins announced that Mr. Tiffany had returned to the house for his notes. The last time he called, he reverted to his original message.

When the phone on Louis's desk rang a fifth time, no one moved to answer it, for the simple reason that they were too stunned by the sight of Louis Tiffany weaving in the doorway, his tie askew and his collar open.

"Ahhh, look who's here—my loyal guard." Louis reached over to hang up his walking stick, missed the hook, and stumbled into the wall. He kicked at the cane and missed.

Before Mr. Thomas or Mr. Platt could react, Clara was on her feet. She leaned in to help him and stopped short. The smell of whiskey that exuded from him was overpowering. "Why Mr. Tiffany, you've been drinking!"

He faced her, his eyes red and wandering uncontrollably in their sockets. "Tho? What do you propose to do about that, Mrs. Driscoll? Call the polith?"

"You can't even stand up straight."

"I motht thertainly can. I'll show you."

In a move that reminded her of a performing circus clown, Louis shoved his toe under the fallen cane and tried to flip it into the air. Teetering backward, he landed on his hindquarters so hard the floor shook beneath their feet.

Mr. Thomas rapidly hoisted him off the floor. "I'll take you home, Mr. Tiffany. You shouldn't be here in this condition."

Louis shook him off. "Get away! I want Clara to take me home. She's prettier than you."

A brief smile flitted across Bond Thomas's face. "I agree with you about that, Louis. However, I'm guessing she doesn't drive nearly as well."

She rushed back to Irving Place, hoping to catch Philip. When he failed to answer his door, she went in search of Miss Owens.

"Let me see." Miss Owens studied the ceiling while she formulated her answer. "Mr. Allen stayed quite a while at breakfast. He drank three cups of coffee while reading the *Times*, and then asked to use the telephone.

I was helping with the dishes, so I didn't pay him much mind, but I did overhear him say he was going to take his wheel up to . . ." Miss Owens frowned and shook her head.

"Up to where?"

"I can't remember. These days, my memory is less like a camel's and more like an unhatched egg."

"Please try, Miss Owens. I want to surprise him. It's his first day off in such a long time, and I won't have this opportunity again for ages. "

Miss Owens snapped her fingers. "Highbridge Park! Came to me just like that. Isn't it funny how the mind plays tricks? Why, my grandmother could remember the name of every one of her schoolmates from the time she was six years old."

"Miss Owens, please! Did he say which part of Highbridge?"

"No," Miss Owens shook her head, "I don't remember that, but I do recall that he asked one of the kitchen maids to pack him a nice lunch. I think she gave him the rest of the ham, with some of that dill mustard my sister made last year, two apples and the last part of that cheese from— "

Calling out her thanks over her shoulder, Clara took the stairs two at a time, already unfastening the buttons on her collar.

Highbridge Park, Manhattan

She found his bicycle amongst the ten or so parked along a low wall at the beginning of a wooded trail. Squeezing her bicycle in alongside his, she bounded up the rocky footpath in anticipation of his surprise at seeing her. He'd break into his slow, crooked smile and pull her behind a tree for a kiss. Later, they'd have dinner at Child's and, if he wasn't too tired, take in a play.

She was thinking of which play they might attend when she spotted his sporty green cap—the one she'd given him for his birthday. She ran a short distance into the woods and hid behind a tree. She'd call out something humorous, maybe something about Danderine and his hair, or maybe she'd just whistle and wait for him to find her.

The cap came closer, bobbing in rhythm with his loping gait. Next his forehead and eyes came into view, then his nose, and finally that sensuous mouth moving in animated speech. She craned forward to get a better view of his companion.

Even from a distance, she could see the woman possessed the delicate flawless beauty that belonged only to the young. Her bicycle suit was cut to show her exceptionally good figure to an advantage.

The woman stayed even with him, moving with a saucy swing, her back straight, and head high. Her voice was clear, the words ringing with a lively spirit. It was the sight of Philip's arm about her waist and the familiarity with which they treated each other, bumping hips and laughing, that robbed her of breath.

For just an instant, she found solace in the thought that the woman might be one of his many cousins, but as they came even to her hiding place, Philip pulled the woman around and kissed her in a manner that could not be considered cousinly by any stretch of the imagination.

Time slowed and stopped. Blind with the pain of betrayal, she saw nothing other than the woman wrapped inside Philip's arms, her mouth on the same lips she'd kissed only a few hours before. She picked her way to the trail, hurrying in the direction of her bicycle as fast as she could without breaking into a run. She hoped by some miracle he might not notice her—but it wasn't a day for miracles.

He shouted her name, the panic in his voice echoing in her ears.

She was within yards of her bicycle, when he caught her by the arm and pulled her around. Over his shoulder she could see the other woman looking a little bewildered, but not threatened—as if she were completely sure of him.

Clara wrenched her arm free. Searching the handsome face that had held her captive for so long, she slapped him hard enough to knock him off balance.

————§————

She remembered nothing of her ride back to Irving Place, except a vague sense of surprise that she could function at all. The shock gave way to anger, anguish, and finally a deep, aching pain that seeped in and overtook her.

Within the hour he was there, nervous, contrite, begging her to listen.

She stood by the window, staring out, seeing nothing. Her hair hung loose in disarray, and she had not yet bothered to change out of her bicycle suit.

"Her name is Ferne Ryan," he began. "We were classmates at the University of Wisconsin. Our parents were good friends, so, of course, our mothers began plotting years ago—probably before we were born. Ferne and I never had a choice."

The curtains billowed in on the breeze, catching on her Tiffany lamp. She pushed them off and lowered the window. "How long have you been betrothed?" she asked, amazed that she could speak at all, let alone be standing without assistance.

"Three years." He turned her around to face him. "Listen to me. It's true that Ferne and I are good friends—like you and Edward—but I'm no more in love with her than she is with me. When I first realized I loved you, I thought I might be able to break away from her, but I wanted to do it gradually, so as not to hurt anyone."

"You are a liar!" she shouted, her voice raw with misery. "I saw you with her. I saw you kiss her and the way she looked at you. Is that what you consider being 'good friends'?" Her voice went raw as she choked out the words. "You've deceived me from the beginning. I thought you were the finest man I'd ever met—a crusader, a paragon of what was right. Now I see you had no regard for me or for anyone other than yourself."

She let the tears run down her face unchecked. "I was happy. I looked forward to getting up in the morning. For once, I had more than my work to look forward to. For once I felt I knew was it was to love and to feel passion." She made herself look at him. "No man has ever known me as well as you. And to think that I almost compromised myself and that you would have *let* me!"

He touched her shoulder. "Please Clara, won't you—?"

"No, I won't!" She slapped his hand away. "I want you to leave and not come back. You've broken my trust, and that's an injury that can never be mended."

He stood with his arms at his sides. "Please don't shut me out like this. Tell me what I can do to make this right with you."

"Nothing. There's nothing left here. Go marry her. Marry your Ferne Ryan, and leave me alone."

——§——

July 26, 1905
Tiffany Glass and Decorating Company

There was nothing subtle about the pain she felt in losing Philip. The work at Tiffany's that she once declared would be the death of her was now the only thing that kept her from wallowing in the memories and what might have been.

Louis was thrilled by the volume and quality of her things, but not so thrilled that he was willing to entertain any further raises in her salary.

To her relief, Edward once again took up the quest of devising new diversions and entertainments. At the moment, she was wishing he would come and distract the whole of the women's department from the terrible heat.

By noon, the temperature inside the workroom had reached an unprecedented 109 degrees, despite the bank of fans lined up like sentinels in front of the windows. Resolved not to have any of her flock succumb to the unpleasant forces of nature, she set up the usual buckets of ice water cut with alcohol in the corners of the workroom. All of the women draped cloths dipped in the cooling mixture over their heads and around their necks, so that at first sight they resembled a group of religious fanatics.

Regardless of their efforts, the women, and finally Joseph and Frank, dropped like flies. By closing time, she and Mr. Bracey were two of four who'd managed to stick it out. As she started for home, her blinding headache grew steadily worse, until she was so caught up in pain and nausea she could not keep her thoughts straight, let alone voice them.

As she crossed Gramercy Park, she came to the frightening realization that she wasn't sure which direction she needed to go to get home. Blurred by the haze of heat, none of the streets or buildings seemed familiar, though she was fairly sure it was the same route she'd traveled every day for years.

She lowered herself onto the nearest bench, desperately wanting to capture and corral her thoughts, a task that proved to be like trying to catch smoke with one's hands. She could make out the figure of a policeman standing on the corner, but when she tried to wave him over, she couldn't lift her arms.

In the middle of trying to find the humor in dying on a park bench in broad daylight, she felt the last of her strength ebb away. Her head slumped onto her chest, and whatever thoughts were left, fractured and floated away into a black void.

Minutes or days later—she had no way of telling—she was conscious of being shaken. "Miss Clara? Are you alright?" The voice sounded like it was coming from the bottom of a deep well.

A woman lifted her chin. Clara opened her mouth to speak, but her tongue was thick, and all that came out was a sound like that of a choking baby.

"Don't you know me, Miss?" The woman searched her face for signs of recognition. "It's Bernice, the housemaid from Miss Owens's. Are you sick, ma'am?"

Bernice? Miss Owens? The names swirled in the fog that had taken over her mind, and then disappeared. Crying weakly, she attempted to wipe away the saliva running down her chin and could not. She sank once again into the murk then came back up to find the woman, Bernice, and a man looming over her, wearing expressions of grave concern. Bernice began chaffing her hands, while the man held a canteen to her lips, forcing her to swallow a heavily sugared liquid.

He pulled off her high collar, and she managed a sigh. There was nothing she loved more than a dress without a collar. His commanding voice forced her back to the surface.

"Clara, wake up! You must drink as much as you can!"

She swallowed a little at a time, the rest spilling onto her dress. The next thing she knew, he had her in his arms and was running. Through the blurred window of her vision, shocked faces flashed by. A door opened, and Miss Owens appeared.

Overjoyed at the sight of someone she recognized, she waved a finger and tried to form the words to say she didn't think she'd be having dinner when, without realizing how, she was on someone's sofa with Miss Owens bent over her removing her clothing.

Stripped down to only a thin cotton chemise, she felt herself being lowered into a tub filled with cool water and ice. The fog that was keeping her mind prisoner slowly lifted.

The man—she saw now it was Edward—removed his shoes and socks, rolled up his pant legs and got into the water with her. He gently rubbed her down, encouraging her to stay with them. A faint smile came to her lips, as she tried to imagine where else she might possibly go.

Miss Owens packed iced cloths under her arms and around her neck, and poured numbingly cold water over the top of her head until her scalp tingled. Alice materialized out of nowhere, alternately spooning salty broth and then sugared water into her mouth.

It wasn't until they lifted her out of the tub that they noticed her chemise had turned diaphanous. A gentleman to his core, Edward averted his eyes even while carrying her to her room, where she lay inside her cotton towel cocoon until the doctor arrived.

It was an easy diagnosis: heatstroke, the same thing that killed dozens of horses in New York's summer streets. The doctor assured them that had she not been found and treated so efficiently, she would have had the distinction of being the first woman to perish on a Gramercy Park bench.

44 Irving Place Prison
July 31, 1905

Dear Ones,

By now you will have received Mr. Booth's letter describing last week's fiasco. The doctor insists I stay in bed and only allows me to be up for one hour a day. I am to eat fruit and drink warm tea at least 6 times a day. I dare not ignore his advice (even though I am PERFECTLY WELL), for I am constantly under the eye of my self-appointed jailer, Warden Booth.

August 2nd is Beatrix Hawthorne's wedding. She's marrying a literary man 12 years her senior. I'm sick about not being able to attend, for I am curious as a cat to see what kind of man was clever enough for her.

On the subject of marriage, I forgot to tell you that I went to Mrs. Cornwell's swanky Murray Hill home for Independence Day dinner. During dessert, she announced to all present that she is bound and determined to marry me off to a rich society man. I haven't laughed so hard in months. I told her I didn't have the time or the correct attitude, but she wouldn't hear of it and said that I was wasting my time loafing around 44 Irving Place.

She went on to say that she'd heard rumors Mr. Tiffany was drinking heavily since the death of his wife, and since he respected me so much, wouldn't it be just the thing for me to help him see the light and perhaps come up married in the process? She kept repeating: "Clara Wolcott Tiffany. It has such a lovely ring to it."

I told her I couldn't think of a worse fate. I can just imagine me chained to the worktable in his private studio, with the valet Simpkins standing over me with a whip and a serving tray of hot cocoa.

The dictatorial Warden Booth tells me my time is up, and I must abandon this strenuous occupation of writing, as it's time for more fruit and tea. (He's so bossy, he watches me until every drop and bite is consumed).

Much love, Clara

P.S. Dear Rev. and Mrs. Cutler and Fair Emily:

I've read over the previous page, and I am not so bad as I have been painted. But, despite these barbed aspersions, I'm doing well and happy in my task of watching over our reluctant ~~prisoner~~ patient. I hope you will come for another visit. Your comforting presence is always welcome here.

Now I must tend to our slightly bruised flower. I bid you adieu and Godspeed.

With love to all, Edward Abraham Booth

August 5, 1905

Dearest Clara,

When you saw the frightful record of 109-degree heat at Tiffany's, why didn't you flee as a bird to the mountains? Don't you ever stay there again under such stress of weather, even if Tiffany's and all it stands for melts to the ground! I thank God for Mr. Booth's presence of mind and his quick actions. What a treasure of a man!

In a few days, we are having a telephone installed in the dining room. We're going to insulate it so that we won't hear the usual hums and buzzes. It will be quite a comfort and help, since we are not able to run about as we once did.

Here is Emily now, pen in hand. I relinquish the robin to her.

Much love, Mama

Clara:

You speak about the dimming of my bulb? How was it possible that you didn't notice you were no longer perspiring? Nevertheless, we are once again in a furious rack against Tiffany's N.Y. I don't know with whom I am more angry, you or that arrogant miser you call your employer.

Remember, you are my only remaining sister. It would not do for you to leave me an only child. Who else would be left to rub my feet in my dotage?

Emily

September 21, 1905

Clara was mildly flattered to be included as an unofficial member of Tiffany's board meetings, though, considering she was responsible for designing the majority of the merchandise sold, it seemed only natural.

Louis sat with his arms folded across his chest, all but his eyes impassive. She could read those eyes better than anyone, and in them she saw his quiet, stubborn fury simmering just under the surface.

"Our objective this morning," Mr. Thomas began, "is to solve the ongoing problem we face every year with the holiday rush and not being able to handle it because of lack of help. At present, Tiffany's employs the maximum number of female glass workers allowed under the union contract. We're here to devise a way to increase the amount of output without increasing the female workforce."

"I've been thinking about this a great deal as of late," Mr. Schmidt said cautiously, avoiding looking in Louis's direction. "What about sending Mrs. Driscoll to Boston to start another company for us? We would, of course, market the product, but she could manage the place."

Mr. Platt gave a nod of approval. "A wonderful idea. In Boston, there would be no limit on the number of people she could hire. She certainly knows enough about the business to do a fine job."

Clara considered the proposition. Going to Boston meant leaving New York and everything and everyone she knew. On the other hand, it also meant having complete control over her own work. With Henry close by, he could introduce her into a new group of friends, and New York was a relatively short train trip. "I *could* do it," she said. "It isn't as though Boston is on the other side of the world."

"Absolutely not!" Louis thumped his cane for emphasis. "I'm well aware you've all been conspiring about this for weeks, and you can put the idea right out of your minds. I want Mrs. Driscoll here. End of discussion."

Mr. Platt cleared his throat. "Think of it as expansion, Louis. We can make twice the money. It's reasonable to assume there's a market for our things everywhere. New York City isn't the universe. My God, man, the Boston Brahmins would storm the showroom, money in hand."

"No!" Louis's jaw clenched. "I won't stand for it. Mrs. Driscoll stays here!"

Silence fell as the men stared down at the table with feigned interest, as if they'd each found their destiny written in the grain of the wood.

"Why not, Mr. Tiffany?" Clara asked with a lift of her shoulders. "Why won't you stand for it?"

They all looked at her, their expressions a mixture of shock and amusement.

"Because, Mrs. Driscoll, I want to be able to direct everything myself. God only knows what trouble you'll get into up there without my oversight."

"You mean the way I get into so much trouble here?"

Mr. Schmidt guffawed and instantly covered it with a cough.

Louis's eyes narrowed. "Are you mocking me, Mrs. Driscoll?"

She gave up. To question him was one thing, but to goad him into a disagreement was altogether beneath her. It would be too much like teasing a cranky child.

"I have a proposal," she said. "I'm thinking that the best way to get around the union, at least as far as the mosaic work goes, is to start a union department inside my department and appoint Mr. Briggs as head man. Mr. Briggs could hire as many men as he needed to do the basic work, which would free up some of my girls to work on things that require more skill and artistic judgment.

"Of course this would need great tact and diplomacy so as not to get the men riled, but we can manage that. God forbid I should have to start sending gift baskets again."

The men looked at each other, and then to Louis, who broke into a smile.

Laurelton Hall
November 17, 1905

Eighteen months is long enough to play this tiresome mourning role! I've ordered Simpkins to burn my widower's clothes. I am not hardhearted—I do miss Louise; she was my anchor even if I sometimes found the rock too weighty to bear happily.

I seem to have failed as a father as well as a husband. My daughters generally look upon me with a wary, distasteful eye. Dorothy and Comfort avoid me entirely.

Clara is frequently on my mind. I am mulling over the idea of formally pursuing the lady, although there are many things to be considered. Right now her value to the company is worth more to me than my need of companionship. I can't imagine she would have objections to such an arrangement. Certainly the difference of 13 years in our ages would be nothing to a woman who once married a man almost old enough to be her grandfather.

The battle over my land and riparian rights drags on. These people seem not to understand that I'm not like them. They must consider that my standing in the world is a universe apart from their own. I am one of an extravagant people who lead extravagant lives. L.C.T.

~24~

February 9, 1906

Dearest Clara and Alice,

The pleasure of your company is requested at Laurelton Hall, on the weekend of February 10 — 12. My chauffeur will arrive at 44 Irving Place promptly at 6 p.m. Saturday, February 10th, to convey you to Cold Spring Harbor.

Dinner will be served promptly at 9 p.m. <u>Be on time!</u>

L. C. Tiffany

February 10, 1906

Dear Mr. Tiffany,

Thank you for your generous invitation to Laurelton Hall. However, it is with regret that Miss Gouvy and I must decline, due to having made previous plans.

<u>With sufficient notice</u>, I am sure we will be able to visit your new home at some future date.

C. P. Driscoll and A.C. Gouvy

MISS GRIFFIN INSISTED on inflicting her new health regime on everyone. Designed to keep them alive far into their nineties, several of the practices seemed to Clara more barbaric than beneficial. Foregoing the water and yogurt enemas and other equally invasive measures, she and Alice decided a spirited walk through Madison Square Park was the least objectionable.

"Mr. Tiffany has been acting peculiar as of late," Clara said, slowing in an effort to match Alice's shorter stride.

"You mean more peculiar than usual?"

"I suppose. He's needing to know what I'm doing every second of the day, constantly asking my opinions on everything from running the business right on down to what I think of his suits and hats."

They came to a bench occupied by two lovers oblivious to everything except each other, and hurried on. "I have some news I think you should hear," Alice began solemnly. "One of the women who works at the factory with me is Philip's cousin. She told me that he and Miss Ryan have set a wedding date for early October. I thought you should know."

Surprised the hurt was still so fierce, Clara said nothing until they reached the park entrance at East Twenty-third. "I suppose you guessed that Philip and I—"

Alice swung around with an air of exasperation. "For God's sake, Clara, *everyone* knew. Did you think we were dense *and* blind? It was almost indecent the way you'd start looking feverish whenever he was around."

"I did have a fever," she said, softly. "In hindsight, you might say I was out of my mind."

"I'm sorry," Alice said, taking her hand. "That wasn't fair of me. It must have hurt you terribly to see them together. I wish you could have been spared that indignity at least."

"You know about *that*, too?" Clara snatched her hand away and rounded on her. "Is nothing private?"

"You aren't the only who was hurt, you know," Alice shot back. "Philip was overcome with grief and guilt over the whole affair. Mr. Yorke told us he was inconsolable for weeks. And what about *us*? You never once came to me about this. It was as if you had no trust in me. We're a close-knit family, Clara. Precious few things are kept secret among us, especially when it so affects one of our dearest members."

"And I don't suppose any of you considered telling me he was engaged?" Clara said, bitterly. "What a low trick—all of you letting me go on making a fool of myself. How could you have been so deliberately cruel? Especially *you*, my closest friend!" She turned onto Park Avenue, walking rapidly in the direction of Gramercy Park.

"It wasn't our place to tell you," Alice yelled, running after her. She grabbed Clara's arm and spun her around. "Even if we told you, would it have made any difference? We kept waiting and hoping that Philip would say something to you about it. Later, when we realized he was falling in love with you, we were sure he'd break his engagement, but he didn't."

Alice's shoulders fell, her anger spent. "By the time we realized how involved you were, none of us had the courage or the heart to tell you, so we kept watch over you. Why do you think we hardly ever left the two of you alone?"

"So the night Edward found us at the cabin, he already knew?"

"Yes, of course. He was determined to save you from making your own misery. Had he missed the ferry that night, I think he would have risked swimming the river."

Clara closed her eyes and sighed. "What a fool I've been. I'll never forgive myself for this."

Alice looked at her in genuine surprise. "Forgive yourself for what? No one is blaming you. Most of us secretly envy you."

"Envy me?" She gave a harsh laugh. "I've made a fool of myself, my friends were put to great tests on my behalf, and I almost ruined myself in the bargain."

"All true," Alice agreed, "but you loved passionately and were loved in return. I would give anything to know that feeling once in my life, even if it did ruin me. Many women go to their graves never having known passion like that. I'm fairly certain that everyone who has ever felt it has made a fool of themselves at one time or another."

She pinched Clara's cheek. "Forgive yourself. Just promise me you don't let this stop you from loving again."

——§——

April 2, 1906

Clara stated her case in no uncertain terms. Beating around the bush with Louis Tiffany was never a good idea.

"I want to go to Europe in May and return in October. It will be slow here, and Mr. Briggs is perfectly capable of handling anything that might come up."

Louis said nothing. It was hard for her to judge from his expression what he was thinking. He held his tented fingers over the lower half of his face, tapping his nose with the point of his index fingers.

"I'll visit all the galleries, sketching everything I see," she continued. "When I come back, I'll be filled with ideas for new things. Actually, you could look at this trip as a sort of investment in future projects." She raised her eyebrows. "What do you say?"

Louis lowered his fingers. "By all means go."

She tilted her head, not sure she'd heard him correctly. "I beg your pardon?"

"It will be a wonderful experience," Louis continued. "I'll give you a list of my favorite sketching places."

Suspicion wound itself around her and squeezed. She knew him too well—his quick generosity would not be without a price. However, if she could make it to the hall without his saying anything more, she just might be home free. She took an experimental step back toward the door. "When I return, I promise to give you wonderful designs." Another step. "Perhaps we might even branch into some new novelty."

"I'm sure whatever inspiration you have will be exceptional—it always is." Louis continued to tap his nose. "However," he paused, "before I agree to let you go, you must find a replacement."

"Replacement? Mr. Briggs is my replacement."

"I'd rather you choose someone else. Mr. Briggs knows the work, but he doesn't have the sensitive, feminine touch you do, nor does he have any idea how to keep the books."

He took the pencil out from behind his ear and began scribbling on his desk pad. "Whomever you find will have to meet my approval. I can't let you leave until you do." He looked off into the middle distance. She could almost hear him plotting.

"If you do manage to find a suitable replacement," he said at length, "I think I'll send Miss Northrop along with you. The two of you can share a stateroom and split the expense."

Her dream of having a nice little stateroom all to herself withered away. Agnes Northrop's heart and soul belonged to Louis Tiffany. That meant that besides always having to be on her best behavior, she'd never be able to complain about him.

"Well then," she said, "I'd better hurry and make my selections, so that Miss Northrop has plenty of time to pack."

44 Irving Place
April 20, 1906

Dearest Mama, et al,

I received the robin tonight, and it was like an oasis in a weary land. I feel as though I've been dragged through a knothole at work. Mr. Platt came to tell me that, to date, greater than 125 of my lamp designs have been made. It's an accomplishment I suppose, although at present I find little joy in it.

Details of the terrible San Francisco earthquake have reached us. Everyone is appalled at the devastation. Edward says it will take years to rebuild.

Emily, you will be relieved to know Mr. Briggs's affairs are looking up. He moved his family into a house he bought outside the city. There's an apple orchard on the land, and Mrs. Briggs has installed three dozen laying hens and planted a large garden. When the apples come in, she plans on selling them to the vendors.

My best news is that on May 12th, I will be aboard the S.S. Prinzess Irene of the North German Lloyd Line, heading for Europe. How I wish you could be there to see me off . . . or better yet, go with me. Edward is green with envy. He so much wants to visit his family and give me a personal tour of London, but cannot take the time from work.

Mr. Tiffany wants to send Miss Northrop along to ensure I don't have too good a time. She'd be full of Mr. Tiffany this, Mr. Tiffany that, every moment of the day and night. I'm not going to worry about it, and I'm not going to let it interfere with my good time either. If she says one word about Tiffany or his studios, I shan't hesitate to push her overboard.

Miss Griffin is giving up her room to one of the other Tiffany Girls and will take my room for the summer, so that I am relieved of that expense.

I'm having a silk evening dress made for aboard ship, and my ecru linen traveling suit is being completely made over with navy blue braid. I've put off shopping for a hat until I can get up the courage. The thought of those evil milliners measuring my head, clucking their tongues and making comments under their breath makes me want to bite somebody.

Now, all that I have left to do is to find my replacement. Mr. Tiffany has rejected my last four recommendations. Everyone at Irving Place is wracking their brains, and I must say, we've come up with some humorous solutions. Edward said the best idea is to put Frank in charge. In all honesty, I agree he would be the best choice, for he's a fine artistic talent with a wonderful sense of color. He has a head for numbers and bookkeeping, and, when Mr. Tiffany or the girls began to harp and chatter, he would remain serene, not being able to hear a word of criticism or complaint.

The bell has rung, and I must go worry some more over my replacement. I love you and can hardly wait to see you this fall.

With all my love, Clara

May 5, 1906
Lenox Hill

The Tiffany Spring Ball, held at the Lenox Hill mansion, was the biggest event of the year for the Tiffany Company employees. Besides giving them a day off to prepare, it provided them with the golden opportunity of seeing firsthand how the other half lived.

In their spring finery, the Tiffany Girls reminded Clara of a flock of beautiful birds. Frank and the boys from the stockrooms looked dashing in their dark suits as they danced the girls around the floor, until all anyone could see were swirling white skirts and flashes of the men's patent leather boots.

Stooped and somber as an ancient egret, Simpkins approached her and bowed. "Mr. Tiffany requests the pleasure of your company, Mrs. Driscoll. He wishes me to escort you to his room."

"His room?"

"Yes, Madam."

"You mean his boudoir?"

"Yes, Madam."

She nodded. "Please tell Mr. Tiffany I'll see him in the library."

"Very good, Madam."

"Is Dorothy here, Simpkins?"

"Yes, Madam. She arrived last night from St. Timothy's. I have already informed her of your presence."

Simpkins hadn't gone five feet when he hesitated. "Madam?"

"Yes, Simpkins?"

"Mr. Tiffany is . . . well, Madam, you should know that Mr. Tiffany is . . ."

"Drunk?"

"No, not tonight. What I mean to say is that Mr. Tiffany is . . . "

She could see how difficult it was for him. "It's all right, Simpkins. You may trust me with whatever it is. I'll not give you away."

The elderly valet nodded. "Thank you, Madam. What I mean to say is that Mr. Tiffany is not happy. I worry for him. He imbibes too much, too often. The children have done with him, and he's . . ." Simpkins hesitated, looking down at his shoes. "He is in need of a wife."

She pursed her lips. "I couldn't agree more, Simpkins, however although I do provide solutions to many of his problems, that is one thing Mr. Tiffany will have to take care of on his own."

For a moment Simpkins looked even more somber than usual, a feat she wouldn't have thought possible.

"Yes, Madam. However, as Mr. Tiffany thinks so highly of you, I thought perhaps—"

"Go no further, Simpkins. I understand, but I'm afraid I must disappoint. I am no fair candidate for marriage, not even for our dear Mr. Tiffany. I'm quite settled on that point."

Simpkins let out a mournful sigh, bowed, and then hobbled away.

She found Edith Griffin at the refreshments table and quickly drew her aside. "In ten minutes have one of the attendants show you to the library. Say that Mr. Tiffany and Mrs. Driscoll are expecting you."

Miss Griffin grimaced. "But Mr. Tiffany hates to be interrupted when he meets with you. What should I say when I get there?"

"Don't worry about that, only make sure you don't leave the library without me, no matter what Mr. Tiffany says."

The library door was ajar when she arrived. Louis was already there, writing at a corner table. Upon seeing her, he came across the room to kiss her hand. In his evening dress, he cut a handsome figure. Any woman who didn't know him well might be swept off her feet. He was so nearly a gentleman, though not quite.

"The girls are hoping you'll come down to the ball." She disengaged her hand and hid it in the soft folds of her gown. "It doesn't seem fair that we should be having all the fun without our host."

"I'll come down after a while, but only if you promise to honor me with a dance or two."

"Of course." She went to the table that held her prize-winning dragonfly lamp. "Simpkins said you wanted to see me?"

"Yes." He edged casually toward her. "I've purchased tickets for the theater next Saturday, and I'd like you to accompany me. Afterwards, I thought we might have dinner at Delmonico's. Would you like that?"

She moved to an adjacent table. "That's very nice of you, Mr. Tiffany, but have you forgotten that I'm sailing for Europe on Saturday?"

Louis stopped in his advance, his expressions revolving from hopeful expectation to disappointment and finally, annoyance. "I've not approved anyone to replace you. My express instructions were that you couldn't leave until you found someone I deemed capable."

She could barely suppress a smile. "But I have found a replacement. She's inarguably the best choice, so I have no doubt you'll approve. She's worked for you for some years and . . . ah, here she is now. Come in Miss Griffin."

Dazzled by the splendor of the library, Edith Griffin stood speechless in the doorway.

Clara took her by the elbow and guided her to Louis. "I was just telling Mr. Tiffany that you'll be assuming my position while I'm away." She gave Louis a look, trying not to sound too delighted with herself. "Miss Griffin was right under my nose the whole time— quite literally. Not only is she an integral part of the women's department, she occupies the room directly across the hall from mine at Irving Place."

Beaming, she placed an arm affectionately around Miss Griffin's small shoulders. "Miss Griffin meets all your requirements. She's a fine critic and her artwork is beyond reproach. She's very orderly; and more importantly, the women respect her. Have I forgotten anything, Miss Griffin?"

"Yes," Miss Griffin said, recovering herself. "I held a position as bookkeeper for two years before I came to work for you, Mr. Tiffany. I am quite able to handle all the accounting for the department as well."

Tiffany stroked his beard, his expression one of a man who had been outwitted and did not like it.

"Oh, and as far as Miss Northrop's accompanying me?" Clara said. "I've already checked with her, and unfortunately she's not able to go right now, such short notice and all that."

Louis danced with her only once, and, to her relief, did not attempt to engage her in conversation. Afterward, he made a short speech about how proud he was of everyone, and then disappeared, not to be seen again.

At one a.m., Clara tucked the last of her flock safely into cabs and was allowing Simpkins to help her on with her coat, when from the corner of her eye, she saw a flutter of green silk descending the grand staircase.

She held out her arms to embrace the lovely young woman with the smoldering looks of a gypsy. "The butterfly has emerged from it's chrysalis, and what a beauty she is. How are you, dear, or shall I begin addressing you as Miss Tiffany?"

"I'll always be Dorothy to you." The girl's eyes sparkled with pleasure, as she led Clara to a sitting room to the side of the entry hall, where a log burning in the grate gave off the pleasant scent of oak.

Clara warmed herself by the fire. "How do you like St. Timothy's?"

"I don't, but my aunt thinks it's the best thing for me. The only thing I do like about it is that it takes me away from here—from him."

"Is he really such a trial for you? Don't you have any love for him?"

"I suppose because he's my father, I must love him" she said plaintively, "but I don't like him very much. After Mama died, we were terrified of what he would do. He didn't disappoint us—he turned into a real tyrant. His tempers kept us terrified.

"Have you been to the Palace yet?"

"The Palace?"

"Laurelton Hall. My sisters and I call it the Palace. We've dubbed Father King Louie the Nineteenth, because we believe he's partly mad. What else can one say about a man who changes his suits three times a day and quotes from Louie Pasteur's papers on the germ theory like he's quoting scripture? And if you ever wondered where all the clocks you designed went, you need search no further than the Palace. His obsession with punctuality forced him to install two, sometimes three clocks in all the rooms."

Clara watched the young woman, noting every detail and change in her. Quick-witted and expressive, Dorothy possessed all the magnetism of her father, but without any trace of falsity.

"He isn't like my friends' fathers," Dorothy continued. "I suppose because he's wealthier than the rest, but the other girls' fathers are so much more devoted to their families than he is. Frankly, Clara, I don't know how you've managed to stay with him. As far as I can tell, you're the only woman besides my mother who has ever stood up to him and his rages." Her lips curled into a mischievous smile. "I'll warn you—he's looking for another wife."

"So Simpkins has already informed me," Clara said. "Don't tell me you would want me to—?"

"No!" Dorothy shrank back in mock horror. "I wouldn't think of it! For as much as I would love to have you as my stepmother, I wouldn't wish that fate on my worst enemy, let alone a dear friend."

Lenox Hill
May 6, 1906

I have half a mind to book passage on Clara's liner. But perhaps it's best to let her have her freedom for a time? There may be something to the saying that absence makes the heart grow fonder. Perhaps when she views the great cathedral windows, she'll find herself thinking of me.

When she returns, I shall barrage the lady with invitations. I've been out of the game for some time, and the rules of courtship are a bit more complicated now. Thank God I no longer have an appetite for coquettish flesh. I don't know how Stanford White keeps up with all his girls. He continues to carry on with the young Evelyn Thaw, née Nesbit. She is barely in her twenties, and he is a man of fifty-two!

I suppose we all have our flirtations with danger— Mr. White with his numerous girls, me with the bottle. I wonder what tempts Clara? Certainly recognition, but I wonder—greatness? L.C.T.

~25~

June 21, 1906

Dearest Clara,

    It doesn't seem possible that my little girl, who used to play tricks on the other children by dressing the cats and dogs in their bonnets and socks, is now sitting in the Forum and Coliseum and being blessed by the Pope—but there you are.

    I have received more lovely letters from our dear Mr. Booth telling us all the exciting news of your Irving Place family. He also sent a kaleidoscope to amuse me. What a wonder of an invention. I sit for hours looking out at a new world of crazy quilt colors and cracked lines.

    Our best news: Mr. Booth has offered to come with Dudley Carpenter and Mr. Yorke to build a new porch and put up an arbor where the old one fell last winter. He has already drawn up the plans and thinks they can be built in four days.

    Maternal advice is sometimes good, but one must be prudent about offering such counsel, especially when that child has done a masterful work of making her own life adorned with success and happiness. I do not mean to be intrusive, but I want to say that I wish you thought as much of Mr. Booth as he does of you. He is such a fine, upstanding man, and I hope that some day you may see him as more than a friend. If it's any recommendation, I believe Emily is half in love with him herself—imagine <u>that</u>!

    Not to worry you darling, but I've had a little twist in my heart that passed as quickly as it came. The doctor tells me I must rest often, so I shall leave off for now and go sit outside with my kaleidoscope.

Have you figured out yet who sent the bouquet of orchids to your stateroom?

We have.

Love, Mama

June 28th

We have been busy. Like a noble and conquering army, your sturdy good men came and built our arbor and porch with precision and aplomb. At the end of day, drooped with weariness, they triumphed over my kitchen as well. Mr. Booth cooked our suppers while Mr. Yorke and Dudley washed and dried the dishes. After dinner, Mr. Booth kept us entertained with witty stories, while Dudley charmed us all by drawing our portraits. We've found Mr. Yorke to be a veritable cornucopia of knowledge.

Four days later, these three miracles of kindness vanished back to their own work as quietly and orderly as they had come. How blessed you are to have such a rich and loving second family.

Your last letter written on the train to Switzerland has been read so many times by so many relatives and neighbors that the paper is worn thin. Your descriptions of Vesuvius and your sail around Capri are being quoted throughout Tallmadge.

You have not mentioned if Tiffany is paying you anything while you are gone, or if this is all dead expense. I ask because Emily came back from Chicago, where she went to a gift shop to buy a $2.50 vase for her room. The shopkeeper asked if she wanted to see the Tiffany ware. Inside the case were all of your hard-worked designs—ink holders, tea screens, vases, jewelry—selling for a king's ransom that certainly no regular mortal could ever afford.

Your two loving families are in a united front against Tiffany and his schemes. He is, in our collective opinion, a scoundrel, one without regard for anything or anyone other than himself and his money.

On the matter of scoundrels, the papers are full of the murder of Stanford White by the cuckolded husband of some misguided girl. If I recall,

Mr. White was the man Mr. Booth threw down the stairs many years ago for his attempted misconduct with you. Now he has been thrown down for good.

Here in Tallmadge we have our own scandal: Ed Hewlett has put his sister, Sarah, in an asylum for the insane. Sarah is about as insane as I am, and there are plenty here who will attest to her sweet nature and <u>normal</u> mind. It made me weep to hear that they cut off all her beautiful hair and took away her clothes, and then practically starved the girl. They will not give her her mail, but open it themselves. I hope to goodness he reads my last letter to her, for his eyes will burn at what I think of him.

I've sold the Jersey cow, so instead of having 18 qts. of milk each day to care for, butterize and sell, we now have 2 qts., just enough for use in cooking and at table. The doctor advises I buy my butter along with my bread, since I am to leave off baking as well. Rev. Cutler is advised not to exert himself, so now we are both in command of our hours to take things easy.

I gave the chickens to Violet Price Talbot. Her little son and daughter are the most delightful children, and how clever is the Lord to have made them in the image of their father. What God did not give to Violet in intelligence and looks, He made up in maternal talent. When I tried to give her little Alfred one of my old waists to be worn as a shirt, he took it outside, flung himself down and rolled around in the dirt yelling all the while, "I won't have it, Mrs. Cutler, I simply won't have it!" We laughed until we wept.

Love, Mama

July 16

I pick up where I left off with good news. The Hewlett affair has been made public, and Mr. Hewlett and his wife are scourged without mercy. God forgive me, but I am glad.

Mrs. Fenn has taken in Sarah. Under that good woman's care, she'll be brought to health and, with God's grace, will be restored to her rightful inheritance that her brother stole from her.

We've received your card about Marcus Aurealius's horse and the Temples at Paestum. You must have been very ill indeed, not to ride the horses at Siena. Your new Paris hat and gown sound lovely. I can hardly wait to see them on the genuine article.

It is hot and I am very tired so must rest for now. I'll write later when I am stronger.

Love, Mama

August 4, 1906

Sister:

I fear Mama is losing ground. She is fainting, and her breathing is poor. The doctor says there is no way of telling whether or not she will rally after this last bad attack of heart congestion. She tries to assure us, but she is failing.

You have been gone almost three months. It's time for you to come home. Rev. Cutler cannot cope alone. Dudley Carpenter and Alice are coming to look after Mama for a week, while I arrange things at school. Mr. Booth has offered to help in any way he can.

One of our neighbors, whom I shall not name, referred to you once (and only once, you can be sure) as ' improperly gallivanting over Italy like a wild horse in need of hobbling.' Upon hearing this blasphemy, Mama, as sick as she was, bolted from her bed and paid the crone a visit to give her a rather harsh tongue lashing. I'm willing to bet the old bat won't make that mistake again.

Mr. Yorke and I are corresponding about the door springs and the adjustments to the new arbor.

Emily

August 15, 1906
Liverpool, England

Dearest Mama,

I sail today on the SS Baltic and will be home before you know it. I long to hold you safely in my arms and look upon your beautiful face.

I love you. Clara

~26~

Dear Emily,

When I arrived, I found sweet Alice and Edward waiting for me at the station, flowers in hand. New York sounded awful, but looked so bright and clean. The subway and everything I saw made me feel seized and held by the old spell, but I shall soon get over it.

Miss Griffin's things are still strewn about my room. She's not had time to fix it up, as Mr. Tiffany has worked her hard in my absence. She had to hire a colored woman for $2 to help clean up and move me back in. In the meantime, I'm sleeping in Edward's clean and orderly room, while he shares quarters with Mr. Yorke.

My first day back at Tiffany's, as I stepped into the hall, there was Miss Northrop greeting me with great enthusiasm. Two of my best girls saw me and spread the news. I was nearly eaten up by the lambs, who rushed out in a body. On this pleasant tide of friendliness I was born into the workroom. Frank nearly had spasms and would have been holding my hand yet, had I not forcibly withdrawn it. Altogether, my heart was quite warmed by it all.

Dudley's exhibition was lucrative. He sold several paintings, one of them the portrait of our beloved Alice in her mother's wedding dress. He is presently doing a full-length portrait of me in my Paris hat and gown, but he's such a perfectionist and so temperamental that I fear it won't be done much before my eightieth birthday.

Oh Em, it's just you and me now. Poor old scrawny robin, no longer a round, proud bird of letters. I open the envelope looking for Mama's handwriting. Not finding it, I suddenly remember and feel the loss afresh. Sometimes I have dreams she is here, and I wake up expecting to see her sitting in my rocking chair, mending.

I burst into tears at the oddest times—at a kind word or when I see a mother being tender with her child. The vision of Mama in those days after she could no longer speak — she looked like a living saint. Her last moment stays in my mind, when it looked like she rallied, and she took our hands and smiled so that her face was luminous.

My regard for Mr. Tiffany has raised a notch, for he's been very kind. I don't think I've seen him like this before, except for a brief moment here and there. Perhaps he has mellowed with age.

Tonight Alice is taking me to Low's for dinner, and tomorrow, to Henry Street Settlement for tea. There is to be an elaborate supper in Chinatown with Edward, after which I'm to read from Pride and Prejudice *for the Irving Place family.*

Now it's back to the mines, dear sister. Be well and take care of yourself.

Love, Clara

P.S. My oculist gave me prisms for my work, a pair of smoked glasses for outside and theater, and a special set of magnifying glasses for your letters. Paper is cheaper than new eyes—buy more paper and write larger.

ALICE RIPPED INTO her Christmas present with all the excitement of a child. At the sight of the gold and garnet broach, she seemed stricken.

"It took me forever to figure out how to work your initials into the filigree," Clara said. "And look here, I've added a bail so you can wear it as a pendant, too."

Breaking into sobs, Alice pulled her into a fierce embrace.

"If you're crying because you wanted diamonds or rubies instead, you'd better go ahead and blubber, Alice. The garnets were hard enough to obtain without going into debt."

"It's beautiful. I'll wear it every day and think of you."

Clara held her at arms length, studying her face. "How can you help but think of me every day? We have adjoining rooms, eat nearly every meal together, and we work for the same company. I would think you'd want to forget me a little."

When there came no response, Clara picked up her gift box and took off the lid. "I think I'd better open my gift, before you tell me why you're crying."

Made entirely of ivory brocade and adorned with clusters of white silk roses, the hat was finer than anything she'd seen.

"It's for your next wedding," Alice said, wiping her eyes.

Clara hugged her. "You've outdone yourself on this one, my dear. If you ever leave Tiffany's, you'll have no trouble making money with your hats, although I suppose you would have to join the Evil Milliner's Union."

"I *am* leaving Tiffany's," Alice said quietly. "I've already given notice. My mother is ill and has asked that I come back to Cleveland. I've applied for a position teaching art at one of the girls' schools there."

Clara felt the legs kicked out from under her, as the last pillar of her world collapsed. Assaulted by a sense of loss and a fear of loneliness, she wept in earnest.

Alice hugged her. "I'm not the only constant in your life, you know; you have Emily, regardless of her disposition, and, you have Edward. I'll take up your mother's place in the round robin and play referee between you and Emily."

There came a soft tap and rattle at the door. Simultaneously, they looked at the mantle clock, then back at each other. It was too late for callers.

"It's probably Saint Nick making his first delivery of coal," Alice said, rising from the couch. Holding her wrapper tight around her neck, she opened the door a crack and looked into the hall.

Muggs, looking perfectly sure of itself as only cats can, meowed his arrival and jumped into Clara's lap. She gently stroked his silky head and was rewarded with an exuberant rumble of purring.

"You see?" Alice said. "There's my replacement. As long as you pet the cat, he'll listen to all your cares and worries and not care two bits about it."

——§——

May 27, 1907
Tiffany Glass and Decorating Company

For the first few months of Alice's absence, Clara wrote every day. The long missives in which she poured out her heart were written with such dramatic fervor, that Alice suggested she might try her hand at writing penny dreadfuls.

Clara dipped her pen and went back to her letter, determined to finish it within the remaining five minutes of her lunch break.

. . .I don't want to belabor the point, dear Alice, but I'm not the only one who feels abandoned. Poor faithful Dudley hasn't eaten for months, and Miss Owens complains bitterly that no one enjoys her pot roast and corn pudding the way you did. Mr. Tiffany has asked about you several times, wanting to know if you're done with your foolish notions of teaching and ready to return to the Corona studio. Edward is inconsolable over having lost his partner in crime, although he and Emily are now in cahoots—mostly about me.

Mrs. Käsebier and I are attending a tea for Women in the Arts to raise—

Louis entered her studio and placed an order sheet on top of her letter. "The whole series of daffodil lamps are sold out. I'll need at least three more of the daffodil and dogwood floor lamps, three daffodil and narcissus table lamps, and perhaps two of the plain daffodil table lamps. That should be adequate."

He rested a hand on her chair so that his fingers grazed her shoulder.

Not daring to move, she kept her eyes on the order sheet. "What about the spreading cherry table lamps? They were popular last spring."

"I prefer the daffodil lamps for now." He moved to the window, fiddling absentmindedly with his pocket watch.

She quickly glanced into the workroom where her girls were seemingly busy at work. She knew better. Anyone who bothered to look closely enough would have seen that every eye was trained on her and their employer. They weren't prying; it was more a matter of a flock protecting their shepherdess.

They'd noticed the increasing frequency with which Tiffany visited her office, and her growing discomfort at being left alone with him. Taking matters into their own hands, they devised a plan to insure she and their employer were never left to themselves for more than a few moments at a time. They made up urgent questions, and when they ran out of those, created minor disasters, from feigning fainting spells to actually breaking glass.

"I'd like you to come to Laurelton Hall the second weekend in June," Tiffany said, once again standing behind her. She could feel his thighs pressing against the back of her chair. "I've invited Miss Griffin, Miss Northrop, and Dr. McIlhiney as well. I want you to see my home. More than that . . ." he bent close to her ear, speaking in an intimate whisper, ". . . I want to see you in it."

Her eyes darted to the workshop. Miss Ring and young Miss Barnes were already on their feet.

She would not deny that the idea of seeing the Laurelton Hall palace excited her. Mr. Platt described it as 'indescribably wondrous,' and the papers reported it as a deserving candidate for the Eighth Wonder of the World, alongside the Taj Mahal. She reasoned (quickly, for Miss Barnes was on her way across the workroom with a rapid, determined step) that in the presence of such respectable company, she was sure to be safe.

"I would like that very much, Mr. Tiffany. Thank you. Shall I expect your chauffer or should I take the train?"

"Excuse me," Miss Barnes stepped into the room, "I was wondering . . . I was wondering . . ." The girl shriveled under Mr. Tiffany's gaze.

"Do you have a question Miss Barnes?" Clara prompted, hoping the girl would come up with something that sounded plausible.

"Um, well, I was wondering if you could tell me . . . tell me . . ."

"Oh, for God's sake!" Louis shouted. "What is it you want?"

Miss Barnes took another step toward Clara and fainted dead away.

———§———

June 8, 1907
Cold Spring Harbor, Long Island, N.Y.

The spectacular beauty and originality of Laurelton Hall was utterly unlike anything she could have imagined. For once, money and artistic ability had been blended to create perfection. From the moment the chauffeured car entered the long, blue gravel drive, Clara had never stopped marveling. After winding past fields of daffodils and honeysuckle, under arches of wisteria and around ponds edged with Japanese iris and day lilies, they passed between the blue K'ang Hsi lions that guarded the entrance. With her first glimpse of the cream-colored palace with the turquoise copper roof, she was filled with awe.

The eighty-four room, eight level leviathan was an eclectic blend of Islamic, Mission-Moorish, and art nouveau architecture belonging to no one but Louis Tiffany. The grand tour was like being in some fantastical waking dream decorated with glassed-in gardens, courts and terraces where marble columns were topped by ceramic poppies, magnolias and peonies, accurate to the smallest detail. For her, the zenith of Tiffany's true architectural genius was the way he'd designed the glass walls to bring sun, sky, storms and the harbor inside—making it all part of the structure.

Exhausted by bowling games and tennis matches, not to mention the lavish seven-course dinner, the guests retired to their rooms. As for herself, she was much too excited to sleep. She wanted to explore as much of the place as she could on her own, and when the multitudes of clocks struck two, she ventured out, praying she would find her way back before breakfast.

She was beginning to tire by the time she came upon an indoor courtyard under a blue glass dome. In the center, water spouted from a glass amphora fountain into a marble pool ringed with quartz crystals. Seating herself, she let the sound of the water lull her into a dreamy trance.

She became aware of him watching her long before he spoke.

"Do you like it, Clara?"

"I do," she said, calmly. "It's one of the most amazing places I've ever been."

Louis sat next to her. She met his eyes, saw what was in them, and looked away. "It's an experience I'll remember for the rest of my life."

"Could you see yourself living here?"

"I'd have to carry a map," she laughed.

His hand closed over hers. "It doesn't have to be just a memory. You could have it as your own, if you lived here with me."

She eased her hand out from under his. "Mr. Tiffany, you must not pursue this idea any further."

He dropped to his knees before her. "From the moment I opened my office door and saw you those many years ago, you have never been far from my mind. I'm a passionate and lonely man, and you are too lovely and talented to be wasting your precious time with clerks and unknown artists. I can't stand the idea of seeing you wither away like some old spinster. If we combined forces, you and I, we could dominate the market in art glass."

"I believe we've already done that," she said, fighting to maintain her composure.

"But we haven't worked side by side as one mind, one talent. Come here and stay. You could work out your designs at your leisure. You can have your own apartments—a whole wing if you prefer. I'll build any sort and size of studio you want. We could begin to know each other on a personal level. You would want for nothing and no one else."

"The clerks and unknown artists you mentioned are not only my friends, they're my family. Without them, I'd be lost. Even this stately palace couldn't replace them."

He took her by the shoulders. "I'll show you a better world, here, with me."

She eased out of his grip. "I can't do that."

"Where does that leave me?"

"It leaves you free to find a woman who's suitable to your station in life."

"But I don't want some silly rich woman who simply wants to spend my money," he pleaded. "You and I are artists of the same mind, the same heart."

She shook her head, unable to get beyond the parts of him that were broken—the missing fragments of human compassion and understanding.

Mercifully, he did not push the matter again, and for a time they sat peacefully together listening to the water flow over the amphora and return to itself. The predawn light was just beginning at the edge of the garden when, as if by some invisible signal, they both rose at the same moment.

He kissed her hand. "I won't give up so easily."

"You never do," she said. "But someday you will have to."

Mr. Tiffany handed each of them an envelope. "Ladies, inside those envelopes you will find an assignment that will commence in July and take two months to complete. You won't be working in these studios, nor will you have Mr. Briggs or the Tiffany Girls to help you."

She bit the inside of her lip. She couldn't imagine having to work with Miss Northrop day in and day out. Two months of that, and she'd either go insane or commit murder.

"Just the two of us?" she asked, hoping her disappointment wouldn't be detected.

"No, Dr. McIlhiney and I will be working closely with you every step of the way."

"Is it a big project?" Miss Northrop asked eagerly. "A window or a mosaic for some international exposition?"

Already Clara's eyes were aching.

"No again," Louis smiled, "but before you look at your assignment, you should know that every expense, including your personal expenses, will be taken care of." He opened the door.

"One last thing, ladies. Refusing the project is not an option, although, I doubt either of you will turn down *this* opportunity. Now, if you will excuse me, I have work to do." As she passed into the hall, Louis gave her a wink before closing the door.

In the hallway, Clara held up her envelope. "Shall we see what fate has in store for us, Miss Northrop?"

"I've too much to do," Miss Northrop answered curtly. "Mr. Tiffany has entrusted me with designing an exclusive piece for his personal study."

Clara tried not to smile. She knew from Joseph that Miss Northrop's 'exclusive piece' was a pipe rest.

Miss Northrop quickly stepped into the lift. "I'll read it some other time, when I'm not so busy." Closing the lift gate, she dropped out of sight, but not before Clara heard the sound of an envelope being ripped open.

She opened her envelope on the spot. Inside were several pieces of paper covered in Louis's messy scrawl.

My Dearest Clara,

Please accept my invitation to accompany me on a sketching tour throughout Brittany and various other European sites.

Enclosed are your tickets and a bank check to cover any expenses you might incur in preparation for the trip. For your comfort and in the name of propriety, I have invited two proper chaperones.

My heart is yours, Louis

Noon at Tiffany's
June 27, 1907

Dearest Emily,

You had best sit down, for you will find my news rather shocking. On July 18th I leave for Europe aboard the S.S. Amerika on the Hamburg Line. It's a new boat, seven stories high, with elevators and restaurants and all the modern improvements—a regular floating hotel.

Miss Northrop, Dr. McIlhiney (Mr. Tiffany's chemist), and I are Mr. Tiffany's guests. We are going in style, with Mr. Tiffany's own touring car. Best of all, I have my own, first-class stateroom on the "A" level, so I'll have a window. Miss Northrop has the adjoining stateroom, but I shall make sure to keep the connecting door locked.

I declined the invitation at first, but at Alice's and Mr. Booth's urging, I changed my mind, and am now resolved to it and feel it will be rather wonderful. I'll love going once in this way—no worries as to what things are costing, and with people who want to see the same things I do. I am to have two new dinner gowns, three new waists and a sturdy but refined suit for the auto trips. We'll put up in the finest hotels and take the automobile from there to picturesque fishing villages for sketching whenever the mood strikes us. Mr. Tiffany says he's too old to rough it in these places.

It might be wise to lower the rent on the farm to $150 per annum. Mama always spoke highly of Mr. West, and I'm sure she would want him and his family there for less rent, rather than having more money from an unscrupulous or dirty family.

I'm glad that Rev. Cutler has found a home with the Carter family. This is a worry off my mind.

It feels so strange, Emily, that the place where we were born and have always known as home will be occupied by strangers. I know I must accept this, but it makes me feel so old.

Mr. Tiffany is here (fourth time today), and so I must leave off.

Love always, Clara

August 18, 1907

Sister:

I received your letter dated August 7th. You are certainly costing Mr. Tiffany an awful lot, but I suppose it's a kind of relief to him to have some way to spend all the money you make for him.

While you traipse about in your luxury car, I'm here at the old house, my fingers wearing to the bone while I scrub floors and set my hand to repairing what I can before Mr. West's brood takes over.

Shall I continue to send my letters to the Misses Tiffany at Laurelton Hall? Are you sure they are all being forwarded unopened? I teach young women and know how irresponsible they can be—especially the pampered ones.

Emily

Rue du Salle, Quimper
August 20, 1907

Dearest Emily,

While Mr. Tiffany and Miss Northrop sketch, I shall rest my artistic mind and scratch a few lines.

Miss Northrop really isn't such an old prune, although I find her somewhat tedious when it comes to punctuality and detail. It makes me wonder if it weren't she who infected Mr. Tiffany with these same obsessions. It seems odd and a little sweet that I have known these people for all these years and am only now getting to know them as friends. Of course, they are very different from my Irving Place family, but they are just as charming and enjoyable at times.

Mr. Tiffany has been the perfect gentleman. If he drinks to excess, he does so after I've gone to my room, for I haven't seen him take more than an after-dinner brandy. He's full of fascinating stories of his travels, which make me long to see the camels and the pyramids and try my hand at surviving a sandstorm.

He's such a strange man at times. He asked to read one of our robins, so I gave him one that was nice. He seemed to enjoy it very much, although I can't imagine what it was about remaking hats and gowns and the price of work aprons that he found so entertaining.

Dr. McIlhiney is a bit dry of spirit, but I've drawn him out several times with scientific questions about chemical reactions in the glass. I don't know where he goes while the rest of us sketch, but he seems to enjoy himself a good deal.

I can hardly wait to tell you in person all the wonderful things I've seen. France is such a beautiful country, and the food must be tasted to be believed. I will be a full 10 pounds heavier by the end of this trip. Thank God Miss Northrop is handy with a needle and thread to let out my seams.

I must stop here, for Mr. Tiffany is ready to move on down the street for another angle of the Cathedral.

Au revoir, Clara

PS: Of course the Misses Tiffany are forwarding your letters to me safely and unopened. What a notion, Emily. I do believe those electric treatments have finally started your brain to percolating.

Paris
September 2, 1907

I have made up my mind. We are to spend the morning on a grand shopping spree, and after lunch retire to the Musée du Louvre. I've asked McIlhiney to distract Miss Northrop while I take Clara into the Tuileries.

I feel like a schoolboy. I have no need of spirits—I'm in a state of natural intoxication. L.C.T.

Le Jarden des Tuileries, Paris

Encircled by diamonds, the large emerald reminded her of the waters at Point Pleasant. Clara closed the velvet ring box and placed it back in his hand. "I'm sorry, Mr. Tiffany, I can't accept this."

He stared at her in disbelief. "But I want to marry you—now—here in Paris. It's not as if we're so young that we have to go by convention and have one of those infernally long engagements. We could have an extended honeymoon and travel around the world. We would have such a life together. Mr. and Mrs. Louis Tiffany—two artists to be reckoned with."

It *was* tempting to imagine what becoming Mrs. Louis Tiffany would be like—never having to think of expense. Making over skirts and hats and worrying over holes in her shoes would be a thing of the past. She could live in luxury, with servants attending her every need, all with a mere tug of the bell rope. To have all that and still be able to work at her leisure, without the headaches of bookkeeping and an angry men's department, seemed like the perfect life.

Visions of luxury were immediately replaced with the image of herself announcing to Emily and the Irving Place family that she was married to Louis Tiffany. She sobered at once. Just as clearly as she could see herself as a woman of leisure, she could visualize the betrayal and hurt in their eyes. Emily would disown her, or, at the very least, refuse to see her. Alice would pretend to be happy for her, but be secretly horrified. Her women would feel betrayed, and Edward—she shuddered—Edward would be devastated.

"I'm honored that you want me as your wife, but I won't marry you. I don't love you in the way a woman should love her husband. I'm guilty of having done that once in my life, and I won't do it again."

Sulky and resistant, he seemed to be searching for some last, magic words to persuade her, when she rested a hand on his arm. "Mr. Tiffany, I believe you aren't so much in love with me as you are with the idea of finding relief from your loneliness."

He pulled away, his jubilation faded. "You speak as though I'm only looking for a companion. The very nature of my position in business and society requires me to be a man on the town. I have more cronies and female acquaintances than I know what to do with. There must be a hundred women in New York City alone who would jump at the chance to marry me.

"What I want is to have you as my wife, damn it!" He slashed the air. "Why do you deny yourself that which would be the remedy to both our ills?"

"I've told you before—because I'm not the sort of woman you want, nor are you the man for me. We would end up miserable together, feeling more alone than we do now. Resentments would grow into hate and worse."

She got to her feet. "Can't we be friends? I promise that in time you will thank me for this."

"No," he said flatly, "I'll neither be your friend, nor shall I ever thank you for wounding me in this way."

"Please, Mr. Tiffany, you mustn't make more of this than it is. We *are* friends. I hope we will always be such."

With a suddenness that startled her, he flung the ring box at her feet. "You can think and do whatever the hell you please," he growled and stalked away.

Noon at Tiffany's
October 16, 1907

Dearest Emily and Alice,

Here I am again feeling like a cat in a strange garret. I don't yet have any great enthusiasm for the work, but shall once I get started. Mr. Tiffany has been indisposed since we returned, so my orders now come from Mr. Thomas.

We all gathered at Point Pleasant a last time before the end of the season. Philip Allen was there, since his wife has not yet returned from her long visit to California. Not being one to hold a grudge for long, I was friendly toward him, which I think he appreciated. He is much changed from our old Philip—hollow-eyed, subdued and not at all what he used to be. He was attentive, but depressed despite all our efforts to get him out of himself.

Edward and Mr. Yorke took me to the Hippodrome—New York's glorified circus. The stage is enormous and the scenic effects spectacular. Although I hate circuses on general principle, I saw the most fantastic ballet with little sea horses and immense crabs swimming in the dance.

Now I must swim back to work.

Much love, Clara

1908 ~ 1933

~27~

Dearest Alice,

I'm designing more jewelry for Mr. Tiffany, specifically necklaces. My salary doesn't increase, but I assure you, with the rate and price at which my necklaces are selling, Mr. Tiffany's income certainly does.

Enclosed you will find several quick sketches of the finished products. I am also sending along photographs of Edward and me on our bicycles, and another of us from last summer on the cabin porch. It would seem that somewhere along the way, I have fallen in love with this wonder of a man. The only thing that amazes me is how I managed not to recognize it years ago.

At the prospect of seeing you in July, Dudley has broken his resolve to never set foot in the 'dangerous wilderness' of Pt. Pleasant. He has sworn to brave the horrors of snakes, mosquitoes, ants and man-eating plants that reside outside of the city. I'm looking forward to watching him squirm at the sight of Edward scaling and gutting his dinner.

I've heard rumors that Mr. Tiffany's daughter, Hilda, is dying of consumption in a sanatorium in Saranac Lake, with but a few months to live. He has scheduled a long trip up the Nile or some such place far away from here. Some might think him heartless to leave his daughter in her time of need, but I don't think he's strong enough to watch another of his children perish.

I pray some good-hearted woman will sweep him off his feet before I ask him again about having my mark on things, or at the very least, on the necklaces, where it will be so small as not to be seen without a magnifying glass. After twenty years of asking, my patience has finally worn through on this subject.

Daniel Bracey stands in my doorway looking exasperated, so I need to see what the matter is. I suspect it has something to do with not receiving the glass we ordered from Corona two months ago.

How I miss you. I hope July comes early this year.

Yours always, Clara

S HE WAS INURED to Louis's furies now, although there were moments when she was sure he was going to forget himself and do her bodily harm. He'd not yet forgiven her for refusing him, and each day he made his resentment known either in his criticisms—which bordered on mad ranting—or in his general lack of civility. That his feelings went from professed love to anger did not surprise her; as her mother was fond of saying, fevered love is just a stone's throw away from hate on a cold day.

He barely glanced at her when she entered his office. "What is it? I'm busy."

Clara debated whether or not to sit down, and decided against it. "Mr. Tiffany, for the last time I'm appealing to you to have my name, or at least my mark, imprinted on some of my designs."

He stared at her with a resentment that chilled her from the inside out.

"No, and I warn you, do not ask again." He came around the desk, stopping inches from her. "I've already told you the only way you'll get to have your mark on the pieces you design."

"*My* mark? You mean *your* name. Tiffany will be on each of my designs, just as it is now. The Clara Wolcott part of it will be sure to disappear. I've given my reasons for not marrying you, and if you had any common sense, you'd give up that ridiculous notion once and for all."

"In that case, Mrs. Driscoll, you may *not* have your name or your mark on anything that goes out of my company."

She swung open the door, intending to leave without parting words, when he held her arm in a claw-like grip. Her eyes went to his fingers. "You're hurting me."

"Not nearly as much as your cruelty has wounded me."

"I never had any desire to cause you misery. Think this through with common sense, Mr. Tiffany. We're both stubborn, independent and strong-willed. What possible joy could ever come from a union between two people like that? It's precisely because I do care for you, that I have refused you."

His eyes narrowed "Is there someone else? Just tell me that much."

She sighed; she may as well have been talking to a rock. "Mr. Tiffany, it shouldn't matter whether there is or isn't someone else. What does matter is that it will never be *you*."

May 10, 1908
44 Irving Place

She was singing *Sweet Adeline* and clearing away the cobwebs that had accumulated in the corners over her bed, when a man's voice joined hers in perfect harmony. Thinking it was Edward come back to search for some lost article, she didn't bother turning around. "What did you forget this time?"

"Certainly not you, Clara. I could never forget you."

Whirling around, she gave a cry of pleasure. "Philip! What are you doing here?" She came down from the ladder, removing her scarf, at the same time tucking escaped strands of hair back into the thick coil of her braid.

He met her with arms outstretched. "I've missed you more than you know."

She smiled, truly glad to see him, but didn't linger in his embrace. Should Edward find them alone in her room, it would undoubtedly bring up painful memories that were best forgotten.

"Come down to the parlor," she said, already heading for the door. "We'll have a cup of tea."

In the full light of the parlor windows, his sickly pallor became apparent. She touched his forehead and drew back. "You're burning with fever!"

He caught her hand and held it against his chest. Through his thin jacket, she could feel him shivering.

"It's a guilty conscience," he said, flopping down onto the sofa. "I had to see you. I started a letter, but it seemed a coward's way out." He stopped to get his breath and began again, his voice rising and falling with each burst of words. "I've come to make things right between us. I should have told you the truth long ago."

She watched his eyes, sunken and ringed with shadow, and grew frightened. There was no one to help her get him to a doctor as everyone was either at church or out enjoying the warm day.

"Let me call the doctor," she said, getting up from the sofa. "He's only a few blocks away and I'm sure he wouldn't mind. . ."

He reached for her hand. "Please, Clara, hear what I have to say. I can't rest until you do."

Not wanting to upset him further, she took her seat.

"I should have been honest with you. I should have told you about—"

"That's all over now. You're married and I'm happy for you."

"You don't understand. I'm talking about Tiffany and what he's done."

"Mr. Tiffany? I doubt there's much you could tell me about him that I don't already know."

Philip raised an eyebrow. "I doubt you know *this*."

She stared at him, startled by his bitter tone.

"At the Paris Exposition," he began, "Tiffany bribed the reporters and the owners of the papers they worked for."

"I don't understand. Why would he do such a thing?"

"To make sure the names of the artisans whose designs won were kept out of the papers. Tiffany insisted on being the only one who received recognition in the press."

His voice dropped. "Do you remember the article in the *Daily News* that printed your name under the rendering of your dragonfly lamp?"

"Of course. I was thrilled. But obviously if Mr. Tiffany didn't mind about that, why would he need to bribe—"

"Because that article was supposed to be about Tiffany, and only Tiffany. Henry Belknap arranged with one of the reporters to have your name appear. The reporter was fired the next day, and there isn't a paper in the state of New York that will hire him. Tiffany made sure of that."

"Mr. Tiffany wouldn't stoop that low."

"Yes, he would—and much lower." Philip rested his elbows on his knees and ran his fingers through his hair. "Did you know that he cheated John LaFarge out of his due for opalescent glass?"

"That was just hearsay," she said. "Mr. Tiffany said that LaFarge started that rumor because he was jealous."

"It was no rumor. After I learned about Tiffany buying off the press, I began going through legal records and public accounts. I found that by the time Tiffany met him, John LaFarge had already developed methods and formulas for making opalescent glass suitable for colored windows.

"Eight months after LaFarge was granted a patent, Charles, acting on Louis's behalf, approached LaFarge, suggesting a partnership between him and Louis for the purpose of producing stained glass windows under LaFarge's patent.

"Lafarge was destitute at the time, so thinking only of the monetary advantages a partnership with Tiffany's would give him, he readily agreed. Charles seized the moment and asked LaFarge for permission to use his formulas for making and plating glass while the Tiffany attorneys drew up the partnership papers. Foolishly, LaFarge gave his consent.

Once Tiffany had the technical information and permission they needed from LaFarge, they never followed through with the partnership. Louis walked away scot-free with LaFarge's work and never once acknowledged or compensated the man. Ten years later, he did nearly the same thing to Arthur Nash."

Unnerved, Clara took her time about replying. "Surely these are exaggerated accounts. You know better than anyone how these stories can get twisted around."

"It's fact, not fiction, Clara. Tiffany may pay you well enough, but he's robbed you and all his artisans in the same manner he has cheated these men. You and your designs *are* the Tiffany Glass and Decorating Company. Leave that place and watch how soon it crumbles to nothing."

Not wanting to hear more, she came to her feet. "You're ill, Philip. Edward and Mr. Yorke will be here any moment. They can settle you in one of the vacant rooms upstairs. I'm going to telephone for the doctor. "

"I don't want a doctor, " he said. "I only came to clear my conscience. I should have told you this a long time ago." He got wearily to his feet and managed his way to the same foyer where they'd first met. "I've been a weak coward. I hurt so many by not saying what I knew to be the truth."

He took her by the shoulders. "I want you to know that I did love you. I still do."

She stared after him until he disappeared from sight. She thought of what he'd told her, and wished he hadn't. The gnawing fear that she had somehow wasted her life began in the pit of her stomach and showed no signs of going away.

Point Pleasant, N.J.
May 27, 1908

Dearest Robinites Emily and Alice,

That lovely blue hydrangea bush that was by the cabin's back door— the one we dump our dishwater on—has been ripped out. They may as well have set fire to the place and let it go to the Devil, for that bush was without doubt the prettiest thing here.

I'm writing this out on the roof, where I can smell the ocean, yet be shaded from the sun. When I close my eyes, it's as if time stops here, and I can't tell one year to the next, for the sea is constant and the sky, though ever-changing, is the same in its beauty.

Philip Loring Allen died yesterday, the spark of his life snuffed out by that diabolic assassin, typhoid. All that talent and life gone in an instant. Yes, I know—life is fleeting, but still, I'll never get used to this idea that someone so full of spirit and intelligence and humor can be here one moment, and gone the next. His obituary in the Times *from the trustees of the* Post *made me weep. It does him no good now.*

It's all I can do to keep ahead and do my work. Short of standing on his head and spitting wooden nickels, poor Edward has done everything he can think of to take me out of my gloom. I think I would perish without him.

With all my love, Clara

June 30, 1908
Corona, N.Y.

Walking from the train, Clara nervously approached the Corona Glass factory resolved to go through with her plan.

For a time after she entered the metal shop, she watched the men do their magic with hammers and pinchers and blowpipes. The ordinary sights and sounds of their work lightened her mood. The metal foreman took her around to see all her metal designs in progress, and then handed her off to Mr. Logan, whom the men jokingly referred to as 'Mrs. Driscoll's Lampshade Man.'

They retired to his office where, over a bag of chocolate pieces, they fell into easy chatter.

"The Pineapple lamps have been selling well," Mr. Logan said. "The Belted Dogwood isn't far behind, but Mr. Tiffany wants to phase out the peony." He leaned back in his chair, making it squeak. "I don't agree with him on that, but once he gets on about something, there's no talking him off of it." He gave her a rueful look "As I'm sure you know."

Without comment, Clara got up and closed the office door.

"You must have something on your mind," Mr. Logan said, picking out a thick wedge of chocolate.

"I do, however it's a task that carries with it a fair amount of risk."

"Short of robbing a bank, I guess I don't mind taking a few chances."

"Good, because this will be a risk that could cost you your job. That being said, I promise that should it come down to it, I'll do everything in my power, including lying, to make sure you're held blameless."

He regarded her thoughtfully. "Tell me what you need done."

"I want you to start printing my name on the invoices for those items that are my design. I want it kept before the public that Clara Wolcott Driscoll is the designer of those pieces and not Louis Tiffany. And when you order my lamps, instead of saying 'we need another ten of number nine-four-zero-seven,' I'd like you to say you want ten of those lamps that Mrs. Driscoll designed."

"Had enough of His Lordship putting his name on your things, is that it?"

"I think, Mr. Logan, it's more that I feel I have to get up a commercial reputation as well as an artistic one before I'm too old. This has been long in the coming, and if I don't go after it now, it will be too late."

"I'll do it," he said. "As of today, your name goes on the invoices. I don't think we need to worry about his finding out, either. I know for a fact Tiffany never looks at them."

She rose, feeling like the cat that ate the canary. "Thank you. You don't know what this means to me."

"Sure I do," he said, "I just don't know why you didn't ask long before this."

"I've been waiting," she said, "But now I think I've waited long enough."

July 15, 1908

Dear Clara,

The more I think about it, the more I'm convinced this new scheme of painting your flower designs on silk is a very marketable idea. If you combine that with your necklaces, you'll be set for success.

For someone who thinks she is dull and boring, you certainly lead a most exciting existence. And to think that Edward manages to add to all that. I stand in awe of you both. As of late, I'm more convinced that we aren't meant to be alone, but rather paired. It makes me question whether I was wrong all these years to turn Dudley away.

As to the invoices and the like, it seems so harmless a way to get your name known, and yet with Mr. Tiffany's present mood, I pray he will see it in the same way— should he ever see it at all.

I've got to go. I'm making two hats, one for Mother to wear in church, and one for sister Aline to wear to her Women's Freedom League meetings. I'm using real maple leaves on both. They will be quite stunning—at least until the foliage dries out or is attacked by an infestation of caterpillars.

Much love, Alice

Dreamland Ballroom, Coney Island

For the last in the 1908 summer series of 'Taking Clara to Places She Has Never Visited,' Edward chose the Dreamland Ballroom. Built on the end of Dreamland's Steel Pier, the two-storey, 25,000 square foot structure was, by all accounts, the largest ballroom in the world, a fact Clara found thrilling.

Bathed in the soft light that filled the mammoth room, they made a stunning sight. Clara, in her best silk dress and Alice's magnificent hat, and Edward in his spotless linen suit, waltzed effortlessly around the ballroom floor. The elegant lift of their heads and their continuous, fluid turns, drew applause from the other dancers and bystanders.

As of late, she'd started to notice how other women looked at Edward when they thought no one was watching. Looking at him now, she didn't think she'd ever seen a face more alive. The intelligent gray eyes that appeared violet in certain light, and the sculpted nose and mouth all went toward giving him an overall refined countenance. Added to all of that, he owned a certain poise that other men did not.

He waltzed her to the side of the orchestra pit and off the dance floor. "Shall we walk along the pier? We have a waning moon, but still, the sight should be spectacular."

"Do you recall the first time we ever spoke?" he asked, looking out over the water.

"I do; it was the night you loaned me your collections. You suggested I use the dragonfly instead of a moth as the motif for my lamp. You were so gracious, and such a gentleman."

"And I thought you were . . . are . . . in possession of a most beautiful and fearless soul."

"I would have thought you divested yourself of *that* notion some time ago," she said laughing.

They lapsed into a comfortable silence, listening to the faint strains of the orchestra drifting down from the ballroom.

"Have you noticed how people have been pairing us in their speech lately?" he said, putting his arm around her waist. "As in, 'Edward and Clara, why don't you sit over here', or, 'Edward and Clara like their coffee with milk', or—"

"Or, Edward and Clara won't like that hideous rug in the parlor," she added.

"Or, Clara and Edward just set the parlor rug on fire with their shenanigans."

"Or, Clara and Edward have run off and joined the circus—no surprise there."

"Or Edward and Clara are going to be married."

"Or, Clara and Edward will—" A startled smile came to her lips. "*What* did you say?"

"Well, we are, aren't we? We're happiest when together. Of course, if happiness isn't enough, then I suppose we might consider the practical benefits of such a match. We'll be millionaires with all the money we'll save by halving our rent and combining our resources. Not to mention that we love each other and get on famously, as long as I do the budget, the housekeeping, the cooking and refrain from telling you how to do anything else."

She bit her lower lip, trying not to laugh. "I can see you've thought this through. I suspect you've already picked out the venue for the wedding."

His eyebrows shot up in surprise. "Then you already know that we're to be wed on our bicycles in front of Grant's Tomb."

"In that case, Alice will have to make me a bicycle wedding ensemble and a hat to match with toy bicycles all over the brim and—"

He stopped her with a kiss. "Just say yes."

She drew him to her again, kissing him tenderly at first, and then with the force of her desire. He eagerly reciprocated, until they remembered where they were and broke apart.

She met his expectant gaze. "Will you wait a year?"

He hung his head and let out a long sigh. After a moment he spread his hands. "I've waited this long, I suppose waiting another year won't kill me, as long as there isn't another Mr. Allen in the works."

"It's nothing like that. It's just that I need to make one more effort at Tiffany's. I know something is going to happen with these new designs. I can feel it."

She saw the gladness go out of him, but when he bent to kiss her again, the smile returned to his face. "All right, have your year to become famous or infamous, whichever comes first."

———§———

December 23, 1908

Clara wanted to give the Tiffany Girls a wonderful Christmas party. It seemed the right thing to do, since Christmas came but once a year and youth but once a lifetime.

Going alphabetically, she carefully considered each person—what they did, their overall personality, and what they liked. She trudged through three-foot snowdrifts to Vantine's and Woolworth's shopping for trinkets she knew would mean the world to them. Every gift was accompanied with a poem written specifically for and about the recipient. It took effort and time, but she was more than repaid by the pleasure it gave them.

Following the quick demolition of cake and ice cream, she stood before the Christmas tree and called Daniel Bracey and Joseph to the front of the workroom. "I've saved the best for last, ladies and gentlemen. Mr. Bracey and Mr. Briggs have agreed to provide us with some lively dancing music on the tin whistle and concertina."

The two men shouldered their way to the makeshift stage with their instruments as the rest of Clara's crew pushed the worktables off to the side in order to give themselves plenty of room for dancing.

§

Louis drank off the last of the brandy and stumbled to the window. He was drunk, but not so much that he couldn't still feel the misery that was his constant companion—no amount of brandy could banish that.

In his reflection, it appeared as though the snow were falling through him. With a grunt he threw open the sash, scooped a handful of snow off the ledge, and rubbed it into his face and neck, letting the icy slush run down inside his shirt.

From somewhere nearby the sound of music and laughter reached his ears.

He climbed onto the sill slowly, first one knee, and then the other, and inched out onto the ledge. He listened, trying to locate the source of the gaiety and leaned out until he could see the street below.

It would be easy to let go, he thought, and wondered if he would still be conscious when he hit the ground. Imagining his obituary as reported by the *Times*, he began to weep. His children wouldn't mourn him, but would be glad of his money. His friends would shake their heads, gather together for dinner, make a toast and smoke a cigar in his honor.

Testing fate, he pushed out a fraction more, thrilling to the combined sensations of power and fear. He wondered if Clara would mourn him and dismissed the notion with a contemptuous bark of laughter that knocked him off balance. For one fierce, terrifying second, he was falling.

Arms flying, he made a desperate grab for the heavy curtain, just catching it as the upper half of him swung out over the street. His muscles strained to their limit in his effort to pull himself to safety, Louis only just managed to catch the ledge with his foot and pull himself over the sill.

He collapsed against the side table, where Mr. Thomas kept the piles of work orders and invoices. The papers flew in every direction.

Extending his hand, Louis grabbed one out of the air.

Joseph and Mr. Bracey gave the revelers no rest. From the moment a song ended until the next began, there was barely enough time to catch one's breath. They danced every reel, jig and hornpipe until Clara was sure the floor would give way.

Arms linked, she and Frank were in the middle of an energetic spin, when the music came to an abrupt end. Sheer enthusiasm carried them on dancing for a moment longer until they realized the room had gone silent. Confused, they looked to Daniel and Joseph.

Tin whistle still at his lips, Joseph stared at the workroom doors.

Clara turned to see Louis Tiffany stagger toward them, blind to everyone but her. His shirt was open and soaked through, his tie and jacket were missing altogether. The crowd parted, giving him a wide berth.

"Merry Christmas, Mr. Tiffany. How are you this—?" Her breath caught at the sight of the invoice clutched in his hand.

"Thought you could lead me down the garden path, didn't you?" Louis bellowed, his tongue thick with drink.

Behind her, she could hear Miss Griffin praying under her breath.

Tiffany crumpled the invoice and threw it at her. It glanced off her shoulder. Frank stepped toward him, fists clenched. She pulled the boy away and shook her head, signing that he should stay calm.

"They are invoices, Mr. Tiffany, nothing more. What possible harm could come from my name being on them?"

"Nobody's name but mine goes on anything that comes out of thith factory!" He squinted one eye. "Did Logan do thith?"

"No! I told him you gave your permission. He didn't want to do it, but I assured him it would be all right."

"*You* assured him? You deliberately went against my orders? You think you own those designs? You don't! I own every design, every pound of glath! Your name goes on nothing!"

Several of the women began backing away.

"You think people would buy anything with *your* name on it? Why, you're nothing!" He swung around, leering at the crowd. "Without me, she'd be in the gutter without a dime."

He poked her shoulder. "You're nothing!" When she didn't flinch, he brought the flat of his hand against her shoulder and shoved. "You aren't worth my—"

Before she could stop him, Frank launched himself, pinning Louis to the floor. Screams went up from the women, as Mr. Bracey and Joseph pulled the boy off their cowering employer.

While Joseph restrained Frank, Mr. Bracey took Louis by the arm and hauled him roughly toward the door. There was a scuffle, with Louis escaping long enough to stagger back toward her, fist raised.

"You think you can undermine me?" he screamed. "Jutht try it, and I'll crush you. I'll make sure you won't be able to find work anywhere in the world! You'll be on the thtreet. I'll . . . I'll . . ."

She didn't get to hear the rest of what he was going to do, because Mr. Bracey had picked Louis up, shouldered him, and carried him out.

The last they saw of Mr. Tiffany was his feet frantically milling the air.

Lenox Hill
December 31, 1908

I've won my suit against the rabble of Oyster Bay. A permanent injunction is now in place restraining them from destroying my dock and jetty. It should be cause for celebration, but I feel nothing but bitterness.

Clara. I can't stand seeing her now. To see her in the breathing, living flesh and know she is the one woman on earth I want but can't have. L.C.T.

44 Irving Place
December 31, 1908

Dearest Alice,

Mr. Tiffany has made himself scarce, and no one talks about what happened. Mr. Thomas insists I send him a note of apology, but I refuse, as I don't believe I've done anything wrong.

Christmas night Edward and Mr. Yorke put on a humorous skit about the three wise men getting lost in the desert on their way to the birth of Christ. I suppose it could be considered sacrilegious, but we laughed until we were sore.

Around midnight, Edward insisted we all run out to see the Christmas tree in Madison Square. A snowball fight broke out, with Miss Owens the clear winner. The old girl has a surprisingly strong pitching arm. She got me in the back of the head—twice.

I must leave room for Emily to add her two cents to this meager robin. Until next year, I remain faithfully yours.

Love, Clara

Alice:

You did not miss much this holiday season. The weather has been beastly, and the prices of everything higher than usual.

Keep it under your elaborate hat, but I strongly suspect there is a plot afoot. Clara and Edward are like two oysters closed up tight around pearls of information. No one can get it out of them for love nor money— not that any of us have enough of either. Try to find out what the secret is, and when you do, tell me, and I will tell everyone else. My one clue to this mystery is that Edward gave Clara a dozen linen handkerchiefs embroidered with a D that looked suspiciously like a B.

I leave for Baltimore tomorrow. Hopefully we will see you at Easter.

Emily

~28~

L OUIS TOSSED A colored sketch onto Clara's worktable. "President Diaz of Mexico has requested a fire curtain for the National Theater in Mexico City." He walked around her studio, looking at sketches and randomly touching half-finished molds. "I hired a young muralist by the name of Harry Stoner to paint this view of Popocatépetl and Ixtaccihuatl mountains as they appear from the President's palace."

She studied the watercolor, her eyes drawn to a lush foreground of bougainvillea, aralia and giant cacti, and then to the two snow-capped volcanoes. The last rays of the setting sun gilded the icy summits below a vast expansive of sky, a dozen shades of blue changing to deep purple as night approaches.

"I want you and Mr. Briggs to translate it into a mosaic fire curtain approximately thirty-six feet in height and forty-eight feet wide. I've already got a special crew of workmen reproducing the colors in Favrile tesserae. I want it started no later than April first."

She put down the sketch and regarded him calmly. "No matter when we start, a work of this magnitude will require two years to complete and twice the staff we have now, if we're to keep up with the regular work."

"I don't care what you have to do. This is an important commission."

She rubbed her temples, imagining the countless hours of close work and the endless criticisms. "They're all important commissions, Mr. Tiffany. Hiring more people means violating the Union contract."

"Have Briggs hire them under his department. Hire as many as you need. The ploy has worked before, and it will work again. However, understand that you are to be in charge of this undertaking, directing all the mosaic work."

"And I suppose when it's finished, it will *all* be attributed to Louis Tiffany and *his* personal efforts." The words were out of her mouth and hanging in the air between them before she even knew she'd said them. She stared at him, her anger and resentment clinging to her like dust.

Louis turned away. "Actually, Mrs. Driscoll, I intend on having yours, Briggs' and Stoner's names on the curtain. Does that suit your unbounded drive for glory?"

She shrugged, not really believing him. "It would be a nice gesture, albeit a little late." She waited for his retort.

Instead, Louis threw back his head and laughed.

May 23, 1909
44 Irving Place

Favrile vase still in hand, Clara opened her door, startled to find Joseph Briggs standing in the hall nervously inching his hands around the brim of his hat.

"I want you to know that I've never been one to eavesdrop," he said, drawing her into a chair and seating himself on the ottoman opposite her.

She nodded. "All right."

"I generally don't approve of people who sneak about listening at keyholes, but I did overhear something that concerns us and our departments."

She glanced over at Edward's latest bouquet of daffodils sitting on her washstand and hoped Joseph wouldn't draw out his story for too long. "May I ask how you came to commit this act of spying?"

"I went to Mr. Tiffany's office with the order sheets for the next batch of tesserae. I was about to knock when I heard him and Schmidt talking about us, so I . . . well, I listened."

"Perfectly understandable," she nodded. "I admit to having done that myself once or twice. What did you hear?"

"Mostly a lot of grousing from Mr. Schmidt about our departments' expenses for the Mexico curtain. Tiffany jumped in and said he didn't care about the expense, because we weren't being paid for all the extra hours." Joseph paused, watching carefully for her reaction.

"All true," she said, her smile fading. "Go on."

"Schmidt asked how he managed to convince you to do that, and Tiffany said it was because he'd told you that he was going to put our names on the curtain."

The muscles in her jaw jumped. "And?"

"He started ranting, saying that Tiffany was insane to do such a thing, because it was such an important commission and the only name on the curtain should be Louis C. Tiffany and not a bunch of unknown hired workers."

Joseph hesitated, biting his lip. "Tiffany said he never had any intention of using our names, but it was the only way to assure that we'd give it our best—as if we didn't always do our best. After that, there was a discussion about how they were going to get around Mr. Stoner, because Stoner and Tiffany signed some sort of legal agreement saying that Stoner would get credit for the original rendering.

"I didn't get to hear much more because Mr. Thomas came up in the lift, and I had to leave off."

She sat quite still, the vase unregarded in her lap. Instead of despair or anger, she was suffused with a sense of freedom born of the notion that she no longer cared whether she pleased Louis Tiffany or not. She'd given him more than enough.

"Well, Joseph," she said getting to her feet, "it's just as Jeremiah said: a leopard can't change its spots. The only thing we can do is to continue doing the best we can, until we can't stand to do it anymore."

She placed the daffodils in the vase. "*We* know who did the work and that needs to be good enough for now."

———§———

Mr. Platt signed Clara's proposed budget for the coming month and handed it back to her. "You have done a marvelous job on all counts, Mrs. Driscoll. I couldn't be more pleased."

"Coming from you, Mr. Platt I take that as a compliment." She started for the door and stopped. "Mr. Platt, who would you say our main competitors are here in the city?"

"Stillwell's Decorating, without a doubt."

"Are they very successful?"

Mr. Platt chuckled, folding his hands over his paunch. "Extremely, although their selection of glass isn't nearly what ours is. But they do a brisk business—enough so that we have to keep an eye on them."

She didn't bother to hide her smile.

July 8, 1909
Stillwell's Decorating Company

Clara couldn't help but note the marked difference between the offices of Victor Stillwell and those of Louis Tiffany. While Mr. Tiffany's office was elegant in its open simplicity, Stillwell's was stiff and formal, paneled in mahogany and glass-fronted bookcases. Depressing dark velvet curtains shut out all light and air.

Victor Stillwell shook her hand with great formality.

It was a struggle for her not to smile; the gleaming dome of his head fringed by wiry gray hair sticking out at every angle reminded her of a clown.

"Please sit." He pointed to one of the leather chairs.

He resettled his spectacles and peered down at her, a slight frown forming between his brows. "I must say, Mrs. Driscoll, I was surprised to receive your letter of inquiry about a position here. You've been with Mr. Tiffany for many years."

"And I assume you would like to know why I'm considering leaving his employ?" she said, glad he'd given her a place to begin.

"I admit to being curious, yes."

She wished the man would sit down. He was making her nervous the way he shifted back and forth on his feet. "I want my name placed on my designs, and I want a better salary."

There, she thought, *I've said it.*

"What salary are you hoping for?"

"I want forty dollars a week for the first six months," she said boldly. "If you're satisfied with my work, and I'm happy working here, I'd like to be raised to fifty dollars a week. Any salary increases after that would be based on my yearly review."

He said nothing. If he was shocked by her demands, he concealed it well, for there was no change in his expression.

Encouraged, she plunged ahead. "I work much better and more efficiently when my hours are my own and I'm not required to clock in. I'll need a bookkeeper and at least twenty cutters and selectors to start, all of whom I want to choose myself. In the names of efficiency and comfort, I'd also like the freedom to rearrange the workshop as I see fit.

"Most importantly," she shot him a meaningful look, "I insist my mark or my signature be on each piece I design."

He remained silent for several minutes, absent-mindedly rubbing his hands. Finally, he cleared his throat. "I agree to all your of your demands. However, before we sign any such agreements, I have one request, though you might find it peculiar considering that I am already familiar with your work."

She waited, promising herself she would walk away if he backed down on any of the things she'd asked for.

"I want you to design a piece—one of your lamps—to exhibit to my board. The piece should be your best effort, a tour de force, if you will. Take as long as you like, and when it's complete, I'll present it to the board along with your terms. If they approve, you can begin work immediately."

A tour de force? The freedom to create whatever she liked without restraints or criticisms? It was a dream come true.

"I'll make sure you have full access to our workshop," he went on. "Mr. Weber, our glass department manager, will get you whatever you need, even if I have to order it from Tiffany's Corona factory. Mr. Lifton in our metal shop will assist you with the metal work.

"If you will return tomorrow, I'll arrange to have Mr. Weber show you where things are and introduce you to Mr. Lifton. Lifton will supply you with keys so that you can come and go when you please."

She rose, a smile hovering about her lips. "Thank you, Mr. Stillwell."

"Thank *you*, Mrs. Driscoll." He ushered her to the door. "I hope this is the beginning of a prosperous arrangement for us both."

August 10, 1909

Dearest Alice and Emily,

The enormity of the Mexico curtain is astounding. It promises to be over 25 tons by the time it's finished. I'm not sure how Mr. Tiffany aims to get it to Mexico City, but I have no doubt he will manage.

Alice: No, the design idea for the Stillwell 'pièce de résistance' did not come in a dream, but from Edward, who one day presented me with the living prototype. Joe Briggs has been my secret partner and guardian angel in this endeavor. I needed several large pieces of Favrile in an unusual color, which he special ordered and I paid for, no questions asked.

Edward accompanies me to Stillwell's each evening and reads to me as I work. It's a luxury that makes the job go faster.

I may have mentioned in the last robin that I sent one of my hand-painted scarves to Dorothy Tiffany as a gift. I received her thank you card, saying that her sister Comfort and two of her friends raved about them and insisted on each having one for themselves. She enclosed $15 and asked that I send them to her for distribution. I was pleased, though I thought they'd paid too much, and sent matching, hand-painted silk fans along to make it a fair deal.

Tonight I shall add the final touches to my 'masterpiece' and send it to Mr. Lifton for finishing. Keep your collective fingers crossed.

Here is my dear Edward, come to fetch me to my work. Tonight he's reading E.M. Forester's A Room With a View.

Love, Clara

Edward's voice lulled her into a state of mind in which she was nothing more than the flow of creativity going from the muse through her soul to her eyes and hands.

He closed the book and rubbed his eyes. "Clara?"

"Hmm?" She cut a cerulean glass petal.

"How much longer should I wait?"

"I'll be done with this last petal in a few minutes. We can go after I put away my tools."

He shook his head. "That isn't what I meant. I want to know how long you intend on waiting before we can be married."

She looked over the tops of her prisms, the tranquility she'd felt only moments before having vanished. It was the question she'd dreaded; the question that woke her out of a dead sleep and threw her into a panic. She lifted one shoulder in a graceful gesture. "I don't know."

"We agreed on a year."

"I know, but I thought—"

"That's only a few days from now."

"I know, but if I'm given this position do you know what that will mean?"

"Another twenty years making another wealthy man even wealthier, while you grow old in a small room at Irving Place?"

"No. It means that I'll finally have my name recognized. My income will make it possible to afford anything I could wish for. Just think, I'll be able to buy a house at Pt. Pleasant within a year."

"Then what will you want? An automobile? A suite of your own at the San Remo? Twenty hats and thirty pairs of shoes?"

"Edward, if you could just wait until—"

"Wait is all I've done for ten years, Clara. When I was sure you'd finally reached the end of your tether with Tiffany, you surprised me yet again with this Stillwell venture, and now you want me to wait even longer."

"But I might not even be hired for the position," she said, desperate to convince him.

"That isn't the point! You've again placed me second in line for your attentions. I want you to love me as I love you. Each night I come here and watch you work yourself into exhaustion, all so that you can have the opportunity to work yourself to exhaustion forevermore. This is an inarguably magnificent piece, but I doubt you are even capable of designing anything less than perfection."

He kissed the top of her head. "I'm sorry, dearest, but I can't spend another year or another twenty years watching you kill yourself. I don't want to share you with Victor Stillwell, who, like Louis Tiffany, will undoubtedly get the lion's portion of you.

"Working yourself into rack and ruin isn't what life's about. We need to enjoy life while we're here."

"We do that now, don't we?" she whispered. "Can't we just go on as we always have?"

He shook his head. "I don't want to go on being boardinghouse cronies with the woman I love. We'll be happier as husband and wife, with you in your own enterprises earning your own money and making a name for yourself.

"Forget about Tiffany and Stillwell—they're your past. Let me be part of your future." He bent his head and caught her eyes. "Please, Clara."

She saw the love in his eyes, and shifted her gaze back to the nearly completed lamp. She was wretched, not wanting to make a choice, and not wanting to lose him. "I beg you not to give up on me, Edward. I'm so close to having what I've wanted all my life. Give me one more year and then I'll—"

His withdrawal from their intimacy was like a curtain falling between them.

Shaking his head, he picked up his coat. "I can't. I'm sorry. I'll change lodgings at the end of next week. I'll room with Dudley until I find something else."

"You can't mean this."

"I'm afraid I do, dearest. There comes a time when *someone* has to get off the carousel and get on with life. I'm going back to Irving Place. I'll return at ten to escort you home."

Stunned, Clara watched him go, wanting to run after him and beg him not to leave her. If she hurried she could catch him before he got to his bicycle. She took a step in the direction of the door, when a piece of iridescent blue caught her eye. She squinted and tilted her head. The piece was a fraction too low—it would have to be reset if perfect balance were to be achieved.

She looked after Edward once again, and then, without thinking, took up her grozing pliers and bent to her work.

August 17, 1909

Clara hurried down Fifth Avenue toward Stillwell's in a confusion of excitement and misery. The sight of Edward's belongs loaded onto a wagon made her want to weep.

His wooden trunk, his books, the oak desk he'd made with his own hands. All his things that she'd found comforting within the confines of his neat and orderly room, looked forlorn, like orphans ripped from their natural home.

She wanted to go to him and tell him she loved him and that she was the happiest when she was with him. She wanted to say she would marry him tomorrow.

But she didn't.

Mr. Lifton had sent her a note saying her lamp base was finished and fitted to her shade, and that she was to meet with Mr. Stillwell at the end of the week. Too excited to wait, she'd decided to go in early to examine every inch of the piece for flaws.

She let herself into the metal shop and headed straight for Mr. Lifton's office, cheerfully greeting each man she passed by name. Many of them returned the greeting, but averted their eyes. Immediately, she sensed an undercurrent of alarm.

The youngest of the metal workers, an excitable man the others called Jumping John, ran ahead of her into Mr. Lifton's office and slammed the door shut behind him.

She quickened her step, entering the office at the same instant Mr. Lifton closed the closet door. Both men's expressions were like that of schoolboys caught at stealing apples from the town grocer.

"Ah, Mrs. Driscoll," said Mr. Lifton, "we didn't expect you until tomorrow."

"I know," she said, removing her gloves. "I came early to check over the finished piece to make sure it's perfect for the showing tomorrow."

Mr. Lifton composed his features into an expression of suitable solemnity and shook his head. "It isn't here. It's . . . it's . . ."

Ignoring him, she opened the closet and brought out the lamp that was wrapped in a velvet drape. She set it carefully on his desk. "Is this my lamp?"

The color came to his face. "Yes, but Mr. Stillwell has given strict orders that I'm not to release it to anyone—not even you, ma'am."

She pushed down the urge to scream and sat calmly in the chair next to the shrouded lamp. "In that case, Mr. Lifton, I suggest you send this young man to fetch Mr. Stillwell, because I'm not leaving here without seeing my lamp."

"Mr. Stillwell isn't here," Mr. Lifton said in a way that told her he wasn't used to lying and didn't like it much.

She leveled her gaze. "Either bring Mr. Stillwell to me at once, or I'll cause such a ruckus, you'll wish you had."

A quick nod from Lifton sent Jumping John running.

Mr. Lifton rubbed the back of his neck with his handkerchief. "This is going to get me in a lot of trouble, Mrs. Driscoll."

"Not as much trouble as I would have caused had you not sent for the man," she assured him.

They waited, Mr. Lifton standing in front of the lamp, arms crossed over his chest, while she tried to stare through the sheet. When she tired of that pointless exercise, she walked to the window and pried it open. There wasn't much air to be had, the way the neighboring buildings crowded up close. The narrow alley below didn't seem to have any exit or entrance. At least, she thought, Tiffany's had a view of the street.

Victor Stillwell barged in, his face scarlet. "What's going on here?"

"Mrs. Driscoll came early so she could preview the lamp for mistakes," Mr. Lifton said, perspiration beading his face. "I've explained to her that no one is to see the piece, but she insists on looking it over for flaws."

Mr. Stillwell's smile was so forced as to look like a grimace of pain. "You mustn't worry about that, Mrs. Driscoll. I've not seen the lamp yet myself, but I'm sure it's perfect in every way. When you come back tomorrow as planned, you will see the lamp as it's being presented to the board."

He took her by the elbow and led her to the door. "Why don't you come up to my office? You'll need to sign several agreements—nothing important, but it helps to get the formalities out of the way."

Clara pulled her arm out of his grip. "I'm not going anywhere or signing anything until I've had a chance to go over my lamp. It's not done any other way—at least not by me."

"Tomorrow will be soon enough for you to see it." Mr. Stillwell lay hold of her arm again. This time his grip was not so gentle as he pulled her toward the door. "You mustn't worry, Mrs. Driscoll, I'll—"

She threw his hand off and spun around. "I *will* see it, Mr. Stillwell, and I'll see it now!"

Before he could stop her, she marched back into Lifton's office and unwound the sheet from the lamp. The instant it fell away, Victor Stillwell drew in a sharp breath, his hand going to his chest. Jumping John gave a low whistle. Even she couldn't suppress a cry of delight.

Thin gold blades of prairie grass in various hues, intersected and entwined into a delicate lace that stretched up and disappeared under a cornflower of rich iridescent blue. Hundreds of glass petals, their lancet tips layered one over the other, ascended from the irregular rim toward a central top cluster of curving purple stamen each tipped by a deep yellow pollen bead

Carefully, she lifted the lamp, searching the underside. Both her name and mark had been buffed out and replaced with Victor Stillwell's signature and his company's mark.

Her eyes narrowed. "Where are my signature and mark?"

"You need to be reasonable about this, Mrs. Driscoll. I thought it best to keep the name Stillwell on our things so as not to confuse the customers who depend on the Stillwell signature as an assurance of quality."

"This lamp is not yours," she said, hardly able to breathe around her fury. "If I'm not mistaken, besides being in blatant disregard of our agreement, your signature on my work constitutes fraud!"

Mr. Stillwell gave a nervous laugh. "Calm yourself, Mrs. Driscoll. I see no need for hysteria. The Stillwell name is synonymous with quality. If the customers see a name they don't recognize, the piece won't sell. Now, perhaps after, let's say, another ten of this caliber design, we might begin engraving your mark on a select few. . ."

She stopped listening, suddenly aware that the lamp was growing heavier in her trembling hands. Without hesitation, she crossed the room, gazed one last time at the lamp and dropped it out the window.

The explosion of metal and glass was enough to drown out Victor Stillwell's outraged scream.

She snatched her design sketches from Mr. Lifton's desk and tucked them into her leather case.

"Have you gone mad?" Mr. Stillwell shouted. "What do you think you're doing?"

"I am neither crazy, nor am I an imbecile, Mr. Stillwell," she said, calmly pulling on her gloves. "The lamp was mine. I would rather see it smashed in an alley than to see someone else's name on my work—someone who will gain all the profit and take the glory besides. I warned you the day we met that I'd had quite enough of that. I'm sorry you didn't take heed."

Halfway to the door she paused. "As I am in the habit of keeping track of materials and labor, I know to the penny what I owe Stillwell's. I'll send you a bank check.

"You've made a terrible mistake, Mr. Stillwell. Hopefully, you will learn from it. I bid you good-day gentlemen."

Eyes bright with admiration, Jumping John opened the door with a flourish and bowed as she passed.

"Hello? Hello? Is that you, Miss Owens?" Clara pushed the earpiece against the flesh of her ear. "No, no—nothing's wrong. Is Mr. Booth still there, or has he already gone on to Dudley's?

"Oh? When did he say he would come back for his bicycle? Wonderful. Would you please give him a message? All right, I'll wait."

While she waited for Miss Owens to find her glasses and something to write with, Clara glanced around her workroom, looking for any of her personal belongings she may have missed. The Tiffany Girls were gathering outside her office, looking at her through the glass. She waved and smiled as the phone crackled to life.

"Yes, Miss Owens, I'm still here. Please tell Mr. Booth to meet me at the bench in Gramercy Park at five p.m. If I'm not already there, tell him to wait. Tell him . . . tell him the carousel is slowing down."

They gathered around her, nervously glancing at the crates holding her personal effects.

"I'm one of the luckiest women in this city to have had the chance to work with you," Clara began in a tremulous voice. "I'm so thankful to you. We've created thousands of beautiful things together, and that alone binds us for the rest of our lives."

She swallowed and waited for the lump in her throat to ease. "I'm leaving Tiffany's and I'm going to miss you more than I—" Her voice broke.

At once, Lillian and Marion Palmié took her hands. Miss Ring and

Miss Griffin stepped up to embrace her, and then Joseph, Frank, and Miss Northrop. And so it went in gentle waves, until every one of them had had a chance to touch her and say good-bye.

Daniel Bracey was last to shake her hand. "God bless ya, Miss. Me an' the Missus will be sayin' a prayer for ya each mornin'." He lowered his head. "What in the name of God are we gonna do without ya?"

"You will continue making exquisitely beautiful things," she said finally. "It's who you are."

The metallic clatter of the lift doors put her in mind of being locked into a dungeon. The car lurched once, twice, and began its ascent. She slipped off her glasses and rubbed her eyes, already feeling her time at Tiffany's was long ago.

It was pure vanity, of course, but she felt a twinge of regret to think that, outside of her family, the Tiffany Girls and a half dozen Europeans, no one would ever know it was she who designed the hundreds of pieces that made Louis Tiffany's reputation.

The lift bumped to a stop. She brought her fist down on the lever and yanked the door open hard enough to make it bounce. Wiping away tears, she swore under her breath. "Damn you, Mr. Tiffany! Damn you straight to Hell."

"What did you say?" Louis Tiffany looked up from his work.

"I said I'm leaving my position. Mr. Briggs and Miss Northrop are prepared to take over my duties. The Tiffany Girls know what is expected of them and are quite capable of carrying on. The Mexico curtain is on schedule, the new autumn lamps are in the works, and the bookkeeping is up to date. All in all, my leaving shouldn't interfere with the production schedule one bit."

Louis frowned, and then started to laugh. "Very amusing Clara, but I'm busy now, so what's the real purpose of your visit?"

"I don't mean to be amusing," she said bluntly. "I'm leaving your employ. I've already packed my personal things and made the announcement to my department. I'll come in next week to review things once more with Mr. Briggs and Miss Northrop, and to tender my formal resignation to Mr. Thomas."

All signs of joviality faded from his expression. "Don't be absurd. You can't leave—you have the Mexico curtain to finish."

"Mr. Briggs has taken charge of that."

"You're just tired," he said, real concern creeping into his voice. A small muscle under the pale skin near his eye twitched. "Take some time away. Perhaps you should tour Europe again, or visit the Near East? Morocco and the Nile are exciting in autumn. I'll pay for your tickets. You could invite your sister or Miss Gouvy to accompany you."

"Thank you, Mr. Tiffany, but I am leaving—today."

"No!" Panicked, he came around the desk. "You can't just up and leave without my permission. You haven't discussed this with me."

"I'm discussing it with you now. I've made up my mind to go out on my own."

"You can't do that! I won't allow it." A bead of sweat rolled off his forehead and disappeared in the thatch of his beard. "What about everything you've worked for?"

"Everything I've worked for," she repeated in a flat voice, "has been stolen by you. Besides building your reputation and fortune, what, exactly, is the 'everything' I've worked for?"

"For God's sake, why are you doing this?" he cried, coming toward her, his hands stretched toward her.

She swung around, and this time there was fierceness in her voice. "Because I want my life back. Just once I want to own what is mine."

The sharp slap of his hand against the surface of the table had no effect on her. "After all I've done for you? No! You will *not* walk out on me! "

"After all you've done for *me?* I was under the impression that it was my designs that made your company successful. *My* lamps! *My* windows! *My* mosaics!

"Or perhaps you're referring to the position of manager you so kindly bestowed upon me? I'll admit I was flattered, that is until I realized that my being a manager meant taking on four times the amount of work that was required of your other managers."

"You took the money easily enough," he said, quieter now. "No other woman receives the salary you earn."

"Thirty-five dollars a week! Forty-five cents an hour to ruin my eyes, forty-five cents an hour to produce thousands of original works of art, each of which you sell for an amount equal to half my yearly salary? Forty-five cents and years of my life so that your name could be etched into my work."

Pulling open his office door, she pointed to the deep groove that now resembled an old scar. When she spoke again, her voice was low and even, the fire gone. "Do you remember the day you did this with your cane? It was the day you told me that my designs were not mine. *That's* the day I should have gone elsewhere. I should have known then that you would continue to rob me of what was rightfully mine."

She stepped into the hall, the pure joy of freedom filling her until there was nothing else. Turning her back on him, she simply walked away.

"How dare you!" he thundered after her. "Come back here this instant. You don't know what you're doing."

"Of course I do," she called back. "I've finally come to my senses."

Clara spotted him on the other side of Gramercy Park. Elegant in his linen suit and straw hat, Edward sat with one arm casually draped over the back of the bench, staring up into the trees. He was tracking the wind, searching among the branches for birds and butterflies, naming them to himself. When he greeted her he would point out some bird or insect she'd never seen or heard of before, and then wait patiently while she made sketches to use in her work.

She slowed, never taking her eyes from him. In that moment the park, the city, the world, belonged to just the two of them and the possibilities for their future seemed limitless.

Edward caught sight of her and raised his hand in greeting, an uncertain smile beginning at the corners of his mouth.

Striding toward him, Clara began to laugh.

~29~

June 21, 1930
Point Pleasant, N.J.

CLARA MANEUVERED THE Model A onto the bare dirt patch that was their lawn and cut the motor. Made drowsy from the heat, she rested her head against the seat and peered up at the sun filtering through the leaves of the surrounding trees. It gave the illusion of a canopy of green lace held against the vibrant blue of a midday sky—a perfect motif for her next series of silk scarves.

The heavy scent of lilac drew her attention to the back of the bungalow, where a harmony of flowers and trees covered every inch of ground. She'd planned out the whole garden during the dark months of nineteen twenty-two while she'd looked after Alice.

As the tuberculosis progressed and her life ebbed, Alice found peace in making watercolors of the flowers she most loved. Clara kept the paintings, and when she and Edward purchased the bungalow, the first thing she'd done was to plow up the backyard and plant what would come to be known as 'Alice's Garden.' She truly believed it was her one-sided conversations with Alice, while she tended to each stem and tree, that made everything bloom so abundantly.

An automobile much too expensive for the neighborhood pulled up in front of the bungalow. Henry Belknap, impeccably dressed in bottle-green blazer and cream slacks, got out and made his way toward her. Leaning inside the car he kissed her lightly on the cheek. "Are you thinking of who you're going to run over next?"

Clara slapped the steering wheel in mock exasperation. "I wish Edward would stop telling everyone that little piece of fiction. You know perfectly well he has a tendency to exaggerate things for the worst. I was only trying to scare him a little. It wasn't my fault he didn't move fast enough.

"It's about time you showed up." She patted his hand. "Seven months is too long between visits, especially . . ." she gave him a withering look from over the tops of her glasses, "since you never answer any of my letters. How are you?"

Henry removed his straw boater and passed a handkerchief around the inside band. "Surprisingly well for a man of seventy. And you?"

"Still kicking," she said, getting out of the car and taking his arm. "Come in and have lunch; we'll catch up on all the news. It's just you and me. Edward's in New York taking care of another snag in Miss Owens's estate."

"She was a lucky woman to have you and Edward looking after her at the end."

"It was the least we could do for the dear, considering she provided us with a home for all those years."

Henry arranged the hardboiled eggs on a plate, and set the table while she made canned tuna sandwiches.

"I've just received another letter from Dudley," he said, pouring the lemonade. "He's moved from La Jolla to take a new position teaching art in Santa Barbara. He says his two boys are growing like weeds."

"He's done an admirable job raising those two on his own since Margaret died. Hopefully he'll bring them back to see us one of these days." Clara cut their sandwiches on the diagonal and put one on his plate. "And what are you up to these days? Last time I saw you, you were writing that book about Salem."

"Good God, it *has* been a while; I finished writing that book ages ago. I'm writing one on my family history now, and after this one, I'll probably write another on photography. McBride and I have a contest going to see who can write the most books in the shortest time. I'm pretty sure he's got me beat—the man is prolific."

"Is he still the art critic for the *New York Sun?*"

"Oh yes, and if you thought he had a swollen head before, he's recently been crowned the dean of American art critics, so there's no living with him. He's hobnobbing with Matisse, Steiglitz, Marin—he's even involved with that Gertrude Stein woman . . . or man . . . or whatever she is."

He wiped his mouth. "Are you and Edward happy with your Ormond Beach house?"

"My bones and various moving parts are ecstatic over it," she laughed. "My body was threatening a revolution if I didn't get out of the snow and ice. Of course, with the Depression Edward's worried about paying the taxes on both houses, but I expect we'll weather that storm better than we could the cold. Since the Yorkes and the Palmiés have moved down, he's been much happier. He and Mr. Yorke have formed a men's bicycle touring club."

Henry held up a hardboiled egg as if making a toast. "That's our Edward—wheeling to the finish line.

"How is the Clara Booth Scarves, Necklaces and Fans Company doing?"

"I had to change the name," she said. "Fans are passé, so now I'm Clara Booth's Scarves, Handkerchiefs and Necklaces Company, and I'm not too sure about the necklaces either, considering the price of materials. I've already lowered my price on the scarves from five dollars to three, and the necklaces aren't moving at all. But who could blame people for wanting to hold onto their money now? If you want, I'll show you my latest scarves after we eat."

"Only if you'll let me buy a half dozen from you; I've become the most popular man among the ladies in my family who receive them as gifts."

After they'd washed the dishes and put them away, she led him through Alice's Garden to a small screened-in studio set in the far corner of the property. Cluttered with jars and bolts of different colored silk, the workshop was nonetheless a sunny, cheerful place. She pulled a large square of painted silk from a flat gift box and held it up. "This one is part of my swamp collection from that time Edward and I ventured into the Everglades."

Arrayed in intricately detailed white feathers and plumes, two herons perched on the branch of a bald cypress hung with Spanish moss. Their bright gold eyes focused on the viewer. All around them, water and sky were alive with the brilliant oranges, reds and yellows of a Florida sunset.

She shook out a second scarf, this one long and rectangular. Painted end-to-end was a sky of purple, orange and lavender radiating from a molten setting sun. Running along the bottom, the lustrous quality of the waves had been perfectly captured.

"The richness of your colors takes my breath away," he said. "These are works of art. They don't belong on shelves, they belong in galleries, for God's sake."

"It's kind of you to say so, but nobody cares about this sort of thing any more. Art has long since moved away from the naturalists and Art Nouveau. Nowadays, everyone wants Art Deco—just look at the new Chrysler Building. It's the reason Mr. Tiffany withdrew his money and left Joe Briggs to run an ailing company that built its reputation on an outdated style.

"Anyway," she sighed, "you can't stop progress in fashion. Young women don't want fancy things." She looked down at her own straight-line rayon pants and plain cotton blouse. "It's all slim-line silhouette styles. Simple lines, no fussy undergarments." She paused, and then added, "Thank God!"

They ambled through the garden and sat on the bench overlooking a sundial surrounded by peonies. Henry filled his pipe, but left it unlit.

"Have you seen Mr. Tiffany lately?" she asked.

Henry nodded. "I visited him at Laurelton Hall two months ago."

It wasn't often she and Henry spoke of him, though she did like to keep up with what he was doing. For a time she'd kept in touch with Joseph, who passed on the rumors, both good and bad. It was he who'd informed her that after she'd left, Mr. Tiffany's drinking had escalated to the point that he'd almost died. A nurse was called in to watch over him day and night, and within months the *Times* was reporting that Nurse Sarah 'Patsy' Hanley, described as 'a young adventurous Irish redhead with vivacious and engaging ways,' was frequently seen about town on the arm of Louis Comfort Tiffany.

When Louis gave over Laurelton Hall, his art collection and 1.5 million dollars, all in support of young artists, Clara was sure the nurse had pushed him to it.

"The nurse," she said, "is she still with him?"

"Patsy? Absolutely. They dote on each other. Louis has done a rather good job of teaching her how to paint, too. She's had a few shows of her own— mostly landscapes and flowers. McBride says she's not all that bad.

"They're still living in that house he built for her next to Laurelton Hall. Being around the art students day and night drove him crazy. Poor Louis—he wanted to keep them strictly within the Art Nouveau camp, but they refused to bend under his cane. I think he's about ready to give up that struggle."

He gave her a sidelong glance. "I suppose you've heard that he's asked Patsy to marry him on several occasions?"

An inexplicable pang of jealousy passed through her. "No. Have they married?"

"Patsy refuses. She thinks his children would resent it, although I doubt that. One of the twins confided that she was just glad Patsy got him off booze and onto her."

They laughed until she couldn't get her breath, and he had to bring her a glass of water. Later, when they'd talked themselves out, they leaned against his car watching the late afternoon sun take on a golden hue.

"Clara?"

She knew from his tone what he was going to say. Closing her eyes, she let out a heavy sigh. "Why do you always bring this up when you know I don't want to talk about it?"

"Because it isn't fair. Without you and the others, his company would have folded like a house of cards." Henry made her look at him. "Hasn't it ever crossed your mind that Tiffany's became a success just after 1888 and went out of production the year after you left? Do you think it was only coincidence that Tiffany's thrived for just those years you were in charge of the designing?

"Why won't you give McBride permission to write about what you did there? Surely there'd be no harm in it now?"

She pulled away, the first stirrings of the old frustrations and bitterness beginning in her chest. "You and McBride have to stop bringing this up, Henry. That was a long time ago. I don't want to stir up the muck."

"But why? What's wrong with letting the world know who you are and what you did?"

"Because it isn't the honorable thing."

He got into his car. "All right, Clara, you win again, but I, for one, sincerely hope that someday you and Nash and all the rest who got nothing for their efforts are given the respect you're due. I can't think of any who are more deserving."

Point Pleasant
August 22, 1932

Dear Emily,

You must not listen to Edward about my driving! I drive perfectly well. The traffic box man came by only to say that I passed through the yellow light and was under it just as he changed it to red. I asked how I was supposed to see through the roof of my car—for this, he had no answer.

I'm glad you approve of our extravagant expenditure on the Westinghouse Electric Refrigerator. Besides saving about $2.50 a month on ice, we're glad to be done with that terrifying Ice Man. We were always on edge when he came around with those ice tongs and that crazed expression. Now we're comparing the cost of oil for our cook stove to the cost of an electric range. (This has nothing to do with the Oil Man—he's a perfectly nice gentleman.)

It sounds like Canandaigua is set for a bumper crop of grapes this year. Are your buyers all one winery, or do you sell to various vintners? In either case, thank God for the Volstead Act, otherwise you'd be selling your grapes for jam instead.

Everywhere we go we see such poverty—mothers and children going hungry, men without work and no savings to cushion their fall. You are correct in your assertion that we are well off comparatively. I found great comfort in your conviction that if the country goes to the dogs, we'll all go together. For my part, I was all set to join the tax revolts, but Edward held me back.

I'm off to the Grand Central Art Galleries exhibit. If I'm to catch the ferry in time, I have to leave off here.

Love, Clara

Dearest Counselor, Friend and Sister Emily,

The Boss left this for me to mail. I figured for the price of a 2-cent stamp I might as well get my money's worth, so here's my two cents:

Now, as for her driving—you might want to pray harder, because she's driving all around the place just as though she knew how. She drove me to the ferry yesterday amid the traffic and wisely, I kept my eyes closed for the duration of the trip. She doesn't listen, but I told her just because she has a license doesn't mean she can drive.

I've been laying down stones for the new driveway, and I don't mind saying that I do feel very tired and full of aches by bedtime.

The Boss got a new commission for a dozen scarves from some fine ladies' store over in Boston. It perked her up. It might be that I'm partial, but her latest work is grand.

I hope you still have enough spare money to get on the bus and come down here before our season closes. I'll leave off now, before I go over the one-ounce limit and have to purchase a 3-cent stamp. I miss you.

All my love, Edward

Clara was admiring Alfred Hutty's *Path in a Southern Garden*, when a slender woman standing by the gallery entrance caught her attention. She touched the woman's elbow. "Dorothy? Do you remember me? I'm—"

"Clara!" Dorothy pulled her into an embrace. For a long time the women stood with their arms around each other, saying nothing. Touched by the genuine warmth of their greeting, tears came to Clara's eyes as she held Dorothy at arm's length, sizing her up.

The ravages of age seemed not to have touched her, though, on closer inspection, Clara saw signs of worry etched around her magnificent dark eyes. "I think the last time I saw you was just after your marriage to Dr. Burlingham. How are you?"

Giving the street a last quick glance, Dorothy pulled her to one of the viewing benches in the middle of the room, talking as she went. "The children and I are doing well. Bob, my eldest, is driving down to pick me up. He's late and I—" She laughed at Clara's shocked expression. "I know, I'm sometimes just as surprised when I think that one of my children is old enough to drive."

"*One* of your children? How many are there?"

"Four. The youngest is twelve. Hard to imagine, isn't it?"

Clara shook her head in wonder. "It doesn't seem that long ago that we were sitting in the Lenox Hill attic sipping hot cocoa. Where are you living now? I read that your sisters and their families are still at Lenox Hill. I assumed you. . ."

Dorothy's features hardened, and for a moment, she looked exactly like her father. "I had no intention of following my sisters' dutiful examples. My father's generosity in having my siblings live there was no more than his desire to remain in control of everyone. As a woman of an independent nature, I expect you, above all, can understand my decision."

Clara smiled faintly, "I do, although I doubt your father will ever comprehend, let alone believe the wisdom of your choice. He was raised in different times with different rules. Still and all, it makes me happy to think that the women of your generation have the freedom to rebel these days. In my time we were bound and gagged; it took a long while for us to fight our way out of the prisons men built for us.

"So if you aren't at Lenox Hill, where are you?"

"The children and I have been living in Vienna, with Dr. Sigmund Freud and his daughter, Anna. I'm studying psychoanalysis. I only came back to New York to see my father, since I doubt very much I'll see him again." She paused. "He's not at all well, Clara."

The news hit her almost as a physical blow. "Your father is ill?"

Dorothy gave her a long searching look then gently squeezed her hand. "He's eighty-four, Clara and very frail. His eyesight and hearing have failed, and at times his mind wanders so that I'm not sure he even knows who we are."

Frail? She couldn't even begin to imagine Mr. Tiffany in any other way than full of life and bluster. Frailty wasn't any part of the man she'd once known.

A good-looking young man came up behind them and touched Dorothy's shoulder. "Mother? Are you ready to go? I have the car parked outside."

Dorothy rose and kissed her son on the cheek before making introductions. She took a card from her handbag and wrote an address on the back. "I'm sorry Clara, but I must run. My family and I are sailing back to Europe this evening. This is my address in Austria. Please write. I promise I'll reply."

From the gallery door, Clara watched after them as they got into the Bentley and drove away. For a moment she felt older and sadder than she'd ever felt in her life, as if she understood for the first time how fleeting life was, and how little time was left.

When her thoughts tangled, threatening to drag her down into desolation, she sought out the one gift that never failed her—the beauty of art that surrounded her.

January 18, 1933
Salem, Mass.

Dearest Clara,

I don't know if you will have already heard the news by the time you receive this, but Louis Tiffany died yesterday after a bout of pneumonia. He went peacefully, surrounded by family, and, of course, Patsy.

I visited him briefly at Christmas and was saddened at how much he'd deteriorated in both mind and body. Nonetheless, there were moments when he perked up, and, at one point—without prompting from me, said: 'I've missed my dear Clara. I wish I could see her once more.'

I wasn't sure I should share this with you, considering I promised not to rile that sleeping dog, but now that Louis is gone, I hope you'll make allowances. Perhaps it might even bring you some bit of comfort to know he was still thinking of you at the end.

I look forward to seeing you and Edward in April. Perhaps we can all meet at Emily's cabin this summer and have a reunion-retreat with whoever else is left from the old 44 Irving Place family. I will write to Emily and begin paving the way for our possible convergence. I'm sure if we encourage her to serenade us on the zither, she'll have no objections.

I'm sorry to be the bearer of sad tidings, but I was sure you'd want to know.

Love, Henry

May 27, 1933
Green-Wood Cemetery, Brooklyn

It was a good day. Clara awoke full of energy—the usual aches and pains that gnawed at her joints, held at bay.

Passing through the cemetery gates, she followed the attendant's directions until she found what she was looking for. With great care, she gathered the flowers from the backseat and made her way up Vale Path.

She spotted him partway up the hill, just below his parents' grave, noting at once the striking contrast between the father's traditional limestone marker and the son's modernistic, prism-shaped stone.

In a nearby tree, a crow watched her with apparent interest, while she took her time breaking off the blades of grass that had grown too tall across the front of Louis's marker. When she was satisfied, she propped the spray of wisteria and peonies to one side of his name and stood back to admire her work.

Still, she could not quite bring herself to believe that he was no longer alive. Twice in the four months since his death, he'd appeared in her dreams dressed in his white pongee suit and Panama hat.

Glancing around to make sure no one was near, she addressed his engraved name. "I'm not sure of what to say, Mr. Tiffany, except that you and I certainly had a roller coaster time of it."

Above, the crow let out a long series of caws that sounded much like laughter.

"You were a clever businessman with a great eye for beauty—I only wish you'd been a better man."

Clara pulled a faded velvet ring box from her pocket and undid the clasp. Under the bright sun, the emerald and diamond ring flamed to life. She stared at it for a long while, then kissed it and pushed it deep into the damp earth of Louis Tiffany's grave.

Brushing the dirt from her hands, she patted the smooth granite top of his headstone. "I forgive you, Mr. Tiffany. Now it's time for rest."

EPILOGUE

January 1, 1945
Canandaigua, New York

My dearest Edward,

Thank you for bringing Clara back to Tallmadge so that she might be buried next to her sisters and mother. When I received Clara's death certificate, the reality of her permanent absence asserted itself with a vengeance. While I understand what a terrible shock it was for you in the misery of the moment, I do take umbrage with your classifying her occupation as 'housewife' on her death certificate. She was never any such thing. If they will let you, change it to her rightful title of 'Artist.'

I went searching for memories and dusted off all the boxes and binders of round robins, starting back in 1853 with Grandmother. I have just come to the letters from 1911, when Clara's company first began making money. Do you remember how gratified she was at finally being <u>known</u>?

I have to stop here for now, as my eyes are not behaving and I am very tired.

With all my love, Emily

A NOTE ON SOURCES

In my efforts to reconstruct the past, I not only relied heavily on the Wolcott women's round robin letters and Emily's, Clara's, and Edward Booth's letters written in the 1920s and 1930s, but also on countless online sites, where I uncovered many obscure and detailed facts about the times, places and people in this book.

My source materials included census records, death and birth certificates, hospital records, social registers, New York State court records, police records, the *New York Times* archives, passport records, real estate records, archived maps, various Sears Roebuck and Co. catalogues from the 1890s and early 1900s, uncountable antiquarian books, and oral histories from Wolcott relatives. I also toured those of Clara's residences still in existence, the site of the old Tiffany studios, and most of Clara's favorite haunts in New York City, New Jersey, and the Hudson Valley.

I frequently referred to *The Last Tiffany: A Biography of Dorothy Tiffany Burlingham* (Atheneum, 1989), by Tiffany's great-grandson, Michael John Burlingham. I also used much information from Elizabeth A. Yeargin's summary, *The Pierce and Wolcott Letters* (1993). Yeargin (1919-2000), was the first to read and organize the entire collection of Wolcott letters. She donated the collection to Kent State University in 1993.

I consulted hundreds of standard histories and source books for the period and characters used in this book, but my use of the following was greatest:

Manners, Culture and Dress of the Best American Society, by Richard A. Wells *(King, Richardson & Co., 1893)*

The Lost Treasures of Louis Comfort Tiffany by Hugh McKean (Doubleday and Company, Inc., 1980),

King's Handbook of New York City by Moses King (1882)

Behind the Scenes of Tiffany Glassmaking: The Nash Notebooks by Leslie H. Nash, compiled by Martin Eidelberg and Nancy McClelland (St. Martin's Press, 2001)

We All Went to Paris: Americans in the City of Light by Stephen Longstreet (Barnes and Noble, Inc., 1972)

A New Light on Tiffany: Clara Driscoll and the Tiffany Girls, compiled by Eidelberg, Hofer, and Gray (New York Historical Society, 2007)

Louis Comfort Tiffany by Jacob Baal-Teshuva (Taschen, 2007)

Louis C. Tiffany, Rebel in Glass by Robert Koch (Crown Publishers, 1988)

In many instances in this book, the dialogue between Clara and her mother, Fannie, comes directly from their letters. However, while Emily and Kate's characters have been formed by the impressions their letters and diary entries made on me, there are no known letters from Josephine. Thus, my character portrayal of Josie was created from the information and inferences gathered from her family's comments and memories of her.

As an added point of interest, the original Lenox Hill Tiffany Mansion (built 1882) on Madison Avenue and East 72nd Street was demolished in 1936 and replaced with an apartment building. Tiffany Glass and Decorating Company at 333-35 Fourth Ave (now Park Ave South) at Twenty-Fifth Street still stands, the ground floor occupied by various merchants. The Corona Glass Factory in Queens, where Alice worked and Clara visited once a week, stands today at the corner of 44th Avenue and 97th Place. The Briars in Laurel Hollow, Long Island, was later owned by Tiffany's daughter, Mary (May-May) Tiffany Lusk. It was torn down in the mid 1930s. Laurelton Hall, Tiffany's architectural masterpiece at Cold Spring Harbor, built at a cost of $2 million, was auctioned off for $10,000 in the 1940s, and was destroyed by fire on March 7, 1957. Miss Owens' Boardinghouse at 44 Irving Place was demolished and is now the site of Washington Irving High School. The San Remo Hotel, at 145-146 Central Park West, where Francis Driscoll died in 1892, is still in existence.

ACKNOWLEDGMENTS

Thank you one and all to the following people and organizations who helped make this book a reality:

National Public Radio (NPR) for airing WKSU reporter Vivian Goodman's January 2007 story about Clara and the Tiffany Girls. Without that broadcast, I would never have met Clara.

Frank Langben, whose research skills greatly helped to make this book as historically accurate as possible. His longstanding support and friendship at every step and turn has been invaluable.

The family of Clara Wolcott Driscoll Booth, especially: Linda Alexander, who has been in my corner from the beginning, supplying me with family information and history. She also generously granted me permission to use the recently discovered photograph of Clara used on the cover of this book. And to Dave Powers of Seattle—the courageous soul who initially challenged the Tiffany experts and brought the Wolcott letters to the public's attention so that Clara might finally have the recognition she has so long deserved.

More distant cousins: Carolyn Atwood Mackey, who directed me to the Wolcott family during my first few days in Tallmadge, Ohio. Dick Pratt and Andy Youngblood who both helped secure and restore the cover photo of Clara.

Robert and Nancy Treichler who were kind enough to give me a complete tour of their home—the Tallmadge 'House on the Hill' where Clara was born and raised and where Fannie Wolcott Cutler lived and died.

Craig Simpson, formerly of Kent State University Special Collections and Archives Library, who guided me in my research of the extensive Wolcott letter collection, and also Amanda Remster Faehnel of KSU Special Collections and Archives Library, for cheerfully and tirelessly photocopying letters, making my many weeks and long hours there easier.

And, to the Brimfield Historical Society, Kelso House Collection, housed at the Kent State University Library Department of Special Collections for kindly giving permissions to use material from their Wolcott-Pierce letter collection..

The Queens Historical Society and executive director Marisa Berman for allowing me access to their portion of the Wolcott letter collection, and for their permissions to use that material in this book.

Liz Fronenberger, who believed wholeheartedly in Clara from the first moment she met her, and for her help with the initial round of editing. Dear friends Ben and Lee Colodzin for providing me with loving support and the means to finish this book. David Weber of Anna Maria Island for his friendship and business expertise.

Editor Ellen Steiber, for helping with the initial structure of this novel. Rosemary Ahern, for her insightful editing, her patience with my many questions, and for her encouragement. Olivia Blumer of Blumer Literary Agency, Inc. for her encouragement. Rachael Garrity of PenWorthyLLC, not only for her copyediting and book design expertise, but for her support and her belief in this book.

Special thanks to Dan Magil of danmagil.com for the logo and his stellar book cover design. Beth Middleworth for tinting and refining the photo of Clara. J. Patrick Heron, Esq., for his counsel on nineteenth century New York State law, and David Simpson of Apple, Inc., for restoring my Mac to health.

And lastly, to Steven J. Vermillion, my incredibly patient, marvelous husband for keeping me laughing and for supporting and loving me during the approximately 2,000 days that I worked like an obsessed madwoman on this book—you, my darling, are a true wonder of a man.

ABOUT THE AUTHOR

Echo Heron is the New York Times bestselling author of eight books, including *Mercy, Intensive Care, Tending Lives, Condition Critical* and the Adele Monsarrat mystery series. *Noon at Tiffany's* is her first historical novel.

Nomads at heart, she and her husband, Steven Vermillion, frequently travel from San Francisco to Here and There.

Made in the
USA
Middletown, DE